A RAVE REVIEW
FOR *CITY INFERNAL*!

"After fifteen some novels, stories selected for over 13 major anthologies, and both critical and popular success, you might expect Edward Lee to show signs of losing the imaginative edge that eventually dulls every author's pen. Yet Lee's latest onslaught, *City Infernal*, is perhaps his most powerful, possessing the frantic pacing and tension of such earlier work as *Ghouls* with an additional emotional earnestness too often lacking in contemporary horror . . .

Lee has penned some of the wettest, bravest terror this side of the asylum. In *City Infernal*, an epic-proportioned urban tragedy of guilt, redemption, and the celestial mechanics of pain, he creates a testimony of human despair and redemption that not only shows the higher effect to which graphic terror can be put, but, in addition, evidence of an ever growing control over craft. . . . Lee's depiction of Cassie, an adolescent struggling with problems of identity and responsibility for her sister's suicide, is no less than remarkable."

—William P. Simmons, *Hellnotes*

MORE CRITICAL PRAISE
FOR EDWARD LEE!

"Lee is a writer you can bank on for tales so extreme they should come with a warning label."
—t. Winter-Damon, co-author of *Duet for the Devil*

"Edward Lee is the hardest of the hardcore horror writers."
—*Cemetery Dance*

"Lee pulls no punches."
—*Fangoria*

"Edward Lee is the living legend of literary mayhem. Read him if you dare."
—Richard Laymon, author of *Island* and *In the Dark*

"Lee is a demented Henry Miller of horror."
—Douglas Clegg, author of *The Infinite* and *Naomi*

"Anyone for a sightseeing tour of Hell? Follow Cassie . . . and have adventures galore."
—*Publisher's Weekly*

ALL ABOARD THE TRAIN TO HELL

The train itself looked like something from the late 1900s—old wooden passenger cars hauled by a steam locomotive. The engine was backed by a high coal tender; however, the chunks of off-yellow fuel were clearly not coal. A man stood on top, shoveling the chunks into a chute. At first he appeared ordinary, dressed in work overalls and a canvas cap as one might expect. He paused a moment to wipe some sweat off his brow, and that's when he glanced down at Cassie.

The man had no lower jaw—as if it had been wrenched out. Just an upper row of teeth over a tongue that hung from the open throat.

"All aboard!"

"Let's try to find a decent cabin," Xeke said and led them down the aisle. He looked into the first cabin, smirked, and said, "Nope." In the cabin sat a man whose face was warped with large potato-like tumors. Cassie wasn't sure, but the tumors seemed to have eyes. Xeke frowned into the next cabin, where an ancient woman sat totally naked, leathery skin hanging in folds. Her nostrils looked burned off.

"Oh my God!" Cassie gusted. She was close to hyperventilating. "This place is *horrible!*"

Xeke sat down. "What did you expect? We're in Hell, not the Mickey Mouse Clubhouse.

EDWARD LEE

CITY INFERNAL

LEISURE BOOKS NEW YORK CITY

For Richard Laymon
Rest In Peace

A LEISURE BOOK®

April 2002

Published by

Dorchester Publishing Co., Inc.
276 Fifth Avenue
New York, NY 10001

ISBN 0-8439-4988-0

The name "Leisure Books" and the stylized "L" with design are trademarks of Dorchester Publishing Co., Inc.

Printed in the United States of America.

Visit us on the web at www.dorchesterpub.com.

ACKNOWLEDGMENTS

Though in debt to many, I would like to particularly thank the following for their help, friendship, and encouragement:
Rich Chizmar, Doug Clegg, friggin' Coop, Don D'Auria, Dallas Mayr, Tim McGinnis, Tom Piccirilli, Matt Schwartz, and Bob Strauss.

Foremost, I need to thank the late Dick Laymon—simply one of the finest and most generous guys I've ever known. I miss you terribly.

CITY
INFERNAL

Prologue

It is an incontestable cycle of human history, 5000 years old:
Cities rise, then they fall.
What of *this* city, though?

The man walks with difficulty down the street. The street sign reads: ISCARIOT AVENUE.

He is carrying a severed head on a stick, and the severed head talks. "Can you spare any change?" the head asks passersby. The man himself can't talk; his body has half gone to rot. One eye is an empty hole; tiny fanged mites rove in his hair. His skin is pustulating from the latest urban infection, and his tongue has long-since been eaten out of his mouth by vermin.

A well-dressed woman in a smart bonnet taps by on elegant high heels. She's wearing a fur-lined trench coat

1

of patterned human skin, and diminutive horns sprout from her smooth, angled forehead. The woman is an uptown She-Demon.

"Can you spare some change, ma'am?" the head asks.

The man holding the head extends a cadaverous hand, and before the elegant She-Demon walks on, she gives him a shiny twenty-five-cent piece.

The coin is embossed not with the face of George Washington but the face of serial-killer Richard Speck.

"Thank you," the severed head says to the She-Demon as she traipses away.

They recycle here.

Hybrid Trolls comprise a municipal reclamation crew, transferring any manner of corpse from the streets into the huge back bins of several steam-powered Meat Trucks. Eventually the trucks will chug past the front gates of the Industrial Zone, emptying their wares into the collection hoppers of a typical city Pulping Station. Blood will be drained for distillation, flesh fileted for sustenance, bones dried and ground for cement. Good value, to say the least.

Barges manned by Golems float atop the brown, lump-ridden surface of a river called Styx, pumping raw sewage *into* the city's domestic water reservoirs. Great furnaces burn raw sulphur for no other purpose than polluting the air, but vents in the furnace silos recycle the intense heat to keep the local prisons roaring hot. The hair of the human dead is used to stuff pillows and mattresses for the demonic elite.

Even Souls are recycled. When one body suffers sufficient destruction, the Soul is transferred to a lower species. Endless life in eternal death.

Most cities run on electricity, but *this* city runs on horror. Suffering serves as convertible energy; terror is the city's most valuable natural resource, where it is tapped as fuel. Industrial Alchemists and civic Warlocks use their advanced means of sorcery to harness the synaptic activity that constantly fires between neurons, the greatest production of which comes from pain. In the humming Power Plants, the city's least useful residents are impounded, hung upside-down against long stone slabs and systematically tortured. The torture never ends—as they never really die. Instead they just hang there, often for centuries, convulsing from ceaseless pain, the energy of which is fed from their exposed brains to the vast power converters.

A single human Soul can generate enough power to light a city block—forever.

Decapitation, evisceration, and summary dismemberment are chief among its public-service skills. Its claws swipe with the efficiency of newly honed scythes. Its jaws, rowed with canine-like teeth, can bite through an iron pipe—or a human throat—as though it were a tube of cardboard.

It is called an Usher, one of several demonic species bred specifically for urban riot control and to counter problems with public disobedience. In a more accurate sense, it is a police officer.

Here, though, the police do not exist to protect and serve. They exist to maintain terror through unimaginable atrocity. Ushers are frequently dispatched in battalions to indiscriminately maim and/or execute citizens en masse.

They keep the populace on its toes.

Sharpened horns curve outward from its anvil-shaped head. It has holes for ears and chisel-slits for eyes, and its skin can be likened to the skin of a slug, darkly spotted, exuding a mucus-like slime.

It eats voraciously.

Its blood is black.

Gumdrop is an ordinary mongrel, part human, part demon—the product of infernal prostitution. She lives in one of the immense public housing complexes in the Ghettoblocks. Her features are attractively human but her skin is green-pocked with white bumps. Her breasts are robust and multi-nippled.

Like mother, like daughter: Gumdrop, too, is a prostitute. Her pimp is an obese Troll named "Fat-Bag." Fat-Bag keeps her in line through any conceivable act of degradation and physical violence. He also keeps her hopelessly addicted to drugs, and around here, the drug of choice is called Zap, an organic distillate that is injected directly into the pulp of the brain via a long hypodermic needle inserted into a nostril. Fat-Bag keeps the 'ho down hard.

She is a streetwalker. In hundred-hour shifts, she walks the decrepit avenues of Pogrom Park, soliciting any species of customer. When she's lucky, a Grand

Duke will pick her up. Grand Dukes pay well.

When she's not so lucky, Broodren rip her off and gang-rape her.

It's all just a day in the life of a prostitute in Hell.

But today she's even less lucky. When she awakes, craving drugs, she rises from the stained mattress that serves as her bed and immediately falls to the floor. She screams when she sees what has happened to her. A Polter-Rat scurries away, barely seen. While Gumdrop slept, the creature ate all the flesh off her feet, leaving only bare bones.

How will she walk the streets now, with no feet?

Tough luck for Gumdrop.

Fat-Bag will wear her out with some kink tricks and then sell her body to a Pulping Station.

The sky churns dark-scarlet. The moon is black. It has been midnight here for millennia, and it always will be. The scape of the city stretches on in a never-ending sprawl. Fires rage, rumbling, beneath the maze of streets. Smoke and steam rise from between endless buildings and skyscrapers.

Just as endless are the screams, which fly away into the eternal night only to be immediately replaced by more of the same.

It is an incontestable cycle of human history, 5000 years old:

Cities rise, then they fall.

But not *this* city.

Not the Mephistopolis.

PART ONE

ETHERESS

Chapter One

(I)

She dreamed of utter darkness, of dripping sounds, and screams.

But first—

The embrace.

The strong hands stroking her body through the hot black satin.

I'm ready, she thought. *I've never felt like this before. . . .*

Her breasts pressed against his sculpted chest—she could feel his heart beating deeply within, and it seemed to beat for her. Their souls seemed to fuse through each ravenous kiss, and soon she felt tingling all over, flushed with heat and desire. She didn't flinch when he pushed up her black blouse, popped the black

Edward Lee

bra, and smoothed his hands over her breasts. The sensation shocked her; she rose up on her tiptoes to kiss him harder—

Then—

The lights flicked on.

The screams exploded.

The blood splattered in her face.

And she saw it all again. Over and over. Every night of her life. . . .

The club's sign—GOTH HOUSE—glowed eerily in dark-purple neon. It was a familiar sight, a landmark for her eye. The line out front wound halfway up the block—another familiar sight—which proved the establishment's popularity as the best Goth club in D.C. There were many, of course, and many more had come and gone over the years, along with every incarnation and reincarnation of the movement. Everything else seemed to change, every aspect of the city and even the world.

But not this.

Not Goth House.

For Cassie and so many like her, the club was a sanctuary, a cultural anchor for the strange ship they all elected to sail, not simply the next big thing in the club craze. Cassie thanked God for that. In a pop society that changed in eyeblinks, where every other week brought some new version of Eminem-like hatred excused as the language of a culture or facile teeny-bopper tramp-glamour divas with shiny pants and blond hair who couldn't even read music, the symbolics of Goth House never wavered. The dark music and dark styles of passionately dark minds. Here, Bauhaus reigned, as they had for two decades. There were no Dixie Chicks, no Ricky Martin. There were no Spice Girls here.

It would be an hour's wait at least, and Cassie Heydon and her sister were three years shy of the posted requirement: YOU MUST BE 21 OR OVER TO ENTER.

Cassie frowned. *It's not who you know, it's who you.* . . . The thought needn't be finished. She knew what her sister was doing; she could see her shadow in the alley kneeling before the fat, slovenly bouncer. Due to this talent, and her willingness to utilize it, Lissa had already gained quite a reputation at school. This just made it worse.

"I do it all the time," she'd told Cassie earlier. "It's kind of fun and, besides, it's the only way we can get in. You *do* want to get in, don't you?"

"Yes, but—"

"You don't want to have to wait in *this* line, do you?"

"No, but—"

"All right already. Leave the rest to me."

There. The matter had been settled, with Cassie's objections diffused. She tried not to think about the image of what must be going on now. Instead, she stood at the curb, tapping her high-heeled foot as dusk lengthened over the city. Distant sirens could be heard in this murder capital of the east, mixed with the collision of music pouring into the street from other clubs. At a strip bar just a block away, a former mayor had picked up prostitutes to smoke crack with. After doing jail time, he'd been re-elected. *Only in D.C.,* Cassie thought with an amused sarcasm. If she peered between the high-rises just right, she could see the White House juxtaposed against dilapidated rowhouses that provided area heroin addicts with their shooting galleries. Another landmark, grandly lit, spired for all to see: the Washington Monument. Just last week another terrorist had tried to blow it up with dynamite strapped around his chest like a girdle. This happened at least twice a year, and along with the drive-bys, the road rage, and the politicians who acted more like mafia lords, nothing shocked the populace by now. It was, at the very least, an intensely interesting place to live.

Come on, hurry up, she thought, still anxiously tapping her foot. Another glance into the alley showed her her sister's gestures hastening, the head of the kneeling silhouette moving back and forth faster and faster. Even if Cassie had a lover—something she *hadn't* had ever in her life—the act she was witnessing now, in the alley, wasn't something she thought she'd ever want to do. Or maybe love would change that some day.

Yeah, she thought coldly. *Some day.*

A few minutes later, Lissa's shadow was standing up again. *It's about time!* Cassie thought. She was waving Cassie into the alley, whispering, "Come on, we have to go in through the back."

The alley stank; Cassie grimaced when she stepped through, hoping not to sully her brand-new black stiletto heels, and she hoped that the squeaking sounds she heard weren't rats. A syringe cracked beneath her sole.

Re-buckling his dumpy pants, the bouncer winked at her. *Not a chance, fat boy,* she thought. *I'd rather hang myself from the Wilson Bridge.* Muffled music trebled in volume when she followed Lissa in through the back door. *Anti-Christ, Superstar,* someone had spray-painted on the door, and *Lucretia My Reflection.* A few quick turns down a few corridors, and they were in the middle of the jam-packed club. The throng of black-clad figures danced wildly to the ear-splitting music. Tonight was "oldies" night: Killing Joke, Front 242, .45 Grave, and the like. Cassie always preferred the material that founded the movement rather than popified stuff that was now ending it. Salvos of blinding white strobelights turned the dance floor into shifting freeze-frames. Stark flesh and bands of black. Vampiric faces and blood-red lips. Inhumanly wide eyes seemed never to blink. In cages high overhead, Goth girls danced through deadpan expressions, in varying states of undress. Couples kissed voraciously in secluded corners. Waves of grinding music made the air concuss.

Cassie felt immediately at home.

"Over here!" Her sister tugged her by the hand through more pressing bodies. As they edged further away from the crush of dancers, heads began to turn.

Of course, Cassie thought, rather morosely.

She and Lissa were identical twins. The only telling them apart was a minute detail: they'd both dyed a white streak in their matching straight black hair, Cassie's on the left, Lissa's on the right. The only other noticeable difference was the petite barbed-wire tattoo that encircled Lissa's navel, while Cassie had a petite half-rainbow around hers. But it was Lissa who always insisted they dress identically whenever they snuck out to a club. Identical black-velvet gauntlets, identical short black crinoline skirts and black-lace blouses. Even their stiletto heels and kidskin wrist purses were identical. It drove their father nuts, but even Cassie was beginning to get bored with the novelty; that and it never seemed to draw any attention to her, just to Lissa.

She didn't dwell on that; it was a rumination that, she'd learned long ago, led to nowhere except the heart of her own lack of confidence and self-image. Her secret envy of Lissa sometimes bubbled up to quiet hatred; she'd never understand how two people who looked so alike could possess such opposite personalities. Lissa the out-going Guy Magnet and Party Chick, Cassie the dour introvert. Five years of psychotherapy and a few months in a mental ward gave her only enough edge to keep going at all. But it wasn't just Lissa, it was everything. It was the world.

For Christ's sake, she nagged to herself. *Just try to have a good time.*

They eventually made their way to the back bar. "Looks like we lucked out tonight!" Lissa exclaimed, still tugging Cassie along.

"What?"

"Radu's working. That means we drink for free."

Radu's real name was Jim—he couldn't get off the vampire kick that seemed a stigma now for true Goths. Shirtless and shaven-headed, he looked like *Nosfer-*

14

atu's Max Schreck—only with muscles. He and Lissa had been dating for several months, but how seriously was a mystery. Radu must know about Lissa's lusty reputation at school, and Cassie supposed that her sister's expertise at bypassing the line at the door was already well-known amongst the club's male employees.

"Welcome to Goth House, ladies," Radu greeted them, and slid them each a can of Holsten. Lissa was immediately leaning over—her cleavage blaring—to kiss him. Pink embarrassment tinted Cassie's cheeks when the kiss protracted into a mutual tongue probe. "Jesus," she complained. "You two sound like a couple of St. Bernards eating a pile of Alpo."

"My little sister's just jealous," Lissa whispered to him, running her finger round the Order of the Dragon tattoo. His toned pectorals, in reflex, flinched.

Cassie seethed to herself. She was actually seven minutes *older* than Lissa but Lissa insisted on referring to her as her *little* sister. And, yes, she was jealous but she hated to hear it. *Be yourself,* her $250-per-hour psychiatrist would constantly compel her. *Stop beating your head against the wall for not being someone else.* Cassie supposed it was good advice, however impractical.

"Ho, little sister!" Radu remarked. "Save some for the alcoholics! They gotta get drunk too, ya know."

Without realizing it, Cassie had finished her beer and had set the empty can back up on the bar. *Did I just down a can of beer in five minutes?*

The answer was yes.

White fizz sprayed when Radu popped open another one for her. "Need a straw for that? Or how about a funnel?"

"Here's a more efficient idea," Lissa chuckled. "Just hook her mouth up to one of the taps."

That's real funny, Cassie thought in response, *considering what you hooked your mouth up to a little while ago.* She wished she could say it, but didn't dare. They'd just get into it again, and she definitely didn't want that. She refaced the crowd, sipping her beer, while Lissa and Radu made more baby talk. Bauhaus' infamous *Bela Lugosi's Dead* started off the next set, riling the crowd. The song was older than Cassie but it never lost its defining power. The strobelights adjusted to the creepy tick of opening percussives, transforming the dancefloor into a chasm of jumpcuts and bladelike flashes. Cassie perused the revelers. Up front, two girls in black fishnet body suits openly caressed each other through the dance, and in a corner two guys in black leather ground groins. Tonight's was a diverse crowd. Sometimes Cassie was perfectly content just to watch— for whatever reason, seeing other people happy made *her* happy. Other times, though—like now—it just threatened to bring on more depression. It didn't help when a handsome guy in a Danzig *blackaciddevil* t-shirt hustled right up to her and said, "Hey, wanna dance? You're Lissa, right?"

"No, I'm her sister," she replied.

Then the guy said, "Oh, sorry," and walked away.

That's just friggin' wonderful!

The two beers on an empty stomach were doing their job. *Screw it,* she decided, *I'm just going to get drunk.* Back at the bar, Radu raised a brow when she signaled for another Holsten.

"Hey, little sister, didn't you know that the beer-chugging contest is *next* week?"

"Just get me another beer," she said.

Now both brows raised. "What's the magic word?"

"Get me another beer *please,* you bald vampire-looking prick."

He threw his head back and laughed. "That's the spirit!" he said, and slid her another beer.

Lissa roughly grabbed her arm. "Would you lighten up! You're gonna get drunk and brood all night and throw up in Dad's Cadillac on the way home like you did the last two times we came here."

"No, I won't. I promise, this time I'll throw up out the window. I just hope we're on Pennsylvania Avenue when it happens. I'll wave to Bush."

Lissa sighed, exasperated. "Cassie, please don't do this."

"Do what? I'm just drinking a beer and looking around."

"Yeah, and whenever you do that you sink right into one of your moods."

"My moods are my business. And speaking of business, why don't you do me a favor and mind yours?"

"Stop being such a bummer. Christ, half the time I feel like your babysitter."

"Babysitters perform fellatio on Goth bouncers?"

"It got you into this place, didn't it?" Lissa shot back at the insult. "Sometimes I don't know why I bother bringing you in the first place. You'd still be standing out there in that line if it weren't for me, moping and looking down at your friggin' shoes like Little Bo-Peep. Next time *you* can blow the bouncer to get us in here."

"Oh, yeah, *that'll* be happening," Cassie said through a strained laugh.

"Sometimes you can be such a chore, Cassie. I'm sick to death of having to worry about you all night whenever we go out."

"You don't have to worry about anything. You do your thing, I'll do mine."

"*Your* thing? What's that, standing in the corner like a wallflower?" Lissa gestured the crowded dancefloor. "Why don't you go out there and mingle. Meet someone. Meet a guy. Go dance and have a good time."

"I *am* having a good time," Cassie said snidely, and drank more beer.

Lissa abruptly took the can away. "Here, take this. It'll mellow you." She tried to give her a small heather-green pill with a Playboy bunny imprinted on it.

"Oh, great. You give me a bunch of crap about drinking and now you're telling me to take Ecstasy."

"Come on, tonight's a rave, Cassie. Everyone's doing it."

"Thanks, but no. I'd rather keep my neurons intact. A mind is a terrible thing to baste."

"It'll put you in a good mood."

"Yeah, and shrink my brain to the size of a pecan by the time I'm twenty-five." She held up her Holsten can.

"At least my liver should last another couple of decades. I'll quit drinking after the transplant."

"Fine," Lissa snapped. "*Be* a wallflower. Get drunk and puke and make an idiot of yourself. Let everybody in the whole place think you're a basket-case and a drunk. If you don't want to have a good time, then *don't*. Have a *lousy* time, Cassie; that's what you want anyway. Just mope and frown like a dejected little dope so everyone feels sorry for you. Boo-hoo, poor little Cassie, she's so misunderstood."

Cassie had heard enough; she tuned it out, let the argument die right there. She let the place take her away as Lissa stormed off back to a peering Radu. The music washed over her, soon leaving her contentedly numb, the sensation she preferred; it seemed to nullify the passage of time. She smiled serenely, looking out into the strobe-lit crowd. She didn't need to take part in all of that—she just needed to take part in whatever small part of herself that she liked. She knew it was rationalization, but the alcohol helped her find that place.

So what if no one noticed her?

So what if no one was interested in Lissa Heydon's "little" sister.

Being by herself in this crowded place was safer than being *part* of the crowd itself. *There's as much unhappiness out there,* she thought, *than there is in here.* Being alone was so much different than being lonely.

At least that's what she told herself.

More music rolled over her in steady waves: Skinny Puppy, Faith and the Muse, This Mortal Coil, and

Christian Death. She danced by herself through the next set and suddenly she *was* part of the crowd. She was being acknowledged as part of the whole. Exotic white faces flashed through the club's wonderful murk; eyes sparkled at her, some keen with drugs or lust but others simply keen with living. A girl she'd never seen before, all tight and leggy in a scarlet corselette, rubbed right up against her, blood-red lips in a woozy grin. She gently stroked Cassie's face as she slipped back into the throng. Next, a boy all in black eyed her forlornly; he smiled at her but then his face disappeared in the next strobe-flash. Barely seen couples were kissing—and more—hidden like daring ghosts in the club's most remote crannies. Cassie's stark black hair fell over her face like a veil, reducing her vision to long swaying gaps. Harder music ensued, deafening her—but she liked it. White Zombie, Tool, and iconic Marilyn Manson. She felt tantalized when bodies bumped into her, smiled dreamily when an errant hand slid across her back or arm. Not-so-errant touches didn't anger her as they usually did; instead, she found them curious, even inspiring. Music and motion grew pandemonic as last call neared. When she drifted back to the bar, Radu got her another beer, but she didn't see Lissa. He shouted something at her, as if to explain, but she couldn't hear him over the pounding riffs and rhythms.

Generally, after so many beers, she'd begin to feel depressed right about now—it always worked that way. But not tonight. Instead, she felt gently enlivened. She'd truly had a good time tonight, in spite of her sister's mordant guarantee to the opposite. Next song up was something by Death in June, a group Cassie had never liked. They seemed cryptofascist so she wandered further back in the club, contemplated going to the bathroom, but shirked away from the chatty line.

She wandered around without really thinking. Getting home late wouldn't be a problem tonight—their father was in New York, yet another business trip. But Lissa would have to drive. *I'm too drunk,* Cassie admitted to herself. And now that she thought of it, where *was* Lissa?

She didn't see her anywhere. The bathroom maybe? Another door off to the side stood open an inch. She drifted in.

No Lissa. It was just a back room, for storage, dark, cluttered with boxes and recycle bins full of empty cans and bottles. Then—*yeck!* she thought. A bitter taste flooded her mouth along with something grainy. She angled her Holsten can under the light and saw a half-dissolved pale green pill at the bottom. *Those assholes,* she thought. She tossed the can away and realized now why she'd felt so wistful tonight. *Oh, well, I'll live,* she supposed. Next, though, she found herself staring at an old Bauhaus poster on the wall, the group's four members standing in what appeared to be an art-deco crypt.

"Can you believe it? Those guys are old men now. Forty, at least."

Radu's voice startled her. He'd walked in without her realizing it. The sudden image of his bare chest and well-toned abdomen caught her even more off-guard than his voice. *He's so good-looking,* she paused to realize. Outside, she could hear the night's last cut come

21

on: Alien Sex Fiend's "The Girl at the End of My Gun."

"You put that Ecstasy crap in my beer, didn't you?"

His hands spread out.

"I confess. Your sister put me up to it. It was a low dose and, besides, it has an anti-depressant effect. Your sister told me you've been seeing a shrink for depression."

Damn her. "That's my business, not hers *or* yours."

"Well, you did have a good time tonight, didn't you?"

A pause. "Yes. . . ."

He stepped closer, nonchalant, the finely shaped pectorals moving beneath tight skin. "That's why we come here, to have a good time."

His voice sounded distant. She tried to shake off the distraction of his lean body so close to her, but when the image returned, of Lissa kissing him, Cassie saw herself kissing him. She wondered what it would be like. *Sweet eighteen and never been kissed,* she thought to herself. *Just drunk again. So what else is new?*

"Where is Lissa anyway?"

His smile mixed with a frown. "We had an argument earlier. One of my ex-girlfriends came in, started flirting. Usually stuff like that doesn't bother Lissa, she's usually more mature about it. But she stalked off somewhere all pissed off."

"She better not have driven home without me," Cassie considered.

"I'm sure she's still here someplace. She'll be back after she thinks about things." He shrugged as if to denote some kind of innocence. "Anyway, the arrangement we have was her idea."

Arrangement? "What do you mean?"

Another shrug. "Well, you know. We agreed that we can see other people and not get all bent out of shape about it. It's nothing new. She acknowledges my needs, and I acknowledge her desire to stay a virgin until she's ready."

The casual comment jolted her. Cassie had no idea. "You mean, you two don't—"

"No. That's the way she wants it for now. And I respect that. I love her."

Confusion whipped around her.

Then Radu added, "We do . . . other things, and that's fine. I'm sure she's told you about our arrangement—"

"No," Cassie said abruptly.

"Oh, I'm sure she has. She even told me that it would be okay. You know. She wouldn't mind if . . ."

"If what?"

"You know. She wouldn't mind if you and I got together."

Another, harder jolt. But all Cassie could do was stand there, struck dumb, immobile as if paralyzed in a dream.

Why didn't she object? Why didn't she leave right then?

"Come on, I know you've always had a thing for me. It's flattering."

She just stood there, dazed.

"I've always had a thing for you too, but I'm sure you know that."

23

He's *lying,* was her first thought. No one had ever had a "thing" for her, just Lissa, her vivacious alter-ego.

But then the doubts slipped in.

There were no precursory words or gestures, no testing of the waters. He was kissing her at once, and the only thing that shocked her was that she didn't pull back. It never occurred to her to do so. The moment lit all of her fuses at the same time, longing that had percolated deep inside since puberty. Cassie could almost hear those fuses burning in the core of her soul. She returned the kiss with no reservation.

What am I—

Her skin tingled beneath her black-satin top; his skin, too, felt hot as her hands rubbed up and down his bare back. She didn't flinch when he pushed the top up and shucked her breasts out of her bra—to the contrary, she was ravenous for more, to be touched more urgently, to be felt, to be wrapped up in him. When he grabbed her hand and pushed it down below his waist, she didn't pull it away. She only stood higher on her tiptoes, to kiss him harder.

His soft whisper warmed her ear. "You're a virgin too, aren't you? Like Lissa?"

She didn't want to hear her sister's name now—not at this moment.

"Yes," she panted back. "But I don't care. I don't want to be."

"I could never take that from you—I wouldn't," he said. He seemed so considerate, so sweet. "I'd have to know that you were really sure. . . ."

I'm ready, she thought. *I've never felt like this before. . . .*

But in her mind, her emotions collided. Guilt tried to ruin the priceless embrace, to put a wrecking ball through a moment that she'd been yearning for for so long.

But then she remembered what he'd told her, that Lissa had said this was all right.

"I'm really sure," she promised him. "I know I am."

His eyes penetrated her. "Let's go over here. . . ." A strong hand urged her toward some boxes in the corner. From his back pocket, he produced a condom. Cassie kissed him one more time, her exposed breasts pressing hotly against his chest. "I want you to do it now, right *now*," she nearly pleaded.

He was just about to lay her down when—

"What are you DOING!"

—Lissa walked in.

Cassie froze. Radu shoved her away as if leprous.

"Lissa, I thought she was you!" he exclaimed. "She came on to me. Honey, I swear—she was pretending to be you!"

Liar! Cassie wanted to yell, but her voice was lost. She could just lie there across the boxes, frozen in dread.

Rage had contorted Lissa's face into an incised mask. Bloodshot eyes watched the condom fall to the dusty floor. "Bullshit!" she screamed. The voice sounded hysterical, insane. Inflamed by drugs, alcohol, and now betrayal, Lissa seemed possessed.

"Lissa," Radu began. "Honey. Calm down—"

"SHUT UP!" Then the twisted face shot to Cassie. "And you, you treacherous BITCH! My own SISTER!"

Cassie's lips barely worked. "I-I'm sorry," she peeped. "I—"

Lissa was shaking all over. Her face was hot-pink, her eyes radiating hatred above streaming tears.

"Well to hell with BOTH of you!" the next scream exploded, and in another second she'd unzipped her wrist-purse, removed a small pistol.

"Holy shit!" Radu yelled and turned to run.

BAM!

Cassie screamed, the world falling in on her. The bullet caught Radu right in the back of the skull. He fell flat, face-first. Within seconds, a frightful amount of blood began to halo around his head and shoulders.

Lissa's red face turned. The gun pointed at Cassie's face.

"I'm sorry, I'm sorry!" Cassie sobbed.

"My own sister. . . ." Lissa's voice could've been a death rattle, and the eyes that looked down already seemed dead. "How could you do this to me?"

Lissa put the pistol to her own temple.

"No!" Cassie screamed and lunged.

She wrapped her arms around Lissa's shoulders, tried to grab for the gun, when—

BAM!

Lissa collapsed, dead, as Cassie staggered backward, her face and breasts splattered with blood and brain tissue and flecks of splintered bone.

Cassie fell to her knees and screamed until she passed out.

Chapter Two

(I)

She shot upright, her heart thumping, skipping beats. Her hands frantically dragged up the bedsheets, used them to wipe the blood and brains off her face.

She quavered, the silent cry on her lips, and then fell back into the pillows. Her heartbeat paced down; she looked at the bedsheets.

No blood.

No brains.

Just the curse of memory.

Two long years and the nightmare still marauded her at least once a week. *Better than every night,* she reminded herself, which had been the case until they'd moved out here. After Lissa's suicide, Cassie's mental troubles had compounded, not just the recurring nightmare, but further introversion, two failed suicide attempts of her own, and a month in a private psychiatric hospital where the regimen of psychotropic drugs had reduced her to a stumbling zombie. The scars on her slim wrists were the only tangible results. Group therapy, hypnotic-regression, and narco-analysis had also failed. Ironically, it had been her father's idea to break away from all of that. "To hell with all these crackpot doctors and drugs," he'd said one day several months ago. "Let's just get out of the city, get out of this shark-tank. Maybe that'll be the best medicine for both of us." Cassie had no reason to object, and with that, her father, the rather famous William F. Heydon, controlling partner of the third most successful law firm in the country, quit his influential—and very lucrative—post with a single one-sentence letter of resignation. The jurisprudential power circles in D.C. had experienced the legal equivalent of a *grand mal* seizure, and her father never went back to the firm again. Clearly, the two minor heart attacks and repeated angioplasties had shown him the light. "Every day above ground's a good day, honey," he told her. "Don't know why it took me so long to see that. We've got everything we need. Besides, I'm sick of the chauffeur, I'm sick of lunch every day at the Mayflower, and the Redskins suck. Who needs this town?"

"But what about all your friends at the firm?" she'd asked, and he just laughed back. "There's no such thing as *friends* in a law firm, Cassie, just more sharks who'd stab you in the back without a second's thought. I wish I could be there to see them fight over the big piece of raw meat I leave in their laps. I'll bet those blood-suckers are even fighting over my office chair."

It was all fine with her; Cassie's own insecurities had barred her from any real friendships herself. Who would want to hang out with someone perpetually half-dazed by psych drugs anyway? What guy would want to date a "Thorazine Queen?" And the city's Goth scene was dead to her now.

She knew she could never walk into another Goth club again because they'd only remind her of Lissa.

Her father's spur-of-the-moment plan had worked. Since the day they'd moved into Blackwell Hall—a month ago now—her emotions seemed to start balancing out. The nightly dream of her sister's death reduced its recurrence to a weekly basis. The dread of seeing her psychiatrist evaporated; she didn't go to her any more. Release from the battery of anti-depressants and other psycho-pharmaceuticals rejuvenated her to a degree she found astonishing.

She felt alive, vibrant, more so than she could remember.

Maybe things will really work out, she thought. *Maybe I'll get past this, and have a real life some day.*

She was learning quickly that one step at a time was the best way to handle things.

She slid out of the high, four-poster bed, drew the heavy drapes, and immediately shielded her eyes. The harsh sunlight seemed to barge into the room. She opened the French doors and sighed at the caress of fresh air. Standing on the balcony in only panties and bra left her with no reservations. *Who's going to see?*

In D.C., that would be another matter altogether. But this was the *country*. All that looked back at her near nudity were rolling hills and distant pastures. The sun rose over the crust of the Blue Ridge mountains a hundred miles away; song birds—not garbage-plump pigeons—lifted off the railing when she stepped out.

It was an alien environment indeed: Cassie preferred the cityscape at night, not late-morning sun shining over farmland and forests. But she wasn't about to complain. The quiet countryside was what her father craved for his own rehabilitation—Cassie would just have to get used to it. *Beggars can't be choosers,* she reminded herself. *It beats the view from a psych-ward window.*

Though she lacked her father's appreciation of country scenery, she absolutely loved the house. Blackwell Hall, as it was called, loomed over a hundred acres of disused grazeland from the summit of a pleasantly wooded incline known as Blackwell Hill. Blackwell Creek burbled at the hill's foot, feeding unsurprisingly into Blackwell Swamp. When Cassie had asked who Blackwell was, her father had answered with a casual "Who gives a crap? Probably some plantation magnate from before the Civil War." His law firm had inherited the house in an estate settlement; his former partners had gladly given it to him as part of his severance when he'd agreed to endorse his client list over to them for no future shares. He'd simply wanted out, and the millions he'd invested throughout his career provided several more million per year in interest income. Dad was rich for life, in other words, and Blackwell Hall, regardless of its history, provided the seclusion he believed was desperately necessary for them both.

The old southern antebellum house had obviously been added to—if not eccentrically—since its original construction. *Gone with the Wind meets the Adam's Family,* she thought when she first saw the pictures. *Works for me.* The front of the original structure—and its polished white-granite pillars—faced west, and around that, the rest of the delightful monstrosity had been built: a three-story manse with a dormer level, a garret level, iron-cresting along the roof, stone cornices, parapets, and off-hanging turrets windowed with stained glass. Ivy crept up the genuine mahogany siding, and great bow windows, complete with functional shutters, seemed to have grown from its fieldstone-walled first story. There was even an old oculus window in the mansion's central garret.

This place is so creepy, I LOVE it! was Cassie's first assessment.

Inside, the expected clash of styles merged well in an overall refurbishment that borrowed from Colonial and Edwardian styles. Whole walls were reserved for deep man-tall fireplaces and slab mantles and hearths. So what if they'd never be used in the nine-month hot season? They looked cool just the same. The floor layout was a fascinating maze, with odd corridors branching this way and that, rooms leading to smaller rooms leading to still smaller rooms, frequent dumb-waiters, and even hidden closets behind hinged bookshelves. The original gas-lamp fixtures remained, having been refitted with electric lights; six-foot-high sconces provided standing room for statutes of southern historical figures such as Jefferson Davis, Lee, and Pickett, plus more brooding unidentified figures. Thirty rooms in all, the house was a clash of stereotypes which brought visions of southern belles fanning themselves alongside stuffy robber-barons from the '20s.

And the ubiquitous multi-layered drapes kept the interior dark—just the way Cassie liked it.

What functioned as the "living room" was more like an atrium, a thousand square feet in itself. Exotic throw rugs covered the refinished natural wood floors. There was a den, a study, a sitting room, and a library, too, not to mention a vast country kitchen which her father had upgraded with high-end appliances. Other millionaire upgrades appointed the house: a hot tub, a 54-inch television and home theater, spacious black-marble bathrooms, and much else. Lastly, the house didn't have a basement, it had a *series* of basements: long narrow cellars of nearly hundred-year-old tabby brick, so low-ceilinged a tall person would have to duck. Perfect stowage for her father's law books, which he clearly intended to never look at again.

Her bathroom was pretty cool too. A brass ring-shower hung above the original claw-foot sliptub. A framed chevaldefrise mirror was mounted in more original brass over a pedestal marble sink. Cassie took a cool, leisurely shower, then meandered around for a while as she dressed. Her room, like most of the estate's rooms, was enormous—all dark paneling, hand-carved friezework, and intricately embossed brass-and-tin ceiling tiles. Sometimes she felt tiny in its near emptiness;

she'd brought no furniture from home, electing to settle for the few furnishings that were already here. The big four-poster—more like a Renaissance Revival bed—an antique chiffonier, and a simple table and cane chair, and that was it. It was all she needed, and she'd declined on her father's offer to furnish the room however she liked, just as she'd declined on his offer to buy her an exorbitant stereo. Her boombox would do just fine. The only other things she'd brought from their former D.C. brownstone were her clothes and CDs.

She'd never felt comfortable with the luxuries her father could effortlessly provide, and that had been a great bone of contention between them for years. Most of her clothes she made herself, with Good Will scraps and overstock fabrics; she'd become quite a designer, and she supposed that's what she might want to be when she "grew up," whatever that meant. But she knew she needn't worry about any of that until she got her head straight.

She still quite often felt the smothering guilt of her sister's suicide; some part of her spirit felt branded. Since the incident, she'd taken to wearing a silver locket with Lissa's picture inside; she never took it off, and every day she'd plead to herself, *Please, Lissa, please forgive me.* The dreams, she supposed, were punishment, but perhaps forgiveness was coming. Out here, the nightmares had declined and so had her depression.

Would she ever be free?

I don't deserve to be, she thought.

Sometimes the days would start like this, steeped in remorse. She even hated looking in the mirror—of course—because every time she'd see Lissa. She'd cut her long hair straight across at the middle of her neck, dyed it lemon-yellow with lime-green highlight lines. It helped a little, but her face was still the same; it was still Lissa who looked back at her through the silver veins. In the mirror, she inadvertently noticed the tiny rainbow tattoo over her navel, which only reminded her of the barbed-wire tattoo her sister had in the same place.

Damn it, she thought. *Not again.* She was getting depressed, and if she just hung around the house, it would only get worse.

"I think I'll go somewhere," she said aloud, "even if there's no place to go."

She grabbed her Discman and swept out of the room.

As she descended the broad stairs, statues scowled at her, backlighted in strange dark colors from the stained glass. She scowled back, and gave one the finger. *You have a good day too.* At the landing, her hand squealed around a carven newel post; she looked into the living room and saw that the television was off. She checked the kitchen, the study, and the back patio but found no sign of her father.

Hmm.

In the foyer, Mrs. Conner was dusting. Cassie's father had hired her from town to keep the house clean. She was a nice, quiet hill woman, all business. Probably in her fifties but a lifetime of hard work had kept her in good shape. Cassie liked her; she never gaped at her bright hair or dark Gothy apparel like most of the locals. Cassie wasn't too keen, though, on the woman's son, Jervis, who came around a few times a week to take care of the yard. Jervis was pure-bred redneck, about twenty-five, and drunk half the time. He tended to leer at her through a shucksy grin, constantly adjusting his Red Fox chewing tobacco hat. Fat and broad-shouldered, he delighted in telling her far-fetched stories about local murders, hoping to scare her. "Had a brother, Tritt was his name. Got kilt in the woods," he'd told her once. "Couldn't reka-nize him when they brung him out."

"Your point being?" Cassie said somewhat rudely.

"Stay out the woods, girl," Jervis had replied.

Cassie laughed.

Tragic as losing a sibling was, Mrs. Conner had told her what really happened, "My son Tritt weren't much fer smarts. Chugged a bottle'a shine one night and up'n died."

At any rate, Jervis was a bane but she supposed he was tolerable.

"Mornin', miss," the woman greeted without looking up from her dusting.

"Hi, Mrs. Conner. Have you seen my father?"

Her feather duster gestured the door. "Out front in the court, goin' someplace. Didn't say where, though."

"Thank you."

Ah, a woman of few words.

Cassie went out through the great, sidelighted front door, sided by high ionic pillars. Later-morning immediately exhaled a gust of humid heat in her face.

35

Edward Lee

God! It's hotter than a Dutch oven out here! When she re-closed the massive front door, the odd knocker on the center stile caught her eye: an oval of tarnished bronze depicting a morose half-formed face. Just two eyes, no mouth, no other features. *Neat!* Cassie thought.

Past the portico, her father was loping away down a flagstone trail.

"Hi, Dad!"

His hand extended.

"Bye, Dad."

He turned around, sweating already in the heat. A ludicrous fisherman's hat looked jammed down on his head. "I'm going down to the creek," he called back, brandishing his collapsible fishing rod.

"Rednecks probably pee in that creek," she jested.

"Naw, from what I can see they just pee in the street. I'll be bringing back a bunch of catfish." He paused, scratched his head. "Do you know how to cook catfish?"

"Sure. I'll cook 'em, but you have to gut 'em."

"No problem. It'll make me feel like a lawyer again. What are you up to this morning, honey?"

She frowned at the *honey*. "I'm bored, so I think I'll walk into town . . . and be *more* bored."

He gestured toward the Cadillac. "Take the car."

"No, I want to walk."

"But it's ten miles!"

"It's three miles, Dad. I want to walk. Besides, my fragile urbanbred constitution craves all of this stagnant, searing, mosquito-infested country air."

"Yeah, it's great, isn't it? It's just like D.C.—only with no buildings."

She squinted at him, disapprovingly. "What's that in your top pocket?"

He guiltily covered the pocket. "Just a box of . . . Altoids."

"Yeah, right, and I groove on Frankie Goes To Hollywood. You told me you quit smoking, Dad. Two heart attacks aren't enough?"

He sputtered, caught cold. "Look, I don't give you crap anymore about your Kool-Aid-colored hair and your Maryland Mansion clothes. So don't give me crap about a few cigarettes a day."

"Fine, Dad. First of all, it's Marilyn Manson. Second, next week when your aorta explodes against a cork of cholesterol deposits and you fall down kicking and gasping and clutching your chest and your heart stops beating because blood can't get to it anymore and you're foaming at the mouth and swallowing your tongue and your face turns the color of beets and you friggin' DIE . . . do I inherit this giant eyesore of a house?"

He smiled wide, parted his hands like a prophet before a congregation. "One day, honey—all this will be yours. Have a good time in town!"

"Bye."

He lumbered off down the trail, stumbling in his clunky hip-waders; Cassie chuckled after him. *He's such a dork . . . but a good dork.*

Since moving here, for sure, they'd both changed for the better. No more awful arguments over conformity

37

and hairstyles. No more blow-ups about her black clothes or his cold conservatism.

I'm all he's got left, she realized, *and he's all I've got left.*

Cassie rarely felt encouraged about anything, but she genuinely *was* encouraged by how well things seemed to be going. He was making a diligent effort to compromise about her ways, which made it so much easier for her to do the same. However square, her father was a good man, and now he was trying to fix himself up for them both. She and Lissa had blamed him terribly when their mother had left; it was a natural prepubescent over-reaction. Daddy's always at work and he doesn't care about us or Mommy anymore. That's why she left us.

The truth was her mother was an uptown golddigger, and she'd left them all cold for another—even richer—man. Cassie knew that now. She only hoped that her father's retirement would finally help him be happy. After all the tragedy in his life, he certainly deserved that.

When she stepped off the front stone steps, the portico's shade retreated. She'd dressed light today—a sheer black sarong and cotton tank top, and good old fashioned flipflops—but after only minutes outside, the heat was basting her. *Get used to it,* she thought. *Never had a suntan in my life—now's my chance.*

Halfway down the front hill, she looked back up at the house. It *loomed* before her, immense, brooding and Dickensian even in the high sunlight. But she laughed when she looked at the south dormer wing:

her father had ridiculously placed Washington Redskins plaques in all the windows, and another sore thumb was the bright-white satellite-tv dish on the highest parapet; her father could live without the routine of a big city, but he couldn't live without SportsCenter, *Crossfire,* and E! Channel. It was funny how he pretended to be paring down his life, as if to turn away from previous indulgences. Once he'd come back from the general store, where he'd bought a bag of dried pinto beans. "Only thirty-five cents a pound," he'd bragged. "Am I cutting down or what?"

"Yeah, Dad," she'd agreed, "you're really tightening up the budget. Good for you."

Then a knock had come at the door, and her father had rushed off. "It's the FedEx truck. I special ordered some fresh New Zealand lobster tails and Ossetra caviar. . . ."

Yeah, he's cutting down, all right.

Now Cassie appraised the massive edifice a moment more, then nodded contentedly. *This is my home now,* she realized. And she liked it.

She slid on her earphones, cranked on some Rob Zombie, and started walking toward town.

She never noticed the face peering down at her from the oculus window in the estate's highest garret.

(II)

Blackwell Hall existed in an odd uncharted rurality jammed into Virginia's southwestern-most tip. Cassie, deciding to cut through the wooded acreage rather than

39

take the road, found herself half-lost pretty quickly, the short journey into town turning into an hours-long march through stifling heat and brambles. Twice she saw snakes, and ran away in alarm, and when she'd turned onto a thin trail, she'd nearly walked right into a fattened woodchuck. It stared back at her, with huge yellow teeth, and in the distance, she heard wild dogs snarling.

Needless to say, she wasn't enthused about the wild-life.

But she found herself slowly favoring the natural landscapes and robust woodlands to the cement and asphalt of the city. The environ reminded her of the Faulkner she'd read in school, people and places so far removed from mainstream society, untouched by any-thing that could be called modern. *It's like walking into a different world,* she thought.

It was late afternoon by the time she actually arrived at her destination. Ryan's Corner could hardly be called a town at all: an intersection bereft of a single stoplight, sprouting a hodge-podge of ramshackle shops, a Grey-hound stop, and a postal annex not much larger than a mini-van. Several miles north an actual municipality could be found—Luntville—which seemed nearly as desolate but at least they had a grocery store and a police department. The nearest real city would be Pu-laski—a hundred miles away.

Cassie sweltered at the intersection. She squinted, astonished, at a wooden sign that read WELCOME TO RYAN'S CORNER, HOME OF THE BEST POSSUM SAUSAGE IN THE SOUTH.

You gotta be shitting me, she thought.

Beyond, sporadic trailer homes seemed to wend their way through trees up into the foothills, many without power lines, and the exclusivity of out-houses made it clear that public sewage and domestic water lines weren't taken for granted. Cassie couldn't imagine people living in such extremes. In these parts, poverty and simply doing without were the status quo. It almost shocked her.

"The Boondocks lives," she muttered to herself. "This place is a cliché." Decades-old pickup trucks sat tireless atop cinder-blocks. A flop-faced old hound dog loped lazily across the street, tongue hanging. Ancient men in overalls sat fixed in store-front rocking chairs, ringing spittoons with expertise or puffing on corn-cob pipes, as they creaked another day away. *This place makes Petticoat Junction look like Montreal,* she thought. When she crossed the street, the old men all looked up at once, their empty-sack faces leaning forward as if two buses had suddenly crashed in front of them. Even the dog looked at her, barked once very feebly, and loped on.

HULL'S GENERAL STORE, read a creaking swing-sign. After the long hot walk, a Coke sounded like a good idea. Inside, a crag-faced old man in suspenders glared at her from a chair behind the counter. It took him almost a minute just to stand up. *Looks like Uncle Joe's movin' kind'a slow. . . .*

"What the hail are you?" the man said, gaping at her hair and dress.

Here we go. "I'm a mammalian biped known as homo sapien," Cassie curtly replied. "Ever heard of it?"

"The hail you talkin' about?"

Suddenly an agitated fat woman with her hair back in a bun came in through a back room. "Gawd, Pa! It's one of them tranvesterites, I reckon. Like we seen on Springer!"

"A *what?*"

"From the city! They call 'em Goths! They listen to devil music, and half of 'em are really fellas tryin' to look like gals!"

The old man stroked his chin, which looked like a pair of arthritic knuckles. "A transvesterite, huh?"

Oh, Jesus, Cassie thought in mute anger. In a place like this, she didn't expect to be well received, but this was too much too soon. *So I'm a transvestite now?* She faced the woman and, without really thinking about it, she raised her sarong and yanked up on the waistband of her black panties, stretching them tight across her pubis.

"What do you think, Aunt Bee? Does it look like I'm hiding a penis anywhere down there?"

The woman brought horrified hands to her lined face. "Good *gawd!*" Then she clumped hurriedly away.

"The hail you want here?" the old man said.

Cassie readjusted her sarong. "Just trying to buy a Coke in a free country."

"Ain't got none. Get out."

Cassie just shook her head, smiled, and left. *Now that's what I call a first impression,* she thought. *Cassie Heydon, welcome to the Deep South.*

She should've known better than to come down here. Back out on the store front, she ignored the hateful glances from the other old men. As she walked along, she noted that most of the stores along the strip were long closed, unoccupied, easily, for years. Cobwebs had adhered to the insides of the front windows. The heat began baking her again; the locket with her sister's picture inside grew hot on her chest. *Rich little Goth girl's first day in Ryan's Corner—a bust. Can't even get a bottle of Coke in this hillbilly hell-hole.* It seemed wisest to just go back to the house.

But then she thought: *The house.*

She'd really hoped to be able to ask someone about Blackwell Hall, but after her first official welcome at the general store, the prospects didn't look good. Several blocks down the street, she noticed a tavern— CROSSROADS, the sign read. *Hmm, a redneck bar. Bet I'd get some* real *funky looks in there.* That would even be a bigger mistake, and even if they served her a few months short of her twenty-first birthday, she knew she didn't need to be drinking. She hadn't had a beer since the night her sister died.

"Hey, girl. . . ."

Cassie turned at the corner of the last shop. An old red pickup truck was parked there; she hadn't realized until just now that someone was sitting in it.

Another cliché. From the driver's seat, a sun-weathered man in a ZZ Top hat was staring at her. No shirt beneath the overalls, a couple of days since his last shave. He raised a can of beer from between his legs, sipped it. Cassie frowned when she noticed the brand: Dixie.

"Bet old man Hull shit hisself when you walked in," the man said. "Folks in these parts don't take too kindly to strangers."

"Tell me about it."

"Cute tatt, by the way," he commented of the tiny half-rainbow tattoo around her navel.

"Thanks."

"I gotta coupla tatts myself, but believe me, you don't wanna see 'em."

"I'll take your word for it."

"My name's Roy. Can't shake hands proper, well, on account. . . ."

That's when Cassie noticed that his right arm was missing. It was just a nub. Then she saw that the pickup was a stick shift.

"How, uh, how do you drive?"

He grinned. "Practice. See, I joined the army 'bout ten years ago, thought it'd get me out of this cracker town. All they did was send me right back a bit later, left my arm in Iraq. Goddamn Saddam. Oh, I got some of his boys, though, yes sir."

I'm sure you did, Cassie thought.

"Lemme guess. You take one look at me and think I gotta be just another piss-poor drunk redneck on welfare. That why you're not tellin' me your name? You don't seem like the type to hold somethin' against a fella on account of the way he looks."

"My name's Cassie," she said. "I just moved here from Washington, D.C."

He laughed over his beer. "Well you sure picked a dumbass place to move to. Ain't nothin' out here. Aw, shee-it. I'll bet it's you who moved into the Blackwell place, huh?"

"Yes, with my father," she said and instantly regretted it. *Smart, Cassie. You just told this PERFECT STRANGER where you live.* He seemed nice, though, in his own hayseed kind of way, and she felt sorry for him about his arm.

"Yeah, I know this guy who works up there with his ma. Jervis. His ma's all right, but you keep an eye on Jervis. He likes to peek in windows'n such. Did thirty days in Luntville jail for peepin' on little girls at the middle school."

Charming, Cassie thought and frowned.

"Oh, I don't mean to scare you none. The county court makes him take some fancy drug as part of his probation. Keeps his mind off things like that. Just stick a wad of paper in your keyhole, if ya know what I mean."

"I appreciate the sound advice."

"Now, if I was you I'd be more worried 'bout the house itself. That place just has some *bad* vibes."

The comment perked her up. "Let me guess. It's haunted, right?"

"Naw," he said and sipped more beer. A moment passed. "It's a damn lot worse than just being haunted. You know. On account of what went on there."

"All right, you've got me hooked now," she admitted.

"Come on, let's go fer a ride. I'll tell you all about the place if ya like."

Cassie just looked at him, and thought, *I'm really not stupid and naive enough to get into a pickup truck with a one-armed half-drunk redneck I just met, am I?*

"Okay, Roy. Let's go," she said, and got in.

(III)

It turned out that Roy could drive a stick-shift better than she could. The flash of his left hand to the stick only took a second before it was back firmly on the wheel.

"Peel me off one'a them beers there if ya don't mind," he asked, "and help yerself to one too."

"No, thanks. I quit two years ago." She pulled a can from the styrofoam cooler in the footwell, opened it and passed it to him.

His knee kept the steering wheel in place when he took the can. "Bet'choo ain't even drinkin' age and you're already on the wagon. More power to ya, I say. You'll find out soon enough, though. Ain't nothin' to do in this town 'cept drink and sweat."

Cassie was already figuring that out. She grimaced over each bump in the road; the pickup's suspension was shot, and by the sound of it, so was the muffler. *Riding in style,* came the sarcastic thought. *Gee, this puts Dad's Caddy to shame.* He took a long narrow road up behind the row of shops. Soon they were in dense woods.

"All'a Blackwell Hill, see, is cursed so they say. Let me ask you something? When you and your daddy moved in, most of the furniture was still there, weren't it?"

"Well, yes," she admitted, and she also had to admit that it was a strange fact.

"After all this time, a lot of it probably looks like junk, but let me tell ya, there are some quite pricy antiques in that house."

"I know. We kept most of it. My father had it cleaned up by some refinishers from Pulaski."

"And don't that strike ya as odd?" Roy cut a sideglance at her, sipping more beer.

"A little. It *is* a lot of furniture."

"Ain't no one lived in that house for about seventy years. All that expensive stuff sittin' in it, but in all them years nobody pinched a single piece. Any other place—shee-it. The rednecks in this burg'd clean the place out in one night."

Cassie thought about that. "Yeah, I guess it is pretty strange. I wonder why nobody ever ripped the place off."

"It's 'cos you can hear the babies cryin' at night. You heard 'em yet?"

"Babies? No. I haven't heard anything funny. And what's with the babies?"

Roy's head tilted. He seemed to be pausing for the right words. "It was Blackwell. Everything south of town's called Blackwell something. Blackwell Hall, Blackwell Swamp, Blackwell Hill, like that. 'Cos there was a guy—Fenton Blackwell; he's the one who bought the original plantation house back before World War One, then built all them crazy-lookin' additions."

47

Great, Cassie thought. *The wing that I live in.*

"Blackwell was a satanist," Roy said next. "Bigtime."

"Come on."

"It's true enough. You can go to the Russell County Library'n read all about it. They still got the old papers on some micro something-or-other. See, right after he had that funky part of the house built, some local gals disappeared a might quick. 'Bout ten of 'em all told, but nobody paid it much mind on account they was just hill girls. Creekers, we call 'em."

Cassie loved ghost stories, and this was sounding like it had all the makings of a doozy. "What about the babies?" she urged him.

"I'm gettin' to it. You seen the basements?"

She remembered them well: long, narrow brick channels beneath the newer part of the house, not like typical basements at all. "Yeah. Big deal," she said.

"Well, it was Blackwell who snatched them hill girls, and it was in those basements he'd keep 'em chained up. He'd—you know—he'd make 'em pregnant."

"And?"

"And then he'd sacrifice the babies lickety split. Soon as the gals gave birth, Blackwell'd take that newborn all the way upstairs, to that room with the funky window—"

The top garret, Cassie thought. *With the oculus window.*

"—and then sacrifice 'em to the devil."

Cassie slumped as if let down. She didn't believe a word of it, but she at least had hoped for a ghostly folktale that was more original that this.

"Then he'd bury the dead babies on the back hill. They found a few, dug 'em up, but it's for sure that there were lots more all told."

"What makes you say that?"

Roy didn't miss a beat. " 'Cos they caught him doin' it, the local cops. They busted into that place and found the women chained down there in the basements. There were ten women, all still alive, and they'd been missing for ten years. The few that were still able to talk, said Blackwell had been doin' it to 'em steady the whole time. Figure it out. Ten women, each havin' a baby once a year for *ten years?* That's a *hunnert* babies he killed'n buried up there."

A hundred, she thought. *Babies.*

She still didn't believe it. If any of it were true, Jervis—in his own propensity for hokey stories— would've mentioned it.

"Screamin' Baby Hill's what they call it."

Cassie rolled her eyes as Roy pulled the truck to a stop. His one hand gestured out the window, toward the vast wooded hill before them. "That's it. Right there."

"I don't hear any babies screaming," Cassie pointed out.

"A'course not. Not now. Only at night."

"Of course."

"You'll hear 'em out here, but you'll hear 'em best up the house. At night. Midnight,'cos that's when Blackwell killed 'em."

"Of course," she repeated.

He shot her a sly smile over his next sip of beer. "I

know. You think I'm just some nutty cracker with a belly full of beer'n bullshit. But I ain't lyin'. It's all true."

"Then how come I haven't heard any babies at night?"

" 'Cos you ain't listened hard enough, or—" Roy shrugged. "Or maybe them babies don't mind ya bein' there."

"Have you ever heard them?" she asked next.

The sly smile fell apart. He looked serious, even bothered. "Yeah. Once."

It was the quick change in his expression that bothered her.

Roy continued without having to be asked. He finished his beer in a long slug, as if to steel himself. "Just before I went into the Army," he said. "Week before basic training. I took a gal up to Blackwell Hall—Halloween Night as a matter of fact. Her name was Carrie Ann Wells, a real beaut, and I don't have to tell ya just what I was takin' her up there for."

"Checkers, right?"

The levity passed right over him. "She goes in before me on account she wants to light up some weed. I'm in the truck gettin' the beer cooler out, but a second later Carrie Ann comes runnin' out that big-ass ugly front door, and she's screamin' at the top of her lungs. Doesn't even get back in the truck, she just ran on down the hill, screamin'. I'm thinkin' it's a joke, so then I walk into the house. . . . Fetch me another beer, will ya please?"

Jesus. Cassie did so, cracked it open and handed it to him. "You were saying?"

Roy seemed to tremble slightly. "I don't want you to think I'm some kind of coward now."

"Why would I think that?"

"Durin' Desert Storm—well, here, let me show ya."

Cassie pressed herself against the springy bench seat as Roy awkwardly reached across her. He opened the glove box, fumbled through papers. She tried not to shirk when he accidentally nudged her with the bald nub where his arm used to be. "I know it's in here somewhere, damn it." The pose left him bent over, and she saw him steal a quick glance at her crotch and thighs. "Ah, here it is. I got this for blowin' up a T-64 tank with a slap-charge." He recovered his position, looking at something small in his hand. "See, we were layin' portable bridges over the trenches Saddam dug. One'a his tanks was takin' pot-shots at us from about a thousand meters, and really fuckin' us up—er, pardon the language. Really pissed me off 'cos they put a HEP round right into the open door of our M88, and two of my buddies bought it. All of a sudden, the whole company is pinned down by one tank full'a rag-heads. So I jump in a Hummer and flank the bastards; they don't see me, and I got my green-eyes on. Parked behind a dune, and rushed the tank. But by then the TC spots me so he cranks around his co-ax and starts spraying bullets at me. I slap an RDX charge on his back deck, see, and start runnin' back. Then the charge goes off, and the whole tank blows up,'cos, see, it's a dumbass Russian-built tank and they got the fuel cells exposed, and—"

51

Risking being rude, Cassie cut him off. "Look, I don't know anything about tanks or slap-charges. Just tell me about Blackwell Hall."

"Well I'se gettin' to that, hon. Lemme tell the story. I blow up an enemy tank by myself, so Uncle Sam gives me this. Keeps my arm, but gives me this." He showed her what was in his hand: a small star with a ribbon.

Cassie peered at it. "That's a Medal of Honor!"

"Sure." He threw it back in the glove box, closed the door. "And that's my point. I ain't braggin' but they wouldn't have given me that medal if I was a wussy, now would they?"

"No, I'm sure they wouldn't," she answered, aggravated.

"When I rushed that T-64, I knew I could die but I didn't care. I did my job. Wasn't scared one bit."

Cassie sighed. "Yeah? And?"

He stared out the windshield when he said, "I was scared shitless when I stepped into Blackwell Hall that night."

Either he's a good actor or— She leaned closer to him. "What did you see?"

Now he looked right at her. "I saw a tall man in a black suit walkin' slow up the stairs. Heard a sound like a bunch'a cats on fire, but it weren't cats, it were babies. You know how when you're fishin' and you have a good day? You come home with a hook-line full of fish?"

"Yeah," Cassie stretched the word.

"That's what this tall guy had . . . only it was a hook-line full of babies, and he was draggin' 'em up the stairs."

Then Roy let out a long breath.

A hook-line. Full of babies. Cassie shivered as if someone had scraped nails across a chalkboard. She still didn't believe it, but the image gave her the creeps. "That's some story," she eventually said.

Roy shook off whatever distress he might be feigning. "I can tell you don't believe it, but that's all right. I ain't lyin'. Never went near that house again and never will."

Something about the long silence that followed made the story even more effective. A moment later, though, she caught his eyes wandering over her top and bare midriff.

"If you don't mind my sayin' so, you're one fine sight. Best-lookin' gal I seen around her in years."

"I'm flattered," Cassie said, though the comment unnerved her. "The people in the store thought I was a man."

"Shee-it. Old man Hull and his sister? Those crackers are nuts. Yes, sir, you're one beautiful girl, that's for sure."

Cassie slumped in the seat. "Roy, you're about the only decent person I've met since I moved her. Please don't disappoint me by putting the make on me."

"Aw, no, it's nothin' like that, and I'm sorry if that's what ya thunk."

Thunk?

"It's just that when a gal as beautiful as you shows

53

up in a place like this, it's kind of a shock. Girls around here are mostly just trailer cows."

Cassie laughed in spite of herself. "Well, thanks for the story, Roy. But I better get back now. The house is right up on the other side of this hill."

"Screaming *Baby* Hill," he reminded her. "Let me drive ya the rest of the way up."

"But didn't you just say you'd never go to that house again?"

"At night, I meant." He smiled, winked at her.

"I'd like to walk. Maybe I'll trip over some baby bones."

"You just might. Take care now. It was nice meeting you. Hope to see you again sometime."

"You will." She opened the truck door and got out.

"Stop by the bar some night," he said after her. "I'll buy you a coffee. Show ya how a one-armed man plays pool."

"I'll do that, Roy. Bye." She crossed the narrow road, waved to him, and then proceeded up. *Whew! That poor guy is baked in the head.* Her flipflops crunched over twigs as she marched further up the incline. Shadows from the dense trees dropped the temperature; through high branches she could see the sun beginning to set. The hot day was fading behind her.

Screaming Baby Hill, she thought, looking around. *Well, here I am.*

The hill was silent, which seemed odd. No mosquitoes here, no signs of squirrels or other wildlife in the woods. It was peaceful, nearly cool. She wasn't quite certain of her bearings but she knew that Blackwell Hall was up the hill somewhere. *I'll get back to the house eventually.* But then a mental note caused her to stop. She was thinking about the story that Roy had told: Blackwell, the apparent satanist who'd made the eccentric additions to the house. She still doubted that she believed a word of it. Usually such things were grossly amended after a not-too-spectacular fact. Sure, there probably was a Blackwell, and maybe some women had really disappeared. *Consider the times, then mix that into the local grapevine, and suddenly you've got a devil-worshiping psychopath sacrificing babies,* she thought. *The women probably just left town without telling anyone, and Blackwell probably looked sinister.* But now that she thought of it, when Roy finished the story, he never did mention Blackwell's fate.

Her curiosity scratched at her. She hadn't gotten far, and when she glanced back down the hill, she could see Roy's pickup truck still parked at the side of the road. *I'll just go back down and ask him what became of Blackwell.*

Her footsteps crunched back down the hill until she was about to emerge on the passenger side of the truck. She stopped abruptly, though, and ducked behind a tree when she heard his voice.

"Aw, jeeze," he was saying to himself. "Aw, man. . . ."

One squint verified her suspicion.

Oh my God!

Roy was masturbating. She pulled herself away from the visual evidence. *I really don't need to see this.* At first she was grossed out but then she regarded the reality. A war hero maimed while serving his country? Spat back into poverty when the Army had no further use for him? What else could he do?

So much for that bright idea. . . .

Continuing now would only embarrass him. Quietly as she could, she turned and tip-toed back up the hill. *What did you do today, Cassie?* she comically asked herself. *Well, let's see. I went into town and got mistaken for a male transvestite, I learned all about a satanic baby-killer, and I saw a one-armed redneck jerking off. Sounds like a pretty full day to me.*

When she'd turned around, she immediately noticed a footpath of flat stones leading up the hill, and as she stepped onto it and began to walk, she felt a bit embarrassed herself. She could still hear some of Roy's fervent utterings as he neared his moment of crisis.

Gee. I wonder who he's thinking about right now?

She smiled the incident off and headed back up the footpath. After about fifty yards, though, she stopped again.

She heard footsteps—someone *else's* footsteps—coming *down*.

It wouldn't be her father; he'd be done fishing now but he'd have no reason to stray this far from the house.

In the woods?

No way.

A mild panic rose up; the unseen footfalls were getting louder. Should she run back to Roy?

A glance over her shoulder showed her the beaten pickup truck driving away from the hill. By now the sun had sunk so low, the woods had darkened to a maze of shadows. Cassie nervously looked back up the path.

A figure was standing there perfectly still.

Staring back at her.

(IV)

Bill Heydon placed the string of catfish in the refrigerator. *Not a bad haul for an amateur,* he assessed. He'd have to dress them later—Cassie was a good sport and a good cook, but one thing she wouldn't do was handle fish guts. First, though . . .

He walked around the downstairs.

"Cassie?"

Then he marched his 200 pounds halfway up the banistered steps and called out louder, "Cassie? You home?"

No answer.

For the briefest moment, he thought he heard music. A couple of distant blares. One thing he'd never understand was this Goth music. *Maryland Mansion, my ass.* It all just sounded like discordant noise to him. When he looked in Cassie's room, though, she wasn't there. Besides, the music had sounded more distant.

Maybe you're hearing things, you old pud.

He stood still, listened harder, and heard nothing. It was probably Mrs. Conner's kid working outside. Sometimes he brought a radio with him.

But where was Cassie?

Guess she's still out wandering around.

At least that meant the coast was clear. He went back down the stairs and walked out onto the stone-fenced back patio of the older section of the house. He lit a cigarette at once. *She'd scream if she could see me,* he realized. But he couldn't stop.

I'll quit some day—just not today.

The sun was a blistering dark-orange blot as it was dragged behind the mountains by the turning of the earth. *This is absolutely beautiful. No sunsets like this in D.C.* The remoteness of the estate only made the surroundings that much more fascinating. The city was an addiction, and he knew that it was not just killing Cassie, it was killing him too. They both needed to get away from everything; it was the only way. He'd been oblivious back in the city, as though the world's survival depended upon his next landmark lawsuit. He couldn't *see.* It had cost him his wife, and when he finally realized that, one daughter was dead and the other was trying to kill herself in between therapy and mental wards.

One day the truth arrived in a flash: Get out or die.

His eyes roved the pristine house, then the vast woodland beyond. He'd never felt so relaxed nor together in his life. *Please, God, just let this fuckin' work.*

So far, it was.

Cassie had her good days and bad, but over the past few weeks, she actually seemed at home with the drastic change. Bill blamed himself for Lissa's death; if he'd been at home nights, being a father to the kids he'd brought into the world, then none of that would've happened. He'd still have a wife, he'd still have a fam-

58

ily, not just pieces of one. It was too late for any of that, but he felt bound to help repair the damage to Cassie, damage that his own neglect had caused.

He stubbed out the half-smoked cigarette against the smooth stone fence-top. Behind him a bleached white statue of some naked Greek goddess burbled arcs of water. The statue's physical features were a bit too explicit to remain classic and tasteful. Nippled breasts jutted like an x-rated cartoon. The legs weren't quite crossed enough to leave the genitalic details to the imagination. It only projected an aboriginal reminder of sex, something he hadn't had in a long while.

Christ, I'm eye-balling statues.

After the divorce, he'd discovered that his wife had been cheating on him for over a year but in truth he'd been doing the same for longer, and much more aggressively. Ritzy high-priced hookers and party girls. He sometimes even did it with associates and interns, girls his daughters' age. *Got what I deserved,* he thought, despondent. One had gotten pregnant, and he knew that the $50,000 she'd demanded was for far more than the abortion.

Jesus. . . .

But Bill was fifty now. His oat-sowing days were over, and they needed to be. It was time to be responsible for a change. What success seemed to equate to these days were fancy private cocktail parties full of millionaires and escort girls, in posh brownstones rented through corporate accounts. It was not the way people were supposed to live their lives.

Through the glass-paned French doors he could see Mrs. Conner vacuuming one of the dens.

She's older than I am but—Christ—what a body.

And there he went again. *Now I'm lusting after the help.* The notion was even more pitiful. Here was an honest hard-working woman who'd never had anything and had been walked on by poverty and misfortune, and here was Bill, if only in his mind, exploiting her all the more. *You're a real piece of work, Heydon,* he told himself. What made it worse was that Mrs. Conner— widowed for years—had clearly taken a fancy to him. *But somehow I doubt that it's because of my good looks.*

"Howdy, Mr. Heydon." It was Jervis, Mrs. Conner's son, coming around the patio. *A bit of a dim bulb,* Bill thought, *but he works hard.*

"I finished up trimmin' the garden," the young man said, scratching his belly. "Got the front-walk edged, the rest of your lawyer books down in the basement, and them leaky pipes sealed up on the second floor."

"That's great, Jervis," Bill said. He'd been just about to pull another cigarette out but then he thought better of it. Instead, he pulled out his wallet. "What is it, twenty an hour right?"

"Yes, sir."

Bill gave him two hundred-dollar bills. "Keep the change."

The boy gave a big pumpkin grin. "Thanks much, sir!"

"Come back day after tomorrow. I think the lawn'll need mowing by then. And I'll have plenty more work for you to do if you want it."

"Sure will, Mr. Heydon. You'se the best boss I ever had."

"Oh, and Jervis—"

"Don't worry, sir. I won't tell Cassie I seen ya smokin'."

Bill nodded, embarrassed. "Thank you, Jervis."

"Have a good evenin', sir! I'll be waitin' out front. My ma's should be finishin' up soon."

Bill watched the boy lope off. He wondered what it must be like for him and his mother. No industry, no decent jobs, just a trailer to call home and a thirty-year-old hunk of junk for a car. He doubted if they'd ever seen a real city at all, or had any idea what the rest of the world was like. It was during times like these that Bill realized how much he had to be grateful for.

He walked back into the house as Mrs. Conner made a few last swipes with the vacuum. She turned the loud machine off when she noticed him.

Her eyes beamed. "I'm about done fer today, Mr. Heydon."

"That's fine," Bill said. "The place looks great." He handed her an over-estimation of her pay for the day and listened to a gush of drawled thanks. He struggled with himself not to look at her in that way again, was succeeding, but then she bent over to unplug the vacuum.

Bill's teeth ground.

The collar of the woman's simple white blouse hung down, and Bill's unconscious tunnel-vision shot right down. It was plain that no form of brassiere encompassed Mrs. Conner's abundant breasts, and just as

61

clear now that the forces of gravity had treated her with kindness. Bill couldn't help himself—he stared down. The image seemed like a vibrant luxury and it only spurred him further to take closer note of the rest of her body when she stood back up. Age-lines were obvious on her face but—

That body!

The word *hearty* came to mind. Blue jeans spread tight across the wide hips. The plush, hourglass figure and thrusting bosom socked him in the eye.

Even when she smiled, showing a missing tooth, the image remained intense.

That there is one hot slab of country pie. If I don't quit looking at her, I'll probably have another heart attack right here.

He fought to distract himself, thought up some small talk. "I had a lucky day fishing at the creek."

"Yes sir, I saw them fine-lookin' fish in the fridge. I'd be happy to clean 'em and cook 'em for ya, Mr. Heydon. I'll just send Jervis on home. You ain't had catfish till you've had it country fried."

It sounded delicious, almost as delicious as the idea of watching her quietly lusty body bending over the range.

Which was why he said, "No, thanks, Mrs. Conner, but thanks for the offer. Cassie really enjoys cooking. By the way, have you seen her?"

"Not since this morning, sir. She was runnin' off somewheres, town I imagine."

Bill looked at his Rolex. "Been gone all day," he muttered.

"I'm sure she'll be along presently," Mrs. Conner offered. "We cain't keep too tight a leash on our young ones—much as we might want to. Gotta let 'em roam, see things on their own."

"Of course, you're right." Bill averted his eyes from her pressing bosom. The nipples shone through her blouse, the size of the bottom of a soda can. "She's probably just walking around with her Discman somewhere."

"You sure you don't want me to stay?"

"No, that's all right, Mrs. Conner. See you tomorrow."

"Bye!"

When she strutted off, Bill was helpless to stare after her.

Christmas! he thought. *I need to get a life!* He chased more distraction, poured himself a soda, turned on the radio for some music. *Ah, Vivaldi. Thank you!* The spacious sonata lulled the edges off his mood.

Better. Much better.

Beyond the fine windows, the sky had darkened further. He glanced again at his watch.

Where the hell is Cassie?

(V)

"Wow!" came a strange, delighted voice. "Who are you?"

"Uh, Cassie," Cassie said. Her first reaction was defensive, to camouflage her fear with aggression, to demand what this person was doing on her property. But—

The figure facing her was a young woman, probably eighteen or twenty, slim but curvy, and with a demeanor that seemed not really butch but definitely tomboyish. What took Cassie most aback was the girl's appearance: shiny leather boots and black leather pants, a studded belt, a deliberately shredded black t-shirt under a black leather jacket. Not Goth but more like late-'70s punk. Buttons on the jacket confirmed the estimation. THE GERMS, THE STRANGLERS, a button of The Cure's first album cover and another of Siouxie and the Banshee's THE SCREAM. White haphazard letters on the t-shirt read SIC F*CKS!

"Wow," the girl repeated. "This is great! A newbie!"

"Pardon me?" Cassie said.

"I love what you're wearing. Where'd you get it?"

"I—" Cassie began but that was all she could get out.

"And your hair's great! I'd do anything to get my hands on some dye like that. Where'd you get it?"

"I—" Cassie tried again.

"We've never seen you before. How long have you been here?"

"A month or so."

"Still getting to learn your way around—it takes a while." The girl reached into her jacket, pulled out a cassette. "Here, have a tape. It's great stuff. We ripped a bunch of them off the other night, in the city."

Cassie reluctantly took the cassette tape. *The city? She must mean Pulaski, or Charlottesville.* "Uh, thank you." The cover was black with silver Gothic letters:

ALDINOCH. "I've never heard of them. What is it? Metal?"

"You'll love it. And it's really the only thing going on in the city right now." The girl seemed effervescent, overcharged. Her hand shot out. "Oh, sorry! I'm Via."

Cassie shook her hand—it felt hot. "Cassie," she repeated. "So where do you live?"

"It's just me and two others—Xeke and Hush." Her thumb pointed behind her, up the trail. "We stay at that big ugly-ass house on the hill."

What! Cassie felt bewildered. "You don't mean Blackwell Hall?"

"Yeah. Right up here. On top of the hill."

This was too weird. "You must mean someplace else. I live at Blackwell Hall."

Via didn't seem at all fazed. "Oh, well that's cool. You can squat with us."

Squatters. That would explain it, but—

"We stay up in the oculus room during the day."

Could this possibly be true? The house was so large that Cassie supposed squatters *could* stay there in some remote area. But how feasible was it that they could remain unheard and undetected for all this time?

"It's the strongest part of the house," Via went on. "The basements aren't bad either, but the oculus room is where Blackwell killed all the babies."

Cassie suddenly felt rooted to the ground. *What is going on? What is she talking about?*

"You have a really strong aura," Via added cheerfully. "Did you know that? Bright blue. Why don't you

65

come with me to the Station? You can meet the others. We're going to the city tonight."

Cassie's thought processes seemed to grind like a series of cogs. Her eyes were fixed on Via's wrist—and the open slit held together by crude black stitches. She could see dried blood in the wound, as if it hadn't healed.

But now Via was looking back just as strangely.

At *Cassie's* wrist.

"That's impossible," she whispered. She grabbed Cassie's wrist and looked at the similar scar, similar only in that it denoted the same intent. But Cassie's scar was—

"Healed," Via muttered. "It's healed." Then her darkly mascara'd eyes looked stupefied into Cassie's.

"Oh my God," Via said. "You're not dead, are you?"

In spite of the compounding strangeness, Cassie blurted a laugh. "What kind of a ridiculous thing is that to say? Of course I'm not dead."

"Well I sure as hell am!" Via exclaimed and ran away down the hill.

Chapter Three

(I)

Delusion. Hallucination.

What else could it be? At the hospital, they'd told her that some of the psych drugs could produce such side effects. She'd stopped taking them rather abruptly; perhaps hallucinosis was the result.

Either that or I'm just going nuts. I'm going schizo.

Memory of the incident clung to her, unpleasant as the day's humidity. Had she fallen asleep in the woods and dreamed it?

No. It felt too real.

"Hi, honey!" her father had called out from the spacious living room. "I was getting a little worried."

"I . . . got a little lost coming back from town," she'd fabricated an excuse. She'd gasped when she opened

67

the refrigerator and saw the hook-line full of catfish. It reminded her of the awful story Roy had told.

That's what this tall guy had . . . only it was a hook-line full of babies, *and he was draggin' 'em up the stairs.*

"Damn, sorry," her father said, hustling into the kitchen. "I forgot to clean the fish." He retrieved the weighty hook-line, thunked it in the sink.

She smelled remnant cigarette smoke, but didn't say anything. She turned away at the wet grisly sounds of him gutting the fish. She needed to get her mind off her own musings: Via, the story Roy had told, Blackwell and the babies.

But she felt more like an automaton as she turned on the stove and prepared to cook dinner.

Via's words slipped back: *We stay at that big ugly-ass house on the hill.*

There is no Via, she told herself.

"So you checked out town today?" her father asked.

She clunked around in the cupboard for the right pan. "Yeah. It's not really even a town. Just a few old stores on the strip."

"Well, I know it's dull around here. Maybe we'll drive to Pulaski this weekend, do some shopping."

"Cool," she said, unenthused.

Her father had piled the fresh catfish fillets on a plate. "You're awful quiet tonight. Are you okay?"

Peachy, Dad. Today I found out that the guy who used to live here sacrificed infants to Satan. I also met a dead girl named Via. Oh, she lives in the house with her friends.

"Just tired, I guess. I must've been out in the sun too long."

"Go lie down. I'll cook dinner."

"I'm fine, really. I want to do it. Go watch your sports stuff."

"You sure?"

"Sure. Two people in the kitchen is one too many. Makes me bitchy."

Her father laughed, retreating back to the family room.

Cassie poached the fish in soy sauce and fresh-ground horseradish. But when they ate, she barely tasted it. "This is great!" her father complimented. "You could be a chef!"

Cassie picked through her food, still bothered. Of course, what she'd seen today—Via—had been her imagination, minor heat-stroke or something.

It *had* to be.

She looked blankly at the huge television: a pre-season football game. Nothing seemed more pointless in the world than grown men running back and forth over grass trying to move a leather bag full of air.

"Fuckin' Leon!" her father suddenly shouted, pounding the coffee table with the bottom of his fist. "Do us all a favor and chicken-walk your ass back to Dallas, you lazy no-talent sham motherf—" He caught himself in the tirade, looked sheepishly to Cassie. "Er, sorry."

She just smiled and took the plates back to the kitchen, washed and dried them by hand rather than using the newly installed dishwasher. Something was

Edward Lee

side-tracking her thoughts, and she knew exactly what it was.

She knew what she wanted to do.

"I'm going up to my room, Dad. Gonna listen to some music for a while."

"Okay, honey. Thanks for cooking. You sure you're all right?"

"I'm fine. Enjoy your game."

She edged out, started walking up the carpeted stairs. Brass flicker-bulb lamps lit the way up, throwing shadows on the various old statues and oil paintings.

Yes, she knew what she wanted to do.

On the second-floor landing, she glanced down the dark hall toward her room. Then she glanced up the next flight of stairs.

Her father's muffled shouting echoed from the living room: "Don't bother trying to tackle the guy, Leon—oh, no! We wouldn't want you to actually break out into a sweat for your EIGHT MILLION A YEAR!"

Cassie looked at the cassette tape. She'd probably just picked it up somewhere, or found it. Or maybe Roy had given it to her. The name on the cover sounded sinister.

ALDINOCH.

No, Roy must've given it to me, and I don't remember. I'm just having some weird drug flashback from all that crap they pumped into me at the hospital.

Now she felt convinced.

There was no Via. There was no dead girl.

More hesitation. She could go back to her room and listen to the tape, or—

70

She started going up the next flight of stairs. Every few steps creaked. A chill crept beneath her skin; if the story was true, she was making the exact same trek that Fenton Blackwell had—with the babies.

Only a few lights glimmered on the third floor. The halls to either side were grainy with darkness.

Another glance upward. Deeper darkness.

The final flight of steps was carpetless and much more narrow. When she flicked on a wall switch, only the most meager light winked on up above.

She took one step up, stopped, then took another.

Oh, come on! Don't be such a chicken! What? You think you're going to go up there and find people there? Come on!

She ascended the rest of the way quickly. There was no door to the oculus room; the stairs merely emerged up into it.

There. See?

A single hanging bulb lit the room. There was no Via, no people waiting for her. Three bare mattresses lay on the dusty floor, and this bothered her a little when she thought about it. Cobwebs festooned the small room's corners, and the walls appeared to never have been papered, just old wooden slats.

The oculus window stared back at her like an odd face.

Then something caught her attention. Against one rickety wall stood an old tea table, and sitting on top of it was a dusty boombox.

She fingered her cassette tape. She could plug it in now, listen to it here. But as she hit the button to pop

71

the cassette lid, she saw that a tape was in there already.

Her guts were already beginning to sink when she pulled out the tape. ALDINOCH, it read.

It was identical to the tape she had.

Her heart rate jumped. "Don't freak out," she slowly demanded. "There's an explanation. Just . . . get a grip on yourself."

She reclosed the lid and pushed the PLAY button. The sudden blare of volume shook her; she quickly turned it down.

Death Metal, just as she'd thought. Multiple layers of abrasive guitars and discordant synth-drums washed back and forth over corroded vocals:

"Inverting every cross toward Hell
This church is now the Goat's!
Praise him, whores of holiness,
Before I slit your throats!"

Cassie's lips pursed as if she'd tasted something sour. She liked the rhythms and the dense cords, but the negative lyrics turned her off.

Next, a chorus roared:

"I have chosen my afterlife
And darkness it shall be
Satan!!! Open wide
the gates of Hell for me!"

The Gothy mix of Hard-Industrial treatment with Slayer-like lyrics didn't work for her. She switched the boombox off. But what could explain this strangeness? It was the same cassette tape that the girl in her delusion had given her. The tape in the boombox was real, and so was the one in her hand.

And there was another coincidence, wasn't there?

I just happen to find a tape full of satanic music . . . in a room where a satanist supposedly sacrificed babies.

She sighed and turned. The round oculus window full of stained glass re-faced her. The faintest light glowed in a scarlet pane—the moon, no doubt.

Something urged her to open the window. The metal hinge squealed when she pushed against the circular frame. Warm air brushed her face. She looked out the window.

And fainted at once.

It was not the rolling nighted landscape that she'd glimpsed when she looked out.

It was a city, miles distant and seemingly endless. A city silhouetted by a luminous dark-red sky.

A city that wasn't there.

(II)

When Cassie wakened, she felt as though she were rising from an entrenchment of hot tar. Some aspect of her consciousness pushed upward, and when she opened her eyes, she saw only strange blurred squares.

"Cassie?"

The voice helped her to focus; the squares sharpened. They were, of course, the fancily embossed brass and tin ceiling tiles in her bedroom.

She was lying inert on top of her bed.

"Cassie, honey? What's wrong?"

The voice, warbled at first, was her father's. He leaned over, his face stamped with worry.

Scraps of memory began to re-assemble.

I was upstairs. . . .

The oculus room.

A breath seemed to snag in her chest.

That . . . city.

A city that didn't exist. A city so immense that it seemed to go on without limit. The south side of Blackwell Hill extended as miles of open farmland and then a gradual rise of forest belts that ended at the mountains.

But when she'd looked out that window . . .

No Blue Ridge Mountains, no farmland, no trees.

Instead she'd seen a cityscape that glowed as if built on embers. She'd seen a starless twilight of raging scarlet. She'd seen bizarre, lit skyscrapers haloed by dense shifts of smoke.

What WAS that?

"I found you upstairs, in the oculus room," her father said. "You had passed out."

"I'm . . . all right now," she murmured, leaning up in bed.

"I should probably call a doctor—"

"No, please. I'm okay."

"What were you doing up in that room, honey?"

What could she say?

"I thought I heard something. I'd never been up there before, so I went up."

"You thought you *heard* something?"

"I don't know, I thought so."

"Then you should've come and gotten me."

"I know, but I didn't want to bug you. Sorry."

Her father sat in a cane chair beside the bed. He looked exerted, which was no wonder because he'd obviously been the one who carried her back downstairs to her room. She didn't like to lie, but how could she tell him the truth? *There're dead people living in the house, and the sky outside is red. I saw a city where there IS no city.* He'd have her committed for observation immediately. No, she couldn't tell him the truth.

She didn't even know what the truth was.

The difficulty of the next question shone in his pinched expression. "Honey, have you been drinking again, or taking drugs. If you have, just tell me. I promise I won't go apeshit, but I need to know."

"I haven't, Dad. I swear." The question didn't anger her as it had in the past. *After all my screwing up, what's he supposed to think?* "It's just the heat, I think. Too much sun. I've felt kind of sick all day."

He patted her hand. "You want me to get you anything?"

"No, that's all right. I just want to go to sleep."

"If you're still not feeling well tomorrow, you're gonna tell me, right?"

"Yes."

"I'll get your old doctor out here right away."

"Dad, she's in D.C."

Her father shrugged. "Then I'll charter a goddamn helicopter and *fly* her out here."

She managed a giggle. "You would. I'll be fine. I just need to go to sleep."

"Okay. You call me if you need anything."

"I'll be fine," she repeated. "Sorry to be such a pain in the butt."

"Yeah, but you're *my* pain in the butt. Remember that."

"I will. Go back and watch your game. I know how much you love to bitch about Leon Flanders or whatever his name is."

The comment instantly set him off. "That lazy, no-effort, non-football-playing son of a bitch! He missed *twelve* tackles in the first half!" He walked out of the room and back down the hall, his complaints fading. "Jesus Christ, I'm a fat old man and *I* could tackle better than that talentless bum!"

Well, Cassie thought. *At least he's back to normal.*

She rubbed her eyes.

But what about me?

She dawdled about in her room, exhausted yet wiry with fret. She turned off the lights, stripped and donned a short nightgown, and next she was walking out the French doors onto the gable-sided terrace. Night-sounds pulsated—crickets, peepers—and then a warm wind stirred. She looked out over the moonlit landscape and saw no smoking, luminous city. Just open land and forests which extended to the crisply edged mountains.

What did you expect?

Sighing, she walked back in and went to bed.

Sleep pulled her down like muggers sneaking up from behind. She felt stuffed in a black ravine as nightmares hulked overhead.

First, as always:

Lissa's face, twisted into a mask of insane hatred.

And the death-rattle voice. "My own sister . . . How could you do this to me?"

Then the gunshot and the hot blood splattering into Cassie's eyes.

No, please. . . .

More fragments of nightmare plodded over her. Yes, she lay immobile in a ravine—or an open grave.

Her mouth felt sealed shut.

She could smell malodorous smoke, could hear muffled cracklings of a roaring fire. Again, she saw the city under the scarlet sky.

The city seemed endless.

Distant screams careened to and fro, like sirens miles away. But with each frantic beat of her heart, the visions lurched closer. . . .

The city raged before the infernal terrascape, a firmament of inversions whose highest edifice winked at its peak like a beacon of luminous blood. Cassie's vision trailed away on stinking, hot winds, shooting through abyssal avenues and abhorrent boulevards as though it were a scream itself. In one avenue, a troop of man-like *things* with chisel-slits for eyes shouldered into a crowd of haggard people, and with inhuman three-fingered hands, these same *things* began to select victims for whatever purpose there was on this horrid night. Faces were dragged by fingers hooked into eyes. Wan mouths opened to scream ejecting innards and blasts of blood. Heads were prized apart, raw brains rowed through by the fat taloned fingers. One man was being seared with prods of white-hot iron, another was eviscerated with one fast swipe of a talon. The guts were then summarily shoved into the victim's mouth as he was being forced to eat. Women faired worse, stripped to emaciated nakedness and plundered for sexual possibilities that defied all human imagination.

Dark chuckles fluttered as the endless workings of this place ground on and on.

Horrid as the images were, Cassie received the notion that these were things she was *supposed* to see.

The eye of the nightmare blinked, then focused more closely on the details of this evil street. Screams were exploding now; Cassie thought of famine-riots in some collapsing Calcutta-like city in the Third World. The vaguely-human wardens plodded on in their nameless duties, tearing into the crowd. One woman was singled out, hauled forward by the hair and thrown into the street. Her clothes were torn off, and as she was being raped *en masse,* two more three-fingered hands vised her head and twisted it round and round and round until it came off. Decapitation did not seem to dissuade the woman's queue of rapists in the least. In guttering glee, then, one of the wardens stuck the severed head atop a street sign for all to see.

The street sign read: CITY MUTILATION ZONE

The severed head was Cassie's.

Silence.

Darkness, like death.

Then—voices, sibilant whisperings:

"See how blue? I told you."

"Cool."

"You can even . . . *touch her*."

Hands felt her body. She was blind. One hand seemed to tremble as it touched her face. Another opened flat between her breasts.

"I can feel it! I can feel her heart!"

Fingers seemed to diddle with the locket on her chest. "I can even feel this. I can *hold* it . . ."

"You were right."

Cassie's eyelids opened. She could not move. She lay like a corpse that somehow continued to see.

The nightmare of the city and its systematic butchery was gone, replaced by this. *It's still a dream,* she thought. *It has to be.*

"You were right. She's an Etheress."

"My God . . ."

A pause.

"Let's go," one of the figures said. "I think she's about to wake—"

—up, her back arched severely as the paralysis of nightmare broke and she lurched upright in bed. Her eyes bulged. Her mouth was propped open and she was screaming but the scream came only as a long barely audible hiss from the back of her parched throat. The faintest light of dawn etched orange around the tasseled front drapes. She felt mutely terrified, the way one might feel upon wakening to realize that an intruder lurked somewhere in the room.

Her gaze jerked left.

Was it her imagination or did she glimpse a shape moving quickly away from the doorway?

She jerked again in bed, snapping on the lamp on the nightstand as if the light would drive away her panic. She waited for her heartbeat to recede but it didn't. Her nightgown felt like tissue paper stuck to her skin by sweat, and when she looked at her locket, she wasn't sure but its burnished silver finish seemed blotched by fingerprint smears.

I am SO screwed up in the head. . . .

She thought of calling out for her father, but what good would that do? She had but one option and she knew it.

She swallowed the rest of her fear and left the bedroom, her bare feet quickening down the hall, to the landing, and then up the next stairwell and the stairwell after that.

This is it, she thought.

Without pause, she ascended into the oculus room.

Three figures sat in a row on one of the mattresses: a girl, a guy, and another girl whom she instantly recognized as Via.

"Hi, Cassie," Via said. "We knew you'd come up to see us eventually."

Chapter Four

(I)

Via smiled cheerily from her seat on the mattress. The other two seemed to have expressions of awe on their faces.

Cassie just froze.

"This is Xeke and Hush. This is Cassie. She lives here with her father."

Cassie didn't even move her head to look back at them; only her eyes darted. Via remained dressed in the leather pants, boots, and jacket that she'd been wearing previously. Xeke, the male, was dressed similarly: late-'70s British Punk and appropriate buttons and patches (BRING BACK SID! and *Do You Get The KILLING JOKE?* and the like). Were it not for her shock, Cassie would've been struck by how handsome he was—lean, toned, dark intense eyes on a face like an Italian male model's. Small pewter bats dangled from his earlobes, and his long jet-black hair had been pulled back into a masculine ponytail. Xeke's eyes appraised her as though she were iconic, and the same went for the third squatter, the other girl. *What did she say her name was?* Cassie thought. *Hush?*

"Hush can't talk," Via said, "but she's cool."

Cassie felt far away as she listened; she felt detached from herself. Her throat clicked as she tried to speak. "Yesterday . . . on the trail. You said you were dead."

"We are," Xeke replied matter-of-factly.

"We can guess what a shock it is to you," Via continued. "It'll take you some time to get used to."

"All three of us are dead," Xeke said, "and when we died, we went to Hell."

People living in my house, Cassie thought numbly. *Dead people.*

She didn't contemplate any of it now. It was either true, or she was insane. Period. Instead, she followed Via, Xeke, and Hush down the stairs.

"We'll just prove it to you now," Via said, "and get it over with."

"Then we can really talk about things," Xeke added.

Hush looked back over her shoulder and smiled.

Yeah. I'm following dead people down the stairs.

"Blackwell Hall is the strongest Deadpass in this part of the Outer Sector," Via was explaining.

"Deadpass," Cassie stated.

"It's because of Fenton Blackwell—"

"The guy who built this section of the house, in the '20s," Cassie latched onto the familiarity. "The Satanist who . . . sacrificed babies."

"Uh-hmm," Via verified.

Xeke laughed when they got to the next landing, his mirthful eyes on Cassie. "Jeez, you must think you're losing your mind about now."

"Uh, yeah," Cassie said. "The thought has occurred to me more than once."

"Just be patient. Follow us."

When they went down the next flight of steps, Via advised, "Don't make an idiot of yourself, Cassie. Remember, *you* can see us and hear us—but *they* can't."

Cassie wasn't sure what they meant until the four of them marched into one of the dens, where Mrs. Conner was busily waxing some antique table tops.

Cassie stood there, looking at her.

The older woman glanced up. When her eyes met Cassie's, there was no way that she couldn't have seen Via, Xeke, and Hush standing alongside of her.

" 'Mornin', Miss Cassie."

"Huh—hi, Mrs. Conner."

"Hope you're feelin' better. Your pa said you had a spell yesterday."

Via laughed. "Your *pa!* Jesus, what a hayseed!"

Mrs. Conner didn't hear the comment.

"Uh, yes, I'm feeling a lot better," she replied.

"She's got the hots for your father," Via added.

The remark startled Cassie. "What?"

Mrs. Conner looked back up. "Pardon, Miss?"

"Uh, er, nothing," Cassie said fast. "Have a good day, Mrs. Conner."

"You too."

"Your father's got the hots for her too," Xeke said through a grin.

"That's ridiculous," Cassie replied.

Mrs. Conner looked up again, a bit more oddly. "What's that, Miss Cassie?"

Instantly, Cassie felt idiotic. "Just, uh, er—nothing." *My father,* she wondered, *has a thing for Mrs. Conner?* The notion was absurd, but then—

So was the notion of dead punk rockers occupying her house.

"I told you to be careful." Via chuckled, leading on. "Oh, and watch your step around her kid—"

"Yeah," Xeke said. "That Jethro Bodine-looking Jervis. He's a peeper."

"A—"

But Cassie was *shushed* when Via brought a finger to her lips. "Don't take showers with your door open anymore. That fat redneck's always looking in on you."

Cassie was mortified. *Yeck!* But her thoughts trickled on. Hadn't Roy mentioned something similar, that Jervis had been put in jail for being a Peeping Tom?

"Something smells good," Xeke said.

It did. Via was leading them into the kitchen, and when the four of them entered, Cassie saw her father puttering at the range, clumsily wielding a metal spatula. When he glanced—and noticed the sheer, short nightgown—he cast her a fatherly frown. "You trying out for Victoria's Secret?"

"Relax, Dad. No one's going to see me," she replied.

"No one except us," Xeke piped in. "Your daughter's got some smokin' hot bod, huh, Dad?"

He and Via laughed out loud.

Cassie's father clearly didn't hear them, or see them.

"You feeling better?"

"Fine, Dad. I was just out in the sun too long yesterday," she tried to placate him.

"Well, good,'cos you're just in time for a Cajun catfish omelette."

"Sounds a little too heavy for me," Cassie said.

"Hey, Dad, look!" Via exclaimed. She walked right up to him, hoisted her black t-shirt, and flashed her breasts.

Bill Heydon didn't see it.

"So what are you going to do today, honey?" he asked, searching for the pepper grinder.

Xeke chuckled. "Yeah, *honey?*"

Shut up, Cassie thought. "I don't know. Probably wander around."

"Yeah, Dad," Via chided. "She's gonna wander around with the dead people living in your house."

"Well, remember. Not too long in the sun this time," her father tried to sound authoritative.

"I won't."

"Still don't believe us?" Via asked her.

"I guess I do," Cassie answered, then immediately thought *Damn!*

More laughter from her cohorts.

Her father looked at her. "You guess you do *what?*"

"Sorry. I was thinking out loud."

"That's a sign of senility, you know." Now her father was dropping pieces of catfish into the fry pan. "You're too young to be senile. Me? That's another story."

"Hush?" Via said. "Show her."

The short mute girl in black drifted across the kitchen. She grabbed Cassie's bare arm and squeezed, to verify it to Cassie. Then she grabbed her father's arm but—

Hush's small hand seemed to disappear into Mr. Heydon's solid flesh and bone.

"All the way now," Via instructed.

Hush stepped *into* Bill Heydon's body—and all but disappeared.

He suddenly shivered. "Damn! Did you feel that cold draft?"

"Uh, yeah," Cassie said as an afterthought. Her fascination gripped her as she watched Hush step back out of her father's body.

"If you don't believe us *now,*" Via said, "then you've *really* got a problem."

"Tell me about it," Cassie said.

Another funky look from her father. "Tell you about what, honey?"

Damn! Did it again!

More laughter.

"Come on, *honey,*" Xeke said. "Let's get out of here before your father thinks you've completely lost it."

Good idea. This was getting way too confusing. "See ya later, Dad," she bid.

"Sure." He gave her another look, shrugged, then returned to his cooking.

She followed them out, back toward the atrium-sized living room. Hush smiled at her and took her hand, as if to say *Don't worry, you'll get the hang of it.*

Cassie had no idea where they were taking her. By the stairs, Via said, "Hey look. Here comes Goober Pyle."

Jervis Conner was bringing some moving boxes down the steps. When he noticed Cassie's scanty nightgown, he tried to hide his gawp. "Howdy, Miss Cassie."

"Hi—"

"Hey, Goober!" Xeke yelled. "Where's Gomer, ya big redneck putz?"

Via stood right in front of him. "I'll bet you wipe your ass with corncobs."

"He's always sneaking up to our room to beat off," Xeke told Cassie.

Via laughed. "He thinks no one's watching. Boy, if he only knew!"

"After seeing you in that nightgown, I'll bet he'll do it five times today."

Cassie blushed.

"Give Shorty a break!" Xeke yelled at Jervis.

Cassie laughed, unable to help herself.

"What's, uh, what's so funny, Miss Cassie?"

This is too much! "Nothing, Jervis. Have a good day!"

"Enough monkeying around," Via said. She led the way down the hall, past the odd statues and oil paintings. Her leather boots thunked loudly on the carpet, but by now, Cassie realized that only she could hear it.

"Where are we going?" she asked when out of Jervis' earshot.

"Someplace where we can talk," Xeke told her, his long black ponytail swaying behind his head.

"Back up to the oculus room?"

"Someplace better," Via said. "The basement."

(II)

"So," Cassie deduced. "You're ghosts."

"Nope." Xeke sat on the cold stone floor, lounging back against the basement's long wall of tabby bricks. "Nothing like that at all. We're living souls. We're physical beings."

Hush sat beside Cassie on a row of moving boxes; she leaned her head against Cassie's shoulder as if tired, her black hair veiling her face. Via remained standing, walking back and forth.

"How can you be living souls," Cassie asked, "if you're dead?"

Via answered, "What he means is that we're living souls in *our* world. We're physical beings in *our* world. In your world, though, we're subcorporeal."

"What's that mean?"

"It means that we exist . . . but we don't."

"But we're not ghosts," Xeke said. "Ghosts are soulless projections. They're just images leftover. No consciousness, no sentience."

Cassie considered this. "So the man who built this house—Fenton Blackwell—he really does haunt this place?"

"Sure," Via said. "But it's just his image lingering, walking up and down the stairs. It's nothing to be afraid of. I'm sure you'll see him every now and again."

Cassie hoped she didn't. "All right, so much for him. What about you?"

Via took off her punky leather jacket and dropped it in Xeke's lap. By her attitude and gestures, it was clear that she was the leader of this little group. She began to diddle with the safety pins holding the tears in her t-shirt together. "It's a long story, but here goes. First, you gotta understand that there are Rules. We weren't really bad people in life, but we were fucked up. We couldn't hack it. So we killed ourselves. That's one of the Rules."

"No ifs, ands, or buts," Xeke said.

"If you commit suicide, you go to Hell. Period. No way around it. If the *Pope* committed suicide, he'd go to Hell. It's one of the Rules."

Cassie touched her locket, felt something shrivel inside. Her sister, Lissa, had committed suicide. *So she went to—*

Cassie couldn't finish the thought.

"This house is a Deadpass, or I should say the newer part of the house, the part that Blackwell built. His atrocities caused the Rive—that's, like, a little hole between the living world and the Hellplanes. If you're like us—if you can find one of the holes—you can take refuge in the living world."

"But no one in the living world can see you," Cassie figured.

"No one. Period. That's another one of the Rules."

Cassie began, "Then how come—"

"*You* can see us?" Xeke held his finger up. "There's a loophole."

A dense silence filled the narrow basement. Via, Xeke, and Hush were all trading solemn glances. Hush held Cassie's hand and squeezed it, as if to console her.

Cassie looked back dumbfounded at them all. "What is it?"

"You're a myth," Via said.

"In the Hellplanes," Xeke went on, "you're the equivalent of Atlantis. Something rumored to be true but has never been proven."

Via sat down next to Xeke and slung her arm around him. "Here's the myth. You're a virgin, right?"

Cassie flinched uncomfortably but nodded.

"And you were never baptized."

"No. I wasn't raised in any particular faith."

"You've genuinely tried to kill yourself at least once, right?"

Cassie gulped. "Yes."

"And you have a twin sister who *did* kill herself." Via wasn't even asking any more; she was *telling* Cassie what she already knew. "A twin sister who was also a virgin."

Cassie was beginning to choke up. "Yes. Her name was Lissa."

More solemn stares.

"In Hell, you hear about it the same way you hear about the angelic visitations here, like these people who see Jesus in a mirror, or St. Mary on a taco," Via went on. "Stuff like that. You hear about it but you never really believe it."

"It's all written down in the Infernal Archives," Xeke said. "The Grimoires of Elymas, the Lascaris Scrolls, the Apocrypha of Bael—the myth's all over the place. We've all read about it, and never really believed it either. But you're real."

"And the myth is true," Via said. "You're an Etheress."

The strange world seemed to flit about the basement like a trapped sparrow. "Etheress," Cassie repeated.

"Just like it says in the Grimoires," Via continued, "you're a physical bond in the Etheric Realm, something that's created by astronomical circumstances. Two twin sisters, both virgins and both suicidal. One commits suicide and one survives. Both born on an occult holiday."

Now Cassie frowned. "Lissa and I were born on October 26. That isn't any *occult holiday*."

Via and Xeke laughed out loud. "It's the date of Baron Gilles de Rais' execution," Via explained.

Then Xeke: "To the Satanic Sects, it's their most powerful day of worship. Makes Halloween and Beltane Eve look like a sock hop."

Via spoke louder now, her voice echoing. "You're an Etheress, Cassie. You're very very special."

Xeke leaned forward. He seemed hesitant. "And because you're an Etheress . . . you could really help us out. . . ."

"Damn it, Xeke!" Via turned and yelled. "Don't be so mercenary!"

Xeke shrugged. "Well, it can't hurt to ask."

Via elbowed him hard, then looked to Cassie. "What *asshole* here isn't telling you is that we can't stay here any more unless you say it's okay. That's one of the Rules, too. If we stuck around without your permission, all you'd have to do is get a priest to bless the place, and we'd have to leave."

Cassie didn't get it. "Why would I want you to leave?" Then it struck her; it was almost ironic. *These people are my friends.* Somehow, it didn't matter that they were dead.

"It's just another one of the Rules," Via said. "You're an Etheress. We have an obligation to tell you."

"Well, I don't want you to leave. As far as I'm concerned, you can stay here as long as you want."

Xeke cracked his hands together in celebration. "I knew she liked us!"

"And what were you just saying?" Cassie asked. "Something about me being able to help you?"

"Yeah," Xeke edged back in. "Do you have any—"

Via shot him another hard elbow. "Damn it! We're not allowed to ask! You *know* that!"

"Sure, but—she can ask us."

"All right," Cassie insisted. "I'm *totally* confused now."

Via stewed over a contemplation. "Be ready, tonight at midnight. But that's only *if* you want to go. You don't *have* to go, and we can't try to influence you. It's one of—"

"It's one of the Rules," Cassie rushed. "I get it. But . . . where are we going?"

"Just so long as you understand. You don't have to go if you don't want to."

"Of course she wants to go!" Xeke exclaimed. "She's an Etheress! It's her destiny to see!"

Cassie had no idea what they were talking about.

Via stood up, put her jacket back on. Xeke and Hush got up too.

"Out here, our energy fades during the day," Xeke said. "we have to go back upstairs and—well, it's what you would think of as sleep."

"Be ready, tonight at midnight," Via repeated. "If you have any jewelry—not gold or diamonds—but silver, with any gemstones like amethyst, sapphire, or pretty much any kind of birthstone—bring it. Onyx is especially important."

"I think I have some of that," Cassie said, still bewildered.

Xeke was nudging Via excitedly. "And tell her to bring—"

"Bring some bones," Via said.

"Bones?"

"Chicken bones, a ham bone, a soup bone. Go down to the diner in town and look in the garbage. Any kind of bones will do."

Bones. *From the garbage?* Cassie couldn't figure it but she consented. "Okay," she said. "So where are we going?"

It was only Hush who looked back at her worriedly. They were leaving the basement now, their forms seeming to fade before Cassie's eyes.

"We're going to the city," Via said.

Her voice was fading. "We're going to the Mephistopolis. . . ."

(III)

Suicide, she thought. *The only unforgivable sin.* Cassie was looking at the scars on her wrists. The healed-over knife slashes looked too insubstantial to carry the consequences that now weighed down on her heart. Back when she'd been suicidal, she'd just wanted everything to be over. Life was just a ball and chain of guilt, failure, and despair—it seemed pointless, masochistic.

Why go on? was the question she'd asked herself a hundred times a day.

Why go on in a world she would never be a part of?

Yes, killing herself seemed the only option that made sense. But now she knew the terrible flaw. Her finger traced a meager scar.

Now she knew the truth. If she killed herself, everything would *not* be over. Her pain and sadness would *not* come to an end. Instead, it would persist forever.

In Hell, she thought.

Guilt collapsed on her, like a brick wall toppling. She would always blame herself for Lissa's death. *She's in Hell now—because of me.* She unconsciously touched her locket. True, Lissa's mental illness had nothing to do with Cassie. *But I was the one who pushed her over the edge. . . .*

"I miss you," she said to the tiny oval picture in the locket. "Please forgive me." Lissa had been her only real friend, and now she was gone.

But she had new friends now, however impossible the circumstances. At this point she couldn't deny the existence of Via, Xeke, and Hush, and her cognizance of that was something she—for some inexplicable reason—found easy to accept. All her life, she knew she was different from everyone else. Perhaps this was why. Xeke had even said it was her destiny.

Etheress, she thought.

She didn't know what it meant, but that didn't really matter. Now she had something to do, and the prospect thrilled her. Her stereo beat quietly in the background as she showered and dressed. (This time, of course, she made sure her door was closed. She didn't want to provide any more scenery for Jervis' perverted eye.) The hot sun blazed in through the French doors; she began her hunt. She'd never been much for jewelry, and she really hadn't brought very much in the way of possessions. One thing she did have, though, was a small felt-lined ring box. *Silver. Birthstones,* she remembered Via's comment. Inside she found a few silver bracelets, a pair of onyx earrings, and an old amethyst pendant on a silver chain. She couldn't imagine what they could want with them—none of it was worth very much—but by now Cassie was getting the picture that things from their point of view weren't easily explained. It was best to simply be shown, and Cassie suspected that what they would show her tonight—the city—would be something to behold indeed.

She turned off her stereo and left her room.

The city. What had Via called it? *The Mephistopolis?* Yes, she was sure that was it.

She was also sure that it was the place she'd seen last night, when she'd looked out the oculus window.

The raging city beneath the blood-red twilight. A city, yes, built on slabs of flaming rock, whose limits seemed to encompass the entire horizon.

Cassie couldn't shake the creeping notion that something was waiting for her there.

(IV)

Dressing for the rural south in the summer was a challenge (the environment simply wasn't *her*). Back in D.C., at this point, she'd scarcely look Goth at all, not with the evident sunburn that was slowly peeling to a tan. And wearing black only amplified the heat. Today she settled for a black bikini top and black denim skirt. Flipflops, she supposed, would remain the exclusive footwear of the season. At least the sun seemed to bleach her already bleached hair, which softened the lime-green highlights. *I'll get used to all of this eventually,* she assured herself.

But now, as she descended past the somber statues that lined the stairwell, she considered her immediate assignment.

Bones.

This request baffled her even more than the request for birthstones—but she oddly refused to question it. Once downstairs, she began to sneak around without fully realizing it, as if she didn't want to be seen. A glance out into the back court showed her father attempting to teach Mrs. Conner how to hit golf balls. *Cozy,* she thought with some sarcasm.

My father doesn't really have the hots for her, does he? Another glance out the front bow windows showed her Jervis edging around the flowerbeds.

Perfect.

She rushed to the kitchen, opened the refrigerator, then the freezer. *Great,* she thought dully. No bones. Not even a steak or a pack of frozen chicken. She really didn't want to walk all the way into town just to root through the dumpster at the local greasy spoon.

Wait. . . .

Via had said *any* kind of bones, hadn't she?

"Well," Cassie talked to herself. "Here goes."

Next, she was on her knees without forethought, rummaging through the bag-lined kitchen waste-basket. *Boy, wouldn't this look great if someone walked in right now? Oh, don't mind me, I'm just looking for some bones. Why? Because the dead kids living upstairs told me to.* But in another moment—her nose scrinched up against the smell—she found her bones.

The bones from the catfish her father had caught yesterday. He'd fileted them, and here were the bones, heads still attached.

She washed the long spines off in the sink as best she could, then wrapped them in foil and put them in a bag. When she went out into the garage, to hide the bag until nightfall, she made another discovery. On a rear shelf, beside weed-killers and bottles of Ortho-Gro, she spotted a sack of bonemeal that Jervis used to fertilize the flowerbeds. *Bones are bones,* she reasoned.

She emptied several cupfuls into her bag.

That should do it.

She hid the bag behind some unpacked moving boxes, then went outside.

All she had to do now was wait until—

Chapter Five

(I)

The tall, chain-driven grandfather clock in the foyer struck midnight, its twelve crisp peals ringing musically throughout the depths of Blackwell Hall. But as unobtrusive as the sound may have been, it surely startled Jervis Conner—to the point that he'd nearly shouted. He bit down on his lip, cursing to himself. If he'd made even the slightest sound, that would be it for this cush job, and he'd probably even get a chance to check back in to the slam for another month or two.

Of course, this bitch wasn't a minor, not like those little sweeties he'd been peeping back when he'd been a janitor at Luntville Middle School. Talk about a great gig for a Short Eyes. Jervis had simply cut a hole in the air duct on the other side of the shower wall. Stuck his

Edward Lee

head right up there and got himself an eyeful of all those little white stringbeans frolicking around in the showers after gym class. Jervis was inventive: he'd rigged some sheet metal with magnets to cover up the hole when he was done, a perfect fit. Too bad the vice-principal had caught him, literally, with his pants down.

This bitch Cassie was twenty or twenty-one, but Jervis doubted that that fact, at this point, would urge a judge to be very lenient. He knew he'd have to be very careful from here on.

First couple weeks working at the house, he'd gotten some great peeps on her. If you stood at the end of the hall and hid around the corner, you could look right into the back end of her room if she left her door open (and she almost *always* left her door open). Better still was that the angle let his glance shoot straight into the bathroom (and she almost always left that door open too). He'd seen her buck naked in the shower at least ten times now. Problem was it was a tad too far for Jervis' liking, and if someone came up the stairs while he was peeping, he could get caught.

And, well, there was a third problem too, but Jervis guessed it was just paranoia. The corner he'd always hide behind was right next to the stairwell that led up to that funny room with the round window. Jervis had used that room a bunch of times, to take care of his need after a peep, but to tell the truth, he always had the weird feeling that someone was watching him. The house creeped him out bad enough during the day. But now, at night—at *midnight*—it was ten times worse.

Not that Jervis was squeamish, mind you.

He just couldn't lick the idea that someone was there, someone in the shadows, looking at him.

Forget that crap, he ordered himself. It would ruin the peep, and peepers had it tough enough to begin with.

He didn't feel the least bit guilty, by the way—peeping on chicks and such. Figured he deserved it, figured that life owed him a little spark now and then. Growing up in this hot sinkhole of a town, busting his ass in one pissant low-pay shit job after another for his whole life? It wasn't like he was knocking over banks or selling crack to nine-year-olds like they did in the city. It wasn't like he was killing folks. He was just taking a peek at pretty things and fetchin' some pleasure out of it. The way he saw it, it was God who made gals good-lookin', so what harm could there be in taking a gander and appreciating the fine-looking things that God made? Seemed a right fucked up, it did, that looking at God's creations could be a blammed *crime* that could land Jervis' fat can right back in jail with the winos and punks and crooks, with the *real* criminals. It just didn't seem fair, not one dang bit.

To hail with the law, he resigned. *I'll take my chances.*

Today Cassie had kept her door closed whenever she was in her room, and that rightly pissed Jervis off because after seeing her this morning—in the practically see-through little nightie—he'd about gone nuts.

But he'd already been working on a fix.

Most of the walls in the house weren't fashioned from sheetrock; they were wood slats with plaster, and wallpaper, while Cassie's walls were paneled. The smaller room next to Cassie's had a big closet with one end broken out. For days Jervis had been slipping into that opening for a little handiwork with his hand-drill and a tiny eighth-of-an-inch bit. He'd gingerly located a slat-seam in the closet that directly adjoined to a seam on Cassie's wood paneling. Just a few tiny holes per day had eventually formed an inch-long line indiscernible to the eye.

But *Jervis'* eye struck Peeping Tom pay dirt.

Kneeling at the gap, he could see right over her big four-poster bed and into the bathroom.

He'd snuck back into the house after dropping his mother off when the work day was done, and now here he was again, hunkered down and waiting in the dark. No one knew he was here, and that secret titillated him; it made him feel charged by some weird hidden kind of power over others: that he could peep on them as he pleased, and they never knew it. Usually Cassie went to bed about ten, and Jervis wanted to be ready when she undressed and slipped into one of those tight foxy nighties. Or maybe she'd do him a *real* favor and sleep nude. In this heat? *Come on, baby! Get nek-it!*

The gig was great. Good money for not a whole lot of work, plus the eye-candy on the side. The kid and her old man didn't fit in out here at all—rich cityfolk, with their weird city ways—but what did Jervis care? *If they want to live in this big creepy place, that's their business*. Most of the furniture had stayed in the place for the whole time it was closed up; the ghost stories kept the thieves away. Jervis didn't believe in ghosts, but he loved the stories. (On the other hand, he'd never quite summoned the balls to come up here and steal himself.) The old man was cool, Jervis supposed—a bit stiff sometimes, but he generally paid twice what the work was worth. And his kid?

Pure fuckin' angelfood cake.

Skin like hot white chocolate and big cherry bon-bons for nipples. And all that skimpy black pinko weirdo shit she wore was just the ticket for any redneck voyeur. Jervis didn't care for that whacked-out Goth crap she listened to; he'd snuck into her room a few times when she was out and looked at her CD covers. Mostly fellas dressing up like gals and wearing make-up and the like. He'd take Charlie Daniels any day. Didn't matter to him, though, what kind of shit she listened to. Jervis just wanted to see the tits and the cookie, and that trim white stomach and little belly-button that just made him want to haul back and do a rebel yell—with his hand in his pants of course.

The life of a voyeur was intricate and bizarre.

But after almost three hours up here, kneeling in the musty closet with his eye to his peephole, Jervis wasn't getting much in the way of treats.

She sat around on her bed or at her desk in a jean skirt and fancified black bikini top, mostly listening to that hippie Goth crap or reading books. Jervis would've liked the short jeans—except the denim was black. *Black denim?* he thought. *Dumbest-ass thing I ever done seen. These freaky Goth kids, all they ever wear*

103

is fuckin' BLACK! Nor did he care for the diminutive rainbow tattoo over her cute little bellybutton. It seemed like vandalism, like spray paint on a gorgeous canvas. Why did gals these days insist on messin' up their bods with all that hippie tattoo business?

Time just kept ticking by. Would she ever get undressed and go to bed?

Aw, come on! Let's get down to it!

At ten o'clock, she gave no indication of turning in. Jervis heard her saying goodnight to her father out in the hall, heard the old man go to bed himself, but after that she just came back to her room listening to more of that weirdo music. At least now she listened with headphones, so Jervis didn't have to hear all the groaning and screaming lyrics about the anti-Christ superstar or some such shit, and kids killing themselves. But Jervis was pretty much trapped in the lightless closet, and wouldn't be able to head back home until after she'd gone to sleep.

Which it didn't look like she had any intention of doing.

Come on, you yellow-hair little city bitch! I ain't got all night! Get them clothes off and give Jervis some stroke time!

It seemed, then, he'd get his wish. She took off her headphones, looked at her watch, and stood up.

Get that shit RIGHT OFF! I want that dumbass-looking black skirt ON THE FLOOR! Get that bra and little panties the fuck OFF!

That's when the clock downstairs struck midnight.

It almost seemed like a signal. When the clock struck, Cassie turned off the light and left the room.

Daaaaaaag-NABIT!

Jervis remained kneeling in the dark, knees aching—with nothing for his effort.

He could hear her going down the hall, her flipflops flopping. Then the flopping stopped at what he guessed must be the landing.

He didn't hear her go down.

Very carefully, he rose, hoping his knees wouldn't crack. He tiptoed to the door and knelt again, at the old-fashioned keyhole. He looked out.

There she was, standing at the landing, right next to the other stairwell that led up to the oculus room.

He knew it was his imagination—simply compounded by the dark and the late hour—but for a moment he actually thought he heard footsteps coming *down* from the oculus room. *Naw, that's silly. There ain't no one up there.*

How could there be?

Yet Cassie remained standing there, looking up now, as if waiting for someone to come down. . . .

He heard her whisper: "My father's asleep. We can go now."

But no one else stood on the landing.

Now who in the HAIL is she talkin' to?

Cassie turned on the barely-lit landing, began to descend the stairs to the first floor.

She was alone.

But she continued to whisper, and the last thing Jervis thought he heard her say was:

"Don't worry, I got 'em. I got the bones. . . ."

(II)

Via, Xeke, and Hush arrived as they'd said, at midnight. Midnight was the best time for a "Pass," Cassie was told, simply due to the human meaning it had accrued over the last millennia. "Where we live, Etherics are tangible," Xeke had said aside. "What's cosmic or spiritual in your world is hard science in ours."

Cassie didn't even pretend to understand.

They traversed the dark, silent house, Via and Xeke leading the way. Hush had clearly formed a bond with Cassie, touching her and holding her hand whenever possible. The contact was not erotic or sexual in the least but something sisterly, as though Hush regarded Cassie as an elder sibling. The younger girl's hand felt hot, which struck Cassie as odd. Hush was dead. Shouldn't her hand be cold?

But then Cassie reminded herself that her new colleagues weren't really dead at all. Dead was a subjectivity. In their own plane of existence, they were very much alive. They were as alive as Cassie was in her own world, the Living World.

"God, your aura's really strong," Via told her.

"I can feel it," Xeke added.

"It's lighting up the whole downstairs!"

Again, Cassie was mystified. On the first floor, she saw nothing in the way of luminescence, felt nothing that could be described as an emanation of her lifeforce. *Guess I'll just have to take their word for it.* "Oh," she said. "And I got the birthstones."

They stopped on their way through the kitchen, and Via, Xeke, and Hush's faces did indeed seem to light up when they saw the pro-offered handful of stone-set jewelry.

"Outstanding!" Xeke said.

"Look at it all!" Via beamed. "And she got an onyx! That's terrific!"

"Here, you better take it," Cassie said to Xeke and made to hand it to him. "I don't even know what it's for."

"I *can't* take it," Xeke told her. "None of us can."

"Not here," Via added. She held out her palm. "Drop one of those earrings in my hand."

Cassie did so, a sapphire.

The gem fell straight through Via's hand.

"See? We won't be able to touch them until we go through the Rive and exit the Deadpass."

Cassie got the point—at least as best she could, and picked up the stone, put it all in her pocket. "The bones are in the garage," she said. She took them out there, and they all seemed just as elated to see the bag of fish spines and ground bone meal. Cassie, however, recoiled when she opened the bag. The bones stunk worse than they had when she'd pulled them out of the trash bin in the kitchen.

"We could probably travel the entire city from one end to the other with all of that," Xeke approved.

Cassie closed the bag, frowning after the odor. "But it's just garbage."

"Where we're going," Via told her, "it's better than cash."

"Bones are how the upper Hierarchals amass their wealth," Xeke went on. "The only way to get bones from the Living World into the city is by the power of the Ossifists."

Cassie's confusion was beginning to make her irritable. "Hierarchals? Ossifists? I don't have any idea what you're talking about."

Xeke grinned in the dark. "You will."

They left the garage through the side door, stepping out into the sultry night. The chirrups of crickets throbbed loudly. Moonlight made the woods fluoresce. They wound around to the front of the house, which faced south. "You said we're going to the city," Cassie stopped them. "This . . . Mephistopolis."

"That's right," Via replied.

"You're talking about Hell, right?"

"Oh, yeah," Xeke answered. "Home, sweet home."

"Sort of," Via amended. "See, we don't live there any more—we can't. We're XR's—ex-residents."

"Same as fugitives," Xeke explained. "In the city, there are two social castes: Plebes and Hierarchals. We're Plebes, commoners, and as XR's we're not allowed to reside in the city anymore. We're considered criminals because we haven't conformed. That's why we have to live in a Deadpass, like your house, or the Deadpasses in the other three Outer Sectors. It's a bitch, but if we stay in the city too long, the Constabularies get wise to us. We wouldn't last very long if we tried to stay in the city limits."

Via could read the confusion on Cassie's face. "Believe me, it's easier to just learn as you go. You still *do* want to go, don't you? Remember, you don't *have* to."

"I still want to go," Cassie said testily. "I just want to know exactly where it is we're going. Hell? Hell isn't supposed to be a *city*. It's supposed to be a sulphur pit, a lake of fire, stuff like that."

Xeke chuckled. "It used to be—several thousand years ago when Lucifer was cast out of Heaven. But just use your common sense. Take New York City, for example. What was New York City several thousand years ago?"

"Woods, I guess," Cassie said, still not getting the point. "Just . . . land."

"Right, undeveloped land. So was Hell when Lucifer first arrived; it was just a hot plain, a wasteland."

Then Via put it this way: "Just as human civilization has evolved over the past three or four thousand years . . . so has Hell."

Xeke: "And just as God's creatures have developed here on Earth, Lucifer and his dominion have developed equally. Progress and technology don't just happen in your world, Cassie. They happen in ours as well. That sulphur pit is now the biggest city to ever exist."

The information quelled Cassie's irritation; she was growing fascinated again.

"Just wait till you see it," Via said and then began leading them down the hill.

Cassie thought about that. "Wait a minute. I *have* seen it. From the oculus window."

"Um-hmm," Via casually responded. "And I'll bet you've had dreams about it too. Living in a Deadpass, and you being an Etheress, it's inevitable."

109

She was right.

Cassie remembered the awful dream she'd had just last night. She'd dreamed of a city raging in chaos and atrocity. And now something else confused her. They were heading down the wooded trail where she and Via had first met. This trail led down the south side of the hill, the front of Blackwell Hall behind them. "Last night, when I looked out the oculus window, I saw it. I *saw* the city. It was south of the house, and we're walking south now." She peered down the trail. Beyond her gaze, where the city *should* be, she only saw the expected rolling farmland and woods. "How come I'm not seeing it now?"

Hush pulled her along by the hand, pointing. Xeke said, "Here's the Pass. Just walk a few more steps. . . ."

Cassie walked out ahead of them now, her flipflops crunching over the trail's carpet of twigs and fallen leaves. But as she progressed, she felt something strange, something that could only be described as variants of pressure and temperature. Vertical layers of hot and cold, an annoying strain in her ears. Then came a sensation like dragging her hand through dry beach sand, only the sensation encompassed her entire body, through her clothes right to her skin.

For a moment, all she saw was utter blackness.

Then—

"My God," she muttered, looking out.

(III)

Just wait till you see it, Via had told her moments ago, just a few yards up the hill. Now, a few moments and

110

a few yards later, Cassie stood at the foot of another world.

She couldn't talk, she could scarcely even think.

All she could do was *see*.

Overhead the sky churned in gradients of scarlet. An exotic, sweet-smelling heat caressed her. A sickle-shaped moon hung in the horizon: a moon that was black and whose black light impossibly lit her face. Indeed, a scrub, smoking wasteland extended from her feet over what had to be the next fifty or even a hundred miles. She could see everything, every detail in a crisp macrovision. And beyond this intricate wasteland stood the Mephistopolis.

The scape of the city—with its buildings, skyscrapers, and towers—seemed forged against the scarlet horizon. It truly was immense. When Cassie looked to the left, the city's face extended further than she could see, and the same to the right.

Smoke—more like black mist—rose from the city into the sky, and so did myriad spears of multicolored lights, which she could only equate to spotlights. Birds—or winged *things*—could be seen sailing away in the distance.

The sight of it all stole her breath.

The others had stepped through the threshold and now stood behind her. They seemed to marvel at Cassie's speechless awe.

"Pretty cool, huh?" Via bid.

"Kind of makes Chicago look like a pup tent."

"I couldn't believe it, either, the first time I saw it. Couldn't believe it's where I'd be spending eternity."

Finally Cassie was able to speak. She glanced again to the left and right. "It . . . never ends."

"Actually it does," Xeke explained. "Ever read the Book of Revelation? In Chapter Twenty-One, St. John reveals the actual physical dimensions of Heaven, so Lucifer deliberately used the same dimensions when he produced the original blueprints for Hell. Twelve thousand furlongs square. That's, like, 1500 miles long and 1500 miles deep—the surface area is over two million square miles. If you took every major city on Earth and put them together . . . *this* is still bigger."

Cassie couldn't really even envision these dimensions. "So, since Lucifer fell from God's grace, he's been building this city?"

"That's right. Or, we should say his *minions* have. Most entrants into Hell become part of the work force in some way. And in a sense, the Mephistopolis is just like any other city. It's got stores and parks and office buildings, transportation systems and police and hospitals, taverns, concert halls, apartment complexes where people live, court houses where criminals are tried for crimes, government buildings where politicians rule. Just like any city, er, well . . . almost."

Via explained further. "In the Mephistopolis, people aren't born—they arrive. And they live forever. And where the social order on Earth is the pursuit of peace and harmony amongst the inhabitants—"

"The social order in Hell is chaos," Xeke informed.

"You have Democracy, we have *Demon*ocracy. You have physics and science, we have black magic. You have charity and good will, we have systematized horror. That's the difference here. Lucifer's social design must function to exist in a complete opposite of God's. Lucifer has built all of this to offend the entity that banished him here."

"So . . . it's not underground like in the legends?" Cassie asked. "It's not on Earth someplace?"

"It's on a *different* Earth that occupies the same space," Xeke informed her. "It's just on another plane of existence that God created. So is Heaven."

"So," Cassie began, "when you die—"

"You either go to Heaven, or you come here. Just like is says in the Holy Bible. Just like it says in most religious systems." Xeke cocked a brow. "Not really much of a surprise when you think about it."

As Cassie continued to stare at the distant cityscape, her mind turned over a thousand questions. How could she ask them all?

"Let's just go," Via said, as if deciphering her thoughts. "Your questions will all be answered."

They started to march ahead, Hush pulling on Cassie's arm. But Cassie was dismayed. "Wait! You mean we're going to walk? It's miles and miles away!"

Xeke tossed his head, flipping his black ponytail back. "Of course we're not going to walk. We're gonna take the train."

Cassie faltered. "The . . . train?"

"Yeah. But it sure as shit ain't Amtrak, I can tell you that."

113

Chapter Six

(I)

The trail descended like a dark slalom. It was nighttime, Cassie was told—it was always nighttime here—but the murky scarlet tinge from the sky seemed more like the beginnings of dusk in a strange, alien terrain. The hill they descended seemed identical in dimension to the hill before Blackwell Hall, but that was it. Nothing else remained identical. "The forests," she questioned, "the farmland and pastures? Where are they?"

"In the plane of existence you just left," Via said. "There were forests a long time ago, but they were all cut down." She pointed distantly. "And if you want to call that farmland . . . go ahead."

Beyond, Cassie saw thin figures laboring in the smoke-misted fields. Plump, hairless beasts dragged plows through reddish-black soil; more thin figures trailed behind, picking twisted roots and noxious vegetables from the dirt. The sight of the laborers shocked her.

They're so thin. . . .

Like people in a death camp.

"It's an Emaciation Detail," Xeke said. "Hell's criminals are brought out here by the Constabulary. They're forced to work until nothing's left on their bones."

"They're starved to death?" Cassie asked.

"They're starved until their Spirit Bodies die. When you die in the Living World and come here, you get a physical body just like you had when you were alive—that's your Spirit Body. But when *it* dies—if you're mutilated, crushed, dismembered, stuff like that—your soul gets transferred to another life form—something born here. Say the Capnomancers burn your body completely down to ash. . . . Your soul—your consciousness—doesn't die; it never does—it *can't* die."

"So what happens to it?"

"If you're in Hell's favor, your soul goes into a demon or a gargoyle, something like that."

Cassie was afraid to ask. "What happens if you're *not* in Hell's favor?"

"It's transferred to the body of a lower species—a Polter-Rat, a Bapho-Roach, or—" Xeke stopped on the trail, pointed aside to what appeared to be a pile of animal waste. "Or an Excre-Worm," he said. "See it? Each one of those things contains an immortal, sentient human soul."

Cassie felt a stab of nauseousness when she looked more closely. The mound of waste was churning with plump, grub-white worms.

"Condemned to eat shit forever," Xeke finished off.

The image, and the remark, nearly finished *Cassie* off. Her face blanched under the red darkness.

"You'll be grossed out big-time at first," Via offered. "Then you start to get used to the way things work around here."

Cassie had serious doubts about that.

Then Xeke was kind enough to add: "Shit and rot and pus and stink, atrocity, horror, mindless violence and non-stop sheer fuckin' terror . . . it's all no big deal."

Cassie choked back more nauseousness.

"You see stuff like that here the same way you see people walking their dogs in the real world, or someone just getting in their car and driving to work. You'll literally see blood running in the gutters the same way rain water runs in them where you live. Horror is the status-quo. It's Lucifer's public order."

It wasn't only the content of Xeke and Via's remarks, it was the nonchalance with which they'd made them that bothered Cassie just as much.

No big deal?

She could scarcely ponder any of it. She took a final glance at the stick-figure laborers in the hot fields, grateful she could not discern their features to any great detail.

Hush could sense Cassie's unease; she gripped her hand tightly, as if to reassure her. Every so often, along the path, bones could be seen, some human, some clearly not. Xeke stopped and playfully picked up a great horned skull. "Check it out. You won't see this very often—the skull of a Grand Duke."

Cassie shuddered at the huge demonic cranium.

"Looks like a Ghor-Hound got him, right in the noggin." He tilted the skull to give Cassie a view of the wide bitemarks. Something had bitten open the skull in one strike. "Sucked his brain right out of his head—that's *some* doggie food."

"In the Outer Sectors, the Ghor-Hounds can grow to the size of horses," Via said.

Cassie could only imagine what a Ghor-Hound was—some hellish version of a dog—and she didn't ask for elaboration. But the obvious danger occurred to her at once. There were creatures that big running around out here?

"How do we know one of them won't attack *us?*" she asked.

"We're Plebes," Xeke answered. He heaved the horned skull away. "They usually only go after Hierarchals."

Great, Cassie thought. *I feel so safe now.*

More bones lay scattered to either side of the path. "Well it doesn't look to me like there's any shortage of bones in Hell."

"There isn't. Spirit Bodies die all the time. I'm sure the Department of Raw Materials will send a crew out here soon to pick all these up. They crush the bones up in the Industrial Sector, mix it with limestone to make brick and cement. Nothing's wasted in Hell."

"Sounds very efficient," Cassie said with sarcasm. "But what I mean is, with all the bones you've got lying around out here, what's so special about my bagful of fish bones?"

"It's not the *kind* of bone," Via said. "It's just the fact that yours come from the Living World."

"Bones from the real world are like gold here," Xeke added. "The Ossifists use chemical sorcery to produce them. Like the alchemists of the Dark Ages on Earth who sought to turn lead into gold, the Ossifists can turn Spirit bones into real bones. But it's a really complicated and expensive process; that's why they're worth so much, and that's why only the upper-class Hierarchals have them."

"But now—" Via seemed hesitant.

Xeke rubbed his hands together. "Now Cassie can provide an endless supply. We'll be rich!"

Via elbowed him. "Don't listen to him. We're not allowed to profit from an Etheress. We can't ask you for anything."

Getting bones out of the garbage seemed simple. "You don't have to ask. I'll get you all the fish bones you want."

"We're rich!" Xeke repeated.

Via's disapproval was plain. "One of these days," she said to Xeke, "you're gonna say one word too much and violate the Covenant of Citizenry. The Ushers'll grind you up into blood pudding, and then it'll be *your* soul that gets transferred to an Excre-Worm."

"I'm so scared," Xeke bragged. "I've killed Ushers before and I'll kill them again. They're just a bunch of big ugly chumps."

"What's an Usher?" Cassie asked.

"They're working-class Hierarchals—demons that exist to torture and kill for Lucifer," Via said. "Think of a psychotic, homicidal gorilla with no hair, whose only instinct is to kill. They've got fangs like lions and claws that can cut through stone."

"Wonderful," Cassie replied. "I can't wait to meet one." Then she changed the morbid subject. "All right, I get it now. Bones from the real world are money. But what about this jewelry I brought?"

"That's mainly for your protection," Via told her. "We pretty much have our own." Xeke pointed to his pierced earlobes, on which stone-fitted skulls dangled. Via brazenly pulled up her t-shirt, showing similar tiny stones on metal stems which pierced her nipples. Hush, too, had earrings set with odd gemstones, and in a silent giggle she stuck out her tongue. A black-streaked stone on a pin pierced her tongue.

"Plus I've got some goodies in here," Via said, wagging a small pouch on her belt. "Some special stones, a couple different kinds of Enchantment Dust, some talismans. It comes in handy."

Xeke grinned. "Via's a punk-rock witch."

"Damn right. Silver can always be used in an emergency, for a Warding or Repulsion Spell. And birthstones can protect you from various demons. You'll see in due time."

Cassie didn't care for the final remark. But as her uneasiness grew, Via added, "That onyx you brought is real important."

Cassie checked her pocketful of stones, then found the tiny black one. "This black one right here? It probably cost less than twenty bucks."

"Doesn't matter what it cost where you come from; in Hell, its priceless, and it'll give you a unique protection. You're an Etheress; you have a living aura, and any drastic emotions you feel can set your aura off. For instance, right now your aura just jumped, kind of yellowy. That means you're scared. Are you scared?"

"Well," Cassie admitted. "A little."

"Any sharp emotion will set your aura off: fear, anger, excitement. The onyx will keep your aura subdued, hidden, but you'll have to try hard to control your emotions."

"I don't understand," Cassie said.

Xeke laughed. "Our auras are dead. But you're an Etheress; you're a living being walking around in Hell. Your aura will light you up like a pinball machine. People will see it, and it'll give you away."

Via enumerated: "If word gets around that there's an Etheress on the streets, the Constabulary will go nuts. They'll put a bounty on your head."

The words sunk in. Cassie's footsteps forward began to retard.

"You don't have to come," Via repeated. "You can turn around and go back right now. We wouldn't blame you one bit."

Xeke stood silent. Hush looked up at her questioningly. When Cassie looked back up the smoking hill, she could still see Blackwell Hall.

"She'll come," Xeke said.

"Shut up!" Via yelled. "You can't influence her!"

Xeke ignored her. "Sure, Cassie, it's cool that you've offered to help us out by getting us the bones and all. But you want something from us too, and we know what it is."

Cassie looked back at him. She hadn't really even consciously acknowledged it to herself yet . . . but she also knew that he was right.

"You want us to help you find your sister," Xeke said.

"You want to find her and tell her you're sorry, right?" Via guessed.

Cassie looked down at her feet. "Yes."

"Then it's your call, Cassie," Xeke said.

It didn't take her long to make up her mind. She touched her locket. "Let's go," she said, and then they all began to continue back down the hill.

(II)

"Coach leaving, Track 4!" a voice shot through some kind of tinny-sounding megaphone. "Boarding now for direct connections to Pogrom Park, Pilate Station, Edward Kelly Square!"

Jarring bells clanged amid rising rust-scented steam. Cassie jogged along behind the others through the outdoor train station that had been built at the foot of the long hill. It had just seemed to appear from nowhere: all gridded iron platforms and pillared canopies. A faded swing-sign hung aloft that read:

TIBERIUS DEPOT
(OUTER SECTOR SOUTH)

Cassie didn't have much time to take in details, but she could see no one else standing on the platform. The train itself looked like something from the early 1900s—old wooden passenger cars hauled by a steam locomotive. The engine car was backed by a high coal tender; however, the chunks of off-yellow fuel were clearly not coal. A man stood on top of the tender, shoveling the chunks into a chute. At first he appeared ordinary, dressed in work overalls and a canvas cap as one might expect. He paused a moment to wipe some sweat off his brow, and that's when he cast a glance down at Cassie.

The man had no lower jaw—as if it had been wrenched out. Just an upper row of teeth over a tongue that hung from the open throat.

"All aboard!"

"Hurry!" Xeke urged.

Their jog broke into a sprint. Hush yanked Cassie forward desperately as the train began to chug forward with explosive gusts of smoke from the engine's front stacks. The smoke smelled atrocious.

They pulled themselves up through the open doorway just in time; the door clanged shut as Cassie pulled her foot in. Another second and it would've been severed.

"Let's try to find a decent cabin," Xeke said and led them down the aisle. Wooden sliding doors lined either side, with wide glass panes. Xeke looked into the first cabin, frowned, and said, "Nope." In the cabin sat a man whose face was warped with large potato-like tumors. Cassie wasn't sure but the tumors seemed to have eyes, and one eye winked at her. "Not a chance, Granny," Xeke said of the next cabin, in which an ancient woman sat totally naked, leathery skin hanging in folds, vagina prolapsed. Cataracts glazed her eyes over, and she drooled as her toothless mouth hung agape. Red spots on the old skin seemed to move—until Cassie realized they were mites.

"Smoking is so glamorous," Via commented.

Something morbid forced Cassie to stare further through the pane. The old woman's hands trembled as she awkwardly stuffed two pinches of raw tobacco into her nostrils. She lit them with a match and began to inhale.

Oh, man, that's SO disgusting, Cassie thought.

Into another cabin she only dared to take a peek. A short demon in tattered clothes—and with scaled yellow skin—was lackadaisically urinating in the corner. But the root-like penis had two coronas the size of plums, and the urine was a steaming mix of blood and minuscule worms.

"Just wait till you see him take a Number Two," Xeke remarked with levity.

"I'm about to vomit!" Cassie said, outraged. "Find a place for us to sit down!"

Xeke, chuckling, finally found an empty cabin. Cassie slammed her butt down on the wooden bench seat, then slammed the door shut, heaving in air.

"Calm down," Via said.

"Oh my God, my God!" Cassie gusted, close to hyperventilating. "This place is *horrible!*"

Xeke sat down next to Via, propped his legs across her lap. "What did you expect, Cassie? We're in Hell, not the Mickey Mouse Clubhouse."

Cassie sat forward, her eyes bugged. "Did you see that man—with all those awful growths on his face?"

Xeke shrugged. "Facio-carcinoma. It's one of Hell's strains of cancer. Eventually those tumors grow full faces. They'll rap with ya."

Cassie gagged. "And-and did you see that old woman with the-the-the—"

"Blood-Mites crawling all over her?" Xeke finished. "Yeah, we saw her. It's nothing to get bent out of shape about. In Hell . . . people are fucked up."

The train clattered on, jostling Cassie in her seat. It took a while for her nauseousness to fade. In the window, more scorched land passed them by. At one point she thought she saw a broad-shouldered demon on horseback, riding a fanged horse over people buried in the soil up to their necks. A glance further on showed her several bats biting pieces out of a man crawling across the dirt—only the bats were the size of buzzards.

Cassie quickly turned away, but then her eyes fell on some bulky object beneath the seat. "What-what's that?"

Xeke pulled it out. It looked like a travel bag.

"Somebody forgot their luggage?" Cassie asked.

"They sure did," Xeke said when he opened it. Cassie almost passed out when she saw what was inside.

The case was full of severed human hands and feet.

Xeke and Via couldn't help but chuckle at Cassie's abhorrence. "Like we told you," Via informed. "You'll get used to the way things work around here." Xeke opened the window for a moment, threw the travel bag out. "Give the Dirt-Chucks something to snack on."

A tapping sounded at their cabin window, then the door slid open. "Tickets, please," came a voice. A thin elderly man stood before then, dressed appropriately in uniform and cap, a ticket-puncher hanging off his belt.

"We don't have any tickets," Xeke told him.

The ticket-taker's face remained deadpan. "Then it's a Judas Note each."

Xeke crossed his arms. "We don't have any cash, either."

"Then I'm afraid I'll have to call a Golem and have you all thrown off the train," the man informed them.

"Hold up, pops. Let me show you what we *do* have." He opened the paper bag with the fish bones in it, and he broke off one single bone from a spine. The bone glowed furiously here, bright as an electric arc. Xeke passed it to the ticket-taker. "That should cover it, huh, pappy?"

"I . . . should say so." The man examined the tiny bone, duly impressed. "Why, I don't think I've ever seen a Real World bone of such quality. You must know a very competent Ossifist."

"I got it from Santa Claus," Xeke said. "And you and I both know that that bone's worth more than you make in a hundred years working on this shit-wagon. So how about punching us up some indefinite rail-passes and beating feet?"

"Yes. Of course." The man quickly pocketed the bone, then handed Xeke four tickets with holes

Edward Lee

punched next to a line that read NO EXPIRATION.

"Thank you for traveling with us," the old man said. "Have a good day in Hell."

"You too, you old stick," Xeke returned when the man had left.

But Cassie just sat there, tremoring. The ticket-taker had appeared perfectly normal—save for one detail. When he'd handed Xeke the tickets, Cassie saw that his hands were long, three-fingered claws.

"Surgical victim," Via explained to Cassie's obvious dismay. "He must've gotten pinched by the Office of Transfiguration. Lucifer's Teratologists are always experimenting on people. Skin grafts, transplants and implants—some really gross stuff. Lately they've been taking in humans and giving them transfusions with demon blood."

Cassie seemed to be choking down the information. "But would that—wouldn't that kill them?"

"Nope," Xeke asserted. "But it sure as hell screws them up. Remember, a human can't really die here. Only when the Spirit Body is completely destroyed does the Soul pass to a lower being."

"If somebody cuts your head off," Via gave an example, "the head continues to live and think and talk until it's eaten by vermin or picked up by a Pulper Detail."

But even before Cassie could reckon what a "Pulper Detail" might be, a sudden scream shot out from somewhere on the car. Her eyes bugged again. "What-what was that?"

"Uhhhhh . . . a scream?" Xeke mocked.

The screamed resounded, higher this time. Cassie ground her teeth at the sound.

It was clearly a shriek of agony.

She stood up, looked through into the next cabin, then sat back down, shuddering. "My God! There's a pregnant woman in that cabin! She looks like she's about to give birth!"

Via took a peek. "Yeah? So?"

Cassie couldn't believe the response. *"So? Is that all you can say? So?"*

Now Xeke took a look. "Wow. That ain't no bun in the oven—that's a whole friggin' *bakery*. Looks like she's gonna pop any second now." Then he merely sat back down.

"I do not *believe* you!" Cassie exclaimed. "That poor girl's in labor! Aren't you going to help her?"

"Uhhhhhhh, how about . . . no?" Xeke replied.

Another scream ripped through the air. "Well damn it!" Cassie rebelled. "If you won't help her, I will!" She jumped up, burst into the next cabin. The lank-haired woman lay spread-eagled on the floor, her face stamped with pain. Cassie had little idea what to do to help; she knelt down, took the woman's hand and tried to comfort her. "Don't worry, everything'll be all right," she blathered. "Take deep breaths. Try to push. . . ."

In the background she heard Via say, "Xeke, she doesn't know. Go get her."

"She's gotta learn sometime," Xeke replied. "This is the best way."

Hush came into the cabin, tapped Cassie on the shoulder. She looked sad, motioning with her hand for Cassie to come back.

"I can't just leave her!" Cassie insisted.

Hush scribbled something quickly on a notepad, showed it to Cassie. The note read:

there's nothing you can do

"She needs help!"

Hush moped away, then—

Yet another scream exploded from the woman's throat. Her milk-heavy breasts shuddered as she heaved out the scream. Cassie pulled up the threadbare dress, saw that the vagina had already dilated.

The baby's head was emerging.

"Push! Push!" Cassie implored.

Then Cassie ripped out a scream of her own.

The little head that emerged was no baby's—at least not a *human* baby's. It was gray and squashed, with nubs at the forehead like precursory horns. When the new-born mouth opened, Cassie saw that it was full of fangs. Blood-red eyes looked right at her.

Then the infant began to bark.

Cassie's own screams followed her back into their cabin. Seeing the head had been more than enough—when the rest came out, she definitely didn't want to be there.

"It wasn't a baby, Cassie," Via told her.

Then, Xeke: "*Humans* can't reproduce here; nothing *human* can ever be born in Hell. What you saw in there was just a hybrid."

"She probably got raped by a Gargoyle or a City-Imp."

"The thing in that cabin doesn't have a soul," Xeke finished, as if that made it all okay.

Next came the squalling, a hot burst of infantile need, but soon the squalls seemed to taper off into a fastidious wet clicking sound—like an animal eating sloppily at a trough.

"First it'll suck all the blood out of the umbilical cord," Via informed, "then it'll eat the afterbirth."

"And then," Xeke furthered, "it'll start to nurse—"

Cassie bolted, threw open the cabin window, and began vomiting.

Xeke raised a brow toward Via. "Looks like this is gonna be a long ride. . . ."

PART TWO

THE MEPHISTOPOLIS

Chapter Seven

(I)

Cassie's revulsion overpowered her, but even in spite of it, she could not suppress periodic glances out the window. Past the wastelands, she soon saw strange acres of farmland where slaves cultivated noxious crops; and ranches pocked with what could only be slaughterhouses processing Hell-born livestock that were better left undescribed. The train clattered over only one bridge—a high suspension bridge—which spanned a mile-wide river the color of bilge.

"Styx," Via told her. "It surrounds the city," and then Xeke charmingly added, "All the city's run-off, waste, garbage, and sewage empty into it. Waste is our biggest resource, even bigger than sulphur."

The visions thinned Cassie's breath. Watercraft of manifold sizes—from canoes to barges—roamed along the river's surface of steaming muck. Fishermen hauled in nets teeming with hideous creatures that would later find their way to market; crab traps were hoisted aboard, yet the crustaceous things they contained could hardly be called crabs. Body parts, innards, and various human and not-so-human organs floated atop the unspeakable river, and these too were harvested with zeal.

The next sight jolted Cassie: a fanged serpent at least a hundred feet long serenely rose to the surface and swallowed a dinghy whole. Moments later, Cassie's guts clenched as she glimpsed another serpent prowling just below the watertop—only this one was at least a *thousand* feet long.

"She's not holding up very well," Via observed.

Xeke concurred. "You can get off at Pogrom Park; it's the first stop on the line. You won't have to wait very long before the next train. It'll take you back to the station, and you can go home."

"Go back to my house alone?" Cassie objected.

"Hush'll take you. But Via and I *have* to get into the city. We have to get food. We haven't eaten in a while."

"I've got food at my house," Cassie blurted. "I'll give you all you want."

"We can only eat the food in *this* world, Cassie," Via explained.

I have to go back, Cassie realized. Her nauseousness was only multiplying; she couldn't take much more. Then she nearly vomited again when she inadvertently took another glance out the window, and saw swollen corpses hanging from the bridge's suspension cables. Liquefied rot ran off of them in thick dribbles, yet the corpses still moved with life.

Oh, Jesus, yes! I've got to go back!

But then—

Then I'll never stand a chance of finding Lissa. . . .

The consideration turned over in her mind. "I don't want to go back," she eventually roused her courage and told them. "I want to go to the city."

"That's a good girl," Xeke said. "And you know what? I've got a *great* idea."

Cassie didn't have time to ask what it was before she heard the conductor's voice: "Approaching city limits. First stop Pogrom Park, walking distance to the J. P. Kennedy Ghettoblock, the Bathym Memorial, and our own beautiful Riverwalk. Connections to the City Center Nexus, Panzuzu Avenue, Athanor Hill, and the brand-new Baalzephon Mall for all your shopping needs."

"This is us," Xeke said.

Cassie squeezed Hush's hand as she forced herself to look on. They were fast approaching the Mephistopolis now, the city's northernmost outskirt: smoke-misted skyscrapers along an endless straight line. In between the buildings, Cassie could see an urban labyrinth that might as well have existed ad infinitum.

When the train chugged to a halt, Cassie kept her head bowed as they left the car; she didn't dare look into the cabin across from them where the woman had just given birth.

Hearing the suckling sounds was enough.

"Ah, I love that great fresh air," Xeke said when they stepped off the train.

"To be honest," Via commented, "I really think Newark was worse."

The air, indeed, stank. Cassie could swear she felt soot clinging to her sweat and adhering to the inside of her nostrils. However, the dense scarlet sky aside, her first look around once they'd exited the train proved unremarkable—or, at the very least, not as horrid as she'd expected. When they got off the platform, she was looking at something like a public piazza. It had park benches, trees, open stretches of grass, and sidewalks branching out. A large statue, surrounded by a fountain, stood at the piazza's center. Pedestrians milled about.

The scene, in other words, seemed normal of any large city. But then Cassie took a harder look.

The trees were twisted, deformed; faces seemed imprinted in the pestiferous bark. All of the grass as well as the foliage in the trees was not the expected green but instead sickly off-yellow. Many of the "pedestrians" milling about displayed an array of disfigurements, emaciation, evidence of incalculable destitution; and some weren't even human. Some were Trolls, some were demons or bizarre hybrids. The "normal" fountain gushed blood, and the statue standing above it was the likeness of Josef Stalin, who'd starved millions of his own people to death because they were Jews.

When Cassie looked down, she saw the "normal" sidewalk, the concrete of which was flecked with bone fragments and teeth.

"Welcome to the Mephistopolis," Xeke said.

Cassie was at least grateful for her nausea's distraction. It kept her from concentrating on the details of this new environ. Hush led her along—a petite tour guide in black—behind Via and Xeke. When they passed a row of derelicts begging for money, Xeke joked, "Did we get off in Seattle by mistake?" but the derelicts, sitting in their own rot, were clawed, horned *things* with amputated legs, dressed in infested rags. From one another they plucked off bugs nesting in the rags, and ate them.

Smoky stenches wafted off the water as they toured the elaborately leveled Riverwalk. It was high, unrailed, and dangerously narrow.

The first thing Cassie saw were a band of devilish children attacking an old man, disemboweling him with a hook. Two of the hideous children threw the old man over the side, while a third ran off with his intestines.

"Broodren," Xeke explained. "Kind of like teen-age gangs in the Living World—real pains in the ass."

"There are no human kids here," Via said, "but we've got several dozen different demon races. They reproduce like rabbits. Even the Hierarchals hate them. The Extermination Platoons barely help at all."

Cassie asked a question, half-gagging: "Why did the one—"

"Run off with the old geezers guts?" Xeke finished. "To sell it to an Anthropomancer or Extipicist. They read the future by looking at entrails, and send messengers to report the results to Lucifer. Divination is the biggest game in town—it runs the economy. There are countless thousands of Divination Points in the city."

"Smoke Divination is even bigger," Via said. "It's supposedly more accurate, and it's easier to sell small pieces at a time."

Small . . . pieces? Cassie thought. She didn't ask.

They passed rows of what appeared to be shops: alchemists, palmists, channelers. "Clip joints mostly," Xeke revealed. "Most of them aren't legit—except the place we're going."

But where *were* they going?

"No way!" Via complained when they arrived. A sign above the shop read SHANNON'S APOTHECARIES & AMULETS: CASH, TRADE, OR PHLEBOTOMY.

"It'll only take a minute," Xeke assured. "I figure a Reckoning Elixir will help Cassie get used to things."

"But we don't have any cash," Via hotly reminded him, "and we've got to be *very* careful with the bones. If you just start throwing those things around, the Constabs'll be on to us! They'll put warrants out!"

"Relax. I'm saving the bones for the money-changer's," and before he could say another word, he was walking into the shop.

Via seemed furious; Cassie and Hush followed her in.

A crystal bell chimed, and at once Cassie was surrounded by exotic scents. The simple shop was mostly old, leaning shelves filled with bottles and jars. "Reminds me of one of those hokey voodoo shops in New Orleans," Cassie said.

"This ain't no damn voodoo shop," Via testily replied.

A cheerful young woman stood behind the front counter. Cassie liked her apparel: a diaphanous black silk cloak and hood. The woman—Shannon, she presumed—smiled warmly at them, with deep dark eyes. "Greetings. . . ." Her eyes surveyed Xeke with some approval. "The handsome rogue returns. Didn't thee trade with me, a wee bit ago?"

"Thee did," Xeke mocked.

"Of course! A Bergamot Shot, was it not?"

"Yeah, I had a stomach ache."

"And such a treat it is for the red night to bless me again with thy striking presence. What can Shannon concoct for thee?"

"Shit-can the hokey medieval witch-talk for starters," Xeke said. "I need a Reckoning Elixir, a good one, not that jive crap they sell to Newcomers on the street."

"Mmmm." The smile widened. "For these I have, and for you, I have much, virile stranger—the finest on the Walk." Her dark eyes thinned on Hush. "Invest to me the short one, to be drained just one-quarter-dry, in return for a full liter flagon of Hell's most potent Reckoning Elixir."

"Not a chance," Xeke said. "I just want one dram, and I've got no cash."

The woman's next words were stalled when she looked to Cassie, saw the bag she was carrying. "Lo, no cash. What have thee, though, in that sack, grasped so limply by the pretty one so fulgent-haired?"

"Nothing for you. Just give me the dram."

"Xeke! No!" Via outraged.

"I got plenty," he dismissed over his shoulder.

The cloaked woman drifted to a shelf, placed a tiny vial on the counter. Cassie, in the meantime, was taking some note of the shop's disturbing inventory. Opaque bottles with corroded corks, and jars full of murky slop. One jar contained severed demon fingertips, another severed testes. THYMUS JUICE, another jar was labeled, and another: GARGOYLE SWEAT. Cassie ceased her examination when she looked into one jar and saw a face looking back.

Now Shannon smiled openly, showing a pair of delicate fangs.

"Goddamn vampires," Via complained. "I can't stand them. . . ."

"So, then, a dram for a dram." Her voice grew plush. "Or . . . we can go in back for a while."

"Xeke, if you do," Via challenged jealously, "I'll punch your friggin' face in! I'll never talk to you again, I swear!"

"Dram for a dram," Xeke replied.

The vampire-woman handed Xeke a pointed stylus of some kind, then raised a tiny silver spoon.

Xeke casually pricked his palm with the stylus. From his fist he squeezed enough drops of his own blood to fill the spoon.

"There, knock yourself out."

Shannon slowly sucked the blood off the spoon, savoring it. Her face took on an expression of serene ecstacy.

"Thanks," Xeke said, and took the vial. "Later."

"Later—yes!" the woman slurred through her bloody smile. "I implore thee, come back soon, handsome one."

"Go crawl back in your coffin, you fanged bitch!" Via yelled.

Xeke just shook his head. He was turning to leave, but Shannon delicately grabbed the sleeve of his leather jacket. "Come back soon," she whispered. She lewdly cupped a breast through the black cloak. "I'll show thee many pleasures . . . and you can show *me* what's in your pretty friend's sack."

"Take your grubby hands off him," Via yelled some more, "unless you want me to throw your trashy vampire ass right into the river! I'll chop your head off and stuff garlic down your neck!"

Xeke was clearly embarrassed. He gestured them all toward the door, but something urged Cassie to look back at the vampire one last time.

The woman's red lips silently mouthed *Bye.*

Cassie shuddered and left.

"I can't believe you were flirting with that spooky bitch!" Via griped to Xeke back on the Riverwalk.

"Oh, Jesus. How was I flirting? Can I help it if she digs me? I just played her game a little. She's the best Elixirist in this part of the city."

"She's probably the best head queen too! You've been there before—she said so!"

"So what? I go to Elixirists all the time."

"You *fucked* her, didn't you?"

Xeke rolled his eyes. "No, of course not. Jesus, Via. I can't even look at another girl without you having a fit."

Cassie interrupted the spat. "So vampires are real?"

"Sure," Xeke said. "But when they get staked and come to Hell, they're under an even worse curse—a Conversion Hex. If they bite a human, they turn into pillars of salt. They're only allowed to drink blood if it's offered to them." He uncapped the tiny vial. "Anyway, down the hatch."

Cassie sniffed . . . and nearly retched. "That smells *awful!* It smells like rotten meat! I'm not going to *drink* that!"

"Of course you are," Xeke said. "Don't be such a creamcake. Believe me, after you drink that slop, you'll be glad that you did."

Hush nodded to give Cassie some assurance. Cassie grimaced and swallowed it. The elixir tasted worse than it smelled, and it slid down her throat like a line of mucus.

But, in another second—

Wait a minute. . . .

She felt completely at ease.

The nausea was gone, and so was the staggering mental trauma inflicted by all she'd seen. Suddenly . . . she understood.

"Feel better?" Via asked.

"Yes—wow," Cassie replied.

"And here comes your first test," Xeke chided.

A naked woman shuffled along the walk, leaving footprints of pus. "Daemosyphilitus," Xeke said. "There are sexual diseases in Hell too. It takes over your whole body until you're just one big walking infection— like her."

The meaty stench blew off her as she sloshed along. Cassie felt sorry for the woman, but was not repulsed by her at all.

"Hey, and here comes a Gut-Job."

A haggard man limped along, shirtless. Where his abdomen should be was just a ragged, empty hole—his entire abdominal cavity emptied. Yellow things, like maggots, infested much of the open cavity now.

"Same as that old man we saw get eviscerated by those Broodren," Via accented. "He was either captured and gutted by a Mancer Squad or he willingly sold his entrails to an Extipicist. People are desperate here just like they are in the Living World."

Cassie wasn't repulsed in the least.

"Good," Xeke said cheerily. "It worked." He nudged Via. "See, I told you Shannon made a great Reckoning Elixir."

Via cut a hot frown. "She's a floozy blood-chugging tramp and I'll bitch-slap her up and down the street if I ever see her checking you out again."

"Yeah?" Xeke dared. "And what if I check *her* out?"

"Then I'll pop your eyeballs out and suck your brain."

Xeke winked at Cassie. "Fatal attraction—I think she means business. Come on, let's go. It's time to give you the twenty-five-cent tour."

(II)

Her abhorrence cured now, Cassie found the city diversified and fascinating—she also found it structurally

143

awesome when she considered that this district represented only one grain of sand in a megalopic sandbox. She remembered what Xeke had told her of the actual dimensions: over two million square miles. "It's bigger than most *countries* in the Living World," he said as he led the group down the Avenue Des Champs-Blóde. Cassie easily noted the Parisian influence, especially when they walked beneath the massive Arc de Miserius, where corpses of Broodren hung upside-down by iron hooks set in the keystones. These corpses, however, showed no signs of movement, unlike those they'd seen on the Styx Bridge. "*Human* bodies can't die here, but pretty much anything Hell-born can," Via explained. "Trolls, Imps, Broodren—most of the lower species of demons. They aren't born with souls. Even Grand Dukes can die."

"So only *human* souls are immortal here?" Cassie asked.

"Humans," Xeke answered. "And Fallen Angels. That's about it."

"Golems don't count, because they're manufactured—they're almost impossible to kill but they're stupid." Via pointed. "There's one now."

The thing stood on a corner, nine feet tall. Its sculpted body of riverbed clay shined wetly in the sulphuric light of a street lamp. It seemed insentient as a statue, until something caught its thumb-holes for eyes, and it turned into an alley.

"Golems are like street cops, the lowest level of the Constabs," Xeke said. "Spells program them what to look for."

"But didn't you say you were fugitives?" Cassie wondered. "Aren't you afraid a Golem might come after you?"

"Naw. They can't identify *people,* just criminal activity. XR's like us are safe from them. Ushers are another story, though, and so are Conscripts. They have brains."

"Ushers are Hellborn; they're the most ferocious genus of demon, and Conscripts are hybridizations of Orges and Nether-Bats. But most of them are recruited into the Mutilation Squads," Via added. "What XR's and other fugitives most have to worry about are other humans who read the District Wanted Boards. The Constabulary is granted a large budget for squealers and spies. It's a big temptation. Treachery is a way of life here."

Several Polter-Rats scurried across the next street. They were larger than city rats, with vaguely human facial features. Cassie noted, too, that their feet looked more like a human infant's hands. "Whenever a Spirit Body is destroyed to the extent that the Soul is transferred to vermin or proto-demons," Xeke said, "some of the human physical traits are transferred as well."

Via kicked a tin can—labeled VIENNA TROLL-BRAIN SAUSAGES—across the street. "Polter-Rats are probably the worst vermin. They have anesthetic in their saliva—so you don't wake up when they're eating you. It's a real problem in the Ghettoblocks. One night you go to sleep as usual but when you wake up, your face is gone, or all the flesh has been eaten off your arms or legs, and all you've got left are bones. Bapho-

Roaches are pretty gross too. They'll lay eggs under your skin; the only way to get 'em out is to cut."

Xeke kicked another can further, which read HUMAN SPAM. "And let's not forget Hell's most notorious pest, the Caco-Tick. They get into your hair and drill through your skull, and what they feed on is your spinal fluid. One tick can suck a human dry in no time. Fucks you *all* up. But don't worry, our gemstones protect us all from most of that."

Somehow, Cassie didn't feel terribly secure.

Across certain intersections, she thought she could feel a rumbling beneath her feet, while smoke and licks of flame gushed out of the sewer grates. But then Xeke and Via explained that Hell's bedrock was indeed sulphur, and subterranean sectors had been burning for centuries—fires that would never go out. After another block, they crossed the street, and Cassie suddenly found herself walking ankle deep in some grotesque, warm liquefaction. "Yuck! What's that?"

"Oh, sorry. Forgot to warn you." Xeke's boots plodded on through the muck. "Sometimes the fires underneath the street are so hot that the Physical Plant Department has to open a sewer line into the street."

Though the potion she'd drunk prevented a reaction of disgust, Cassie still felt outraged. "You mean, we're walking in—"

"Satanic sewage," Xeke casually replied.

Lovely, Cassie thought, cringing at the wetness around her feet. *Mental note: Don't wear flipflops in Hell.*

Hush tapped her side, pointing up. Past more buildings, Cassie saw a dingy Gothic clock-tower spiring up at least fifty stories. But the tower's clock-face had no hands.

Xeke sounded jovial when he said, "Hey, everybody. Let's set our watches!"

It was then that Cassie noticed the next oddity. Via, Xeke, and Hush all wore watches—but they were all like the clock in the tower. Blank.

"Watches without hands?" she queried, confused.

Via explained, "It's one of the first Public Laws. You have to wear a watch that doesn't tell time, and every city district has a clock-tower, like that one there. It's so we never forget that we're here forever."

"Time is illegal in Hell," Xeke said. "There's really no way to keep track. It's always nighttime here, and the moon"—he pointed up into the dark-crimson sky, where a black sickle moon hung—"is always in the same phase. Look at your own watch."

Cassie glanced at the tiny Timex she generally wore. It no longer ticked, and its hands had stopped at several minutes past midnight, when they'd crossed the Deadpass.

Time . . . doesn't exist here.

Cassie grew more and more fascinated with every new thing she learned. Eventually, Xeke led them all into a broad brownstone. NEWCOMER'S POINT, the transom sign read; another sign deeper inside read, WELCOME TO THE POGROM PARK GALLERY! KNOW YOUR CITY! LOVE YOUR CITY! The long empty room walled by glossy photo-murals reminded

Cassie of a tourist center, displaying pictures of local attractions. Frame by frame, then, she looked at photographs of Hell's greatest landmarks:

The Industrial Zone and its hundred-foot walls of iron girders. Inside this vast complex lay the city's Central Power Plant, the Foundry and Slag Furnace, the Flesh-Processors and Bone-Grinding Stations. One shot showed thousands of destitute workers cutting the flesh off of corpses. Endless conveyor belts then delivered the cuttings to the Pulping Plants for further food processing; more conveyors delivered the bones to be ground up for bricks and concrete. In the Fuel Depot, wheeled hoppers delivered large chunks of raw sulphur by the tons, to be manually chopped into smaller chunks by stooped laborers—the city's endless fuel supply.

De Rais University extended over countless acres and appeared almost campus-like in its layout. Here, the finest Warlocks in the land taught their pupils in the blackest arts: divination, psychic torture, spatial transposition, and the latest in vexation.

The Rockefeller Mint provided the city with all its currency: brass and tin coinage featuring the embossed faces of all the Anti-Popes, and Hellnotes printed on processed demon skin.

Osiris Heights stood proud and posh, the residential district for upper-Hierarchals who lived an eternity of privilege in pristine highrises. A typical suite boasted the latest conveniences: harlot cages, skull-presses, iron-maidens, and neat personal-sized crematoriums. Television, too, powered not by electricity but by psychical theta-waves, offering up all the best torture channels.

Boniface Square encompassed whole city blocks in its leisure services. From the finest restaurants specializing in the best demonian cuisine to the most common street vendors pushing carts of flame-broiled meat skewers. Opulent nightclubs to rowdy hole-in-the-wall bars. From strip joints, bordellos, and peepshow parlors to the opulent Frederick the Great Opera House, all manner of abyssal entertainment could be found in the Square.

The J. Edgar Hoover Building existed in the Living World as well as in Lucifer's; here, though, the immense Gothic edifice housed the million-occupant Central Jail, the Drug Perpetuation Agency, the Commandant of the Mancer Divisions (headed by an articulate gentleman named U. S. Grant), the Tamerlane Emergency Response Battalion, and, of course, Satan's official police department—the Agency of the Constabulary.

Other landmarks included Tojo Memorial Hospital, the John Dee Library and Infernal Archives, St. Iscariot Abbey, and the infamous Office of Transfiguration and Teratologic Research.

And wealthier Hierarchals who enjoyed beachcombing could always open their cabanas along the beautiful blood-filled Sea of Cagliostro.

Cassie's fascination didn't abate. The gallery's final mural occupied the entire back wall, showing different angles of the most spectacular skyscraper she could ever imagine. Monolithic and pale gray, the building must have spired miles into the smoky air, looking out on the city with hundreds of thousands of gun-slit windows. Gargoyles could be seen prowling the stone ledges of each level; Caco-Bats nested in the iron trestle that crossed to form the structure's fastigiated antenna-mast. One shot from the highest ledge made Cassie dizzy just looking at the city's panorama.

"The Mephisto Building," Via identified. "That's where Lucifer lives. It's 666 floors straight up."

Cassie squinted at a lower shot of the Devil's metropolitan abode. The bottom of the building seemed to be surrounded by a perimeter of something shining and pinkish. "What is *that*?" she asked. "Around the building? It almost looks organic."

"It is," Xeke answered. "The Flesh Warrens, they call them. It's a maze of connecting city blocks that are *alive*. It's like an organic security zone, a catacomb of manufactured living flesh that has its own immune system. Think of it as Satan's home burglar alarm; it's impossible to penetrate. Every once in a while, a terrorist group will go in, try to get to Lucifer. But they never come out."

But this sparked another query. "Why would anyone want to attack Lucifer?" Cassie asked. "Isn't he the god here in Hell? Isn't he worshiped?"

"He's worshiped by order of public law, but billions hate him. There are literally billions of humans and demons alike who'd love to get their hands on him."

"But he's a Fallen Angel. He can't be killed."

"No, but he can sure as shit be fucked up. Lucifer rules over this entire burg, but if you want to know the truth, he lives every second of his immortality in fear. Maybe that's his own Hell. Anyway, that's why he had the Flesh Warrens grown around the entire building. So no one gets in."

The explanation made her think of what he'd said a moment ago. "And what did you just say? There are *terrorists* here?"

"Oh, sure. Most of them are pretty rag-tag, not very well armed or organized. They're insurgents, rebel militias that wage a little guerilla warfare on Lucifer's army and the Constabulary. There have been revolutionary movements in Hell for as long as it's existed." Xeke seemed downcast. "But the groups always get their asses kicked. There'll never be a terrorist force that can stand up to Lucifer." Xeke pointed to a sign on the wall right next to the mural. The sign read:

WANTED:
EZORIEL, PUBLIC ENEMY NUMBER ONE
(COMPOSITE NOT AVAILABLE)

"Ezoriel?" Cassie asked. "The name almost sounds angelic."

"It is," Xeke replied. "Ezoriel was Lucifer's right-hand man, the second Angel to be cast out of Heaven by God. But he didn't dig the way Lucifer was running the place, so he started a riot in Satan Park, and from there began to form his own rebel group. It's called the Satan Park Contumacy, and it's now the biggest terrorist organization in the city. Ezoriel swears that he'll depose Lucifer some day, but all I can say to that is good luck. He's launched a bunch of attacks on the Flesh Warrens, but they're always repelled."

Terrorists, Cassie thought. *Revolutionaries in Hell.* It all sounded marvelously fascinating. Then she looked again at the photos on the mural; she couldn't even contemplate the sorcerous biological technologies that must've been involved to create such a thing as the Flesh Warrens. A labyrinth—made of flesh. "Jesus," she muttered in awe.

Xeke laughed. "You won't find Him here, but every now and then you'll see Judas bopping around town. Come on. Let's get out of here. We've got business in the Ghettoblocks. . . ."

(III)

"God, I *hate* coming here," Via complained. "Why do we have to come *here?*"

"I've got some moves to make," Xeke replied. "I'm hip in these parts. I've got connections."

"Oh, you're such a player," Via groaned. "Did you hear that? Xeke's *hip* in these parts. He's The Man."

"You just wish *you* could be as hip."

"Oh, right."

The area they traversed now—the Ghettoblocks— smelled worse than anything yet. Endless drab high-rises, many on fire or gushing smoke from shattered windows—lined the litter-strewn main drag. The starved and the hollow-eyed sat in desperate limbo on equally endless front steps. Haggard humans, wielding knives, chased Polter-Rats through alleys that reeked of urine and far worse. Others simply scraped up dirt or gutter filth with their hands, for food.

"This is where the poorest human residents live," Xeke informed. "There are millions of apartments. No running water, no sewage or power—it ain't Rodeo Drive, that's for sure."

They had to walk nearly in the middle of the street, for man-tall heaps of garbage consumed the sidewalks. Wet splattering resounded from all sides, wan residents emptying buckets of waste from high windows. From an alley, several mocha-skinned demons emerged and dispersed; moments later a human woman appeared, adjusting a soiled, threadbare skirt. Aside from dirty hair and flinty smudges on her skin, she could've been attractive. When she saw Xeke loping on the other side of the street, she whistled, "Hey, stud-muffin! Gotta penny-piece for the best action in town? Come on, let's party!"

Then she teasingly raised her rotten skirt.

"Uh, no thanks," Xeke said.

Next, she showed an emaciated breast. "All right! For you it's free!"

"Naw, gotta run. Next time, maybe."

"*Next time,* maybe!" Via yelled at him. "You ass-hole!"

Xeke scoffed. "I was just being polite. She's a Zap whore. I wouldn't touch her with a ten-foot pole."

The woman continued to wave her skirt. "Come on, cutie!"

Via glared at her. "Keep your trap shut, you demon sperm-dump! I'd come over there and kick your ass, but you're not worth getting shit on the bottom of my boots."

"Fuck you, bitch!" the prostitute yelled back.

Via's rage exploded. She took off across the street, hate in her eyes.

"Aw, Via, just leave her alone," Xeke groaned.

Via continued to sprint across. The prostitute squealed and ran off back down the alley.

"Yeah, you *better* run, you whore!" Via shouted. "Next time I see you, I'll mop all the shit up off this street with your face!"

"Was that really necessary?" Xeke complained when she came back. "She's got it bad enough."

"She won't have it *bad* until I get my hands on her," Via sputtered. "Damn street whores. And you just make it worse by flirting with them."

"I wasn't flirting with her!" Xeke objected.

"Bullshit. You love it. All you do is walk around thinking you're some Don Juan from Hell. Yeah, you're hip, all right. Even the *street whores* are whistling after you."

Xeke smiled to Cassie. "Women are so jealous."

But the notion seemed alien to Cassie. *I've never been jealous over a guy, because I've never HAD a guy.* The sudden thought instantly depressed her.

The only boy she'd ever even kissed had been Radu— that night at Goth House. The act that had triggered Lissa's suicide. . . .

She refused to think about it any further.

They passed more massive slums, more fire and smoke. In another few minutes, Xeke was leading them into a place called THE GHOUL'S HEAD TAVERN.

"Great," Via continued to complain. "Now we're going into a bar. Let's see how many girls put the make on Xeke *here*."

"Women don't menstruate in Hell," Xeke said. "Then how come you've got PMS all the time?"

Via responded, "I wish I had a dick so I could tell you to blow me."

Hush smiled up at Cassie, shaking her head as if to say *Situation normal.*

As they were about to enter through the two cliched swing doors, a thin, sharply dressed man was coming out, whistling "The Summer Wind." Billiard balls could be heard clicking within. In Hell's ghetto, Cassie didn't expect much, but she found the taper-lit darkness inside to be comforting. Upholstered benches lined one side; a long brass-railed bar stretched across the other. In the back, she saw two shabby men playing pool, and in a high corner, a television flickered with the sound off.

"This place almost seems normal," she remarked.

"Does that look normal to you?" Via pointed to a high mantle over the bar. The severed head of a monster had been propped there on a spike. Bottles on the glass shelves behind the bar all seemed to be full of muck rather than liquor, and then there was a sink full of green mold over which a sign read: EMPLOYEES MUST NOT WASH THEIR HANDS.

A chalkboard announced the day's specials: HUMAN CHILI (SPICY OR MILD), HUMAN SAUSAGE, HUMAN MEAT LOAF WITH FIXIN'S.

"Those are the *specials?*" Cassie questioned.

"Sure. In the Ghetto, *Human* meat is rare. It's usually shipped to the ritzier districts, which means this place has some mob ties. Nine times out of ten, you'll only find demon meat in the Ghettoblocks." Then Via gestured toward the pool table. "The balls are kidney stones from a Nether-Pig. Oh, and check out the tube."

Cassie looked closer at the oval tv screen in the corner. It was a boxing match between two demons. Instead of boxing gloves, the contestants held carpenter's hammers in each hand.

Via reached up and changed the channel, a game show where a cadaverous host in a tuxedo spun a great clicking wheel. Wedges on the wheel bore words: TOTAL DISMEMBERMENT, LUXURY SUITE, BONE-REMOVAL, $50,000 CASH, and the like. A giddy She-Demon watched as the wheel spun. "Here's your chance, Magnolia!" the host celebrated. "Will it be riches, or will it be the end of the line for you?" The wheel slowed, ticking. The pointer turned through a wedge that read LUXURY CRUISE FOR TWO ON THE SEA OF CAGLIOSTRO, but—

One more click and the pointer stopped on: HEAD-PRESSING.

"Oh, no, that sure is some bum luck, huh, Magnolia?" the host said, and at once the woman was dragged off the stage by tuxedo'd demons. Her head was forced into a metal box with a hand-crank on it, and soon the woman's arms and legs were flailing. One demon was vigorously turning the crank, crushing the woman's head. The audience cheered as blood and pureed brains began to run out of a tap in the box.

Where's Wheel of Fortune *when you need it?* Cassie thought.

"And you wouldn't believe the soap operas they've got here," Via added.

Behind the bar a handsome man with a pompadour was polishing highball glasses with a blood-stained cloth. "Xeke, my man. How goes it?"

"Like half a dog, Jimmy D.," Xeke answered.

"Half a dog?"

"Yeah, I'm still standing on two legs so I suppose I'm doing all right."

The barkeep leaned over. "The heat's been up around here lately. Keep an eye out for the Constabs. Oh, and the meat supply's down; they're trolling hard for XR's and Plebes on the wanted boards."

"Those punks'll never get me," Xeke bragged. "They *wish* they could get me."

But the keep seemed very serious. "Word is Nicky the Cooker is looking for you and Via. Word is you scammed him out of five grand."

"That goombah greaseball can sit on a Caco-Dragon's horn for all I care," Xeke said, "Now gimme a shot of your best sour mash, not the rail stuff, the stuff from the back."

"Oh, so it's *Grand Duke* Xeke now?" The barkeep laughed. "Don't bust my balls. You and I both know you ain't got the cash for that."

Xeke opened the paper bag. "I'll have plenty of cash once you exchange *this* for me. And don't try to jive me with the city exchange-rate. I want it from *your* people on Trafficante Street."

The barkeep's eyes shot wide when he saw the catfish spines and bone meal. It all glowed in the bar's darkness like lime-green fire. "Holy shit! That's worth a quarter-million Hellnotes on the street!"

"Which is why I'll take a hundred and fifty large from you." Xeke acted as though he expected a haggle, but all the barkeep did was go into a back room and reappear with a sack of cash. "My people will *shit* when they see this, and I'll get a kick-ass commission. Thanks for coming to me, man."

Xeke downed his drink and grabbed the sack. "No problemo. Keep your mouth quiet about this and I'll have you up to your eyebrows in commissions."

"You mean . . . you've got more bones?"

Xeke just winked and turned back to the others. "Let's get out of here."

"But I thought you guys were hungry," Cassie pointed out. "Why not eat here?"

Xeke frowned at the specials board. "With the kind of cash we're packing? Hell, I wouldn't eat that slop . . . with *Via's* mouth." Then he laughed and slapped Via hard on the back.

"Yeah?" Via retorted. "I've got something for you to eat—" But before any more insults could be traded, Cassie noticed the barkeep staring at her.

"Oh, hey," he said, "I didn't recognize you with your hair that way."

"Are you—" Cassie looked behind her confusedly—"talking to me?"

"Yeah, sure, you been in here a bunch of times, said you worked the cages at the S&N Club. Wasn't I talking to you the other night?"

Uh, no. I wasn't in Hell the other night. She couldn't imagine what he was talking about. "Sorry. You must be mistaking me for someone else."

"You don't say?" The keep smiled, shaking his head. "There's this chick, comes in here all the time for Desolation Hour, and I mean she looks *exactly* like you, except her hair's different. Spittin' image of you."

Cassie stood mute for a moment, then Xeke whispered, "He might mean your sister. Ask him." Then Hush pointed to her locket.

"Her hair? Is it long and black, with a white streak?" Cassie's heart was already racing. She rushed to the bar, opened her locket with Lissa's picture inside, and showed it to him. "Is this the person you're talking about?"

"Yeah, that's her. Ain't that weird?"

The implication slammed into Cassie's consciousness. *He's talking about Lissa! He's SEEN Lissa!*

"What were you saying? You said you know where she works?"

"Yeah, that's right—"

"Where!" Cassie exclaimed.

Her excitement took the barkeep aback. "She was telling me that she worked—" His words paused, then he looked up at a keening sound. "Ask her yourself."

159

Then he pointed over Cassie's shoulder. "There she is."

Cassie turned very slowly. All she could do was stare, a lump in her throat.

There, standing in the tavern's doorway, was her twin sister.

Chapter Eight

(I)

At first she couldn't believe it—she couldn't believe *any* of it. She wasn't in this bar. She wasn't in Hell.

And it wasn't Lissa standing there looking back at her.

No. This was crazy. She was dreaming. She was hallucinating everything. There was no Via, Xeke, or Hush. Her house wasn't a "Deadpass" and there was no such thing as an Etheress.

"Cassie?"

Lissa's voice.

Lissa's face and body.

Lissa's hair, down to the white streak on the right side. She wore black-velvet gauntlets, a short black crinoline skirt and black-lace blouse. The same thing she'd been wearing on the night she shot herself in the back room of the Goth House. The tiny barbed-wire tattoo around her navel was the final proof.

Cassie knew then that she wasn't dreaming. It was all real.

But when she opened her mouth, to speak to her sister for the first time in over two years—

Lissa turned and bolted, ran out of the bar.

"No! Come back!"

Cassie disregarded all else. She ran out of the bar, too, and manically followed her sister.

Why is she running? came the anguished question. *She should be happy to see me*—

Then again, maybe not. Maybe the opposite.

I'm the reason she's in Hell, Cassie reminded herself.

Her flipflops carried her across the wretched street; she hurdled piles of garbage and nameless waste. A pack of Polter-Rats dispersed, squealing, as she leapt over them. Overhead, the bloody sky squirmed, and down the dark avenue, Lissa dashed onward, as if fleeing a certain terror. She was easily out-pacing Cassie.

"Lissa! Come back!"

A huge carriage rattled down the intersecting street— not drawn by horses but by rotund, rhinoceros-looking beasts with shiny, pustulating skin. Lissa crossed their path and darted into an alley. Then the carriage inconveniently stopped as the beasts paused to feed on a demon corpse in the road.

The alley was blocked.

"Damn it!" Cassie shouted. "Lissa, come back!"

But her sister was gone.

Cassie didn't dare follow. That would mean skirting the swollen things that hauled the carriage, and she suspected they might prefer eating *her* to the dead demon.

The others caught up to her on the corner, out of breath.

"Cassie, don't ever do that!" Via warned her.

"You need to always stay with us," Xeke said. "You don't know the turf; you wouldn't last a minute on your own."

Cassie knew they were right, but—

She was close to tears. "That was my *sister!* She was standing right in front of me and now she's gone!"

"We'll find her." Xeke seemed confident. "She figures she lost you—"

"But *she* doesn't know that *we* know where she works," Via added. Even Hush's little smile seemed assuring.

Cassie's mind reeled. "I-I forgot what the bartender said. *Where* does she work? Some kind of club?"

"The S&N Club," Via confirmed. "Sid and Nancy's place. It's in Boniface Square."

"And you'll love the club," Xeke said.

"Why?"

"It's a Goth club." Xeke grinned. "In Hell."

(II)

A groaning escalator took them beneath the street, where the temperature must've shot up fifty degrees; it was like being in a sauna. Fires could be heard roaring behind fungus-traced tile walls. Their rail passes were good here—*here* being the Rasputin Circle subway station. In the ticket cage, a fat woman with leprosy waved them through the turnstile, waved them, that is, with a skeleton arm.

Cassie barely took note of this latest bit of sight-seeing; she was too pent-up over Lissa.

Why did she run away? the question tormented her.

But Via explained some more dismal realities: "This place changes people. Most can't hack it at all. It changes every aspect of their personalities. You need to be aware of this."

"You really can't expect Lissa to warm up to you," Xeke added.

"Consider what she's been through since she got here. And *how* she got here."

Cassie shuffled despondently toward the platform. "I know. She's in Hell, and it's my fault."

"It's not *your fault. She* killed herself."

Yeah, but it was because of me. . . .

"One thing's very important, though," Xeke added. "When we do find her, you have to let her think that you're dead too."

"Yeah, you can't let her know you're an Etheress," Via forewarned. "There'd be a riot. If Lucifer ever got wind that there was an Etheress on the street, then he'd be after you with everything he's got. He'd activate the entire Constabulary to hunt for you."

"Why?" Cassie asked.

"According to the legends, if an Etheress is captured alive, Lucifer's Arch-Locks at the College of Spells and

Discantations could use your body in a Transposition Rite. Satan could fully incarnate demons into the Living World. He could even incarnate *himself*."

"So," Cassie wondered. "You mean Satan's never really set foot in the Living World?"

"Oh, sure he has, a bunch of times," Via continued, tapping her leather boot as they waited for the subway. "But only as a Subcarnate, not fully in the flesh. And the subcarnation rites never last long, they're real hard to perform properly, and real expensive."

Then Xeke: "That's why we have to be real careful. No one can know that you're an Etheress. A full incarnation is Lucifer's holy grail, and if he finds out you're an Etheress, he'll do *anything* to get his hands on you."

Only now did the implications start to sink in. *Satan,* she realized, *will put a dragnet out for me. . . .*

The prospect made her stomach clench.

More from Xeke: "You can't let on to your sister that you're different from everyone else here. So when we catch up to her, you'll have to be real careful. I know you want to see her, and I can imagine you won't rest until you do. But we gotta be honest with you. Like Via was saying, Hell changes people."

"You might not like what those changes are," Via said. "She probably hates you, she might even attack you."

"I don't care," Cassie told them. "I just need to . . . tell her I'm sorry."

The silence that followed made it clear that they all understood her motives. Several rag-tag demons and a few humans waited at the stop. One man stood by smoking a cigarette, though his rib cage was missing; black cancer-ridden lungs leaked smoke when he inhaled. A woman in a football cheerleader's outfit peeled crusted scabs off necrotic skin; she seemed to be selling them to an Imp in an overcoat. When Cassie glanced down off the platform, she noticed an abundance of crushed bodies and body parts: people thrown onto the tracks.

A deafening roar approached, augmented by loud metallic clangings and screeches. The string of subway cars that pulled in looked more like a procession of iron boilers with rivet-seamed porthole windows. The black metal hissed from intense heat. When the subway stopped, a human in a Ted Bundy t-shirt shoved a crippled demon against the car's exterior surface. The demon howled, its face sizzling against the scalding iron, and when it recoiled, half of its face remained on the car, frying.

"Where do we sit?" Cassie asked, noticing no seats in the coach.

"Nowhere," Xeke told her. "Grab the hand loop. The subway travels through the underground fires; it's super hot."

"If you sat down," Via suggested, "you'd literally cook your ass off."

Cassie grabbed the overhead loop, then glanced down in dread. "My flipflops are melting!"

Xeke and Via chuckled at the oversight, while Hush tugged Cassie forward to stand on the tops of her boots. Then the awkward ride began.

"I feel idiotic!" Cassie exclaimed, embarrassed. She hung partially from the hand-loop, balancing her feet on Hush's boots, while Hush hugged around her waist.

"It's only a few minutes to Boniface Square," Xeke said. "You'll like it, it's a pretty hopping part of town, lots of action."

Cassie frowned; she was pretty sure she'd seen enough "action" already; she couldn't even contemplate what she'd feel like by now if she hadn't taken the Reckoning Elixir. The subway jerked periodically, and seemed to be accelerating at a phenomenal speed. Soon, the sound of its wheels clattering over the tracks was completely drowned by the sound of roaring flames. A glance to the port-hole window showed her whitehot fire. Next, she glanced around the car itself. Someone had etched some graffiti on the inside of the hull:

Jesus saves. . . . He passes to Moses, shoots. . . . HE SCORES!

And as in any subway, advertisement panels ran across the top of the car. One was a photograph of a demon-child grinning as he threw a rock through a window. JOIN THE MOVEMENT TO RID HELL OF THIS SOCIAL OUTRAGE. GIVE GENEROUSLY TO THE "KILL THE BROODREN FUND." Another showed a solemn cloaked and hooded man holding a handful of gemstones: SICK OF POLTER-RATS EATING YOUR FLESH? TIRED OF BAPHO-ROACHES LAYING EGGS IN YOUR BODY CAVITIES? CALL PIP BOYS NOW! THE BEST IN CRYSTALOGICAL PEST EXTERMINATION!

And another: DO YOU HAVE AN UNWANTED HYBRID? ARE YOU TIRED OF ALL THAT SQUALLING, ALL THOSE DIAPERS, AND ALL THAT MESS? WE PAY **CASH** FOR YOUR BABIES! WHY WAIT? VISIT AN URBAN PULPING STATION NEAR YOU! THAT'S RIGHT! **CASH** FOR THOSE UGLY LITTLE CRITTERS!

The heat was insufferable; Cassie felt like a piece of raw clay baking in a kiln. But when she feared she might pass out altogether—and flop to the griddle-hot flooring—the subway had ground to a halt, and in another moment they were helping her out. Cassie paid no mind to the amputated derelicts plodding around the platform on their stumps, nor to the pack of Broodren beating a She-Troll down with crowbars near a vending machine that sold Skin Jerky. Cassie began to revive as the grinding escalator ferried them up into an open park. A statue of Lizzie Borden—bearing an axe—greeted them on the street. It seemed darker here—long twisted tree limbs from malformed branches overhead blocked out the eternal twilight. Cassie noticed ill-colored fruit hanging from some of the trees, fruit the size of footballs.

"Don't stand under the Uter-Gourds," Via warned and pulled her away. But Cassie noted that the bizarre things were churning as if to dispel their contents through a suspiciously vulvalike groove. Cassie didn't care to see what came out.

"Make way," Xeke said. "Don't piss him off."

Cassie nearly screamed when she looked at the thing that trod down the sidewalk: a great fleshy mouth a yard high, walking on a pair of human legs.

"A Dentata-Ped," Via identified. "They made thousands of them at the Office of Transfiguration before they decided to cancel the project. At first Lucifer wanted an entire army of them to supplement the Mutilation Squads."

"But they don't have much for brains." Xeke chuckled. "They were chomping up Ushers and humans alike."

The thing strode by, teeth the size of paperback books and a huge lolling tongue.

On the side of its burgeoning head, great orbs for eyes gave Cassie a lusty glance.

"And speaking of Mutilation Squads," Via pointed out, "here's something you should know."

At the corner a sign stood: CITY MUTILATION ZONE.

Cassie stopped, remembering. She remembered her dream.

"I saw that," she said, "or something just like it."

"In a nightmare?"

"Yes."

Then the ensuing carnage replayed in her mind, the phalanx of demons tearing into a crowded street to dismember, rape, and destroy.

"They have the Zones to keep things from getting dull around here," Via mentioned. "Without any warning, the Squads will Nectoport into a Zone and go on a rampage, just for fun."

"Anything goes in a Mutilation Zone," Xeke added. "But don't worry; they did this street not too long ago. Probably won't hit it again for a while."

Cassie tried to feel confident as they passed the sign and stepped into the street. "What did you say a minute ago? They . . . *Nectoport?*"

"It's the most advanced form of spatial displacement. Kind of like the transporters on Star Trek, only the Sorcerers at the De Rais Labs use tapped psychic energy from their Torture Factories as fuel for the process. It's the same sort of power that Hell uses in place of electricity, except the Nectoports use a lot more energy."

They were in the middle of the street when Cassie asked, "So these Squads could appear—anytime—on any street in a Mutilation Zone?"

"Uh-hmm."

"Even *this* street right here?"

"Uh-hmm."

Flipflops snapping, Cassie ran the rest of the way across the street as the others laughed after her. Eventually they all crossed.

"So where are we going now?" Cassie asked.

"Munchies," Xeke answered.

The short walk seemed as pleasant as it could be, considering that this was Hell. Open-air cafes lined the street, wafting awful scents over the heads of their patrons. One waiter prepared a tableside dish on a red-hot iron plate: small mice-like rodents jumped on the plate, squealing, as they were flambee'd in smoking oil. Espresso machines hissed, expelling steaming blood into dainty cups.

"Careful here," Xeke said.

One by one they carefully stepped into a large revolving door, as one might find at the front of a ritzy Manhattan hotel—only the edges of the door were sharpened cutting blades. Dried blood and skin on the blades proved that some hadn't been so careful.

Shortly thereafter, they were sitting down at a table in what was, by initial appearances, a high-class restaurant. The Alferd Packer Room at the No Seasons Hotel.

"This is the best restaurant in any human district," Xeke said, "and finally, we have the money to eat here."

A waist-coated busboy—with white warts all over his face—politely filled their water glasses, but the water looked full of rust. Cassie noticed maggots frozen in the ice cubes. "Almost all of the entrees are human-based but it's not that ground-up stuff that comes out of the Pulping Stations," Via said with enthusiasm.

"I'm not going to eat *human meat!*" Cassie whispered hotly across the table.

"It's not like cannibalism in the Living World, Cassie." Via perused a shiny black menu with gold tassels hanging off the spine. "Here it's just . . . meat. It's an everyday resource."

Xeke grinned. "And it tastes just like chicken."

Not even the Reckoning Elixir would remedy this. "Please," she pleaded. "Don't eat *human* stuff! Not in front of me!"

"I guess it's only proper that we humor her." Xeke ran his finger down the menu. "Hmm. Let's see."

They were attended by a shapely waitress in black slacks and a pretty white blouse with puffed sleeves;

however, the front of her face looked collapsed as if beaten in with a pitted bludgeon.

"We'll start off with an order of Caco-Crabgut Rangoon," Xeke told the waitress, "the Nether-Worm Tenders in Mustard-Sorrel Sauce, and the Creole Spiced Gargoyle-Liver Pate on toast points."

For main courses, Xeke ordered Demon-Brain Flambee in Pesto Lung Puree, Via the Troll Wellington Au Jus with E. Coli-Cream Baked Bilge Apples, and for Hush the Spotted Sewer-Fish Sushi and Abyss-Eel Bowel Tempura with Pickled Ginger.

"There. Satisfied?" Xeke asked Cassie. "We won't scarf any human meat."

"Thanks a lot."

"You don't know what you're missing, though. *Human* ribs beat baby backs by a long shot."

"I'll remember that next time I'm at Ruby Tuesdays."

"What are you going to have, Cassie?" Via asked. "Veggies? You'd love the Devil Plantains. They deep-fry them in Gargoyle lard. Better than French fries at McDonald's, no kidding."

The cycle of culinary grotesqueries made Cassie feel exhausted. "Oh, nothing for me. I'm watching my calories today."

The "food" arrived amid indescribable odors—but at least the presentation was nice. Cassie averted her eyes as her companions dined, and then she exclaimed "No way! You've had enough!" when Xeke jokingly asked if anyone cared for dessert. Then he paid the bill and tipped the waitress a Nero Note, bidding, "This is Be

Kind To Mirrors Week. Treat yourself to a new face, babe."

"Why, thank you, sir," she mumbled through a mouthful of bloody spittle and tooth fragments.

The red-coated doorman, a well-bred Imp, nodded when they left the restaurant and went back outside. The hotel's entrance looked as exorbitant as any five-star operation in Washington's power-lunch district; the long canopy and red carpet could've made Cassie forget she was actually in Hell . . . until a throng of derelicts encircled them. Humans and demons in advanced states of emaciation tugged at them and held out gnawed and rotten hands, begging for change. Cassie noticed many with ears missing, eyes, fingers and sometimes whole hands missing too: pieces of themselves that they'd cut off and sold to the Diviners.

"Beat it!" Xeke yelled with authority and shoved them off. They squalled, cursing, but eventually dispersed.

Cassie's first reaction was one of pity. "Can't you give them some money? We've got plenty."

Via explained, "They're Zap-Heads, Cassie. It's their own fault."

"Only dopes do dope, especially in Hell." Xeke brushed muck and debris off his leather jacket. "Zap is Hell's version of heroin. It's a concoction of infernal herbs boiled in Grand Duke urine until it's cooked down to paste at the Distillation Vats. The bodily waste of anyone in the Hierarchy is of great value."

Via added, "Zap is the most addictive substance in either world. One mainline and you're hooked for life,

173

and here that means eternity. Zap-Heads are great business for the Smoke Diviners. They systematically amputate parts of themselves, to sell in exchange for Zap money."

"Only a fraction of one-percent of users ever get off it. If a former addict is ever caught clean, they take them straight to a Re-Tox Center." Then Xeke pointed to a Public Service poster hung in a window.

DO YOUR PART! HELP MAINTAIN THE MISERY! A grainy photograph showed several Zap addicts inserting long syringes into their nostrils. SUPPORT YOUR LOCAL DRUG DEALER!

More tragedy. The worst of Cassie's own world seemed reflected here as well. Or perhaps it wasn't a reflection at all, but a source. Before she'd come here she'd always believed that evil was just a word, an excuse that the gullible used to define misfortune. But now she could see that evil was an entity, a grand design exercised to offend God.

That was the only purpose of this place.

And now she knew where the evil in her own world really came from.

Back out on the streets, the red twilight seemed to darken as queer yellow clouds moved in overhead. The effect only amplified the brightness of the streetlights and myriad lit building windows. From high poles, just like in any city, she noticed power cables, only these were much more stout. A block away, some sort of juncture of cables sprouted from one of the poles and led into a large cement edifice with a fluttering neon pyramid on top. "What is that?" Cassie inquired. She could hear a heavy, resonant humming.

"It's a district power transformer," Xeke answered.

And Via added, "There's no electricity here—we've got *agonicity* instead."

"Agon—"

"Come on, I'll show you. We can see through the vents." Xeke led her down the block, toward the strange pyramidic structure. The humming grew louder as they approached, and intermittent crackles could be heard. A sign came into view:

MUNICIPAL POWER PLANT #66,031
(Boniface District)

"They're really efficient," Xeke went on. "Lucifer really nailed a big problem when his Bio-Wizards came up with the technology."

Agonicity? Cassie repeated the odd word in her mind.

"There's one in every district in the city, and all it takes is a single unit to provide all the necessary power to an entire district." Xeke stopped right in front of a drab brick wall. Metal vent slats studded the wall, and Cassie could feel their slow gusts of heat. "And all it takes is one person to run the whole unit," Xeke went on.

Cassie was astounded. "One employee runs the entire station?"

"No, no. I'm not talking about maintenance personnel. One *victim*."

Victim? Cassie didn't see his meaning.

Until she looked into the vent.

When Xeke propped the metal slat open with a finger, the steady humming began to mix with another sound:

Screaming.

Cassie looked into the vent and she saw the most macabre thing. Large capacitors—probably ten feet high—pillared the brick-walled room. A figure in a dark hood and cloak stood aside as if in supervision, and at the center-point of the room was a simple stone column.

Lashed to the column was a naked human man.

From a smoking cauldron beside the column, two uniformed demons took turns removing ladles of boiling water. The water was then splashed onto the naked man's skin, each splash understandably causing him to scream and convulse from the pain.

"Who needs turbines and dams and nuclear power plants," Xeke proposed, "when the brain of a single human being can generate an enormous amount of convertible power? See that wiring harness?"

Cassie squinted, got a better look. The top of the man's skull seemed to have been sawn off, and situated over his raw brain was a contraption of narrow cathode tubes and wires, the wires sunk deep into the brain pulp.

"The boiling water lights up the pain centers in the brain, and those impulses are then converted to energy that's processed by all those capacitors. Sorcery works into it too, sort of an electric alchemy.

The torture that that poor sap suffers is turned into power for the district. And since a human can't die in Hell—"

Cassie denoted the rest. *They power the entire city with human pain, and the power source can't die. . . .*

"Agonicity," Xeke said again. "It's theoretically eternal."

"You mean . . . they'll torture that man forever?"

"Well, not forever. Probably just for a hundred years or so. Then they'll put a fresh human in there and start all over again. In Hell, agony is product, pain is a fuel source."

Cassie pulled her eyes away from the vent; the barking screams faded. She'd seen enough.

With every new vision came more verification of the pure evil of this place. Exploitation was maximized for an ultimate effect.

It made her mad.

They walked back over to Via and Hush who waited for them at the corner of 1st and Attila. *Lissa,* Cassie remembered. She struggled to regain her focus. "When are we going to—"

"Soon," Xeke said. "The S&N Club is across the Square. In Herod's Alley."

"Okay, then. Let's go—" but when Cassie began to cross the street, Xeke grabbed her arm, held her back. Hush looked absolutely woeful as she pointed across to the decrepit park. The Polter-Rats were scurrying away, and strange fanged birds lifted out of the trees in black flocks. The image reminded Cassie of how birds and animals sometimes sense a coming storm.

The air felt still.

"This isn't good," Via said.

"Yeah," Xeke agreed. "It might be a—"

Then a man, whose upper body looked as if it had been clawed, stepped into the middle of the street, holding a sack. From the sack he withdrew fistfuls of crisp Hell-Notes and began to throw them up into the fetid air. "Hell-Notes!" he shouted. "Come and get it! Hell-Notes for the poor! Thousands of dollars in Hell-Notes!"

Each fistful blossomed overhead, then rained down like confetti. In just seconds the street was mobbed, hundreds of the destitute—mostly humans—shouting, scrabbling for the money.

"This is a set-up," Xeke said.

Cassie didn't understand. "It's just a man giving money to the poor."

Via pointed hotly to the sign—

CITY MUTILATION ZONE

"Run!" Xeke said.

They sprinted off, Cassie still confused. Now the street was a literal riot as hundreds more struggled into the desperate fray.

Before Cassie and her friends could get away—

Sssssssssssssssssss-ONK!

—a terrifying sound popped in the air. Cassie felt her ears pop too, like an airplane descending, and next came a flash of throbbing green light. The flash seemed to grow into a stagnant, shuddering blob at one end of the street, and then she noticed an identical blob at the other end. The blobs grew, painting everything in their eerie green glow.

"Nectoports!" someone screamed.

Too late.

Within each blob of light, an aperture formed . . . and out stormed one Mutilation Squad after another. Armored Conscripts with great, webbed wings led droves of ferocious Ushers and clay-bodied Golems into the crowd. Strange edged weapons were raised along with hooknailed three-fingered hands. Screams crashed like heavy surf, and soon the tumult turned into pure chaos. By the time the green Nectoports closed and faded away, the Squads had completely enveloped the crowd and then began to move in. Great scythes swept this way and that, mowing down lines of humans like weeds. Hewers fell, dividing people completely in half from head to crotch. Golems crushed whole heads—and whole bodies—with intractable hands and beneath anvil-like feet. Ushers tore into the horde with their claws, dismembering, decapitating, and disemboweling with each swipe.

Where moments ago, the air had been raining money, it was now raining gore.

The meld of sound was deafening: metal clanking through flesh to the pavement, the ceaseless whistling of scythes, and of course the throat-flaying screams. Ironically, across the street, Cassie spotted the man who had lured all those people into the street by throwing cash. He greedily stroked his chin as a demonic sergeant paid him off. *The whole thing was a trap,* Cassie realized. *The Constabulary paid that guy to throw*

Edward Lee

money around, and draw everyone into the middle of the street—bait for the Mutilation Squads.

"If we don't get out of here now," Xeke said worriedly, "we'll be lunch meat." They sprinted down the sidewalk, behind the surging rank of mutilators. "If we're lucky we can—"

Via and Cassie screamed in unison, while Hush's mouth shot open in her own silent scream.

"Fuck," Xeke said.

A rabid Usher came out of the street, charging Xeke. When its claws grabbed him, Xeke deliberately fell to the ground, dragging the demon with him. He fell and rolled, and when they were both on the pavement, he'd managed to jump on the Usher's back, all the while slipping something long from his pocket. It looked like a piece of rope, only with handles at each end.

The Usher roared. Before it could regain an advantage, Xeke got the rope around its neck and began to yank back and forth on the handles.

Screams exploded from the Usher's throat, and eventually its head came off.

That's when Cassie realized that the implement was no mere piece of rope. It was a rope-*saw*.

The creature's body ran off headless and blind, blood black as hot tar spraying from the severed arteries in its now-exposed neck. The hideous head rolled into the street, where it was trampled at once.

"That took care of him," Xeke said. He was winded but seemed pleased with the gory job he'd done. But then—

"Behind you!" Via yelled. "Holy shit! Look out!"

180

A reptilian-skinned demon in a visored helm broke from the ranks and was trotting right for them, a wide-bladed hewer held at port arms. A monstrous smile could be seen below the helm. At the end of each of its curving horns a severed human head had been planted, warrior decor.

"Stay right behind me!" Xeke ordered. "Get ready to move quick. When I get him out of the way, run your asses off to the corner till you're out of the Zone!"

"But, Xeke!" Via began.

"Don't argue with me! Just fuckin' do it!"

Xeke rushed the demon—

Cassie couldn't believe what Xeke was about to attempt. "Xeke! No!" she shouted.

The great blade's first swipe blurred a silver line across the air. Cassie had never even imagined a hand-held weapon so large; it was wide as the pendulum blade in the Poe story, shining like lightning at its sharpened edge.

Swooosh!

The blade cut crosswise through the air, so fast it could scarcely be seen. Xeke ducked beneath it, then sprang back up and somehow managed to grab the hewer at mid-shaft. A vicious kick to the demon's groin stunned it—then Xeke twisted the hewer out of its monster-hands.

"Now! Run!" he shouted over his shoulder. "Get the hell out of here as fast as you can!"

Cassie, Via, and Hush ran, their feet splattering in the fresh blood that was overflowing now from the gutters, stumbling on chopped limbs, heads, and various body parts that lay forth. When they got to the corner—out of the danger perimeter—they all peered back in focused terror.

Xeke had already hewn the demon's head in half, through the helm. It staggered about, its split cranium spurting green blood and lumps.

Swooosh!

A second swipe cleanly severed the creature at the waist, whereupon strangely shaped organs twirled in the air. However horrific, it was a magnificent sight. But when Xeke did the same thing to a Golem, the thing's upper half just kept coming at him, walking on its hands.

"Try this on for size, Gumby. . . ."

Swooosh-swooosh!

But even when two more swipes of the great blade divorced the thing from its arms of black-gray clay, the arms continued to flop forward:

"Persistent little dickens, ain't he?"

Finally Xeke hacked the arms into chunks, and that was the end of the Golem.

"Come on!" Via yelled. "Get out of the Zone!"

Xeke was about to retreat, but then a pair of primeval-faced Ushers broke rank and came after him. Suddenly there was no effective point to retreat to. His only option was to charge into another fight.

"Go on without me!" Xeke yelled back. "Just go! I'll meet you at the club later! The Constabs'll be here any minute."

"Come on," Via said. "We have to get out of here."

YES! ☐

Sign me up for the Leisure Horror Book Club and send my TWO FREE BOOKS! If I choose to stay in the club, I will pay only $8.50* each month, a savings of $5.48!

YES! ☐

Sign me up for the Leisure Thriller Book Club and send my TWO FREE BOOKS! If I choose to stay in the club, I will pay only $8.50* each month, a savings of $5.48!

NAME: _____

ADDRESS: _____

_____

TELEPHONE: _____

E-MAIL: _____

☐ **I WANT TO PAY BY CREDIT CARD.**

☐ VISA   ☐ MasterCard   ☐ DISCOVER

ACCOUNT #: _____

EXPIRATION DATE: _____

SIGNATURE: _____

Send this card along with $2.00 shipping & handling for each club you wish to join, to:

Horror/Thriller Book Clubs
1 Mechanic Street
Norwalk, CT 06850-3431

Or fax (must include credit card information!) to: 610.995.9274.
You can also sign up online at www.dorchesterpub.com.

*Plus $2.00 for shipping. Offer open to residents of the U.S. and Canada only.
Canadian residents please call 1.800.481.9191 for pricing information.
If under 18, a parent or guardian must sign. Terms, prices and conditions subject to change. Subscription subject
to acceptance. Dorchester Publishing reserves the right to reject any order or cancel any subscription.

JOIN NOW

"We can't just leave him here!" Cassie exclaimed, even though she realized there was little they could do against such creatures themselves. What, spit at them? Say bad words? Cassie cringed at her own sense of helplessness as the Ushers surrounded Xeke.

"Don't shit a brick just yet," Via said with some confidence. "He can take care of himself. Look."

A frantic glance showed her that Xeke had already eviscerated the first Usher and beheaded the second. More came after him from the chaotic ranks.

"Come and get it, you ugly fucks!" he laughed and charged them.

Cassie couldn't watch the demonic slaughterfest. Via tugged her away and they began to run, the cacophony of screams fading behind their frantic footfalls.

Chapter Nine

(I)

It was not a nightmare that snapped Bill Heydon out of his slumber. What was it then?

Suddenly his eyes were open in the high, valance-trimmed bed. Something had terrified him, but he could recall nothing in the way of dreams. Often, images of his dreams lingered at times like these—dark, late at night—but this was not an after-image.

Then he realized what it was.

Creep me OUT! he thought. He sat upright immediately in bed and switched on the small tulip-shaded lamp on the night stand.

No, it wasn't an after-image, it was an after-*touch*.

He jumped out of the bed; the bedside lamp wasn't

enough. Next he clicked on the chain-mounted swag fixtures that hung overhead.

Now the room bloomed with light.

And, of course, no one was there but him.

Jackass, he called himself.

The lagging sensation remained spooky nonetheless. It felt as though someone had touched him, shaken him, while he slept.

"Must've dreamed that someone touched me," he muttered. The whole room seemed to look back at him in his fading fear. "Then I forgot the dream."

Now the bright light was *too* bright, bringing a sudden headache; he turned them off and walked in the much dimmer light from the nightstand to the broad mahogany armoire in the corner. He opened the frame-tiled doors and dug his pack of cigarettes out from behind rolls of socks. The antique parliament clock on the wall ticked nervously. *He* was still nervous, from the dream-touch or whatever it had been. It seemed very late but then the clock told him it was only a few minutes past midnight. He looked at the half-empty pack of cigarettes and thought, *To hell with it. I might as well do this right.*

Next he was shuffling out of the first-floor bedroom, in his underwear. The headache pulsed; he kept the lights off, preferring a dark trip through the foyer to the pantry behind the kitchen. Moonlight through the back bow windows barely gave him enough light to see by, but eventually he got his hand around the bottle of Glenlivet that he kept stashed behind some sacks of flour. Given Cassie's former drinking problem, he didn't want any hooch sitting around to tempt her. Thank God, though, that she'd worked hard to put all that behind her. As far as Bill knew, his daughter hadn't touched a drop of alcohol since Lissa had died.

He took the bottle into the kitchen where the moonlight was brighter, carefully retrieved a glass from the cabinet, and poured himself two fat fingers. The first sip sang down his throat. *Ooo, yeah!* Then he sealed the ritual by lighting a cigarette. *Yeah, momma!* In his retirement, at least, this seemed appropriate. Nothing wrong with a man who'd worked hard all his life having a drink and a cigarette.

At midnight.

In the dark.

In his underwear.

Well . . .

To hell with it, he thought again.

He downed the drink, poured himself another. Just a finger and a half this time. Hell, he'd heard on the health shows a bunch of times that a few drinks a day could even be good for you, lowered the cholesterol count or some such. What could be the harm, especially to a man with some heart troubles?

He took another edgy sip.

And that's when he heard the footsteps.

Shit! Cassie's coming down the stairs!

The last thing he wanted was for her to catch him sneaking a nip and a smoke at midnight. In his underwear. He stashed the glass in the cabinet, doused the cigarette in the sink. Then he walked back out into the foyer, trying to seem as casual as possible.

Casual, yes. At midnight in his underwear.

Strange.

The hall lights on the second-floor landing remained off. And the long stairwell was empty.

Jackass, he called himself for a second time. *I must have one grade-A class of the willy's.* He was certain he'd heard Cassie coming down the long stairs.

Back to the kitchen, to retrieve his drink.

What the hell is going on! Is this some kind of a damn joke?

Not two seconds back in the kitchen, he heard it again.

Footsteps. Slow but deliberate footsteps.

Only this time they were going back *up* the stairs.

He dashed back to the foyer. Turned on the crystal chandelier.

There was no one on the stairs.

All right, I'm still shook up over the dream, or whatever the hell it was. It was the only explanation possible . . . or so he thought. *I'm like a little kid, scared of the dark and wanting mommie to make the monsters go away!*

Out went the chandelier and back went Bill to the kitchen. He finished his drink but then—

Holy MOTHER—

—dropped the glass when he felt a hand gently touch his shoulder from behind. The glass shattered, spewing wet fragments across the kitchen floor.

He spun around, and in spite of his fear, he knew there'd be nothing there.

187

And was wrong.

In the moon-lit darkness, a slender young woman stood before him.

Grinning.

She was nude, her skin pale as cream. Just standing there.

Bill couldn't move a single fiber of muscle.

The young woman's slender arms reached out. Her white hands touched his chest but the touch seemed to *dissolve*. Her hands seemed tangible for only a moment, then they disappeared into his chest.

A ghost touching him.

But now he knew who the ghost was.

The long black hair with the white streak on the right side.

It was Lissa, his dead daughter.

Worse was the obvious mutilation.

Her breasts were gone, as if sliced off, leaving only two angled lines of black stitches in their place.

"I'm in Hell now, Dad," she said, but the voice flowed from her mouth like some corrupted dark fluid.

Then the apparition disappeared.

I'm fucked up, Bill concluded, wiping his brow on his t-shirt sleeve.

There'd been no ghost, of course. There were no such things. But there were hallucinations, optical illusions, and horrible images produced by the subconscious. There were powers of suggestion from unknown and undeciphered traumas and stress. There were alcohol-induced visual tricks.

Bill regained his breath. He refused to let this bother him. He was a mature man, not a nut. He poured the expensive, eighteen-year-old scotch down the drain in the fancy brass-and-porcelain-fitted kitchen sink. It gurgled away, leaving its warm aroma floating in the air.

That's enough of that, he thought firmly.

Lissa was dead. It was the worst tragedy of his life, and it had obviously left its mental scars. True, the entirety of those scars would probably never go away altogether, and he realized that.

But she was dead and buried and gone now.

There were no ghosts. There were no spirits haunting the dark.

He walked stolidly back to his room, turned off the bedside lamp, and got under the sheets.

Jackass. Just go to sleep.

He was determined to do exactly that, but when he rolled over he saw that someone else was in bed with him.

(II)

Cassie felt distressed as she, Via, and Hush trotted away from the abattoir of the park, their gory footprints trailing behind. As they ran off, Constabulary platoons marched in the opposite direction, followed by Collection Crews pushing their wheeled hoppers to pick up the carnage and deliver it to the Pulping Stations. In spite of the gruesome incident, the rest of the district seemed back to normal only minutes afterward, as

189

though such outbursts of atrocity were as routine as a fender-bender in any other city.

Evidently, they were.

"We'll be pretty safe here," Via suggested to her. "The Constabs don't generally pay much attention to the heart of Boniface Square. Lucifer likes all the money that pours in from the clubs, restaurants, and stores."

"It's like a shopping district?" Cassie asked.

"Entertainment district is a better way to think of it. The better-heeled residents of Hell come here to party. It's like the Hollywood Boulevard of Hell."

"But as ex-residents—XR's," Cassie ventured, "I thought that makes you fugitives, right? Doesn't that mean that the Constabulary will be looking all over the place for you?"

"Technically, yes, but there aren't any official warrants out for us here. The Ghettoblocks and Industrial Zone are another story,'cos we've committed a lot of crimes there. Mostly stealing, and things that would be considered Crimes of Nonconformity."

"Crimes of—" Cassie began to question.

"Resisting arrest, killing Ushers and other Constabs, ripping demons off—stuff like that," Via answered as though it were no big deal. "One time Hush painted *Satan Sucks* on the front door to the Westminster Church of the Anti-Christ, so the Constabs but an APB out on us. Then there was another time when they sent an entire regiment of Conscripts after us 'cos Xeke blew up a police station near Baalzephon Mall."

"So . . . you're like urban guerillas?" Cassie saw the association. "Like the terrorists Xeke was talking about earlier?"

"We do our part, but it's all nickel-dime compared to the real revolutionaries. Like Xeke was saying, there is a bona fide resistence movement—the Satan Park Contumacy—but they operate mainly in the City Center. We don't have the guts to join them."

This sounded fascinating to Cassie. "Why not? It seems to me that if enough people banded to-gether—"

"We could overthrow Lucifer?" Via laughed at the idealism. "It'll never happen, Cassie. The Contumacy is led by Ezoriel, one of the Fallen Angels, but even with half a million volunteers, he can't beat Lucifer's security forces. They've been trying to break into the Mephisto Building for a thousand years, but even with the power of a Fallen Angel, they've barely been able to penetrate the Flesh Warrens. It may sound cowardly, but if we joined them, we'd just wind up in the Torture Factories eventually. We gotta spend eternity here— eternity's a long friggin' time. Why would we want to make it even worse for ourselves?"

Cassie couldn't very well argue. After all, she was still a member of the Living World, and as-yet Un-Damned. She only hoped she could keep it that way.

"Well, at least that's something of a relief," she ob-served, "that we're safe from the Constabs in this dis-trict."

Concern on her face, Hush pulled on Via's punky leather jacket and silently mouthed the word *Nicky*.

"Oh, yeah," Via was reminded. "There *is* one guy we've got to look out for, though. Nicky the Cooker. He's not in the Constabulary; he's a Mob guy. A while back, we ripped one of his shylocks off for five thousand."

"Like a loan shark, you mean?"

"Yeah, same thing here. Nicky's one guy who'll *always* be looking for us, so we've got to be careful. 'Cos of the strip clubs and bars, he does a lot of business in Boniface Square."

Cassie hated to ask, but she asked anyway. "Why do they call him 'The Cooker?' "

"If you cross him and he catches you, he cooks you."

"*Cooks* you?"

"Yeah. He owns a sulphur pit in Outer-Sector East," Via calmly explained. "They put you in a big metal drum, seal the lid, and throw the drum into the pit. So you just sit there in that drum and *cook*. Forever."

Jesus! Cassie thought.

"It's real funny how a lot of the Mob guys in the Living World kick off, go to Hell, and continue being Mob guys here. Live or dead, I guess you are what you are. Lucifer loves organized crime and all the corruption that comes with it."

Cassie imagined so, and Nicky the Cooker was one person she hoped she'd never have to meet.

Soon they were walking through an urban maze of strip malls and commercial buildings boasting a multitude of enterprises. "Boniface Square is huge," Via said. "Where we just came from—the restaurant and hotel district—is the Square's ritzy area. From here down, things get kind of seedy. Bars, strip joints, porno parlors, and bordellos, like that. It's where wealthier citizens buy their drugs and get their jollies. The music clubs are all mixed in here, too."

Music clubs, Cassie reminded herself. *Like the place where Lissa works.* The endeavor to find her sister remained foremost on her mind, but then there was always the issue of Xeke. Cassie was terribly worried about him, but Via seemed unperturbed.

"Aren't you even a little worried about Xeke?" she asked.

"A little? Sure. This is Hell. There's lots to worry about. But I've seen Xeke rip his way through Mutilation Squads and Constabs a bunch of times. The smartest thing for us to do is simply follow his instructions. He knows what he's talking about. He told us to meet him at the S&N Club, so that's exactly what we'll do."

"Yeah, but what if he doesn't *make* it to the club?" Cassie had no choice but to challenge Via's confidence.

"He'll make it," was all Via said.

More questions arose, a force of habit. "I'm a little confused, you know, about you and Xeke—your—"

"Relationship?" Now Via seemed subtly displeased. "I'm in love with him. How's that?"

It seemed so. "But—"

"Is he in love with me? Hell, no. To him, we're just pals, we're 'buds.' Jesus. We've never even gotten it on, never even kissed, which pisses me off 'cos I've given him every chance." A dolorousness crept into her voice.

193

"Fuckin' men—in either world they're supreme pains in the ass."

"Why don't you—"

"Make the first move?" Via kept finishing Cassie's questions. "He'd just think I was a tramp if I did that. And, no, I've never told him that I love him. That'd just drive him away. Isn't that how it always works?" She sputtered to herself. "He's actually right, though. He doesn't want to have a relationship with me because he knows what everybody here knows. Relationships never work out in Hell. I wish I could be as strong and as smart as him."

Cassie felt bad for her. She could easily tell that Via's genuine feminine feelings were seeping through the harsh, tom-boy veneer. Another thing that seeped through was just as plain: in spite of Xeke's street-smarts and combative prowess, Via was truly worried about him.

A long fence topped with rolls of razor wire lined one side of the block. Demon sentries marched guard posts along the interior perimeter. Beyond the fence, Cassie could see long rows of dark concrete buildings.

"This almost looks like a military compound," she said. "What's it doing in an entertainment district?"

"Every district has at least one government facility," Via replied, walking along. "That's a Supernatural Services Installation. Lucifer can't *live* in the Living World, so he takes any opportunity to mess with it."

Cassie squinted at bizarre stenciled signs:
AUTOMATIC-WRITING BARRACKS
SEANCE PROJECTION

CHANNELING POST

"Seances, channeling?" Cassie questioned. "Doesn't all that have to do with communication with the dead?"

"Sure does. And it's all fake."

"What?"

"It's all bullshit for gullible minds in the Living World," Via said. "It's all an instigation of Lucifer's sorcery technologies. Ouija boards, phone calls from your dead relatives, trance-channelers who think they're writing notes from Edgar Cayce, stuff like that. It's all fake. It's all manufactured here. When people fool around with Ouija boards and become convinced that they're in contact with their dead Uncle Harry, it's really just a Necromancer on this end, manipulating the board so it seems real. Remember that guy who claimed that Mozart was contacting him to finish his last symphony? They even compared the hand-writing to letters and sheet music that Mozart wrote himself, and it matched. But it was really just a technician in the Automatic-Writing Barracks, forging it all and channeling it to this moron."

Cassie was astonished by the information. "That's fascinating." Another sign loomed by:

N.D.E. GENERATORS

"N.D.E. stands for Near Death Experience," Via went on. "I'm sure you've read about the stuff. All these people who get brought back to life in emergency rooms, or drown and get revived by CPR—and they all say that they saw a great white light and their dead relatives are all waiting for them in paradise afterlife?"

Cassie was well familiar with the stories.

"It's all manufactured bullshit. Imagery Spells are projected to the people who get revived, and since the imagery is all the same, their stories sound credible. Doesn't matter if they're good people or bad, Christians or Jews or Muslims or Atheists. The experience is the same so it suggests that there's this wonderful non-Bible-oriented place of perfect peace waiting for us when we die. But it's really all just a trick. Same thing with alien abductions—Jesus. Imagery Spells are randomly projected to people in the Living World; the images make them think they've been kidnaped by aliens. If you get people to believe in aliens—"

"They won't believe in God," Cassie got it. "And if people think aliens are real and God is a myth . . . they reject the notion of salvation."

"And their asses land right here the minute they die."

They passed the creepy compound, Cassie's fascination brimming. Lucifer's schemes were intricate and brilliant. She wondered how many millions had been deceived by him.

Suddenly Hush was pulling Cassie along harder by the hand; she seemed giddy with excitement.

"Hush loves to window-shop," Via said.

Here, odd store fronts lined the sulphur-lit street. EVITA'S SECRET, one window read. Behind the glass, hellish skeletons served as mannequins, displaying the latest lacy fashions. INFERNAL CONCUBINE? PROSTITUTE? OR JUST AN UPTOWN GIRL? LOOK YOUR SEXIEST IN OUR NEW COFFIN-WORM-SILK NIGHTIES!

The next store read CROWN OF THORNS BOOKS, whose window display showed an array of books, *The Glyphs of She, Cultes Des Ghoules, Megalopisomancy, The Gospel According to Judas*. Another sign blared, DON'T MISS OUR NEXT SIGNING! CAPOTE AND LOVECRAFT AUTOGRAPH THEIR LATEST RE-LEASES, *PORTRAIT OF THE WRITER IN HELL* AND *THE SHADOW OVER PROSPECT STREET*. Between the next two shops a midget Gremlin tended to a tuxedo'd demon as might a shoe-shine boy: the demon was having his horns sharpened. Another Gremlin sold smoking nuts of some kind from a wheeled stand. Cassie doubted they were chestnuts.

Big-screen televisions were displayed in the next shop, with strangely oval screens. *Sony they ain't,* Cassie thought. The grainy screens flickered in washed-out color. One screen showed what appeared to be a bikini contest, with demonic contestants. A game show flickered on the next. "And what's behind Door Number Three?" a handsome human host with hook hands announced. The door raised, revealing a torture chamber, complete with squirming bodies shackled to racks and quivering in spiked iron maidens. Yet another screen showed an arena with packed grandstands. On the field, huge birdlike demons ripped strips of flesh off naked humans. The crowd roared with applause.

I guess football doesn't make it here. . . .

Next, Hush was beaming at a shop whose transom read TRANSPLANT PARLOR (AN AUTHORIZED COMMERCIAL ANNEX OF THE OFFICE OF TRANSFIGURATION). It reminded Cassie of a realtor's, where an audio tape was triggered by a motion detector when browsers walked by. An energetic voice announced: "Don't trust your body modifications to an unlicensed surgeon. Come in and meet one of our government-approved Transfigurists for all your transplant needs. Get rid of those insufficient human arms and let our doctors give you a pair of powerful Troll arms. Get revitalized with a demonic transfusion. If it's Nether-Wolf fangs you want, we've got them. And don't forget about our easy low-interest payment plan."

"Capitalism at its finest," Via said. "Things actually aren't that different. If you've got money, you've got privilege. Hierarchals enjoy an eternity of luxury, on the backs of the poor. Just like the Living World. See? Even the government's in on it."

"Hush seems very interested in this place." Cassie noted her friend's longing eyes.

Then Via explained, "Hush can't talk because the Constabs caught her stealing a piece of Ghoul Sausage from a vendor. They cut out her voice box as punishment."

The answer seemed simple to Cassie. "Well, by the looks of things, we can buy her a new one."

"Ain't gonna happen. It's a government annex," Via explained. "To get services, you have to register. Me, Xeke, and Hush are XR's—we're fugitives. You have to prove residency for any government service."

Damn. It distressed Cassie when she considered the predicament. Hush would spend eternity wanting something she could never have.

"Here's another Annex," Via pointed out when they crossed the next block. The elaborate neon sign read: SUCCUBIC SERVICE CENTER! RENTALS, LEASES! AN AUTHORIZED SUBSIDIARY OF THE LILITH SUBCARNATION CONSERVATORY.

"The Conservatory is another government project," Via said, "but this annex rents succubi and incubi to all the downtown strip joints and escort services. Lilith herself is the Conservatory's CEO—Lucifer's had a thing for her for eons; she bore Adam's children after Eve left him, and the children were half-bred sexual demons. At the Conservatory, she uses Conversion Spells to turn humans into succubi, to subcarnate them into the Living World where they haunt men's dreams. Just like the legend."

By now it was occurring to Cassie that many myths, legends, and occult lore must actually be true. Behind the glass, several naked "samples" sashayed back and forth in a plush parlor. Glowing yellow eyes glinted back at her. The women had flawless physiques, every aspect of female desirability accentuated to supernatural perfection. They were bald, however, and bereft of any body hair, and their poreless skin shined as if shellacked, not flesh-toned but a rich, exotic violet.

"And you say they *rent* them out?" Cassie qualified.

"To titty bars, live-sex shows, massage parlors and whorehouses." Via chuckled sardonically. "Sounds a lot like L.A."

They continued on down the maze of dark streets. Via hadn't been kidding earlier, when she'd said they'd be going to the seedier parts of the district. Wan pros-

titutes enticed customers from bordello windows; some
were human, some succubi, and some crossbred demons. Peep show parlors flashed like Las Vegas casi-
nos, promising live sex shows, private booths, and the
latest pornography. Beneath a garish yellow sign that
read JACK RUBY'S ROMP-HOUSE, an eager Imp
barked at them: "Step right in, ladies! Dancers wanted!
Jack'll take your applications *personally!*"

"No, thanks," Via smirked.

DEAD PORNSTAR LAP DANCES! boasted an-
other sign, and then another, CRIPPENDALES! FOR
LADIES ONLY! GET A PRIVATE DANCE (AND
MORE!) FROM JOHNNY THE C-MAN HIMSELF!

Lastly, the Onan Theater sported a flashing marquee:
"HELL-TRAMP 666" STARRING CATHERINE THE
GREAT! PLUS EVA BRAUN IN "GARGOYLE
ORGY A-GO-GO!"

Cassie grew weary of the parade of smut. So much
revolved around sex, just like in her world. Hush
seemed to sense her impatience, pointing to the next
block.

"The S&N Club is right over there," Via said. "In
Herod's Alley."

But when they crossed the street, Via slowed. A Golem was hulking down the street, stopping at each
street lamp and sign post. The huge, clay-bodied thing
seemed to be attaching sheets of paper to each post.

"What's he doing?" Cassie asked.

Via didn't answer; instead she trotted to the first
street sign. "Shit, I should've known," she muttered.

Cassie looked at the paper that the Golem had fixed to the post. *It's a Wanted poster,* she realized when she read it.

POSTED BY ORDER OF
THE AGENCY OF THE CONSTABULARY
(BONIFACE DISTRICT)
WANTED
FOR THE MURDER OF 16 MUTILATION
OFFICERS
REWARD
OF 1000 HELL-NOTES FOR INFORMATION
LEADING TO THIS CRIMINAL'S ARREST

And below that was a picture of Xeke.

Via was laughing softly. "How do you like that? He killed sixteen of them and got away."

"Yeah," Cassie remarked, "but now they've got a bulletin out for him."

"At least he's still alive. We can only hope he'll make it to the club."

Cassie saw her point. Xeke being wanted by the police meant he was still out there somewhere.

So long as they were looking for him, he was still alive.

"Let's get going," Via urged and led on.

When they arrived at the alley's entrance, Cassie noticed an endless line of rundown buildings pressed together. It reminded her of the Goth block in D.C.: black-painted brick-fronts and bouncers standing with their arms crossed in front of battered propped-open doors, but these bouncers were either deformed or demonic. Low bassy notes and a familiar voice eddied from one door: "Since my spirit left me, I've found a new place to dwell. I drugged out and croaked on a toilet seat and—went straight to Hell."

Cassie paused. *No, it . . . couldn't be!*

Or could it?

Before another club, a severed head on a stick talked to them. "Hey, girls! No cover! Robert Johnson and Grieg are JAMMING!"

NEVER MIND THE BOLLOCKS! HERE'S THE S&N CLUB! a sign down the way alerted them. *Finally,* Cassie thought.

"Crap!" Via exclaimed. "We can't get in! I just remembered that Xeke has all the cash!"

"And there's no sign of him," Cassie observed around the entrance. "If he was here, he'd be waiting outside for us, wouldn't he?"

"Yeah. *Damn* it!" Via looked down at stained pavement, scuffed a boot. Cassie could imagine what she was considering: that Xeke wasn't coming, because Xeke was being apprehended by the Mutilation Squad right this instant.

"He'll be here," Cassie tried to sound hopeful. "He's probably just hiding out for a while, until the Constabs leave."

Via just nodded. Then she asked the weirdest question: "How long are your fingernails?"

"Huh?"

"It's the only thing I can think of that can get us in the door. We can't trade our train passes, in case . . ."

Via gulped at the reality. "In case Xeke never shows up."

Cassie looked at her long black-lacquered nails, then hesitantly showed them to Via.

"Those are great. Bite one off."

Cassie winced at the thought but when Hush made the universal gesture—rubbing her thumbs against her first two fingers—Cassie knew that the fingernail from an Etheress would serve as money. Less than delicately, she bit the nail off her pinkie, gave it to Via.

The instant that the nail was no longer part of Cassie's body, it glowed a harsh lime-green.

"Cover charge is a De Sade Note each," croaked the bouncer at the door. He was shirtless, everything from the waist up covered with third-degree burns. He looked at them with lidless eyes.

"Three for inside, Romeo," Via said and gave him the luminous fingernail.

The bouncer examined the nail, impressed. "Where'd you get this?"

"I'm a concubine for Grand Duke Charles the First. Why don't you be a sport and slip us some drink tickets too?"

The bouncer produced the tickets without a quibble, and let them pass.

Inside, at first, Cassie was reminded of all the wonderful Goth clubs she'd gone to in D.C. Completely inchoate surroundings, subdued chatter, a dance floor filled with faces and murk. Dim light flickered from corners and around a long, congested bar in the back. All the walls were black-painted brick.

Cassie noticed crude graffiti: SEE U SOON, JOHNNY! JIM WAS HERE, AND I NEED AN L.A. WOMAN. . . . I FUCKED UP—JANIS

Music she'd never heard before ground out from a high DJ station and occult speakers driven by Hell's version of electricity. The DJ himself appeared to be some species of Troll. Beneath wavering phosphor lamps, the stage extended, bereft of a band as yet, guitars on stands and a drum set in wait.

Mostly better heeled humans filled the dance floor, some dancing to the current set, some chattering with acquaintances, odd-colored drinks in hand. One couple made out not-so-discretely while they danced, a male demon with a thin chain joining the tips of his horns, and slick green skin over his twelve-pack abs and Mark Wahlberg pectorals.

"Here. At least look the part," Via said and extended a warm metal can to her. Cassie sniffed it; it smelled like rotten hops, and the label read HELL CITY BREWING COMPANY. *Ugh!* she thought, not daring to taste it.

Next, she stared. A spritey woman bopped past, with a navel where her mouth should be. Cassie couldn't resist to look further, to the woman's midriff. Where her navel should be was a mouth, complete with lip piercings. "Hi!" the mouth said to Cassie.

Good lord . . .

"It'll probably take a while to find Lissa," Via proposed. "I doubt that she'll come on until the band starts."

"Didn't the bartender at—what was it called?"

"The Ghoul's Head Tavern."

"Didn't he say that Lissa was an employee?"

"Yeah, I think so. Said she worked the cages, but as you can see . . ."

Cassie's gaze followed Via's upward. Hanging over the stage were four dance cages—all empty.

"Hush," Via instructed, "you go hang by the front door, watch for Xeke. Me and Cassie'll snoop around."

Cassie tried to appear normal in the hellish club, scanning the crowd and deformed bar-staff for Lissa's face, but she saw nothing. *She works here,* she thought in fragments. *An employee. A dancer. Where would dancers be before their set?*

In the back.

"Where are you going?" Via asked.

"In the back," Cassie said and pulled away.

"Be careful!"

Via's objections were drowned out by rising shouts. The crowd in front shoved their fists in the air, demanding "Sid! Sid! Sid!" as Cassie shouldered her way through more decadently displayed bodies. She was grateful for the distraction. Eventually a deathly thin man appeared on stage, tight jeans and studded boots, spiky black hair. His shirtless chest revealed crisscrosses of razor cuts.

"I'm fucked up!" his cockney accent blared into the mic. "Can barely walk or talk—yeah!"

The crowd exploded.

"Anybody got some smack? *Fuck* it! Here's the hottest band in Hell! Aldinoch!"

The band she'd heard on the cassette tape.

A human trying hard to look like Trent Reznor grinned slyly and rubbed his groin against her side. Cassie sneered at the crude gesture.

"Hey, doll baby. Just got a new rig at the Transfigurist's." He brazenly displayed his hips to her; the crotch of his black slacks looked as if he'd stuffed a puppy in them. "Wanna try it out?"

"I'd rather be damned to Hell," she replied.

"Hey, that's a good one!"

She smirked off. Dirge-like guitar riffs meandered through the air; drums began to pop as the band—four figures in black cloaks—began their first number. Cassie found a black door further back, opened it a crack, and peered in.

WHACK! WHACK! WHACK!

A fat Troll in suspenders was beating a small Imp with a truncheon. The Imp had been peeping through the keyhole of another door.

"Freakin' pervert! Get back in the garbage hopper unless you want me to fire your ugly ass!"

Several more blows of the truncheon, and the Imp squalled and shimmied away, blood running from its pointed ears. When the Imp was gone, the Troll—obviously a manager—peeked into the keyhole himself and chuckled.

Then he, too, was gone.

Cassie slipped in, looked in the hole.

As she'd hoped, it was a dressing room. Several dancers in slinky outfits were filing out another door. Cassie noticed another violet-skinned succubus, a four-breasted She-Demon with modest bat-wings and a scarlet corset, and two human women in black bikinis, both of whom sported outbreaks of yellow tumors on their faces.

But no Lissa.

Then, all the girls left the room through a rear door.

Damn it all!

Had Lissa filed out of the room before Cassie had peeked in?

She snuck back out. The band's sonorous mix of Goth and death metal was grinding out in full as the dance floor rocked.

"The house of God in flames, protect me Father Satan, in Hell I'll be your slave!" the lead singer croaked.

Cassie could scarcely hear herself think over the infernal lyrics. But now the dance cages above the stage were occupied—with the girls she'd seen previously in the dressing room.

Another girl—a human with a white pageboy haircut—stepped right up to Cassie, hugging her. "Let's dance!" she said.

"Uh, no thanks," but as Cassie struggled to pull away, she felt hands clumsily kneading her breasts.

What the hell?

Then she saw how this could be. The woman snickered and stepped back. She pulled up her blouse, displaying human hands, which opened and closed, sprouting from where her nipples should be.

This place is REALLY a trip!

But just as Cassie was admitting to herself Lissa was likely not working tonight, she felt a tug at her skirt. It was Hush, excitedly pointing upward, behind her.

207

Two dance cages that Cassie hadn't previously noticed hung behind them, over the bar. An attractive redhead with a face bloated from elephantiasis danced sultrily in one cage.

It was Lissa who danced in the other.

The long shining black and white streak blurred before her face. She danced to the grim waves of music, still dressed as she had been the last night Cassie saw her alive: the black-velvet gauntlets, the short black crinoline skirt and lacy black over-blouse.

It's her. She's really here . . .

"You see her!" Via yelled from the other side of the bar.

Cassie nodded.

But now . . . *How do I get to her?* A small hatch in the wall led to the opening of the cage, and Cassie could only guess where the access was. Somewhere in the back, along with the truncheon-wielding Troll. Should she risk it?

A second later, though, she knew she had no choice.

Lissa had stopped dancing. She was staring down through the cage bars, right at Cassie.

"Lissa! Don't run! I just want to TALK to you!" Cassie did her best to blare over the music.

Too late. Lissa was already out of the cage and crawling away into the hatch.

Got to cut her off! Cassie knew. She bulled back through the dancing crowd, slammed through the back door and slammed again through the door to the dressing room. Toward the rear was an open doorway next

208

to a ladder on the wall, and just beyond that a fourth door, marked EXIT.

Lissa was climbing down the ladder, her face twisted into dread when she saw Cassie.

"Lissa! Please! I'm sorry!"

Cassie was about to run to her—until a heavy scaled hand grabbed her from behind by the hair. All her breath slipped out of her as she was spun around, to stare into the runneled face of the Troll.

The inhuman voice gurgled: "Aw, this is gonna be sweet! Got me a little human bitch back here tryin' to steal!"

"I wasn't trying to steal!" Cassie pleaded. "I just need to talk to my—" and then her voice was severed when the taloned hand grabbed her throat and squeezed.

Pale-green eyes glimmered back in homicidal lust.

The other scaled hand raised the truncheon.

"Let's see how fast it takes me to whip your brain into pudding. . . ."

Her fear felt like electrocution; she couldn't breathe. But as the truncheon raised higher for its first strike to her head, another emotion surged up from her heart.

Anger.

Suddenly the room seemed tinted in sparkling light. The Troll, amazed, let go of her and backed off, and the truncheon thunked to the floor. Cassie's face burned back at the creature, and when she yelled, "LEAVE ME ALONE!"—

Splat!

—the Troll's head exploded.

209

Cassie fell back; the strange sparkles fading. Her eyes widened at the convulsing corpse on the floor and the goulash of brains running slowly down the wall.

What the hell just happened?

There was no time to figure it out now. Her focus crashed back: Lissa!

But when she turned back around, her sister was gone.

And the exit door had just slammed closed.

(III)

The hot kiss drew Bill Heydon into a cloud of urgent bliss. The saliva off his mysterious new lover's tongue melted in his mouth like opium smoke. He breathed her scent and just kept sailing away in the warm luxuriant darkness of his bedroom. When he'd come back to bed, shaken from the macabre hallucination of a breastless, grinning Lissa, he'd turned to find a strange figure in bed with him.

The initial shock had nearly stopped his already faulty heart. The figure leaned up, gently pulled off his t-shirt, then smoothed her hands over his bare chest. The sensation enraptured him.

When his eyes re-adjusted to the dark, he saw who it was.

Mrs. Conner, the housekeeper.

Her nakedness proved what he'd already suspected. She was a robust, attractive woman, with a high full bosom that hadn't sunk with age.

Any semblance of rationale escaped him, and if he'd been able to give it any logical thought at all, it would've occurred to him just how wrong this was. The steel trap of his lawyer's sensibilities would've remembered that Mrs. Conner was an unbonded employee, an uneducated hill woman. The courts wouldn't care that she'd snuck to Bill's bed of her own volition. Tomorrow she could cry rape; she could sue him for millions. And no backwoods jury would ever side with a big-city attorney in a rape or sexual exploitation case when the plaintiff was one of their own.

It never occurred to him to put an end to this right now.

Instead he lay there, his eyes sucking up that natural naked beauty of hers, that down-home desire in her eyes, that lusty, working-woman's need.

Bill just let her do it.

He had some needs of his own, needs that he'd ignored for a long time.

She didn't say a word; the hot smile on her face said enough. She kissed him with fervor, her lips sharing his breath, sucking his tongue. His arms slipped around her naked back and pulled her closer, and when her breasts pressed against his chest, he moaned into her mouth.

Her hot hand slithered down, and that's when any chance of resistence on Bill's part shot away altogether. Her own urgency was clear; he could hear it in her breath, see it in the glint of her eyes.

Then she rose up, moved a knee over his hip, and straddled him. . . .

211

Chapter Ten

When Cassie banged out the exit door, she found herself in a narrow brick alleyway that stank of the most infernal odors. Fire licked up from the iron grates in the pavement. At first all she could hear was the crackle of flame, but then—

Sharp, rapid footsteps.

Cassie squinted through the smoke and saw her sister in the distance, running down the alley.

"Lissa!" Cassie bellowed at the top of her lungs and began to give chase.

Skittering Bapho-Roaches crunched like nuts under her footfalls. After more sprinting, she slipped on some slime and fell, her face landing inches away from one of the iron grates in the pavement.

Another face looked back at her—"Help me!" it pleaded from the flames.

But Cassie couldn't. What could she do? She dragged herself back up off skinned knees and returned to her chase.

"You go, girl!" a severed head cheered from where it had been left astray. As Cassie sprinted on, an obstruction emerged from the smoke: an adolescent City-Imp obviously addicted to Zap. The creature convulsed where it lay, whining, its clumsy paws manipulating the long hypodermic needle. Cassie hurdled over the thing, just as it inserted the needle into a nostril, injecting the drug deep into its brain.

Up ahead, Lissa reached the end of the alley and turned off.

"Lissa! PLEASE come back!" Cassie hollered.

She slipped over more vile slime then accidently stepped on a Polter-Rat as she ran on. The rodent squealed, ejecting its innards from its fanged mouth when Cassie's heel slammed down. As she approached the end of the alley herself, she heard more footsteps behind her: Via and Hush.

The alley emptied into an intersection glittery from phosphoric street lamps. A mephitic fog had set in, diffusing the strange yellow light. From a building ledge across the street, several Gargoyles gathered, peering at her, and then she jumped in startlement when a decaying human tending a vendor's grill barked, "Step right up! Get your piping hot Manburgers right here! Two-bits, honey! Best Manburgers in the Square!"

She stole a quick glance at the strange patties sizzling on the grill. "Did you see a girl just run out of here?"

"Buy a Manburger and I'll tell ya," he grinned.

Cassie's rage flared. "I don't have any money for a FUCKING Manburger!" she yelled. "Now tell me if you saw—"

But in an instant, a sourceless burst of bright sparkles flashed before her and—

"Holy shit, honey!"

—the vendor's head blew apart like a rifle bullet through a watermelon. A flop of brains landed right on the grill and began to sizzle.

It happened again! Cassie thought in shock. *What was that?*

But there was no time to reflect. She glimpsed Lissa again, on a corner a block away. Cassie resumed her chase through the ill-smelling fog.

"Damn it, Lissa! Don't run!"

But Lissa ran, dashing into the street. The fog consumed her, then came a sound like screeching tires—

"LISSA!"

A scream and an ugly THUNK! followed, then a metallic chugging. Cassie's heart plummeted in her gut. Even without seeing what had happened, she knew.

From the fog, some sort of a long automobile emerged, speeding down the street. A stout, horned Grand Duke sat in the back of the bizarre, steam-powered vehicle, while a lower demon drove. The iron bumper was shiny with blood.

Oh my God!

Cassie dashed into the middle of the street. When she was close enough, she could see Lissa lying in the road, amid the fog. Already some Polter-Rats were encroaching; Cassie kicked them away, horrified.

"Oh, please, Lissa! Don't be—"

Via and Hush darted up behind her. "Hurry! Get her out of the street!"

They dragged her to the sidewalk—

"Get out of the road, ya dizzy whores!" a voice grated and a horn honked.

Another speeding steam-car clattered by, missing them by inches.

But Cassie felt mindless now. Lissa wasn't moving. They dragged her to a park bench fashioned from demon bones, lay her down on it. A street light burned through the fog.

"Shit," Via said. "She's dead."

"No!" Cassie sobbed and fell to her knees.

She grabbed Lissa's still hand—if felt cold. Then she drooped her head onto Lissa's bosom and cried.

"I'm real sorry," Via said. Hush put her arm around Cassie, to console her.

"I came all this way to find her and tell her how sorry I am about her suicide," Cassie sobbed, "and all I do instead is get her killed! If I hadn't been chasing her—"

"It's not your fault. You can't blame yourself."

Cassie brushed her sister's hair back, and when she looked at her face, she cried harder. Lissa looked as pretty and vibrant as she ever had in the Living World.

And now she's DEAD! Because of ME! Now her soul has been transferred into a bug or a rat and it's ALL MY FAULT!

215

"Wait a minute," Via said, a suspicious edge to her voice. "This is fucked up."

"What?" Cassie sobbed, incoherent.

"I mean, *look* at her. There's some blood but . . . that's about it. She's not in bad shape at all."

"What are you talking about!" Cassie blared. "She's dead! She got run over by a car!"

"Step back," Via said sternly.

Cassie moved back, bewildered.

"Just as I thought," Via said when she knelt for closer inspection. She was pressing her hands down against Lissa's chest. "No ribcage."

"Whuh—*what?*"

"Cassie? What's one of the first things we told you about Damnation? When you go to Hell, the first thing you get is a Spirit Body that's exactly the same as your body on Earth. But, here, it takes a lot more than this to kill a Spirit Body. It has to be completely destroyed before your Soul can be transferred to something else. This is nothing."

Cassie was wiping tears off her cheeks. "I have no idea what you're talking about!"

Via stood back up, nodding. "Shit, I've been run over by steam-cars a bunch of times, but I didn't *die*. It's impossible, Cassie. It doesn't inflict anywhere near enough damage."

"I still don't know where you're—"

Via silenced her abruptly. "That's *not* Lissa. That's what I'm trying to tell you."

This was just too much confusion. Cassie looked again and knew that the body on the bench was Lissa's.

Her midriff was exposed, revealing the exact same barbed-wire tattoo around her bellybutton. The face was the final proof: Lissa's face looked exactly like Cassie's.

"It's a Hex-Clone, Cassie. It's *not* Lissa."

"You mean, this isn't—"

"It's not her. It's a *fake*. Trust me. We've seen these things before."

Hush was nodding too, to assure her friend.

"It's a Hex-Clone," Via repeated. "They make them in the Industrial Zone for the Constabs. Animation spells and organic molding. Lucifer's Houngan Priests at the Department of Voudou Research make these Hex-Clones from a flesh sample of the real person. It's sort of like genetic engineering in Hell. What I'm saying is that thing on the bench isn't Lissa—it's not a Spirit Body. It's just a sack of animated meat that was made to look exactly like your sister, right down to every last detail."

Could this be true? But Cassie couldn't believe it. How could she?

"Show her, Hush."

Hush looked consoling as she produced a short knife with gems in the handle. She reached forward and—

"Are you crazy!" Cassie yelled.

"Calm down," Via said and pulled Cassie back.

Hush stuck the knife in Lissa's abdomen, then drew it up all the way to the chin. Cassie expected to see bones and organs, but when the knife cut in, the body seemed to collapse.

217

From the incision, out spilled billows of what could only be described as organic *mush* that made Cassie think of ground pork. The mush overflowed in a pile onto the sidewalk, leaving an empty bag of skin.

"See?"

They're right.

How could Cassie argue, with the evidence all in a wet pile?

It's not Lissa. It's just some thing they made to . . . But she could think of no *reason* for this. Why would the authorities go to the trouble of producing a clone of her sister?

"The good news is, Lissa's not dead," Via said. Even Hush looked worried about the insinuation. "The bad news is, the Constabulary is onto us."

"But why—er, how—"

"There's only one reason why they would make a Hex-Clone, Cassie. They're using it as bait, and that's why we have to get out of here right now," and then Via dragged Cassie up, and the three of them ran off into the fog.

"Bait?" Cassie questioned, huffing as she ran.

"Bait to set a trap!"

"What are they setting a trap for?"

"You!" Via answered.

(II)

Bill Heydon made love to the woman ferociously, first, on the bed, then a second time right on the floor. The experience rejuvenated him, made him feel decades

218

younger. After the second time, they collapsed in one another's arms, their sweat shining like a primitive lotion, both sighing in spent bliss.

Bill had still not yet regained his sense of reason and, evidently, Mrs. Conner never *had* a sense of reason. *She'd* seduced *him* right? *She'd* snuck into *his* bed.

And from there, it was all basic human impulse.

They were cave-people ten thousand years ago, using each other to slake their needs.

She lay with her head on his chest, his arms draped flaccidly around her. Another part of his body was just as flaccid, and he assumed it would remain so for now. *Christ Almighty,* he thought. *This woman sure can f—* but then her knee slid up between his legs, and the tip of her tongue was encircling his nipple. He was breathing in the herby soapscents of her hair along with their shared musk, and as her breasts pressed harder against him, he could feel her heart beating. What Bill wanted more than anything was to do it again but then he was reminded of the realities of age. *The old crane won't be rising again any time soon.*

But Mrs. Conner's desire was even more plain. She wanted to do it again too, and the insistency of her attraction to him only made him feel better. Since his wife had left him, and considering the continued accrual of middle-aged pounds, it had been a while since any woman had wanted him. But tonight, Bill Heydon was definitely re-finding a lot of long-lost confidence. Only hours ago he was pretty much consigned to the fact that he was a pot-bellied, over-the-hill duffer who'd spend the rest of his life scratching his ass through his shorts and watching football on tv. But now here he was sprawled out on the hot hardwood floor with a beautiful naked woman who *wanted* him.

Little moans began to escape from her lips, and her affectionate afterplay was soon growing into something else. Her mouth drew up and opened over his, and then she was sucking his tongue again. A breath lodged in his chest; his hips flinched at the re-emerging waves of sensation. Then her warm fingers walked down across his belly to his groin.

Bill chuckled. "Honey, don't think I don't want to 'cos I do. But nothing much is going to be happening down there for the rest of the night."

Mrs. Conner's smile defied his statement. Her hand worked on a while longer in the most clever ways, and soon Bill's *body* was defying his statement too.

God, I can't believe this. . . .

Her smile disappeared for a time as her mouth occupied itself elsewhere, and now Bill was staring up in the dark. The intensity of pleasure caused him to move his head back and forth. At one point his eyes fell on the parliament clock, but he was too exhilarated to notice that it had stopped ticking an hour ago.

Even beyond his own belief, he was ready again. He looked down at the proof—*Holy smokes! Is that mine?*—and then she was straddling him, gently but urgently. She was *taking* him.

The moment froze in the most erotic image. She was sitting on him, the perspiration on her skin glittery as gold dust, the lines of her robust body and breasts etched in the finest edges of moonlight.

"God, you're beautiful," he muttered upward.

Mrs. Conner just smiled, her wanton eyes fixed on him. She didn't say anything in response, and it never occurred to him that she hadn't said anything *at all* since he'd found her in his bed. But when a simple hitch of her hips brought him into her again, she spoke for the first time tonight, the same word several times. . . .

"More . . . More . . . More . . ."

Bill eyes widened. Something wasn't right.

When she'd spoken the craving words, it hadn't been in Mrs. Conner's familiar soft drawly voice at all.

The words gushed out in dark, sultry sub-octaves. No, not Mrs. Conner's voice.

It was the voice of sheer lust.

The voice of utter sin.

It was the voice of all the whores of Gomorrah.

(III)

"Why are we going here?" Cassie asked quizzically when Via led them into a corroded brownstone off of Lady of Kadesh Avenue. The tacky flashing sign out front blinked THE ASTORETH INN. LOW RATES!

"This looks like a—"

"It's a flop-house," Via said. "We have to lay low."

Renting a room from the old woman behind the counter cost another of Cassie's fingernails; when the old woman said "Thank you," blood bubbled from a deep slash across her throat.

In the dank stairwell, a tri-breasted She-Imp in a nightie paid them no mind as she rifled through a wallet she'd taken from a corpse's pants.

221

A flop-house? Cassie thought when they entered the squalid room. *More like a slaughterhouse. . . .* The room itself stank of the most foul odors. Bloody handprints walked up the yellowed walls; more blood drenched the lice-ridden sheets on the bed. Perhaps the Reckoning Elixir was wearing off; the room made Cassie feel nauseous again.

When she looked in the bathroom, she saw that the toilet was full to the top with demon feces.

Cassie did her best to block it all out. "What did you mean? If that thing back there wasn't the real Lissa, then where *is* the real Lissa?"

Hush sat down on the edge of the bed, turned on the TV. Via slouched in a chair by the window.

"The Constabulary's got her somewhere," Via responded. "They're the only ones who can order a Hex-Clone."

"Then what did you mean when you said that the clone was a lure?"

"They were using it to trap you, but it got run over by a steamcar by accide it. If that hadn't happened, it would've led you right into the middle of a squad of Constabs. Is any of this starting to sink in yet?"

"No," Cassie shot back. "It doesn't make sense that *I'd* be wanted by the Constabulary."

"Cassie, that's the only thing that *does* make sense. The simple fact that they manufactured a Hex-Clone of *your* sister proves beyond a doubt that they know about *you.*"

Cassie pondered the assertion—then it dawned on her that Via had to be right. *There'd be no other reason for them to make the clone. . . .*

"It means they know about you, Cassie. They know that you're in the Mephistopolis, and they know that you're an Etheress. *That's* why they want you. An Etheress in the hands of Lucifer's Bio-Wizards could wreak havoc in the Living World. You're *alive,* Cassie, in a domain of the dead. They want you for your Etheric energy. It's a power they've never had before."

"You never told me that!" Cassie shouted.

"There wasn't any need to because there's no way the Constabs could find out."

"Well, they *did* find out! How?"

A queer silence yawned over them. Suddenly Via and Hush were exchanging solemn glances.

"What *is* it?" Cassie hotly demanded. "Why are you looking at each other like that?"

"Someone told them about you, Cassie," Via said despondently. "And the only people who could've done that are me, Hush, and Xeke. Hush and I have been with you the whole time. Which means . . ."

Cassie blinked. "Xeke? You're saying that he . . . ratted me to the Constabs? That's impossible!"

Via's head was bowed. "There's no other explanation. Xeke's a traitor. For someone to turn over an Etheress to the authorities? The rewards would be untold. It was Xeke. There's no one else it *could* be."

Cassie felt dazed. "But we just saw Xeke fighting the Mutilation Squad. We saw the wanted poster, we—"

"Xeke killing those Ushers and demons was just part of the act. He was putting on a show—for us. And the wanted poster? They put it up to make us think that Xeke's on our side. But I'm not buying that shit for a

223

second. If it hadn't been for that Hex-Clone, we'd be none the wiser."

Cassie couldn't believe it, but then . . . what other explanation could there be? Who else *but* Xeke could've told the Devil's police that an Etheress was in town?

But the weight of that revelation—hard as she tried to remain strong and objective—was clearly crushing Via. *She's just realized that the man she loves has sold her out,* Cassie realized. She couldn't imagine how that felt.

"So what do we do now?"

Via flipped idly through the *Gideon's Luciferic Bible* on the nightstand. "Lay low here for a little while, till the heat's down. Then we get you back to your own world, where you won't be in danger anymore."

"But I don't want to go back," Cassie insisted, "not yet. I need to find my sister!"

Hush looked at her forlornly, then so did Via. "That's out of the question now. We've got to get you out, and you can never come back."

"I'm not leaving this screwed up city until I see my sister!" Cassie was quite adamant. "I didn't come all this way, through all this—" she glanced fiercely about the malodorous room—"*crap* just to go back without seeing her."

"We'll argue about that later," Via said. "But now let me ask *you* something. What the *hell* happened to the Troll back at the club? When Hush and I ran out of there, he was dead. It looked like someone redecorated the place with his brains."

That's right. The Troll, and that vendor.

All this commotion had pushed it to the back of her mind. "I did it," she confessed. "At least I *think* I did. But I'm not sure what actually happened."

"Were you mad?"

"Well, yes. He was trying to kill me."

"Did the room fill with weird light?"

"Yes."

Via and Hush were nodding, smiling. "It's just more of the Etheress Myth that's turning out to be true," Via went on. "An outburst of emotions will amplify your aura. You can project violence with your thoughts, and that's good because we're gonna need it, considering what's happened."

Cassie didn't want to project violence; she just wanted to find her sister. But she also considered this: *With every Constab in the district looking for me, I'm probably going to have to project A LOT of violence. . . .*

"You have a tremendous amount of power, Cassie, and once you learn how to use it, that'll greatly increase your chances of getting out of here in one piece. But there's a bad side. Your aura itself."

"I don't understand."

"When you walk in Hell as a living human being, your whole lifeforce glows off of you. That's why we told you to bring an onyx stone; it'll keep your aura hidden most of the time, except when you get really mad or frightened—like with that Troll. But there's an exchange of energy. Show me your onyx."

Cassie dug the stone out of her pocket, examined it between her forefinger and thumb. "It's tiny!" she exclaimed. "It's only half the size it's supposed to be."

"That's because your aura's using it up. It won't be long before it's all burned off, then you'll be walking around here lit up like a Christmas tree. Shit."

"Then we need to get another onyx," Cassie deduced.

"Yeah. Too bad there aren't any in Hell. We have our own stones for certain kinds of protection—Bloodphire, Totenstone, Nektaphyte—but they don't work on someone who's alive."

"Then we'll go back to my house—the Deadpass. I'll get more onyx there, and more bones and anything else we need." Then Cassie decided to stand her ground. "And you can't tell me I can't come back. I know where the trail is, I know how to get here. You can't stop me— I can do anything I want. I'm an Etheress."

"Great," Via said to Hush. "Now she's getting a big head. But you're right; we can't stop you. You can come back here and search every block in the Mephistopolis for your sister if that's what you want."

"That's what I want," Cassie asserted.

"We have to rest for a little while," Via said, droopy-eyed. Hush was nodding off too, in front of the bizarre TV. "To us, we've been on the move all night, but to you, only one second of your life has gone by."

Cassie didn't fully understand, but that was a given by now. Via and Hush both curled up atop the atrocious bed and were sleeping within seconds.

Cassie felt the opposite: energized, raring to go. She dawdled about the room, ignoring the bloodstains and other signs of remnant horror. *What else could I expect in a whorehouse in Hell?* She looked out the window. Below, prostitutes of many species pranced up and down the street, looking for clients. The black moon crept along, inching between the monolithic skyscrapers in the endless distance. A Gargoyle sat hunched on an opposing building ledge. Thousands of years of devolution had apparently left their wings useless; they spent their lives crawling about on buildings. The Gargoyle snarled at her, baring fangs, but when Cassie focused her thoughts, the feeble mental projection went nowhere.

The Gargoyle cackled.

I did it before. How come I can't do it now?

Then a furor rose from below: high-pitched subhuman shrieks bursting into the night. Cassie looked down and saw a devilish pimp stomping on a young prostitute that seemed part-Troll and part-Imp. "Stop that!" she shouted down, but the pimp just looked up, extended a taloned middle finger, and kept stomping.

Cassie shouted again, her aura flashed and the pimp's horned head exploded with a grisly *pop!*

Still works, she thought, satisfied.

The prostitute waved up to her. "Thanks!"

Cassie just smiled and nodded.

She tried to occupy herself with television but it was difficult. A Ghoul in a white apron hosted what appeared to be a cooking show. "Render the fat at precisely 375 degrees," the hideous woman instructed. "We'll want to fry the baby Nether-Swine brains in quadrants, to ensure even cooking, but before dredging

227

them in the flour, we'll need to marinate them briefly in milk. Milk from freshly pressed Cacodemon moles is preferable, but if you don't have that—be resourceful!"

Now the woman was deftly kneading one of her own leathery breasts, letting the dark milk drip into the bowl of greenish brains. *Emeril would dump in his pants if he could see this!* Cassie thought and switched channels.

Next came a show called SELL YOURSELF FOR ZAP! White-cloaked Neptomancers stood perfectly still as lowly Zap addicts severed parts of themselves for divination. One man sawed his foot off and placed it into a censer full of hot coals, while the cloaked diviners took notes, reading the smoke. Applause rose from the studio audience. The contestant was rewarded with a single syringe full of the drug, which he immediately inserted up his nostril and injected. Next, a woman was rewarded with *six* syringes after she willingly lay naked upon a red-hot iron grate. Her flesh sizzled, producing a large billow of smoke. More applause. Then the woman got off the grate to take her reward, the entire back of her body charred black.

Cassie was about to turn the set off, but a sudden beeping sound ensued and letters began to roll across the screen. ALERT! ALERT! ALERT!

Then: DO NOT TURN OFF YOUR TELEVISION! STAY TUNED FOR AN URGENT BULLETIN FROM THE LUCIFERIC EMERGENCY BROADCAST SYSTEM. . . .

An anchorwoman whose face looked segmented like a turtle shell sat stolid behind a news desk. Pointed ears protruded from the sides of her neatly flipped brunet hair. "The most shocking news to ever be reported has rocked the Mephistopolis tonight. The Agency of the Constabulary has just told us that a genuine Etheress has entered Hell—"

Cassie leaned closer, eyes wide.

"—and is now hiding out somewhere in the vicinity of Boniface Square. All citizens of the Mephistopolis are ordered to keep a look-out for this woman. . . ."

Now the screen flashed something akin to a police composite—of Cassie's face.

"Oh, Christ!" she exclaimed. Then she turned and was harshly jostling her friends on the bed. "Via! Hush! Look!"

When they awoke, they groggily stared at the TV, but they didn't remain groggy for long.

"Holy shit," Via muttered. "Word sure got out fast. Now we're *really* screwed."

"The offender's name is Cassie Heydon," the saurian anchorwoman continued, "and she is in Hell as I report this. Spokesdemons from the Constabulary recently learned of Ms. Heydon's infiltration of the Mephistopolis after the fluke capture of this lowly XR—"

Next, the screen flashed the wanted poster they'd seen earlier, sporting Xeke's face.

"I knew it!" Via hissed. "I *knew* that back-stabbing son of a bitch ratted us out!"

"This dire information was extracted out of him after routine interrogation at the Commission of Judicial Torture. . . ."

Now the screen showed the dismal torture chamber where Xeke lay strapped to a rack of iron spikes. Two uniformed Golems were placing heavy, flat stones on his chest. Xeke was bellowing in pain as the points of the spikes surfaced through his chest. The camera zoomed to Xeke's agony-twisted face; he looked frantic-eyed to the lens and hacked out: "Cassie! I'm sorry! I tried not to squeal but I just couldn't stand the pain! Please forgive me!"

It crushed Cassie to witness the torture. *Xeke didn't willingly go to the Constabs,* she realized. *They tortured him for the information. . . .* She would do anything to make the torture stop.

But then, on the screen, the Golems began to remove the rocks, and Xeke groaned in relief. Suddenly a vaguely recognizable face appeared, a narrow face with a monocle in one eye. "Cassie Heydon," the figure said in a sharp nasally voice. "I am Commissioner of Torture Himmler. I'll have you know that there is a lofty bounty out on your head. My Constables are hunting you this very moment; they are on every street corner, in every alleyway, and in every subway station. It is impossible for you to escape the city, so let me appeal to your better judgment. As you can see, I have stopped all torture procedures against your friend. If you turn yourself in, I will guarantee your safety as well as the safety of your confederates. You will all be rewarded handsomely—"

"Don't listen to him, Cassie," Via said.

The Commissioner continued: "I have also ordered all torture to cease upon *this* person too. It's someone I believe you know. . . ."

Cassie gasped. The station cut to another studio—another torture chamber. In the dark stone room, a woman hung suspended from shackles.

Lissa.

Cassie's stomach clenched. *Oh my God, no. . . .*

The scene cut back to the Commissioner's narrow face. "Your sister will also remain safe—*if* you cooperate."

Xeke's voice boomed in the background: "Don't do it, Cassie! Don't believe him! Get out of the city as fast as—"

A sudden *whack!* and then Xeke's outburst was silenced.

"Please comply quickly," the Commissioner suggested. "I'll be waiting for you."

A final cut back to Lissa, whose face looked terrified through tresses of black hair. The camera panned down to show what Lissa had been suspended over: a vat full of squirming Razor-Leeches.

"You sick BASTARDS!" Cassie yelled in outrage, and then her aura flashed brighter than ever and—

"Damn!" Via shrieked.

—the television exploded.

Pieces rained down on them. When the cloud of smoke cleared, Cassie stared around in the silence. "Sorry," she peeped.

"Try to control yourself," Via said, coughing in the smoke.

"How can I? If I don't do what they say, they're going to torture my sister—for *eternity.* And you saw what they were doing to Xeke."

231

Via and Hush exchanged more suspicious glances. "I'm still not too confident about Xeke," Via revealed. "It's all too convenient. I still think he's in on it."

The notion seemed absurd to Cassie. "How can you say that? They were *torturing* him, for God's sake! We can't blame him for telling the police about us! He was suffering incredible pain!"

"That's not even what I'm talking about. They *want* you to think exactly what you're thinking now—that he's still on our side. And when you refuse to turn yourself in, what do you want to bet that we'll run into Xeke somewhere along the line? And he'll have some jive about how he escaped."

"That's crazy," Cassie objected. "And who said I was *refusing* to turn myself in?"

Via and Hush grinned at each other, Hush laughing silently, Via aloud.

"What's so funny?"

"Jesus, Cassie. You're the most naive person I ever met," Via went on. "You *believe* that guy?"

"Why not? I'll turn myself in, then we'll all be safe. He even said we'd be rewarded."

More laughter. "Cassie, you'd buy tea from Lucrezia Borgia. If you turned yourself in, Lucifer's Warlocks would put you in an Auric Press in two seconds. They'd squeeze all your Ethereal energy out and transfer it right into a Power Dolmen. That's why they want you, to use you like a supernatural battery so that Satan and his most powerful demons can be fully incarnated into the Living World. And your sister? They'd drop her into that vat of Razor-Leeches and leave her there for a thousand years, and me and Hush too."

"Well . . ." Cassie had to think. "All right, here's what we'll do. We'll *act* like I'm turning myself in, but then we'll rescue Lissa and Xeke."

Another round of laughter. "Right. We're gonna rescue Lissa and Xeke from the Commission of Judicial Torture, the Constabulary's biggest stronghold. You'd have an easier time busting someone out of a supermax prison. It's impossible."

"No it's not," Cassie insisted. "I'll just use my—my—" She pointed to the exploded television. "My projection powers. Anyone who gets in our way, I'll-I'll . . . blow up their heads."

Via and Hush couldn't stop laughing, which was really beginning to piss Cassie off. "Against Bio-Wizards and Warlocks? They'd eat you for breakfast, Cassie," Via told her. "And the security troops all wear incantated armor. If you projected against *them,* it would be like shooting paperclips with rubber bands at a cinderblock wall. Believe me, it won't work."

Cassie flared, "Then what the hell good are my Etheress powers!"

"You're an *untrained* Etheress. You don't even know how to use what you've got. You'd have to practice for years before you could take on the Constabulary. It's an intricate psychic art; you've got to train your mind and your spirit. You don't just walk into Hell one day and start blowing up heads."

Cassie's enthusiasm deflated at once. But then Hush got up quickly, whipped out her pencil, and began writing on the wall:

What about an inversion hex?

"That'd be great, Hush," Via said. "But we'd need a Power Relic, and we don't have any way to—"

Her sentence stopped as if guillotined. Then her face beamed. "You're right! With Cassie, we *could* do it!"

"Do what!" Cassie demanded.

Via got up. "We have to go back to your house right away."

"But how?" Cassie asked the logical question. "The guy on TV said that every Constab in the district is hunting me. They're even staking out the subway stations. How can we get back to Blackwell Hall without being caught first?"

This time, the glances that Via and Hush exchanged were downright grim. "How do we do this, Hush?" Via asked.

Hush wrote:
draw straws, I guess

"No, I'll do it," Via decided.

"You'll do *what?*" Cassie insisted. Once again she felt like everyone knew what was going on but her.

But before an answer could be made—

tap tap tap

The three of them all looked fretfully to the door. Someone was knocking.

"Hold tight," Via whispered. "If it was Constabs, they wouldn't bother knocking." Then she went to the door, looked out the peephole. "What do you want?"

A gruff male voice replied. "It's the manager. You breakin' stuff in here? Open up."

Via rolled her eyes at the broken television. "Ah, just a little accident. We'll pay for the damage."

"Open up," and then a key could be heard in the lock.

"Damn it!" Via muttered and stepped back. "Everybody be cool, he's coming into the room."

The door opened and in walked a fairly normal looking bald man in a suit. He didn't look happy to begin with, and when he noticed the shattered TV, he looked even *less* happy.

"What the hell are you silly bitches doin' in here!" he complained rather loudly. "What's this look like? A pig sty?"

"Uh, no, not a pig sty," Via said. "A whorehouse in Hell."

"Don't get smart, missy," he pointed a finger at her. "You wrecked a perfectly good TV! You know how much those things cost? You think we put 'em here just for you to bust up? Huh? You think televisions grow on trees? Judas J. Priest, that was a *brand new* set."

"It was a piece of shit. The reception sucked."

"Oh, so that means you silly bitches can just trash it? You pay up right now—two Brutus Notes—or I call the Constabs. They won't fuck around with the likes of you—they'll throw all three of your asses right in the lezzie tank. Then you can spend a couple hundred years being some butch demon's bitch and munching Troll carpet. See how you silly bitches like that."

Via looked duped, and Cassie quickly realized the predicament. A fingernail would easily pay for the damage, but if she bit one off in front of him—

He'll know I'm an Etheress, Cassie thought.

"Look," Via faltered, "we don't have any cash right now but we'll have some soon. I promise we'll pay you back. I'll write you an I.O.U."

The manager gawped at her. "What am I, an asshole? You silly bitches come in here and trash my motel and I'm supposed to take an *I.O.U?*" Now he was stalking around the room, his hands up, ranting. "Judas J. Priest! I am just so fuckin' sick of bein' taken advantage of by every pimp, hooker, and hustler to walk down the street! I try to be a nice guy, and look what happens. Try to give you whores a decent place where you can make some money, and look what I get for my effort. There *ain't no way* I'm gettin' ripped off by a bunch of silly bitches like you!"

Guess he's having a bad day, Cassie thought.

But when the man turned around—his back to them—Hush jerked on Via's sleeve and then scribbled on the wall:

Bi-facer!

Via stared at the man's back, and then Cassie noticed something too. There seemed to be some strange fold of skin around his neck, showing within the back of his collar.

"Run!" Via yelled, and then the entire room was a frenzy. Three Trolls, seven feet tall and dressed in tidy three-piece suits, had burst into the room, wielding hatchets. Before Cassie could even react, she, Via, and Hush were cornered.

The manager stood before them, chuckling snidely.

"Who the hell are you?" Via demanded.

"You silly bitches sure are dumb. This is *too* easy, ain't it, boys?"

The three Trolls chortled and nodded. Then the "manager" placed his hand on his bald head, and his fingers seemed to be pulling the skin up off his scalp.

"Bi-Facer motherfucker," Via muttered.

The man pulled up on the skin of his scalp and in a moment his face began to move upward, until it was replaced by the other face he'd kept hidden under his collar. The first face hung in a loose flap, and now he was grinning through his *real* face.

"Nicky the Cooker," Via revealed.

"Had ya going there, didn't I? When my stoolies on the street spotted you, I about shit my pants. It's been a long time, Via, and a long time that you and that punk boyfriend of yours have owed me money. Nobody rips off Nicky the Cooker. *Nobody.*"

"I can pay you back," Via stammered. "We just need a little time. I know it sounds like bullshit but it's true, I swear."

Nicky laughed out loud, gesturing his crew. "Can you believe the balls on this silly bitch? Huh, boys? She rips me off and now she thinks she can deal her way out!" Then his true face turned dark. "I got a reputation to maintain, and you and that punk embarrassed me. I'm Nicky the Cooker, not some pissant chump you can hoodwink."

"Let us go. I swear you'll get your money."

Nicky just shook his head. "It ain't even about the money now. Don't you read the papers? Ain't you seen the TV? The Constabs got a dragnet out for you, and they already got that punk boyfriend of yours." His steely eyes darted to Cassie. "That Goldilocks little friend of yours there is an Etheress, and *I'm* gonna get the reward for turning her in."

"Cassie?" Via said.

Cassie trembled. Her fear was paralyzing her. She tried to project a violent thought at the man but . . . nothing came out.

"Uh, Cassie? A little help?"

Cassie tried again.

Nothing.

"But you and that little mute bitch," Nicky said to Via, "you two don't count for shit. My boys'll chop your arms and legs off, then we'll put the both of ya in a couple of drums. See how you silly bitches like being cooked alive in a sulphur pit for a thousand years." Nicky crudely rubbed his crotch. "But, ya know what I'm gonna do first? I ain't had me no nookie in a while—" and then he grabbed Via by the hair and threw her squealing onto the bed. Chuckling, he crawled on top of her, grabbing at her belt—

That's when Cassie's fear turned to rage.

The room glowed with silver light—so bright, the three Trolls stepped back, shielding their inhuman eyes. But then, one by one, those same eyes popped out of their sockets. One roared, blindly raising his hatchet, and when Cassie focused her gaze on his arm, the arm flew off before a geyser of ill-colored blood. "Fuckers!" she yelled. She looked at one's abdomen, and the abdomen popped open, spilling entrails. The third Troll loped sightless about the room. Cassie focused on his waistline and then suddenly the creature was on the floor, cut in half.

In less than five seconds, Cassie's Ethereal rage had butchered all three Trolls and left them bleeding to death on the filthy floor.

Now your turn, she thought.

Nicky the Cooker was already off of Via, cowering against the wall.

"My name's not Goldilocks," she said.

"Look, look, wait a minute," he pleaded, his second face flapping behind his head like a rooster wattle. "I can give you money, a *lot* of money." He feebly thrust out a stack of bills. "Just let me walk out of here, and you can have it all."

"Oh, don't worry," Cassie told him. "You can walk out of here."

"Yeah?"

"Yeah. ON YOUR HANDS!" she shouted, and then cut both of his legs off with one swipe of her gaze.

Nicky screamed and fell off the bed, legless.

"Damn, girl!" Via celebrated. "You're already getting the hang of it!"

"I-I guess so," Cassie said when she took a closer look at all the carnage she'd produced. "Jesus, did I do all that?"

"You sure did. You're a walking meat-grinder!"

Cassie felt less than flattered. Next, Hush was pointing across the room, where Nicky the Cooker was indeed trying to walk out of there on his hands.

"What about him?" Cassie asked.

"Oh, I'll take care of him. It'll be a pleasure."

Via stepped over a Troll corpse and picked up one of the hatchets. Then she got down on her knees and shoved Nicky against the wall, pinning him there with one hand.

With her other hand, she swung the hatchet.

"We—" she said, and hacked off one ear.

thwack!

"—are not—"

She hacked off the other ear.

thwack!

"—SILLY BITCHES!"

Blood sprayed outward as the last thwack of the hatchet cleanly divided Nicky's head into two halves.

Via stood back up and grinned at Cassie and Hush, blood flecking her face like freckles. "Think he got the message?"

Chapter Eleven

(I)

Bill had no way of knowing that he'd been hexed. How could he? The harder he tried to focus on what was wrong, the weaker he became. Some sort of energy of opposites had overtaken him, some mental parasite of the dim night. Bill Heydon was a sensible modern man with a keen perception of reason but something, now, had taken hold of his 21st Century common sense and retarded it to the most primitive stratum.

A sexual impulse and nothing more.

No, it was not Mrs. Conner's voice that had issued out of Mrs. Conner's mouth. It was a feminine *vox inhumana,* the voice of some diabolical *thing*.

A *thing* that was, essentially, raping him.

He lay spread out, immobile, as if invisible fetters had bolted his wrists and ankles to the hardwood floor. Mrs. Conner seemed silently delirious, sitting on his hips, riding him like some mindless beast over a fast, rocky trail. She was ravenous, frenzied and intent in this cryptic pagan lust. Her plush white body was a slow blur in the moon-tinted dark. Her breasts rose and fell, rose and fell, with each impact of her loins against his. She was savaging him. She was impaling herself on his genitals. Bill's body was the inanimate object that she was using for her own pleasure. But he experienced pleasure too, a stark, terrifying pleasure that mingled with his utter helplessness. He was the rocking horse that raced along with his frantic heart.

His climax paralyzed him. He lay locked in rigor, gasping open-mouthed while his suitor purred in the dark. His testicles pulsed, blazing raw lumps in his scrotum. His nerves felt like a thousand hot wires twisting through every fiber of flesh. By now he was sopped in sweat, and so was she. Their bodies shined like heavy lacquer in the musk-scented darkness. Bill's sheer exhaustion was dragging him over the edge of consciousness, but as his eyelids drooped to slits, he heard the course, throaty chuckle—a sound like rocks being ground together—and his hips were flinching, his raw sexual nerves being accosted yet again.

She was fellating him now, demanding more of the impossible—and she was getting it.

No more. . . . I can't go on. . . .

The arcane ministrations of her mouth had him erect again in moments, erect but numb, ready to be re-used, re-violated by the monstrous need.

Still chuckling, she sat back on his groin and began again.

The coitus hurt now, searing hyper-sensitivities blazing, forcing his teeth to clack together in the fidgety agony. Her sex was a devil's maw intent on devouring him until there was nothing left.

Bill was being *drained*.

The next round drew on for what seemed an hour, an hour of her body throttling him, an hour of her steepening lust with no release in sight. But Mrs. Conner's own climaxes were clear: first rising animal pants, her nails digging into his chest, the channel of her sex clenching, then her abominable shrieks exploding all around the room.

Then silence, as she rode on for more.

Bill could only stare glassily upward, a piece of meat with eyes that couldn't close against the atrocious coupling. And that's when he began to see. . . .

His thoughts barely held together:

What is . . . that. . . . THING . . . behind her?

Yes.

Some . . . figure seemed crouched immediately *behind* Mrs. Conner—a lissome figure only half-real, an amalgamation of shadow and flesh.

Not a figure. A woman.

A woman made of night.

Her movements traced Mrs. Conner's exactly, a macabre puppeteer, and as the brutal thrusts drew on, this spectral consort—this Night-Whore—seemed to grow minutely more whole. And now the woman's face was peering back at him, over Mrs. Conner's bare shoulder.

It was the face of a phantasm, the visage of sex and death.

A slender black arm—half-substance, half-ghost—reached around Mrs. Conner's body, reached out and down, the elegant obsidian fingers of which stroked the side of Bill's face. The contact felt nauseating, like slugs on his skin. Then the loathsome hand opened flat on his chest as Mrs. Conner's body began to ride him faster.

Bill's heart was thudding, banging like a gavel deep in his chest. His breath grew thin; he was wheezing, shuddering.

The half-felt hand pressed down harder, and the spectral grin sharpened.

"You're killing me," he croaked.

The unholy mouth opened, mimicking Mrs. Conner's, and the Night-Whore hissed, "Yessssssssss-ssss. . . ."

Bill's heart began to miss beats, and as he lay there, with no recourse, he knew he was about to die.

(II)

Cassie, Via, and Hush dragged the corpses—and the *pieces* of corpses—into the revolting bathroom and closed the door.

"Out of sight, out of fuckin' mind," Via commented.

Cassie would have agreed in slightly more delicate terms. "How did he manage to get *two* faces?"

Via plopped down on the bed; she looked at her blood-and-gruel-covered hands and wiped them off on the sheets. "It's an expensive trick. We call them Bi-Facers. The Constabulary uses them as spies and confidential informants, and half the humans in the Mob are already in cahoots with the police. The Surgeons at the Office of Transfiguration cut your scalp off and stitch another face on. Then you pull it down like a stocking mask and—presto—you walk the streets and nobody knows who you really are. But you can spot them if you look close; the original face'll be kind of bunched up below the collar. That's how Hush caught on that Nicky was a Bi-Facer."

Bi-Facers, Cassie thought. *Yuck.* What else might they have in store for her in this city?

She didn't want to think about that.

"So *what* is it we're doing now?"

"There's this thing we can do called an inversion hex," Via explained. "With all the excitement going on lately, it completely slipped my mind. If we do it right, we can rescue Lissa."

That was all Cassie needed to hear. "Then what are we waiting for?"

"We need this special thing called a Power Relic—it's one of the most ancient talismans—and because you're an Etheress, there's a good chance that we can get one. That's the good news. The not-so-good news is that we have to go back to your house to get it, which means we have to get all the way back to Pogrom Park and take the train, without getting caught by the Constabulary."

"You heard the guy on the television. They're on the lookout for us. The Constabulary's everywhere."

"You ain't kidding," Via agreed. "You can bet that those sons-of-bitches are searching every street and alley in the district."

Cassie's zeal popped. "So how can we possibly get out of the city and all the way back to my house without being caught?"

"No pun intended," Via said without much enthusiasm, "but there's only one way I can think of, off hand."

"What? Some spell or something?"

"Not quite. . . ."

Hush and Via looked melancholy, then Via picked up one of the hatchets off the floor. She went to the small table by the window.

"What are you—"

"We have to make a Hand of Glory. Unfortunately, in Hell, you have to use your *own* hand to do it."

"What?"

Via leaned her left hand on the table, raised the hatchet with her right.

"Don't!" Cassie exclaimed. "Use Nicky's hand, not yours!"

"Won't work. It'll only work when you're motivated by the same thing." Via raised the hatchet higher, squeezing her eyes closed.

"Wait!" Cassie gulped. Then she grabbed the hatchet from Via. "This whole mess is because of me. It should be my hand."

She didn't know if she could bring herself to do it, but to her it was the only acceptable alternative. Why should Via be the one to have to maim herself?

This whole mess is my fault, so it has to be me. . . .

Now it was Cassie who was raising the hatchet, over her *own* hand.

"But you're an Etheress, Cassie. Don't—"

Cassie wouldn't hear of it. She grit her teeth, struggled to summon the courage and prepare for the pain but—

thunk!

She and Via glanced aside.

The matter had been settled before Cassie could do it.

Hush, frowning, flopped her own severed hand onto the table, and dropped a second hatchet to the floor.

"Thanks, Hush," Via said.

Cassie winced at the sight. "It should've been me," she lamented. "I'm sorry, Hush."

Hush shrugged, a gesture that said *No big deal.* There was little bleeding—human hearts didn't beat in Hell—but the wound would never heal. Cassie and Via tied a piece of cloth around Hush's stump.

"Poor Hush," Cassie murmured, a tear in her eye.

"You're an Etheress," Via reminded. "You need *your* hand. And if we're lucky and our plan works, we can get an unlicensed Surgeon to sew Hush's hand back on later."

It seemed like a terrible consolation.

"Let's get on with it," Via said.

A wooden match was struck. Via held the hand as Hush ran the lit match back and forth under her former fingertips. Via incanted something in Latin, then finished with: ". . . and let slaves be barons and stone be cloud and blind all eyes against us, so mote be it."

Magically, the fingertips of Hush's severed hand burst into five tiny flames.

"There. . . ."

"What's this going to do?" Cassie asked.

"It's an Eclipsion Rite," Via said. "Come on. Let's grab the first subway back to Stalin Station. We'll be at your house in no time."

Cassie expected something bombastic, something spectacularly occult. She didn't understand, and pointed to the fiery hand. "How is *that* going to protect us from the Constabulary?"

"Easy," Via answered. "We're invisible."

(III)

And invisible they were.

At first, Cassie didn't believe it, but as they walked down the busy street toward the subway stop, no one seemed to notice them. Via simply held the severed hand up as they walked. The wanted posters they'd seen previously for Xeke had all been replaced now, with this:

POSTED BY ORDER OF
THE AGENCY OF THE CONSTABULARY
(ALL DISTRICTS)
WANTED
FOR ETHEREA, AND FOR CRIMES AGAINST
LUCIFER'S TYRANNY

REWARD
OF ETERNAL WEALTH
AND TRANSFIGURATION TO GRAND DUKE
STATUS

The detailed composite of her face looked exactly like Cassie, but as she stood next to the sign, passersby, be they human or demon, didn't see her.

Even with this proof, though, she wanted more. She waltzed right up to a nine-foot Golem, jumped up in front of it, waving her hands before its dead clay face. The Golem merely stood there, looking on. She waved even more vigorously at a group of winged Conscripts flying down the street in a low-level formation.

No reaction. They just flew right by.

Through a steaming park riddled with vermin holes, an entire Mancer Squad marched in ranks, their standard mission clearly redirected for the search. Cassie ran up to the horned squad leader and marched alongside of him, sticking her tongue out right in front of his deformed face.

The squad leader didn't see her, nor did any member of the squad.

She stopped and let them march by.

"Enough fooling around," Via whispered. "The subway terminal's right around the corner. Let's get moving."

It wasn't a long wait; if anything, mass transit was far more efficient in Hell than it was in the nation's capital. They hopped invisibly over the rusting turnstiles and then rushed into the first open car. Citizens of every variety stood grasping the overhead handles, completely oblivious that the city's most wanted fugitives were on board with them.

Cassie was used to it now. *What a cool trick.* She contentedly baked in the heat, standing on top of Hush's boots, as the infernal subway took them back to the outskirts of the city, and soon after that, they were back on the clattering train, chugging back across the noxious River Styx.

Heading back to the Living World.

Chapter Twelve

The darkling sighed.

She was called many things:

Lilû, Lilitu, the Goddess of Ardat, the Mother of Harlots and All Abominations of the Earth.

But her real name was Lilith.

Opportunities such as this were few and far between; for the first time in decades she breathed in earthly air. It intoxicated her, almost *too* rich a luxury compared to the familiar mephitis of her home. It gorged her, made her happy and light-headed.

The incarnation was nearly complete.

She could feel her own flesh now as the subcarnation continued to ferment. Unlike her succubic progeny, her skin was not violet—it was a fresh, blushing pink, like just-bloomed begonias, like the inside of a newborn baby's cheek. Her sleek hands slid up, caressed her erect breasts, teased the darker, extruding nipples. She ran a long finger up the furrow of her sex, and hissed in bliss.

She was real in the world again, but she knew her precious time here would be all too short.

The female she'd been machinating sidled over and collapsed, leaving the male peon spread-eagled and perfectly still on the floor, his flesh white as a skinned tuber. Lilith hunched over, grinning in delight with beaming eyes.

She pressed her hand again to the peon's chest, felt a few slow, feeble beats.

He was more dead now than alive—hence the incarnation's finish—but any life at all, even an inkling, offended her.

Her hand pressed harder. . . .

Yessssss. . . .

Harder.

Yessssss. . . .

Harder.

Die. . . .

The sodden heart beat one last time, then stopped, and at the same moment her mouth opened over his and she sucked out his last breath.

The taste of death was sweet, like warm honey.

She stood up in the dark and stretched serenely, her bosom jutting. The clock on the wall stared back at her with its proof that the conjuration had succeeded in full: it didn't tick, its hands didn't move.

She gazed out the window, drank up the vision of the star-lit night and the moon pregnant with its worldly yellow.

Thou art fallen from Heaven, O Lucifer!

Then the darkled seductress turned and slipped silently out of the room.

Her illumined eyes marveled at all she saw: the mansion's foreboding furniture, portraits, and dark wall-coverings. On the stairs she saw a wraith, which paid her no mind because it *had* no mind.

Ghosts were just more of her Master's wondrous props, and they served evil well. They'd been striking fear into the hearts of God's paltry creatures for thousands of years.

But they weren't real enough for Lilith's liking.

The ghost—the former owner of this place—had served evil well too. Back in the Mephistopolis, his Spirit Body had been rewarded richly for his unspeakable deeds. Fenton Blackwell was a Grand Duke now, slaying mongrel offspring for eternity, while here, an incalculable distance away, his ghost remained.

It trudged hauntingly up and down the stairwell in its endless travail, dragging behind it the bundle of roped infants.

It was an imposing sight.

But Lilith wished for a real man—a living man—with whom she could quench her lust, someone to suck dry of all will and life-force and faith, a vessel of real flesh that she could drain like a goblet of sweet wine.

Too bad the dark house was empty.

But just as God was known to answer the prayers of His faithful, perhaps Satan could too. For only a moment later, the darkling's black heart sung with joy. Just as she had determined that the brooding house was devoid of anything she could use for her pleasure—

Oh, what a wondrous gift!

Another figure appeared on the stairs.

Not the ghost. . . .

"Who the . . . *hail* . . . are—"

But he never even finished his query, having already succumbed to her potent gaze. He was slovenly and fat and stupid—but he was *real*. She could scent his crude, unsophisticated lust like a snake tasting the air with its forked tongue, and her voice was like crystal water rushing over stones in a brook when she looked up at him, said, "Come down here."

(II)

"*Whose* bones?" Cassie asked in alarm.

"Blackwell's," Via replied, slouched in the train seat. "You know, Fenton Blackwell, the guy who—"

"Yeah, yeah, you don't have to tell me the story," Cassie made the grueling recollection. The mansion's previous owner. "He killed all those . . . ," but then she didn't even want to think about it anymore.

"He sacrificed babies to Lucifer only minutes after they were born—dozens of them. He did it up in the oculus room at midnight. Service has its rewards— human sacrifice is the greatest homage that can be paid to the Devil. Blackwell was made a Grand Duke the second he descended into Hell."

This made sense but it also confused Cassie. "But I thought he was a ghost, in my house."

"A ghost is just a projection, like we told you." Via seemed tired and bored. "It's an image left over—part of the Deadpass. Blackwell's ghost is soulless. It's like a movie that switches on at certain times."

"But Blackwell's actual damned soul is in Hell now?"

"It sure is, partying hard somewhere. I heard he lives somewhere in Templar Cape; that's where a lot of Grand Dukes live. It's sort of like the midtown Manhattan of the Mephistopolis. Penthouse suites in luxury skyscrapers, every amenity. Those ugly fuckers live like kings—forever."

Cassie wasn't seeing the connection. *What's this got to do with—*

"And that's why we need his bones. In Hell, bones from the Living World are of great value," Via repeated what had already been explained. "But the bones of someone truly evil—like Blackwell—can be used as Power Relics."

The Hand of Glory still provided them their invisibility, and they needn't worry about their voices being heard because they shared a separate booth on the train. The bilge-filled River Styx behind them, Cassie glanced out the window at the red twilight and its thin black scythe of a moon hanging over the wastelands.

"Power Relics," she muttered, back to the point.

"Not simply bones but very *powerful* bones," Via said. "We can use them to rescue Lissa."

Yes! Cassie thought. "And Xeke."

Via frowned. "I told you. That bit with Xeke on the television—it was all an act. He's a traitor."

Cassie was too confused to argue, but deep in her heart, she knew it couldn't be true.

"End of the line," Via said when a bell started ringing. The train's speed began to slow over the clattering iron tracks, and then the conductor's voice rattled: "Last stop, Tiberius Depot, Outer-Sector South. Thank you for using the Sheol Express."

"Remember," Via said, "no one can see us but they can still hear us." She got up and held the severed hand forward. "No talking till we're on the trail."

Cassie and Hush followed her out. Filing off the train before them were two horned military demons in leather armor, leading a pair of naked humans—a man and a woman—who were preposterously obese. The humans were chained in leg irons, misery stamped on their bulbous faces. Hush seemed alarmed when she pointed further ahead. Getting off the train first were two hooded figures in long white cloaks. . . .

Diviners, Cassie thought.

Hush held a finger to her lips as they got off.

Via ushered them to a corner of the outdoor train platform, and when out of earshot, she whispered, "This could be trouble. Those two guys in the white hoods and cloaks are Extipicists from the Sacred College of Anthropomancy—Lucifer's personal Diviners."

"What are they doing here?" Cassie whispered back.

"Lucifer must've sent Extipicists to every exit point in the Outer Sectors. He's not taking any chances; he's calling every card."

"Meaning?"

Hush awkwardly scribbled in her notepad:
they're looking for us
they think we might be here, at this depot
Cassie's stomach clenched.

"Let them all get off the platform," Via whispered.

Several Trolls with suitcases hulked by and boarded the train. In the distance, the Extipicists and their crew left the station.

"Jesus," Via whispered. "This sucks."

"I don't understand," Cassie ineptly asked.

"The shit they do works. They're gonna cast a divination, and when they do, they'll know we're here. . . ."

"Should we get back on the train?"

"I don't know. Maybe. Damn it!"

Cassie peered around one of the platform's lichen-stained pillars. The Diviners were walking up the same trail they'd have to take to get back to the house.

To add to the confusion, a sudden beeping sound began to emit. Hush pointed upward: an oval television mounted on a pillar displayed a commercial for branding irons, but then words they'd already seen began to roll:

ALERT! ALERT! STAY TUNED FOR AN URGENT
BULLETIN
FROM THE LUCIFERIC EMERGENCY
BROADCAST SYSTEM

It was the same turtle-face anchorwoman whose face appeared next. "Military authorities have just reported an insurgent attack in the outskirts of the city's revered Mephisto District. Illegal Nectoports are being activated as I report this. . . ."

Cassie watched, astonished. A news clip flashed on the screen, showing hordes of figures in black metal armor wielding swords and axes against platoons of Ushers. In the background, buildings were on fire.

"Divination sources speculate that previous news of a genuine Etheress in Hell triggered the outbreak by inciting the infamous Satan Park Contumacy, headed by the national traitor Ezoriel, but the Joint Demons are confident that the poorly planned attack will be no match for our security forces. Mutilation Squads have already been Nectoported to the scene and are soundly defeating the rebel troops. . . ."

Another flash showed more of the fray; phalanxes of the black-armored troops mowing down Ushers and Golems like weeds. What immediately occurred to Cassie was that the Mutilation Squads didn't seem to be defeating anyone.

"What a bunch of propaganda bullshit," Via chuckled. "The Mutilation Squads are getting their asses kicked. This is great!"

The anchorwoman gulped. "Uh, and, uh, meanwhile the hunt for Etheress Cassie Heydon goes on." Cassie's composite briefly flashed. "She still has not cooperated with the Constabulary, and it's only a matter of time now before the generous Commissioner Himmler has no choice but to sentence the Etheress' twin sister to eternal torture."

Cassie's heart flinched at the next clip: Lissa hanging by her wrists over the squirming vat of Razor-Leeches.

"To make matters worse," the newscaster went on, "this human XR—a long-time fugitive—has escaped custody after having brutally murdered five detention officers."

It was Xeke's composite that appeared next on the screen.

"Rewards for this criminal have been doubled. He is believed to be a confederate of the Etheress and her party."

"More bullshit," Via whispered.

"To viewers who have just tuned in—war has broken out in Hell. Stay tuned for more updates—"

"The shit's really flying now," Via said. She put her arm around Cassie and grinned. "How's it feel to be famous?"

A final terrifying newsclip showed more of the black knights butchering slews of Ushers in the flaming street. One knight, spattered in demon blood, walked right up to the camera and held up a sign:

ETHERESS! JOIN US IN VICTORY!

(III)

The darkness licked her immaculate pink skin, and so did her ecstacy. She drooled into the peon's agape mouth as she rode him—in the flesh.

He had little for her to take but she took it regardless, unhesitantly, hard and fast, right there at the foot of the stairs. She was a nimble leopard, running down a clumsy moose in the field, taking it for her whimsy.

The act was so refreshing to feel it all for real, not as a subcarnation but genuine flesh on flesh, his real blood so close, her own Hellborn skin sweating along with his as she raped him in his frenzy. Her blood surged, gorging her breasts and nipples, glutting the maximum capacity of every nerve and unearthly blood vessel.

Abstain from fleshly lusts! she quoted St. Peter in a mocking thought. Her lissome legs clenched, the perfect pink abdomen tightening in feminine ripples. Her bliss hissed out between her teeth like steam from a kettle. *Thy fleshly lusts which war against the soul!*

She took him a second time, pulled him atop herself, and wrapped her sleek, pretty legs around his back. Fetid breath gusted into her face, but to the darkling, it was cologne. She crossed her ankles and mused.

I could snap the peon's spine if I so desired. Let him drag his pitiful self around after me!

Her elegant hands girded the fat throat and squeezed till he choked and his face ballooned.

I could strangle him this very second. . . .

Indeed, now that her spells and machination hexes had made her fully *incarnare,* this voluptuous woman of the Dead could slay the Living. But—

She knew she mustn't forget her purpose here.

It was a divine purpose, and a sacred one. She mustn't let her own appetites obscure the crusade she'd been intrusted with.

A final thrust, then—

There. That was good.

When she was done, she shoved him off of her; let his plump and pallid body slap to the floor. He lay there gasping, a fish out of water.

"Goddess," he croaked up at her, trembling hands reaching out. "Don't leave me! I am your unworthy servant forever. . . ."

"My servant?" her windswept voice returned. "Then kneel as I anoint thee."

The peon knelt and bowed his head as she stood and covered him with her abyssal urine.

"Make homage," she demanded.

It was laughable how the enspelled human frantically hauled his pants up from his ankles and fumbled through his pockets. Eventually he produced a small folding knife. He opened it and held it up to her.

"Good little peon. Now cut your throat to the bone."

With no reservation, he put the blade to the side of his neck, and just as he began to cut, she said: "Stop. This world would be far better off without a useless sack of flesh such as yourself but . . . I may need you. Be at my call."

"Yes, yes! Thank you, my Goddess!"

Now, she thought, looking around with her bottomless eyes. *For the task at hand.*

She traipsed to the long room where the humans prepared their meals, examining the strange implements concealed in the many drawers and cupboards.

Her grin faded.

But there were no torches here, no candles or oil lamps or flint.

"Sperm, sweat, spit, and blood," she whispered the elements of humanity, and then the elements of nature: "Air, water, earth. . . . But no fire."

This Deadpass must be destroyed by fire—of this she'd been commanded. *But how?* she wondered, frustrated.

Her ungainly acolyte shuffled to her, preposterously holding his pants up to his waist. "Goddess! Goddess! I'm here!"

"Go away, you useless drone," she replied, contemplating the predicament. "You should be fed to lions. You should be trussed and cooked on a spit. Do not annoy me further, or you'll receive far worse."

"But-but," he blabbered, "I live to serve you! Is *this* what you need?"

His fat fingers held up a tiny silver box.

Curious, she thought and took it. *And what might this worldly trinket be?*

The darkling wasn't quite sure. The box had the strangest word engraved on it. "What does this word mean, peon—" her sleek finger pointed—"this word right here?"

The word was: ZIPPO

(IV)

"Fuckin-A," Cassie muttered a rare profanity. The newsclips of the rebel war in the city blurred in her mind. *It's all happening because of me. . . .*

"Watch out," Via said, alarmed. "It's a Were-Jackal—it can smell us."

262

They'd skirted the trail up to a stand of scaled trees. But Cassie could see what Via meant. Some doglike beast was trotting across the scorched soil, heading right for them. A foot-long red tongue hung from a wide lower jaw rimmed by teeth like masonry nails. White foam hung off the jaw in dangling strings.

"Do it," Via ordered. "Hurry. That thing'll give us away to the Diviners."

Cassie, confused, tried to direct her energy. She continued to peer at the animal as it trotted closer. "But—I can't. It's a dog. It'd be like killing somebody's pet."

"That *pet* is a Were-Jackal," Via sternly said. "It'll eat your liver. If it gets up here, our cover's blown. The three of us'll get scarfed down like a bag of Snausages. Then you'll never get to see your sister again."

Now Cassie noted the animal's features. It had something akin to a human head on a jackal's body. She gritted her teeth and glared at it.

The beast stopped, backed off a few feet. But that was all.

Then it re-commenced its trek up the hill.

"Try it again!" Via insisted. "We don't have till friggin' Christmas!"

Cassie let her mind be filled with the most vicious image: the Were-Jackal tearing into them, snarling, its great jaws pulling their innards out like stuffing from a pillow.

Then she glared again—

The beast yelped once, then fell over, its rib cage suddenly crushed by the force of Cassie's mind. Its eyes popped and its mouth vomited a slew of maggot-ridden blood.

Oh, man. I am really getting sick of this Etheress stuff.

But it was a smidgen of good luck for a change. The beast's lone yelp hadn't been heard by the Extipicists.

Cassie, Via, and Hush glanced down the hill's smoke-misted slope and saw that the pair of attendant demons had lashed their victims to a single pole in the ground. The two human subjects tremored in terror, their body fat quaking. The Extipicists stood aside, perfectly still in their white hoods and cloaks.

Then the demon conscripts began to flense the subjects.

Aw, GROSS!

With great curved blades, the Conscripts began to deftly shear the fat off the chests and bellies of the subjects. The subjects, understandably, screamed to high Heaven. When the fat had been parted and trimmed off, this left the bare abdominal walls, which the demons then sliced into with vigor.

Armfuls of entrails were removed from the rents.

"Come on," Via urged. "We'll be back at the Dead-pass by the time they get the reading."

The three of them began to jog up the trail and disappeared into more malformed woods.

"What were they doing?" Cassie asked.

"They throw the guts on the ground and the Extipicists analyze them. It's an ancient art that goes back to Mesopotamian times, the most accurate form of telling the future," Via explained. "We're safe for now and because we'll be through the Deadpass by the time they make their reading, they won't know we were ever here. In other words, they won't be waiting for us when we come back."

This at least sounded heartening.

They were approaching the Rive, Cassie could sense it now, her Ethereal perceptions ever sharpening. Via blew the tiny flames out on the fingertips of the Hand of Glory. She gave it to Hush. "Here's your hand back. Put it in your pocket."

Hush silently mouthed a sarcastic *Thanks a lot!*

Cassie went first. She wasn't afraid this time, she was eager. The Rive sucked against her, bringing its variants of temperature and pressure. The red twilight behind her turned momentarily black. She felt gritty friction against her skin, and suddenly—

Home at last . . .

Via and Hush emerged behind her. Now they stood back in the Living World, amid its *normal* forest, and its *normal* moon and night sky.

Just up ahead stood the house, Cassie's home.

"Wait a minute," Via said. "Do you see that? What's—"

But Cassie had already noticed, and she was already running up the hill. In a side window, she spotted the licking orange light.

The house was on fire.

PART THREE

MACHINATIONS

Chapter Thirteen

(I)

Smoke billowed from an open window on the lower level, and when Cassie barged into the house through the side door, the kitchen wall was being rapidly eaten by flame.

"Fire!" she screamed. "Dad! Wake up!"

Smoke stung her eyes. The fire was crackling, crawling noisily up the wall and moving outward. Desperate, she feebly filled a pot with water from the sink and threw it at the flames.

There was just a faint sizzle, and the fire kept moving.

"Cassie, you've got to put this fire out!" Via yelled. "*They* did this!"

Cassie hurled another useless bucket of water. "Who!"

"Lucifer! He sent someone to do this. If the Deadpass burns down, you'll never be able to get back to the city!"

Unfortunately, there was nothing Via and Hush could do to help; back in the Living World, they were discorporeals.

Or were they?

"There!" Via said. "Cut yourself!"

She was pointing to the set of kitchen knifes in a block holder.

"What?"

"Just nick your hand with a knife, then we'll be able to help!"

The fire was growing before her eyes; it wouldn't take long before it consumed the room, and even if she called the fire department right now, there was no way they could get here before the house was gone.

Having no idea what she was doing, she took a steak knife and flinched as she made a half-inch cut on the top of her hand. Via immediately licked some blood off the cut, then so did Hush.

Then they too were hurling buckets of water at the fire.

There was no time to ponder the details. As her friends cycled pots of water from the sink, Cassie rushed into the utility room and returned with a small fire extinguisher. Within a few minutes, the three of them managed to douse the fire.

"We did it!" Via celebrated.

"Damn," Cassie said. She opened several doors and windows, to vent out the smoke, then sat down on the kitchen table, exhausted. "I thought you were just spirits on this side, can't touch anything."

"Blood from an Etheress gives us a temporary incarnation," Via explained. "But it only lasts for a few minutes." She held up a pot, and after a few more seconds, it fell through her hand. "But one thing I'm sure of—there's been a *full* incarnation here tonight."

Hush tugged on Via's leather jacket, pointed to the small pouch that hung from her belt.

"Good idea," Via said. She dug her fingers into the pouch and retrieved a small purplish gemstone. "This is a Delueze Stone. If anyone from Hell has been here, this'll prove it." She leaned over, walking slowly around the kitchen, the stone thrust out between her fingers. It was as if she were wielding an ultraviolet light. The stone itself didn't glow, but the marks on the floor did.

"See? Footprints?"

Cassie squinted down. On the kitchen floor, a line of bare footprints led out. Each print gave off a faint purple glow.

"How do you know they're not *my* footprints?" Cassie questioned.

"You have six toes?"

Another squint. Via was right. *Someone with six toes on each foot had been walking around in here*. . . .

"A succubus," Via muttered.

Cassie looked at her.

271

Hush was nodding grimly. "Lucifer sent a succubus here, to try to incarnate herself," Via went on. "It's rare but it can be done. That's one of the things they do at the Lilith Conservatory. And the incarnation obviously worked. Succubi are demonic sex spirits that invade the dreams of men." Suddenly Via broke from her stance. "Shit! Where's your father?"

"My father?"

"Hurry! Take us to him!"

Cassie rushed to the only logical place her father could be at this hour: his bedroom.

Via explained as she followed: "The only way a succubus can achieve a full incarnation . . . is to kill a man during a possession! Hush! Check the rest of the house!"

Hush ran off. Meanwhile, Cassie's heart felt like it would explode at the information.

Then it sunk when she rushed into the bedroom and switched on the light.

Her father lay sprawled on the floor, perfectly still.

"Dad!" She knelt, pressed her hand to his chest. "There's no heartbeat!"

"Do CPR!" Via yelled back.

Cassie's emotions spiraled downward. All she knew of CPR was what she'd seen on TV. Nevertheless, she performed the procedure as best she could, alternately blowing breaths into his mouth and compressing his chest.

"Keep doing it!"

Cassie did, not knowing if it did any good. Tears welled in her eyes. *No, please, Dad! Don't be dead!*

"Oh, but he is," a bizarre, hissing voice flowed into the room.

Via's face paled with dread when she looked at the sleek, hairless woman who'd entered the room. Her naked skin shined, the color of human lips. Her eyes seemed a thousand colors at once.

"Lilith," Via muttered. "In the flesh. . . ."

The demonness grinned, then—

SLAM!

—grabbed Via by the collar and threw her clear across the room. Her body hit the wall so hard, the wall cracked. In a pink blur, Lilith straddled Via, pinning her to the floor, grinning, ever grinning.

"This will be so sweet."

Via fought back, to no avail. As the hands of the Whore of Revelation encircled her throat, she managed to croak out: "Cassie! Keep doing it. . . ."

"I think I'll eat your face off," Lilith remarked. "But, look. Poor Cassie, the poor little Etheress. She's got no company while we play. . . ."

Then the beatific monster called out: "Acolyte! Serve me now!"

Cassie didn't notice the shadow behind her until it was too late.

Rough hands grabbed her hair, yanked her away from her father. She squealed and looked up.

It was Jervis Conner.

He towered over her, shirtless, his jeans unbuckled. He looked down at her through an insane grin.

"I been peepin' on you," he drawled. "Pretty little virgin." Then he pounced on Cassie. "Ain't gonna be a virgin much longer, not after I tear up that little cherry you got."

Cassie threw the most violent thought at him . . . but nothing happened. Her Ethereal powers seemed only valid in Hell. She screamed, pushing up against his clammy chest, punched at his face, clawed at him, but all her possessed attacker did was chuckle. He lay between her flailing legs; he was pulling his jeans down.

"Don't let him!" Via croaked from the other side of the room. "If you lose your virginity, you won't be an Etheress anymore."

But this fact escaped her. Cassie knew that she wasn't fighting for her powers—she was fighting for her life. A mindless glance aside showed Lilith's jaw coming unhinged, lowering to Via's face, the rows of petite glasslike teeth shimmering.

At the same time, Jervis was pawing at Cassie with a dirty hand, trying to tear off her panties—

But then another shadow seemed to appear.

Hush!

But what could Hush do against a corporeal?

Cassie shoved her hand out—the hand she'd previously cut with the knife. Hush sucked at the still-wet wound and—

THWACK!

—kicked Jervis so hard between the legs he literally launched off of Cassie. Jervis wailed, clutching his groin. He blubbered like a baby.

"Help Via!" Cassie shouted at her and crawled back to her father. She blew more air into his mouth, beat her hands against his chest. "Go help Via!" she screamed at Hush again, but Hush just shook her head. She began pressing down hard on Mr. Heydon's chest, and mouthed to Cassie, *Keep giving him air!*

Cassie did so, nearly insane herself after all this. Then they began working together. . . .

Behind them, though, Jervis was recovering. "Now I'm *really* mad," he growled. "I'm gonna have me a good old time, yes sir. Think ya can mess with me? I'm gonna fuck both you bitches up real good."

He lurched forward, hauled Cassie back and grabbed her throat. Cassie gagged. The grip felt tight as a tourniquet. Either her neck would crack or she'd be strangled. As the blood to her brain was shut off, the room darkened quickly.

"Ain't gonna be no Etheress no more. Not when you're dead. . . ."

Cassie's struggles turned limp. She could barely move. All she could do was lie there and be murdered by this possessed redneck.

"Yeah, lights out, bitch. And after you're dead, I'm still gonna—"

But then the guttural voice ceased. The hands came off Cassie's throat, and he collapsed to the floor. Hush had thwocked him in the back of the head with a lamp.

It took several moments for Cassie to regain her senses.

I'm . . . I'm still alive, she realized.

Jervis lay unconscious now, and Hush had returned to pushing away on Mr. Heydon's chest.

Via was screaming.

Cassie's gaze shot across the room. Lilith's razor-toothed mouth was just about to close over Via's face and peel it all off but then—

It was Lilith who was screaming.

The demonness jumped up, outraged. "You BITCH!" she exploded at Cassie. "No one humiliates me in front of Lucifer!"

"Yeah, well we just did, you bubble-gum-pink tramp," Via said, leaning up on her elbows.

The house began to shake, and Lilith . . . began to disappear.

"Bye-bye, asshole," Via grinned. "Go find some *other* house to haunt, and do yourself a favor. Get a wig."

Now the monstress' voice was fading. "I'll see you back in Hell very soon, and I shan't forget this. . . ."

"Just shut up and shan't your ass out of here. Lucifer's gonna have you turning five-dollar tricks on the street when he finds out you fucked up."

A sound like the wind whipped through the room, and then Lilith was gone.

Via smiled at Cassie. "Did we kick ass or what?"

Cassie didn't understand. The parliament clock on the wall caught her eyes, its hands frozen at a few minutes after midnight, the exact moment that Cassie had initially left the Deadpass.

But as she stared, the clock suddenly began ticking again.

Then she turned. "Dad!"

Her father was leaning up, coughing.

"It worked!"

"Lilith's incarnation fell apart the second your father was revived." Via stood back up. She pointed to Mrs. Conner, who lay naked and unconscious on the floor not too far from her son. "She obviously put a Machination Hex on the woman—that's how she got to your father in the first place. And after the incarnation, she threw an enchantment on the redneck. That's why she came here—to burn the house down and trap you in Hell forever. But she had no way of knowing that you'd come back when you did."

Cassie dismissed the details. She was overjoyed just to see her father alive. His eyes blinked a few times and he coughed some more. Then he fell unconscious.

"He'll be all right, and so will the woman and the redneck kid," Via assured. "They'll just be unconscious for a while. Come on, let's go."

"Let me at least put him to bed, or cover him up or something." Only then did it occur to her that they were all looking at her stark naked father.

"No time for that. They'll be fine where they are. We've got work to do."

Cassie, Via, and Hush began to file out of the room, but Via took one more peek back at Mr. Heydon.

"Hey, Cassie. Tell your father to lose some weight. Jesus."

"So where do we go now?" Cassie asked in the ornate foyer.

"Well, the first place we're going is the garage," Via answered.

"The garage? For what?"

"For a shovel, that's what."

(II)

Cassie carried the shovel as they loped down the moon-lit hill. This was no doubt the strangest task she'd ever been charged with.

I'm on my way to dig up a psychopath's bones. . . .

Of course, she had no idea where Blackwell had been buried after his execution, and she only knew one person to ask.

"How far is this place?" Via asked. "If it's more than a couple miles, Hush and I will have to stop. The energy of the Deadpass only goes so far."

"It's about two miles away, but if we cut through the next hill it's a lot shorter." She was taking them to town. She only hoped the place was still open.

The next hill was steep and heavily wooded. Cassie could barely see. But eventually they stalked all the way down and found themselves on Main Street in good old downtown Ryan's Corner.

"What kind of a shit-pit town is this?" Via asked.

"A *redneck* shit-pit. But we lucked out."

She pointed across the street to a run-down tavern whose neon sign spelled THE CROSSROADS. BIL-LIARDS! DARTS! BEER!

"I've seen better looking outhouses. How come we're going into this dive?"

"There's this guy I know," Cassie said. "And that looks like his pickup truck right there. He said he hangs out here. And he knows *all about* the Blackwell stuff; he's the one who told me about it in the first place."

Via shrugged. "All right. Let's check it out."

Cassie wasn't surprised when the few cowboy-looking dopes in the bar stared at her. The place was long and dark. Some dismal song by The Judds twanged from the juke box.

"An intellectual mecca!" Via proclaimed.

Cassie laughed but then caught herself. She had to remember that Via and Hush couldn't be seen or heard by anyone else.

"Ooo-doggie!" some rube whooped from the bar. "Looky what we got here!"

"A jen-you-ine city hippie!" someone else called out.

"Hippies haven't existed since the seventies, Tex," Cassie said. "Nice overalls, by the way. You do *all* your shopping at K-Mart?"

The guy didn't get the joke. "Why . . . yeah."

She could sense herself being felt up by their stares but she didn't care. She walked right up to the bar and addressed a barrel-chested keep with a Red Man cap. "You know a guy named Roy?"

"One-armed Roy? Shore," the barkeep said. "He's in back playin' pool." His gaze poured over her scant, black attire. "But . . . who the *hail* are you?"

"The fairy godmother," Cassie said. She looked around. "*Hail* of a nice place you got here."

The keep seemed taken aback. "Well . . . thanks."

Cassie kept drawing stares as she flipflopped to the back of the bar. A line of women on bar stools grimaced at her—obviously the girlfriends of several patrons—

and they didn't exactly look like members of fine society. They all wore cut-off shorts and cowboy boots, trashy tops, and all sported dark roots in their platinum-dyed hair. *Where's the rodeo, girls?*

Cassie could see Roy awkwardly leaning over the well-lit pool table. Another guy in overalls chuckled, chalking his cue. "Miss this shot," the guy said, "and you lose. Again. You leave me the eight-ball wide open."

"I know, Chester," Roy said. He drew the cuestick one-armed across the inside table edge, lining up a difficult bank-shot.

"That's your friend," Via asked. "The one-armed guy?"

Cassie nodded.

Chester was chuckling. "You know, Roy, you might wanna take up somethin' you'd be better at. Like archery."

The whole bar laughed.

" 'S'shame, you know. First ya get whupped by Saddam Hoo-sane, and now you're gettin' whupped by me."

"I didn't see you in Kuwait, Chester."

"Naw, ya didn't. And ya didn't see me gettin' my arm blowed off by a bunch'a ragheads neither. Shee-it, Roy. You ain't gonna make that shot, so why don't'cha just pay me my fifty right now?"

"No way. I'll make it."

"Shee-it, Roy. Another fifty says ya don't. *If* ya got the balls to take me up on it, but then I guess you let Saddam blow them off too."

"No, just the game, like we started," Roy said, not very confident himself.

Chester chuckled again. "Shee-it. If ya won, ya just might walk away with enough to buy yerself one'a them rubber arms, ya know? Then we all wouldn't have to look at that skinny stump no more. 'Course, if ya ain't got the balls to make the bet, it wouldn't surprise me none. . . ."

"All right, you're on," Roy cracked.

"Watch this," Via said, and sucked a little more blood off Cassie's hand.

The cue ball was off when Roy made his shot—

"Damn!"

—but when it nicked the seven ball, Via invisibly flicked it in the pocket with her finger.

The bar cheered uproariously.

Roy's brow rose in disbelief.

"Fucker lucked out," Chester grumbled.

"Rack 'em," Roy said, but then he noticed Cassie waving at him. "Well, hey there, Cassie," he said, and came over.

"Nice shot," Cassie said.

Roy leaned over, whispered, "He was right, I lucked out. Lemme get'cha a beer—oh, that's right, you don't drink. How 'bout a Coke?"

"Sure, Roy. Thanks."

"So what brings ya to this dump?"

"I came to see you," she said. "I want to ask you something—"

"Hey, Roy!" Chester interrupted. "Who's that jailbait litle piece'a tush you got sittin' with ya there? Your sister?"

"Just ignore him," Roy said. "He's the biggest asshole in town."

Cassie believed it, but then Chester continued to goad, "Hey, Roy? How many women you get with that stump? Bet it wiggles while you're humpin', huh?"

"Shut up, Chester."

"Well, shee-it, Roy, ya know what? I ain't payin' ya your money. Guess you'll just have to kick my ass for it. Got the balls, Stumpy?"

Cassie felt bad for him. "Don't fight him. It's not worth it."

"I ain't no coward, but—"

"Don't worry about it."

"Hey, Roy?" Chester kept on, and this time he gave Roy a shove on his stool. "Why don't you just go on home now and take yer stump with ya. I'll give that little yellow-haired city ditz the kind of lovin' she *really* needs."

"That's it," Roy said and got up.

Oh, shit, Cassie thought.

The two men began to fight, Roy at a distinct disadvantage. For each blow Roy landed with his single fist, two harder blows were returned. The bar crowd gathered around, hooting.

Roy was getting pummeled fast.

"Watch this," Via repeated, and this time it was Hush who licked some blood off Cassie's hand.

Roy's face was already bloodied, but when he threw a feeble punch, Hush poked Chester in the eye at the same time.

"Oooow! You fucker!"

Then Roy landed another blow, and Hush simultaneously kicked Chester in the solar plexus. He toppled over.

"Damn," Roy murmured.

"Why you one-armed son of a whore!" Chester roared. He got up and lunged forward.

Now Hush stood on the pool table, grinning. Roy's fist shot out once again, connected, and then Hush rammed her bootsole right against Chester's face as hard as she could. He crashed against a table and fell over.

"She's a *violent* little thing, isn't she?" Via said, grinning wickedly.

The crowd was cheering.

"Fuck this shit, man," Chester babbled when he picked himself up. Both eyes were black, and his nose was broken. When he stumbled clumsily out of the bar, Hush gave him a final invisible kick behind the knee and sent him sprawling face-first into the gravel parking lot.

"About time someone gave Chester a whuppin'!" somebody shouted. Now several of the girls were smiling at Roy.

"Damn," he said when he came back to his stool. "Guess I don't know my own strength."

Via and Hush were laughing like hyenas.

"I don't think that guy'll be hassling you anymore," Cassie suggested.

Once the bar settled back down, she continued, "I wanted to ask you something. Remember the other day, you were telling me about Fenton Blackwell?"

"Sure," Roy said. "And I wasn't jivin' you when I said I seen his ghost in your house."

"I believe you."

"Ya-ya do?"

"Yeah, and I need to ask you a favor."

Roy shrugged and sipped his beer. "Sure."

Cassie whispered her request in his ear.

Roy pulled back and glared at her with unbelieving eyes. "You want me to help you do WHAT?"

(III)

Nevertheless, Roy agreed to Cassie's request.

"I done some *dumbass* things for women in my time but this takes the whole damn cake," he said when they were driving off in his pickup truck. Cassie didn't feel too good about using his obvious crush on her to get something, but what else could she do? Via and Hush sat in the truck's back bed, along with the shovel Cassie had brought.

"I really appreciate this, Roy."

Roy seemed dumbfounded. "So you're . . . what? You're into *satanism?*"

"No, no, it's nothing like that. I just want to see the grave. Show me where the grave is, and you can leave."

"You want me to leave you alone in a friggin' *grave-yard* goin' on *one in the morning?*"

"Yeah. Don't worry about it."

Roy just shook his head as he drove.

As it turned out, Fenton Blackwell had been publicly hanged in the town square and then buried at the tiny cemetery near the house. Even though the stone was unmarked, Roy knew exactly where it was and even said it was easy to find. But he seemed understandably troubled as he drove on.

Back up towards the house, he pulled around on the other side of the hill. Sure enough, right there and drenched in moonlight, was a small graveyard surrounded by a weedy iron fence.

The truck stopped, idling.

"Look, Cassie, this is a mite weird," Roy said. "You ask me to take you to a graveyard and you throw a shovel in the back of my truck. Please tell me you're not fixing to—"

"I have to dig up his bones," she said.

Roy closed his eyes, thinking, tweaking the bridge of his nose between forefinger and thumb. "Whatever this shit is you're into, it just ain't right. I don't want no part in diggin' up graves. . . ."

But then he sat bolt upright, suddenly staring out.

That's when Cassie noticed that Via, standing at the open driver's window, had blown something gritty into the cab. She was holding the little pouch she kept on her belt.

"It's Dermot the Love-Spot dust," she said. "It causes an enchantment spell. He won't remember anything, and he'll do whatever you want."

Okay, Cassie thought. "Roy, show us where Blackwell's grave is."

"Right over yonder."

He sluggishly got out of the truck and led them across the cemetery. Cassie dragged the shovel along.

285

The dust had somewhat zombified him; he walked slowly, trodding forward. "Right here," he eventually said, and pointed down.

The moonlight revealed the small blank stone. Someone had painted SATANIST! on it in red.

"Here goes nothing," Cassie gave in. She stepped forward and began digging into the soil. She grunted at the effort and toiled for several minutes but barely made a dent in the stony earth.

"This is hard as shit!" she complained.

"Tell Roy to do it," Via suggested.

"He's only got one arm! He can't dig a grave!"

But then they all looked aside. Roy wasn't to be seen.

"Where did he go?" Via wondered.

"Probably back to his truck!" Cassie fretted. "He's probably going to drive back to town to get the police!"

"Relax. The enchantment spell will last for hours." But Via looked back at the truck just in case.

Roy wasn't there either.

The three of them jolted when a sudden loud chugging sound rang out in the cemetery. "What the hell—" It sounded like a tractor or something, and then a pair of lights flashed and around came Roy.

He was sitting on top of a mobile trencher whose stout chainsawlike blade was pointed in the air.

"A grave-digging machine!" Via exclaimed.

Roy drove the trencher right up to the grave plot, then worked a lever which lowered the digging blade into the soil.

"Stand aside, ya'll," he said. "Grave-diggin' ain't no work for a pretty gal to be doin'. Not while I'm around."

The engine groaned as the blade cut into the ground and began to tear up the soil.

This wouldn't take long at all.

(IV)

"So. We've got the bones. Now what? We go back through the Rive, back to the depot, take the train back to Pogrom Park, then find this Commission of Judicial Torture? Is that right?" Cassie asked rather testily.

"Right," Via said. "Simple."

"Oh, yeah, that sounds *real* simple."

They were back on the trail behind the house, near the egress point. Cassie hauled along the bones of Fenton Blackwell in a potato sack.

Jesus, bones are heavier than I thought. . . .

"The Hand of Glory will still work, won't it?" she asked.

"Sure will," Via assured. Hush held her own severed hand while Via re-lit the fingertips with a match. "Without the Hand of Glory, our gooses would be cooked. We wouldn't even be able to get back on the train without being spotted. So just relax. We'll make it to the Commission in no time."

The words reassured Cassie. The sooner they rescued Lissa, the better.

"One minor problem, though," Via said. "Your Reckoning Elixir has long since worn off, and we won't have time to get any more. Hope you don't mind, but you'll just have to rough it."

That's just dandy, Cassie thought, her stomach already queasy just from the idea. She was grateful she hadn't eaten anything in a while.

"Let's go."

Entering and exiting the Rive was something she was almost used to by now, as though crossing the threshold between two worlds were matter-of-fact. It was past two in the morning, but she knew that time would stop for her again, and in the Deadpass too, when she stepped in.

The world turned black, then she was staring up at the strange maroon sky. She tried to formulate a plan, some tactic or strategy to follow. "Shouldn't we be thinking about how we're going to pull this off?" she suggested when Via and Hush came through behind her. "We're not going to be able to just waltz into the Commission's prison, find Lissa, and waltz back out."

"Sure we will," Via disagreed. They began walking down the smoking trail. "And I'll tell you how. With this—" she held up the Hand of Glory—"and with that," and then she pointed to the sack of bones that Cassie was carrying.

"You mean we *buy* our way in?"

"No, no, nothing like that. This isn't like the fish bones."

"But I thought bones were money."

"The bones in that potato sack are worth a lot more than money. They're an incredible Power Relic. Just wait. You'll see."

So far Via had pretty much been right about everything. But perhaps these jaunts into Hell were turning Cassie pessimistic.

The whole thing almost sounds too easy.

Via raised the severed hand as they emerged from pestilent forest. But then she stopped. She was sniffing the air.

Hush was sniffing the air, too.

"You smell something?" Via asked.

Hush nodded, and then Cassie also smelled it. "Smells like leaves burning somewhere," she said. "Something like that."

But Via looked far more grim. "Hush, are we smelling what I *think* we're smelling?"

Another nod from Hush.

Cassie was annoyingly confused. "What? What is it?"

"It's Serroroot," Via said. "Shit. Someone's initiating an Expossen Rite."

"What's that mean?"

Via sighed. "It means we're not invisible anymore."

"What!" Cassie exclaimed.

"It's the only ritual in Hell that could counter a Hand of Glory."

Cassie was outraged, but then she put two and two together. "Then that must mean that the Constabulary—"

"Is waiting for us," Via finished.

Hush pointed frantically beyond the low branches, to the wasteland that stood between them and the train depot.

At least a thousand demons were waiting for them.

Chapter Fourteen

(I)

They ran panicked back up the trail.

"I thought you said they wouldn't be here when we came back!" Cassie shouted.

"Well I guess I was *fucking wrong!*" Via shouted back.

It went without saying, though: their only option now was to abandon everything and go back through the Rive, to the safety of the Deadpass.

"Goddamn Xeke must've told them where the Rive is!" Via complained further. "It's the only way they'd know!"

But then—

"SHIT!" Cassie yelled. They all stopped cold on the trail. "What in God's name is THAT?"

"Flamma-Troopers!" Via yelled. "Duck!"

An orb of fire the size of a beach ball rocketed toward them. Via ducked just in time to avoid being struck in the face. The fireball exploded against a stout tree and burnt it to a pile of ashes in seconds.

As the three of them crouched in a gully, Cassie looked closely at the two *things* standing less than fifty feet ahead of them.

Their human heads sported horns, but they walked on three legs and had no arms. They wore shiny slate-gray uniforms which were crisscrossed by heavy black straps. On either side, hooked to the straps, were dull metal tanks, like scuba tanks, and tubes from the tanks led up under their jaws.

"They're Hybrids," Via said in a rush. "A type of Ter-rademon that they make for Lucifer's special forces. They vomit fire. . . ."

Another flaming orb crackled down the trail. Cassie could feel its intense heat as it passed only a foot over their heads.

"Jesus! They're blocking the trail! We can't get back to the Rive!"

"No duh," Via said.

Now the two unearthly figures were coming down the trail. One's scorched voice ordered, "Etheress! Come out and your friends will be spared."

The other: "But if you don't, our orders are to incinerate you all."

"That's bullshit," Via whispered. "They need to take you alive. But me and Hush . . ."

When Cassie projected at them, another fireball intervened, and Cassie's most violent thought was stopped in its tracks and burned up. "I can't get to them!" she shrieked in frustration.

One of the Troopers took a deep breath, leaned back and opened his mouth. But just as he would belch another fireball—

"Who's that?" Cassie exclaimed.

Two knights in coal-black armor jumped down from the trees. The first Flamma-Trooper's head was promptly covered by an iron pot at the same moment it would vomit its next fireball.

The Trooper exploded into flame.

The second one was beheaded with a single blur of a black knight's sword.

"Get behind us, Holy One."

"Huh?" Cassie replied.

"That means you," Via chuckled. They walked around behind the knights. "They just saved our asses. They're soldiers with the Contumacy. . . ."

Cassie watched in relief. The two knights affixed a strange iron pipe to the beheaded Flamma-Troopers stump—a make-shift cannon. One knight held the limp body out straight while the other injected something with a syringe.

"We're ready, Holy One!"

A plume of fire shot from the pipe, stretching a half mile all the way down the hill. The flame splattered like napalm across the first row of demons. It was like hosing them down with fire.

"Pretty cool, huh?" Via said.

Cassie looked down the hill and saw the figures thrashing in the flames. Black smoke rose in the air. Dozens had just been burned alive.

But there's a whole army of them down there, Cassie realized.

The front lines were regrouping quickly. A demon on some horse-like beast raised a sword and yelled, "Charge!"

And now the army was trotting up the hill.

The pair of black knights drew their swords. One said to Cassie, "Our eternal duty is to protect you, oh holiest Etheress."

The gesture was flattering, but Cassie yelled, "You're just two guys! There's a whole friggin' *army* of demons coming for us!"

"I think they just might have something up their sleeves," Via suggested.

Then came the queer sounds. Cassie had heard them before. Bizarre popping sounds followed by a loud:

Sssssssssssssssssss-ONK!

Sssssssssssssssssss-ONK!

Sssssssssssssssssss-ONK!

Sssssssssssssssssss-ONK!

Nectoports, Cassie remembered.

Four of the strange green blobs of light appeared on the field, two ahead of them and two more behind the demonic army. The blobs grew, tinting much of the field in their eerie, throbbing green. Then the churning channels formed.

When she'd witnessed this phenomenon the first time, it had been regiments of Lucifer's Mutilation

Squads who had rushed out of the channels.

This time, though, it was regiments of the black-armored rebels.

"Talk about front row seats," Via remarked.

Cassie just stared at the spectacle.

"It's the Contumacy," Via said. "The same rebel forces we saw tearing up the Mephisto District on TV."

"We have allies, in other words."

"Yep. The Satan Park Contumacy is the biggest revolutionary force in Hell. Their army is half a million strong."

"We're much larger than that now," the lead knight corrected. "Three to four million." He pointed his huge sword downfield. "Behold the wonder of Ezoriel. . . ."

Cassie doubted that *wonder* was the best word to describe what came next. In only a matter of minutes, the army of a thousand demons was completely surrounded by the rebel soldiers, and what followed looked more like a threshing operation. Demons were mown down like wheat by the whir of insurgent blades. The screams alone sounded like a coming earthquake.

In the end, the vast circle of black knights joined lines completely, having butchered everything in their way.

Then the cheers rose up.

"Wow," Cassie muttered.

The entire field was now a pile of meat. Ushers, Golems, and Conscripts alike all lay dead in a long mound yards high. The generals and sorcerers had been slaughtered, too, without bias. It was a wall of dismembered corpses.

"Praise Ezoriel," one of the knights whispered.

"Hey," Via asked him. "How did you guys know about us?"

"Ezoriel has Diviners too. Our war against Lucifer knows no bounds. It is written in the Infernal Archives that one day the true Etheress will walk in Hell and bless us." The knight's black-visored face turned to Cassie. "You."

Cassie felt a chill walk up her back. "I'm just . . . here to find my sister," she peeped.

"Then you shall, Holy One, even if it means that every soldier in the Contumacy be slaughtered in your name."

"Well . . . I hope it won't quite come to *that*."

Via tapped on his black armor plate. "We need to get to the Commission of Judicial Torture. Can you help us?"

"We would freely drain our blood into the mouths of Cacodemons to assist the Etheress and her confederates. We would willingly bathe in the Lake of Fire—"

"Yeah, yeah, I know. Thanks. But we need to *get there,* and that's not gonna be easy with every Warlock and Diviner and armed Conscript in Satan's legions gunning for us."

"Come and meet our commander," the knight said, "and all your worries will be allayed."

The knights led them down. Via explained the details: "The Fallen Angel Ezoriel is the leader of the Contumacy. He was one of the Angels, like Lucifer, who rebelled against God and got cast out of Heaven. But—"

"Ezoriel realized the error of his ways, repented?" Cassie guessed.

"Exactly. Unfortunately, once you're in Hell, you can repent your sins all you want but you still stay here. Ezoriel is Satan's greatest enemy. The rumor is that his rebel army is hidden in a secret place beyond the Outer Sectors, a place called the Nether-Spheres. And over the last couple of thousand years he's been able to not only train and equip his army, he's developed his own sorcery and has been able to steal a lot of Satan's technology."

"Like the Nectoports," Cassie figured.

"Right. You can bet that Lucifer was royally pissed when he found out about that. Nectoports were one of his most guarded secrets, his pride and joy. But now the Contumacy has the ability too. Their ultimate mission is to burn down the Mephisto Building and depose Lucifer."

That sounded like a big job to Cassie. All she wanted to do was find her sister, but she'd take any help she could get.

When they came fully off the trail, the field before them fell pin-drop silent. The mass of soldiers all stood up at attention and looked at Cassie as she stumbled along in her flipflops.

This is . . . awkward, she thought.

Then someone shouted, "Holy One!" and the rebel army cheered, raising their weapons and waving flags.

"See what a big hit you are," Via said.

But Cassie whispered back, "Yeah, but it's almost like I have an obligation to them."

"You do. They saved your life."

Cassie couldn't disagree, but . . . "I know, but, look, I'm just a Goth girl from D.C. I'm not into all this Etheress stuff. All I want to do is talk to my sister and then go back to where I belong."

Hush grinned up at Via, as if sharing a joke.

"What?"

"Cassie, you have incredible powers. With the Contumacy behind you, you could really change things around here. Don't be so selfish. With power comes responsibility. You think George Washington *wanted* to fight the British? No. But he did anyway 'cos it was his responsibility."

"I'm not responsible for people in Hell!"

"Take my word for it. The longer you're here, the more your powers develop. Pretty soon you'll be spending more time in Hell than you do in the Living World. These people are right. You really are a holy one."

Cassie slumped in frustration. *I don't want to be a holy one. I just want to listen to Rob Zombie and read Goth Times!*

But at least Via seemed a lot more confident now about finding Lissa. Another Nectoport opened on the field and out filed several hundred pretty girls. They wore sheer white dresses and had flowers in their hair, and they all skipped happily along the line of butchered demons, retrieving their fallen weapons and stripping off all armor. Next, a white-cloaked Wizard appeared, holding a pair of crystal balls. He was chanting something, and when he clacked the balls together, they shattered and all at once the nude bodies of the dead burst into flames.

"Magnificent, isn't it, Holy One?" the knight remarked.

"Uh—yeah," Cassie replied, wincing at the mammoth burst of flame. It rose upward in a booming mushroom cloud. "That's, uh, some slick trick."

"Disgrace to Lucifer. Death to all enemies of the Angel of Repentance. May the souls of those who died here tonight be consigned forever to the bodies of Excre-Worms."

In moments, the dense black smoke began to block out the scarlet twilight overhead. The long fire roared and crackled. Distant shrieks could be heard from the blaze, from the few demons who were not quite dead yet. . . .

Many of the black knights now began to retreat into the radiating Nectoports. Next, several platoons of queer-looking Dentatpeds—giant mouths walking on human legs—began to eat the smoking corpses.

"So," Cassie said, getting a bit impatient. "Where's this guy, Ezoriel?"

But then a voice that could only be described as bright light issued behind her. "Here am I, Holy One. I live forever to serve you."

Cassie turned with a start and found herself facing a figure who must've stood eight feet tall.

"It's . . . him!" Via whispered in awe. Even Hush seemed shocked as she looked up. All Cassie could think was, *Holy SHIT.* . . .

Ezoriel, the Angel of Repentance, the Defier of Lucifer the Morning Star, looked back down at them with luminous blue eyes. He wore a battle tunic akin to a Roman legionnaire, strapped with black leather armor. His sheathed sword was a foot wide and five long. Behind him were the stems of his once-great wings, little more than a web of bones, charred by his fall from Heaven. He wore a classic Greek helm of highly polished brass.

Cassie couldn't help but notice the Angel's perfect, muscled physique. *That's some bod!* she thought.

"It is written that you would come . . . and now you have," the voice glimmered. "Your presence here has bestowed upon us the most magnificent blessing, you, Cassie the Etheress, the Holy One from the Living World come to consecrate the Damned."

"How's that for a title?" Via said.

The huge sword sang as it was pulled from its sheath. Cassie's eyes widened. Something unconscious compelled her to kneel.

"It is the greatest honor of my eternal life to dub thee Saint Cassie, the First Saint of Hell. . . ."

The tip of the sword touched her head and each shoulder.

"We are at your command."

Cassie stood back up, flabbergasted. When she looked around, everyone else on the field was kneeling.

Wow. . . .

"So," she said, "you're going to help us?"

"With every fiber of our might."

Great answer! "Well, you're the commander here. What do we do next?"

Ezoriel raised his hand, and another Nectoport opened at once. "We shall strategize now. At my secret post."

"Cool," Via said. "Let's go!"

They followed the Angel toward the port, but then something occurred to Cassie. "Excuse me? Ezoriel?"

The Angel turned.

"Would you mind taking off that helmet? It's kind of creepy looking."

Without a word, Ezoriel removed the helm.

Cassie stared.

Jesus Christ! He looks just like Brad Pitt!

(II)

"Tough life, huh?" Via remarked.

Upon their entrance to Ezoriel's chateau-like fortress, Cassie, Via, and Hush quickly found themselves surrounded in luxury worthy of a medieval queen. They lounged nude in a wide marble pool full of cool, sudsy water; after all this running around in Hell, the baths were well-appreciated. Broad banded feathers formed fans, connected to poles that moved slowly forward and back, a cool makeshift breeze. Exotic flowers floated in the scented water. Cassie just lay back with her eyes closed, enjoying it all.

"And this is *pure* water," Via remarked. "It's an extreme luxury, very hard to come by in Hell."

"Where do they get it? Is there a stream or a spring around here?"

"In Hell?" The notion amused Via. "They make it, from those big distillation vats over there."

Hush's head seemed to be floating on suds. Her remaining hand rose from the fragrant water and pointed across the long tiled atrium. Knights were indifferently packing chopped-up demon corpses into great iron kettles set over fires and tamping the pieces down with heavy wooden shafts. Then tubed lids were latched down.

"The heat turns all water moisture in the corpses into steam," Via explained. "Then the steam travels through the tubes, and once it's cooled—presto. All the pure water you could want."

Cassie blanched at the grueling sight.

The Nectoport had brought them here straight from the battlefield, and their host, Ezoriel, had extended every regal courtesy. The Angel's command post extended as a vast stone-walled fortress full of turrets, minarets, and even a moat. A great keep, for prisoners, occupied an entire wall miles long, while the chateau spired grandly from the perimeter's center. Literally thousands of the black knights comprised the compound's security force.

"This really is some dynamite crib," Via said, luxuriating in the water.

Cassie noticed the foggy sky beyond an open, stone-framed window. It didn't look like Hell's dark-red sky at all, and the breezy air blowing around from the fans and in through the stone windows smelled enticingly

301

Edward Lee

fresh, with no trace whatsoever of the city's urban stench.

"Where is this place exactly?" she inquired.

"The Nether-Spheres" Via replied. "We're still in Hell, but you can think of it as a different plane of existence from the Mephistopolis. There are several Spheres, but nobody knows much about them. It's a secret that only the most powerful Fallen Angels know. According to the legend, Ezoriel won this Sphere from Lucifer on a bet. There's another rumor that the Nether-Spheres exist on the same line as the Sphere of the Seven Stars. That's where Heaven is—supposedly, at least."

"Strange," Cassie remarked.

"Sure, but who cares?" Via lazily rowed her feet in the perfumed water. "You can't beat this place for a well-needed change. I could spend all eternity here, no problem."

"That'd be real nice, but we've got quite a bit of work to do," Cassie reminded, knowing that this gentle luxury would soon be finished. She enjoyed it too, but she also knew she wasn't here for bubble baths.

When they were done in the spacious tub, more of the white-toga'd flower girls came in, dried them off with soft, newly sewn towels, and dressed them. Next, they were taken to a long banquet room whose tables were heaped with exotic fruits. A second salvo of servants—boys this time, Cassie's age—massaged them on long scroll couches and hand-fed them the delectable fruits. The boys were all very handsome, like male models.

"Kind of sucks for you," Via said.

"What do you mean?"

"You have to stay a virgin."

Cassie hadn't thought of that, though it wasn't exactly foremost on her mind. Being wanted by the authorities in Hell had a way diffusing one's sex drive. Instead, Lissa remained the focus of her attention.

I've got to get Lissa.

But how would they do it?

Several knights escorted them next to Ezoriel's War Room. The preposterously attractive Angel and his senior officers bowed on one knee when Cassie and the others entered.

This royalty treatment is starting to get on my nerves. . . .

"Holy One. Have your needs been adequately attended?"

"Yes, thank you."

"Then I'd be honored, my Saint, if you will hear my plan."

"Let 'er rip, handsome," Via said.

Cassie just shook her head. A huge map, drawn in ink on bleached demon skin, stretched across the front of the room, and Ezoriel raised a long thin wing-bone of a Nether-Bat as a pointer.

"A delayed two-front attack is my suggestion, Holy One," Ezoriel said in his light-like voice. "The Constabulary will be expecting you to initiate an incursion here—"

He tapped the pointer on the mark for the Commission of Judicial Torture.

"—and I recommend that you do so. After you've infiltrated the Commission, we wait. Give the enemy time to focus, let them think a second wave will strike the Commission. It is then that I will lead my largest force here—"

The pointer roved across town, and landed on the Mephisto Building.

"Lucifer would never expect a second attack here."

Cassie remembered the explanation of the Mephisto Building's defenses. "But isn't that a suicide mission? The Mephisto Building is surrounded by the Flesh Warrens. Aren't they impenetrable?"

"Ordinarily, yes," Ezoriel answered. "But in this *extra*ordinary circumstance? I think we can take a tremendous advantage. The Warrens will be weakened as Lucifer will most certainly divert the mainstay of his Warlocks to the Commission—in hopes of capturing you. This transfer of phantasmic energy will leave the Warrens at a reduced strength."

"The Flesh Warrens are an organic entity," Via reminded. "It's like an immune-system. Think of it this way: at full strength, it will never catch a cold. But at reduced strength?"

"A massive simultaneous attack into multiple orifi could overwhelm its defenses," Ezoriel projected. "We could penetrate the Flesh Warren and lay siege to the Mephisto Building itself. The first step in deposing Lucifer. The risk is high, but with no risk, there will never be victory, and the Morning Star's reign will go unchecked as the obscenity it's always been."

It seemed like an awful lot of trouble. "Why not just use Nectoports to go into the Mephisto Building? Bypass the Warrens altogether?"

"Nectoportation won't work over the Warrens. The sorcery doesn't exist to achieve such a feat. Air transportation is likewise impossible. We once dispatched an entire division of troops on Nether-Bats to try to fly over the Warrens. The result was catastrophic. Lucifer's psychic-power generators are much too strong. The only way in is through the Warrens."

But then another point popped up in Cassie's mind. "How do Via, Hush, and I get to the Commission? Do we use the Hand of Glory?"

"By now, Lucifer's Warlocks are well aware of the ploy," Ezoriel said, "and their counter-measures will render any Hand of Glory useless. Instead, I shall Nectoport you and your friends to the Commission's grounds."

This seemed kind of weak. "And . . . that's it?"

"With a hundred of my best trained soldiers to lead your assault."

That sounds a bit better. Cassie tried to keep all of the plan's pieces sorted in her mind.

"Okay, great. We attack the Commission and then you attack the Flesh Warrens—a sudden two-front invasion. But if Lucifer's diverting so much power to protect the Commission—" Cassie could think of no better way to put it. "Won't our asses be grass?"

"Holy One, what you don't yet understand is that you and your two confederates will enjoy the most powerful weapon of all." The Angel held up the sack of Fenton

305

Blackwell's bones. "This. The greatest Power Relic to ever be activated within the dominion of Hell."

"It's just a bag of bones," Cassie complained.

"It's a lot more than that," Via countered. "That's why we went to all that hassle to bring it."

"This Power Relic, buried in the Living World and stolen away into ours, will make you invincible," Ezoriel said.

"How?"

"You'll see," Via said and looked excitedly to Hush. *Don't worry!* Hush mouthed to her.

Cassie shrugged. Better to just take their word for it.

"Theoretically the only potential flaw," Ezoriel went on, "regards the supernatural nature of the Power Relic."

"But you just said it'd make us invincible," Cassie complained. "Either we'll be invincible or we won't. Which is it?"

"You'll be invincible to any force in Hell save for one: Fenton Blackwell himself. Once you energize the Relic, the real Blackwell will know; he'll be able to feel it at the core of his damned soul."

"Like I told you on the train," Via said, "Blackwell's in Hell now, and Lucifer transformed him into a Grand Duke. When we start using the Relic, Blackwell will sense it and he'll come after us. Since the bones belong to him, he's the only one who won't be affected by their power."

"Well that screws up the entire plan!" Cassie exclaimed. "What good is a freakin' Power Relic if Blackwell comes after us?"

"He's too far away," Via said. "By the time he gets to us, we'll be long gone. He lives on Templar Cape. That's at the farthest corner of the Mephistopolis. It would take him *days* to find us."

"Actually," Ezoriel interrupted, "it would take quite longer than that. Grand Duke Blackwell no longer resides on Templar Cape."

"He . . . *doesn't?*" Via worriedly inquired.

"He now resides in my dungeon," Ezoriel said with some satisfaction. "I ordered my troops to capture him not hours ago." Ezoriel turned on a familiar oval television which showed a ten-foot-tall figure, with an angular head and horns, bound neck to ankles in stout iron chains. Surrounding him was a squad of the black knights on watch, bearing spears and battleaxes.

"Blackwell's not going anywhere," Via said excitedly. "And with Ezoriel's plan, we get to kill two birds with one stone."

Ezoriel augmented, "You will be reunited with your sister, and we will strike the worst blow yet against Lucifer and his reign of tyranny."

Now everyone in the room was looking at Cassie, awaiting her approval.

"Sounds cool to me," she said. "Let's do it."

(III)

The Nectoport ride reminded Cassie of seasickness. It was like standing in a long curving tunnel made of dark-green lights. The tunnel swayed back and forth as it invisibly traversed space; Cassie thought of a snake whipping wildly around, and *she* was in the snake.

It's too bad they don't have vomit bags in these things, she thought as her stomach tossed and turned.

But Via and Hush seemed to be enjoying the ride. The three of them stood at the rear of the port, behind the battalion of Ezoriel's heavily armed black knights.

"Groovy, huh?" Via said.

"Uh, no. I'm close to barfing."

"Save that for later, after Ezoriel's soldiers turn every demon in the Commission into hash."

Can't wait, Cassie thought. "So when are you going to tell me what good these bones'll do?" she asked and held up the bag. "What, it produces some kind of energy field?"

Via and Hush grinned at each other. "Better than that. It'll be awesome," Via said. "It's so cool, you'll crap."

"Via, I think I've *already* crapped," Cassie said. "I hope you know what we're doing."

"Don't worry. I'm a witch, remember?"

Fine.

Soon the throbbing green light began to darken, and the Nectoport swayed so intensely that the inertia pressed Cassie against the soft wall, off her feet. The port seemed to be whipping downward now.

Then the motion ceased.

"Battalion!" a knight shouted. "Prepare to attack! Death to Satan and his minions! Glory to St. Cassie, our Savior, our Holy One!"

Now the troops roared with deadly fervor.

"Stand safely to our backs," a knight said to Cassie. "We live to die for you, Holy One."

"I don't want anyone to *die* for me," Cassie complained. She wagged her hand. "Just go out there and—and—do whatever it is you do. Make 'em stop being bad. Chop 'em up. Whatever."

Via and Hush laughed.

"Attack!" someone commanded, and then came the bizarre sound—

Sssssssssssssssssss-ONK!

—and the Nectoport opened, and the knights charged out.

A small detachment stayed behind, bidding Cassie and her friends to wait. The Nectoport's mouth hovered; Cassie could see that it had opened right in the middle of the Commission's booking room.

I guess that means we're here.

The first wave of Ushers, Golems, and Conscripts were swiped down in minutes by Ezoriel's soldiers. When the room was cleared, they began to disperse to various defensive points.

"Now," Via said.

They jogged out of the port, which sucked shut behind them. Suddenly Cassie was stepping over gore, steaming piles of innards, and body parts. When their guards found a clear area, Via up-ended the sack and let the bones clatter to the floor.

"What now?" Cassie asked.

"Command it?"

"What, the *bones*?"

"Tell it to stand up."

Cassie looked puzzled at the small heap of bones. "You're kidding me, right? You want me to *talk* to a pile of friggin' bones?"

Via sighed exasperation. "You keep forgetting. You're not on Primrose Lane any more—you're in *Hell*. Things are a little different here."

You can say that again. . . .

"You're an Etheress. Use the power. Look at the bones and say 'stand up.' "

Cassie felt foolish. She looked at the bones. "Stand up."

Then, the bones . . . stood up.

Now I've seen everything.

Upon her command, the bones assembled themselves, forming a complete skeleton which now stood up straight before her.

"Get it yet? *You* become the bones."

Cassie's eyes held wide on the skeleton. The skeleton was alive. *I . . . become . . . this?*

"Now touch it," Via instructed.

Cassie looked back, her face pinched. "Oh, I don't know—"

"Touch it!" Via exclaimed, and then Hush grabbed Cassie's hand and urged it forward.

Her fingers reluctantly reached out—

Cassie squeezed her eyes shut. *I don't know what's going to happen, but SOMETHING sure as hell will.*

Her fingers rubbed against the skeleton's rib cage.

sssssssssssssssssssssssssssst!

Cassie looked around, dumbfounded. Her angle of vision was suddenly different. When she looked at her hands—they were the *skeleton's* hands.

"Believe me now?" Via asked.

Cassie's physical body stood upright, blank-eyed. It was as if her body were in a trance.

But now she knew what had taken place.

Her spirit now occupied the body of the skeleton.

When she talked, it wasn't her physical mouth that moved, it was the jaw on the skull.

"You gotta be shitting me!" she swore. "I'm a friggin' skeleton!"

"You're not just a skeleton, Cassie. You're an *invincible* skeleton. Nothing can hurt you. If a demon stuck a sword through your ribs, you wouldn't even feel it. If somebody dropped a fucking cement truck on your head, *nothing* would happen. And now your Ethereal Powers are a hundred times stronger than when you were in your own body."

Cassie looked down at her body of bones. The bones were glowing. Somehow, she could see through two empty eye sockets.

She could *think* . . . with a dry, brainless skull.

The few knights that remained with them raised their visors in astonishment.

"We'll stay back here with these guys," Via told her, "to protect your physical body."

"But what am *I* supposed to do?" Cassie's bone jaw quivered.

Via pointed outward, toward the sounds of battle.

"Go break bad," she said.

311

Chapter Fifteen

(I)

Cassie broke some *serious* bad.

The only thing she couldn't quite get used to was the annoying *clinking* sound her skeletal feet made when she walked forward across the stone floor, that and the sight of her fleshless arms moving back and forth.

Everything else was a breeze.

A squad of black knights led her down a service corridor. Flamma-Troopers at the corridor's end immediately ejected plumes of flame at them, but all Cassie need do was look at the flame and it bounced straight back to its source.

The Flamma-Troopers exploded like sticks of dynamite in gasoline drums.

Up ahead, a knight was having a hard time hacking at a pair of tall Golems, but when Cassie turned her gaze to the Golems, they immediately melted to pools of bubbling clay.

"Ushers!" someone shouted.

Around another corner, a pack of at least twenty fanged and taloned Ushers rushed forward. The knights raised their weapons, were about to charge, but Cassie said, "Stand back."

She glared at the approaching pack, and as she did so she could actually *see* the violent thought forming before her eyes. The thought fired down the hall like a white-hot blade.

It cut the pack of Ushers in half at their waistlines, gore flying.

This ROCKS! Cassie thought.

But on to business.

"We've got to find the room they're holding my sister in," she said to one of her guards.

"It's the central Torture Cell," she was told. "This way!"

As Cassie followed the detachment in her body of bones, her thoughts effortlessly cut down anything in their way. More Ushers, more Golems, more charging Conscripts and a variety of demonic hybrids that had been manufactured for Satan's military—they all fell butchered. At one point she felt a modest force of pressure push against her, then saw a queue of cloaked Bio-Wizards attempting a hex.

Cassie's thoughts immediately turned them into worms.

Next, they rushed past an intersecting stone corridor a bit too quickly; Cassie's guards were ahead of her, but suddenly she was being attacked from behind. She turned and nearly laughed at the Conscripts bearing down at her. When their swords and halberds struck her bones, the metal shattered. When they grabbed at her skeleton, their hands burned off.

Then she looked at them and simply thought: *Mush.*

A second later, the Conscripts had corroded to something like goulash on the floor.

Open, she thought when they encountered a high security door of heavy iron grate. The grate flew apart. Further down, an immense door of tremendous stone blocks was being wheeled shut, but then Cassie thought, *Rubble,* and the door exploded, falling to pieces.

Before the door, though, was a security moat full of acidic bilge. Cassie thought, *Bridge,* and at once the great stone blocks of the fallen door tumbled out of the chamber and filled the moat. Cassie and her guards easily walked across.

The sounds of battle could be heard rumbling from all corners of the facility. The walls quaked. What they stood in now was a wider corridor with a tall iron door at the end.

A sign read: CENTRAL TORTURE UNIT. RESTRICTED!

One of the guards gestured at a television mounted on the wall.

"Ezoriel's attack has begun!"

On the screen she could see a city block ablaze and columns of Ezoriel's troops rushing out of multiple Nectoports.

". . . unprecedented in the history of Hell," the same newswoman's voice could be heard. "The Mephisto Building's strongest line of defense—the Flesh Warrens—are being stormed by Ezoriel and his Satan Park Contumacy. The massive attack began shortly after a vicous assault on the Commission of Judicial Torture, and intelligence reports are already telling us that wanted criminal, the Etheress Cassie Heydon, is behind the assault."

A cut showed the Commission's front gate, and the buildings behind it in flames.

Yeah! Cassie thought.

"The Etheress and the traitorous Fallen Angel Ezoriel seem to be involved in a blasphemous conspiracy," the newswoman said. The next clip cut back to the woman's turtle-like face in front of the camera. "But Lord Lucifer himself has assured us that reinforcements are already arriving at both sites, and that Ezoriel's barbaric troops are already in retreat." But then the anchorwoman went bug-eyed. "What!" she exclaimed. She jumped up from behind her news desk but wasn't even standing for a second before a sword swooshed down and shore her in half from head to crotch.

Black knights were rushing into the newsroom, destroying everything in their sight.

Finally, one knight stared into the camera.

Then the screen turned to fuzz.

Kicking ass and not taking names, Cassie rejoiced. Her skeletal finger pointed to the huge iron door. "That's it, right?"

"Yes, Holy One! That's where your sister is being held. We await your command."

Cassie chuckled at the RESTRICTED warning on the sign. *Restricted, huh?* Then her thoughts blew the entire door out of its hinges.

A great roar exploded from within.

Even Cassie, in her invulnerable state, had to gasp at what she saw.

With swords, axes, and claws held high, *hundreds* of demons charged out of the chamber—

(II)

Deep in the most remote chamber of the dungeon, Grand Duke Fenton Blackwell—all ten feet of him— tensed against the heavy iron chains that girded him from his neck to his ankles. He'd been propped back on a stone slab, a humiliating display. For good measure, they'd blinded him with red-hot stokers, and they'd sawed off his great horns—the worst insult that could be paid to a Hierarchal Grand Duke.

"I don't know why we don't just chop the unholy thing into pieces," said the black-armored Lance Corporal Flavius. "Let me chop its evil head into chunks and dig its heart out with a trowel. The thing offends all that is righteous, just being allowed to live. It's just another of Lucifer's obscenities."

But Flavius was young and hasty. His hatred for the Morning Star made him brash. It was General Galland who commanded Ezoriel's dungeon, and in his vast experience he knew well the effect of imprisonment. "It is much more a slight to Lucifer to keep the beast humiliated in chains than it is to slay it," Galland said. "Ezoriel's wisdom is our law. We shall not forget that."

The two guards eyed the Grand Duke with satisfaction. With equal satisfaction they monitored Ezoriel's two-pronged attack on the oval television by the sentry desk. *Glorious,* Galland thought. Not only were his Master's troops effectively penetrating the Flesh Warrens, the Etheress was routing the Commission of Judicial Torture and leaving only rubble and death in her holy wake.

"It's a wondrous day in Hell," he whispered to his aide.

"Glory be to St. Cassie and Ezoriel!"

But their glances shot immediately to their charge; the blasphemous Grand Duke Blackwell . . . began to laugh.

"Silence, you vile thing!" Flavius approached the prisoner and yelled. He raised his sword.

But Blackwell just continued to laugh, his broad chest heaving against the strapping chains.

Galland walked up closer, raising his visor. "You laugh? As Satan's stronghold is on the verge of destruction?"

The laughter boomed like cannon fire. The walls of the cell shook till mortar dust sifted from the seams of each stone.

"Fine," Galland decided. "See how hard you laugh when we rivet your evil mouth shut. Lance Corporal! Heat up some rivets for our jovial friend here."

"It would be a pleasure, sir!"

But Flavius would have no time to prepare any rivets, because—

CHINK!

Blackwell's next burst of laughter expanded his chest to the extent that the widest length of chain snapped.

"Call for reinforcements!" Galland ordered. "And fetch a halberd shaft!"

Now the dungeon walls tremored as if an earthquake were rocking the entire fortress. Galland stepped back when another length of chain broke.

CHINK!

Then another, and another—

CHINK! CHINK!

Galland drew his sword.

It's impossible! The chain could bind a Caco-Dragon!

The laughter roared, then—

CLACK!

—the remaining chains exploded off the Grand Duke's body.

Now Galland was scared. . . .

"Bring that halberd!" he shouted. "The beast is escaping!"

Galland expected the dehorned thing to get up off the slab and attack. Grand Dukes could be destroyed but it took the greatest might—such a monster's heart

318

must be cleaved from its chest, and then its head must be severed and pulped—and Galland knew that it would take many soldiers to achieve that feat.

He and Flavius alone didn't stand a chance.

The alarm was blaring in the compound now, and Flavius rushed back, the blade of his halberd high in the air.

But Grand Duke Blackwell did not rise from the slab. Instead, he just lay there, laughing so hard and loud that Galland was deafened.

"Why isn't it attacking us!" Flavius shouted.

I don't know, Galland thought.

And then he leapt up onto the creature and rammed the point of his sword directly into the thing's heart.

"God save us," Flavius muttered and dropped his halberd in the limpest surrender to terror.

The laughter abated when Galland's sword sunk. *Lucifer has tricked us,* he realized in a despairing surprise.

The thing on the slab *deflated* as a pestiferous effluence gushed from the wound Galland had inflicted.

"It's a Hex-Clone," Flavius croaked.

Yes, Galland knew in total disgrace. He threw his sword down. "We've been wretchedly deceived. Summon some messengers posthaste. We must notify Ezoriel at once and tell him to retreat. And we must get word to the Etheress also—if she's not been captured already. . . ."

For it was clear. This sack of putrid meat was not who they believed it was, and there was only one place that the *real* Grand Duke Blackwell could be. . . .

319

Edward Lee

—and as *hundreds* of demons charged out of the Commission's best-guarded chamber, it was *hundreds* of demons that lay slaughtered before them a few minutes later. Cassie was now harnessing her Ethereal skills to a terrifying exactitude, and the amplification of those skills via the Power Relic made her pause to wonder if any force in all of Hell could stop her.

As a skeleton charged by the Power Relic, she might even be able to penetrate the Mephisto Building itself, and throw Lucifer out of his 666-floor penthouse window.

But that was for later. Now her duty was at hand.

Rescue Lissa, get her out of here.

The last defender of the chamber—Cassie was happy to see—was Commissioner Himmler himself. The little man cowered before her, his narrow face agape. His monocle popped out of his eye, and then he was on his knees before the raging skeleton.

"Spare me, please. I'll do anything you command," he sobbed.

God, I can't stand to see a grown man cry, she thought, and then—

splat!

—her returning glance flattened the Commissioner to a smear of gore on the stone floor as effectively as if a steam-roller had driven over him.

Her feet of bones began to climb over the mounds of bodies before her. *I'm glad I'm not the janitor here.* Her squad of knights followed, but when she stepped finally into the central chamber—

No!

Lissa was nowhere to be seen.

Instead, all that occupied the chamber was the vat of Razor-Leeches, and suspended upside-down above the vat was a familiar face.

The body squirming there had been skinned from the feet to the neck, but the intact face wailed at her—

"Cassie! Help me! For God's sake please HELP me!"

It was Radu, her sister's boyfriend.

The man who had seduced Cassie the night that Lissa had committed suicide at the club.

Cassie had no time to think before—

splash!

—Radu was dropped head-first into the cauldron of Razor-Leeches. His screams wheeled away, his skinned arms and legs thrashing amid the leeches.

No love lost there, but Radu's mindless torture was hardly relevant. The bald bartender has been deliberately left here in Lissa's place, and Cassie realized all too well what this actually meant:

The whole thing was a set-up! We all just walked into a trap!

(IV)

From his field post at the intersection of Adam Street and Eve Avenue, Ezoriel's grim stare never averted. Even Angels have bad days, and this was starting to feel like exactly that. He knew that something was wrong. He could sense it.

The first part of the attack couldn't have gone better;

initially he'd deployed a dozen battalions to establish a defensive perimeter, and from there his search and destroy companies had attacked outward, into every corner of the district. Government buildings had been razed, weapons depots and armamentariums ransacked, Constabulary barracks destroyed as were any local command and control centers. Ezoriel's troops had cut off all supply lines and communications posts before any defensive measures could be engaged.

It was magnificent.

Ezoriel knew that any immediate counter-attacks would be weak and disorganized, and of this he took full advantage. His own troops quickly surrounded all pockets of resistence and sealed them off. The result was sheer carnage. Thousands of Conscripts and other Constabulars had been butchered in place. It was a turkey-shoot but, here, demon loyalists served as the turkeys.

Then, when his own defensive perimeters had been sufficiently secured, the *real* battle began.

Ezoriel had opened more Nectoports to either side of his command post, and then rank after rank of his best knights stormed the Flesh Warrens.

Behind him, now, much of the district was in flames, the smoke rising so densely that the Fallen Angel could barely even see the face of the spiring Mephisto Building just ahead. Instead he watched veined pink walls of the surrounding Flesh Warrens tremor.

The Warrens appear healthier than ever, he thought. *How can this be?*

He'd sent a thousand knights into each orifice of the Warrens. . . .

All he could hear from within were screams.

At first it had been Ezoriel's angelic sensibilities that had told him something was wrong.

But now he saw it with his own eyes.

I don't like this at all, he thought. *This reeks of a doublecross.*

"Lord, I don't understand," he said aside to General Barca, his second-in-command. "I guessed that Lucifer would have diverted so much sorcoriel power to the Commission that the Warrens would be drastically weakened."

"Instead, we've been drastically misled," Barca commiserated. "The Flesh Warrens have never looked so strong. They should be at the brink of decay by now, yet instead, they seem to thrive."

"Our troops aren't providing the blight we had hope for. Instead, the Warrens seem to be using them for food, digesting them with a gusto. That organic monstrosity appears to be primed and ready for an attack such as this."

"But at least we've destroyed the rest of the district."

"Satan will simply rebuild it," Ezoriel said. "Anything less that total defeat he regards as a victory for himself. I just can't conceive of what went wrong. How could we possibly have made an underestimation this grave?"

"Lord!" a foot soldier rushed up. He handed Ezoriel a roll of vellum. "A terrible missive has arrived from our messengers!"

The answer to Ezoriel's questions were given to him right there in the burning street.

He read the script . . . and slumped.

"Order a total withdrawal at once," he told Barca. "We've lost the day."

"I'm afraid it's too late for withdrawal, Lord," Barca told him, pointing forth.

The vast snakelike body of the Flesh Warrens was constricting, and each orifice began to expel the red slush of digested knights.

It was abominating to watch.

Ezoriel's troops were indeed being digested, heartily. Enzymes poured forth from the inner channels of flesh, arteries gorging with more and more blood in order to take away more and more raw nutrients. The soldiers who had entered last fled screaming from the gaping orifi, their armor—and faces—half melted by the Warrens' version of stomach acid; some crawled out on dissolving limbs, flesh falling off the bone like hot wax. Others merely collapsed upon their exit and sizzled down to liquid.

Then the orifi widened, expelling the rest.

The thousands that had entered, hoping of victory, were now being vomited out, in defeat.

"I've failed utterly." Ezoriel's voice now fluttered like a dimming light. "I've let myself be outwitted by Lucifer. I can only pray to the God I abandoned that the Holy One will not be captured for my recklessness. Open the Nectoports at once. I will personally lead the counter-attack on the Commission."

After the latest field orders had been dispersed, the troops preparing for full retreat, Barca seemed hesitant. "You realize, Lord, that the Power Relic has more than likely already been defeated."

Yes, Ezoriel thought. *And I will be to blame for the enslavement of the First Saint of Hell.*

Chapter Sixteen

(I)

The screams and sounds of battle never abated within the labyrinthine walls of the Commission of Judicial Torture, but they were certainly beginning to fade. Via took this observation to be a great sign, an indication that they were winning.

Cassie's tearing the crap out of this dump, she felt assured, *and Ezoriel's soldiers are cleaning up shop. By the time they're done, this whole place'll be a big stone box full of demon meat.*

And, hopefully, Lissa would be rescued.

Hush seemed antsy, though, disconcerted when several more troopers hustled into the expansive room. It was the Homing Griffin that had brought the blackest news. The ugly winged thing sat perched on a knight's arm, and it was with some serious trepidation that another knight informed Via of what had really happened back in the Mephisto District . . . and at Ezoriel's dungeon.

"A Hex-Clone!" Via yelled. "That can't be true!"

"I regret that it is," the knight sullenly replied. "It's been officially confirmed; there can be no doubt."

"Then that means the *real* Blackwell—"

"—is probably already in the compound," the knight feared.

"Shit!"

A moment ago, Via had been convinced that the assaults here and near the Mephisto Building were succeeding, but in one second she learned not only that she was totally wrong but also that the entire plan had somehow been sabotaged in advance.

Xeke, was the only word she could think.

Cassie's physical body remained standing upright next to them, the blank eyes of her trance staring outward.

And Cassie's spirit, Via thought further, *is still out there, wandering around in the Power Relic.*

Only four knights were here for protection. That wouldn't be enough, she knew.

"We have to get Cassie's body to a safe place," she insisted to the knight. "All Blackwell's got to do is touch her, and the Power Relic dies."

Hush was peeking out the front entrance of the Commission. Then she agitatingly began to point.

Via glanced out too—and saw what thundered down the street.

327

It was Grand Duke Blackwell, tall and horned, his wedgelike face set in a hideous grin.

"He's already here!" she shrieked. Apart from the entrance, there was only one other doorway, which led into the facility. "Grab Cassie!" she ordered the knights. "We'll go this way."

One knight threw Cassie over his shoulder, and they all rushed for the inner door until—

SLAM!

—an iron portcullis slammed down over the doorway. The first knight who'd stepped ahead of them was crushed immediately.

There's no way out, Via realized. *We're trapped.*

Cassie's skeleton legs took her swiftly back through the Commission's stone-walled maze of corpse-clogged corridors. She knew she had to get back to Via and Hush, and to her inert physical body as well.

Something was *all* messed up.

She could even feel it: she could feel herself weakening, going sluggish. The pace of her steps forward began to drag as though she were trudging through hip-deep mud. But she knew one thing at least, that this "surprise" attack had been no surprise at all.

Lissa had been taken away in advance, and Radu had been left for them to find in her place. It seemed as if Lucifer had staged the entire scenario, allowing thousands of his defenders to be slaughtered just to make the ploy seem authentic.

And she didn't even want to *think* about what might be going on at the Flesh Warrens. . . .

That dragging sensation against her empowered bones persisted, heightening. Even as a skeleton animated by the darkest magic, Cassie felt fatigued; she felt like someone obese trying to mount a high flight of stairs. Even though her heart was not within the skeletal chest, she could feel it racing against the accelerating waves of exertion. Her vision began to dim.

What's WRONG with me!

Then she stopped.

The cessation of her movement was not of her own volition. Suddenly, the bones of her body seemed frozen, not budging an inch in spite of her efforts; it was like trying to walk through a brick wall.

Worse was the sickening sensation that followed. . . .

She felt . . . hands.

Someone's . . . touching me. . . .

Hands, *large* hands that she couldn't see, were vigorously molesting her. She could feel them quite intensely, slithering up the cage of her ribs, pressing against the area of space where her breasts would be, pawing up between her legs and squeezing her there.

After that, she simply collapsed.

The bones of Blackwell's skeleton disassembled and all at once fell to a pile on the floor.

Cassie's consciousness hovered bodiless now, in thin air; it was as though her spirit were encased in a transparent balloon, and the balloon wobbled upward. Without eyes, she was looking down at the toppled bones.

Then—

Jesus Christ!

—her spirit seemed to turn to smoke, and the smoke was being sucked away down the corridor at hundreds of miles per hour. She could feel the mad velocity, could feel herself being drawn out to a thin nonsolid string, like a stream of cigarette smoke being drawn away by a hard fan.

She was drawn through piles of corpses, drawn through stone walls and closed doors. She was a roller-coaster flying off its tracks. . . .

And next—

zzzzap!

She was in her physical body again, back in the Commission's entrance hall.

The dizziness made her senses swirl; everything she saw at first was little more than a spiraling blur. But then the sensation of being touched trebled.

It was no longer a sensation.

She *was* being touched—

Oh my God.

She was being touched by something absolutely monstrous.

Hook-nailed hands the size of baseball gloves held her physical body aloft, cupping up under her armpits.

Now she *knew* she was back in her own body; when she feebly held up her hands, she saw them, not bone hands but her real hands of flesh. And that's not all she saw.

She saw the face of the thing that was holding her up.

The face seemed composed of wedges and angles, with skin the color and tone of sanded granite. Trapezoidal eyes burned blood-red, and the angular mouth grinned at her, showing teeth like long white nails, behind which a stout black tongue shined. The breath that gusted from the thin, saliva-glossed lips smelled like something that had been dead in the sun for days, and dark, awl-sharp horns, each over a foot long, sprouted from the flattened forehead.

The voice sounded like a pack of snakes sloshing in a swamp. . . .

"Hello, Cassie. I'm Grand Duke Fenton Blackwell, and I'm very pleased to make your acquaintance," the thing said.

Cassie's consciousness winked out.

When the monstrous thing had bulled into the room, its huge booted footfalls left cracks in the stone floor. Then it bellowed, and the cacophonous sound hit Via and Hush with the impact of dynamite.

They were blown across the room, slammed to the wall.

Via looked ahead, dipping in and out of consciousness. The small squad of black knights fearlessly charged the Grand Duke, swords high, but . . .

Oh, no. . . .

The Grand Duke chuckled throughout the entire skirmish, pulling the knights apart like straw dolls. Their pieces were strewn aside with glee.

Via knew what would come next.

Us. . . .

Grand Duke Blackwell turned, its red eyes glaring at Cassie's physical body which remained where it stood, still immobile in the trance. Based on what she'd read in the Witchcraft tomes, Via knew that all it would take to break the transposition spell was the slightest touch, and Cassie's spirit would be pulled instantly back into her body, leaving the Power Relic useless.

Via also knew that once that happened, the after-effect of the severed spell would leave the Etheress unconscious for hours. . . .

The only way to kill a Grand Duke was to cut out its heart and quarter its head, but right now neither Via nor Hush were in any shape to even move.

When Cassie had fully returned to her body, she passed out after one glance into her abductor's primeval face.

Her body hung limp as a wet rag in the Grand Duke's grasp. "Oh, what luxuries I could have with thee," it croaked. Its black tongue emerged from the demonic lips, and slowly licked up the side of Cassie's neck. Then it slithered across her eyes and roved inside her hanging mouth. "I could suck the delicate organs right out of this pretty mouth, swallow them whole like sweet meats. But first I would plunder your living womb, use it for—say—a hundred years or so until I tired of it. . . ." The Grand Duke sighed. "But, lo, it shall not be. You are Hell's greatest prize, and my Master covets you. When his Bio-Wizards are finished leeching your Ethereal energy, Lucifer will walk upon the earth again. And for this he will surely reward me."

Sssssssssssssssssss-ONK!

A Nectoport opened in the room, its glowing-green maw widening. Blackwell threw Cassie over its wide

332

shoulder and began to step toward the port.

But then he stopped.

He turned, grinning, and looked to Via and Hush who still lay collapsed in the corner.

Via dragged herself up. *It's useless,* she realized, *but I've got to try. . . .*

She grabbed a fallen ax, struggled toward Blackwell. Hush was straggling up behind her.

"Such amusements," came Blackwell's spiccato chuckle. "But how could I forget such lovely vessels for my need?" A thin kaleidoscope of light sparkled across the room when Blackwell's immense hand opened. "A Paresis Spell for you two—"

Via and Hush collapsed, totally paralyzed.

"We'll have such pleasures together," and then the monster grabbed Via and Hush by the hair and hauled them into the Nectoport.

Again, Via was sucked into the wormlike churning of the Nectoport, the sorcerous passage folding space and distance in a dark glowing whirlwind. It was like a manic plume of smoke bending in the air. But as the mad motion and twisting seemed to increase to the point that her body would fly apart—

It stopped.

Sssssssssssssssssss-ONK!

A few dreadful moments ticked by; Via was being dragged again by the hair, and so was Hush, like someone carrying two plastic bags of groceries one-handed. The pain barked at her scalp but, still, every attempt she made to move her own muscles faltered.

"Welcome to my abode," Via heard. The Nectoport emptied into a vast room of Victorian decor, though it didn't take Via long to realize what the place actually was: a beautifully-appointed torture den. Her eyes moved around in their sockets, but that was all the movement she could muster. The Paresis Spell left Via and Hush as dormant as if their necks had been broken.

The beast that was Fenton Blackwell dropped them both on the floor. Careful not to damage the treasure, he placed Cassie down on a long cushioned récamier couch. The red hellborn eyes lingered on the delicate body. A taloned finger stroked Cassie's cheek.

"Lucifer's servants will come for you shortly, with a worthy reward, no doubt. I'm sure my Master will be pleased with me, and with this gesture of ultimate faith. After all, most Grand Dukes, with their greed, would surely keep you secreted away for themselves, to play with you for eons. But not I. You're a very *special* toy— the first living human in Hell—and it will be with eternal devotion that I will give you up to the Lord of the Air." The monster bowed, to lick her face again with the stinking black tongue. "The taste of *life,*" it guttered. "Like fine wine. It's such a shame I can't empty the entire bottle. . . ."

The place they'd been abducted to smelled of a nauseating meld of rich perfumes and human filth. Via's eyes darted to the end of the room, where she noticed the most harrowing sight. Amid the vast room's plush tapestries, carpets, and marquetry, amid its fine statues and grandly framed portraits, the classic furnishings and adornments, her eyes fell in horror upon a row of naked females—some demonic, some human—hanging from the wall by ornate hooks.

Not the corpses of a madman's gallery—no, they were all alive, squirming in place as they hung by fettered wrists. The ligaments and shoulder sockets of several had long-since failed, stretching feeble muscles and skin between the detached joints. And the skin of several others had turned to great masses of wet festering.

But despite each individual condition, these women had all clearly been hanging here for decades, like a collection of oddities, the gimcracks of Blackwell's obscene pastime.

All of the women were possessed of a single commonality, and by now it came as no surprise to Via at all. Their bellies all stretched grossly forward.

They were all pregnant.

Another flick of her eyes and she noticed another of the room's details: the long stone dolmen in the center of the room left no doubt about what Blackwell did with the offspring of these women.

He's doing the same thing he did in life, Via understood. *Siring babies . . . and sacrificing them to Lucifer. . . .*

The red eyes roved to Via and Hush. "My Transfiguration allows me to impregnate any kin in Hell. You'll have the honor of being raped by me for eternity, and providing me endless infants for the sacrificial slab. Please take heart, though. You'll get to watch it all over and over again. Indeed, the miracle of creation, the gift of *your* god exploited for the homage of *mine*. . . ."

A heavy metallic clicking resounded when Blackwell walked out of view; a moment later he reappeared, hovering over Via. The unspeakable hands slowly descended, manipulating a pair of iron cuffs joined by a few links of chain, and then Via's wrists were quickly shackled after a few more clicks.

"Think of these as wedding bands, my love," the Grand Duke amusedly remarked. "By the powers invested in me, I now pronounce us husband and wife, through lust and hatred, through indulgence and abuse—and you can rest assured that death will *never* do us part."

Via was picked up effortlessly and carried across the spacious room. She was then hung from a hook next to a shivering pregnant She-Troll.

"You'll hang here forever—how quaint!"

The huge hands reached forward then, to begin stripping off her clothes.

"The pretty package, now, needs to be unwrapped. Let your beauty be appreciated by all of your new companions. Congratulations, dear. You're now a part of my sacrificial harem!"

Via hung paralyzed, but her mind felt even more numb. This, she knew, was how she would spend eternity: being raped by this *creature,* and mothering its mongrel children for the satanic slab. She wished she could just die, but that was the height of fantasy. Here, she'd live forever, to be another charm in the monster's display case, to be a permanent receptacle for the Grand Duke's hobby. And she didn't need to be told that an identical fate awaited Hush, too.

But, still, she could hope, couldn't she?

"Don't bother," Blackwell said. "There *is* no hope for you. . . ."

Via ground her teeth together, tried to squeeze her eyes shut. First, her legs were lifted, her boots pulled off and cast aside. "Mmmm," the sound slipped from Blackwell's throat; before he would strip her, his hands felt at her trembling body, squeezing her legs as if to test their firmness, sliding up her sides and then cupping her breasts. "Mmmm, yes. A trim young mare, hot and fit for the stud farm." One demonic hand pressed flat against her belly. "We'll be filling this up right away, I assure you, and then your wan little friend. Don't worry, I've enough love for the both of you—more than enough."

The nailed fingers delicately unfastened Via's belt and slipped it off her waist. Then, just as delicately, they popped the center snap, pulled down the zipper in a slow rasp, and slid around behind her, hooking under her waistband, preparing to pull off her pants.

"I so enjoy unwrapping presents. . . ."

Her dead stare hung as limply as her body, but . . .

Who is . . .

In this position against the wall, Via could see to the Grand Duke's rear.

She could see the figure entering the room.

She could see—

Xeke! Cassie thought.

She lay on the strange couch in this even stranger place, every muscle in her body singing in pain. The pain nailed her against the curving couch; whenever she tried to move, though, the flare of agony in her head and body shoved her right back down as if a two-by-four had been brought hard across her chest.

She saw the ornate room and its decor of Victorian horror. She saw Hush perfectly still on the carpeted floor, and she saw Via hanging from a hook against a long wall at the back of the atrocious room.

She saw the thing that had brought her here: Grand Duke Blackwell, the only figure in Hell with the potency to foil the Power Relic.

And then she saw—

Xeke.

Worse for wear since she'd last seen him, his jacket in tatters, his pants scuffed and bloodied. He'd been gone for so long that Cassie thought for sure they'd never see him again. Not to mention that Via and Hush had suspected him of complicity with the police, or selling them out.

But how could this be true?

I don't believe it, she felt certain. *I don't believe that Xeke's a traitor.*

If that were true, what would he be doing here? And why would he be *sneaking* into the room?

Xeke moved ever so slowly across the carpet. When he saw Cassie, he gave her a brief smile and held a finger to his lips to signal her not to say anything.

I knew it! He's still on our side!

Xeke crept right up behind the Grand Duke, slipping something out of his pocket as he did so, something long and loopy.

Cassie recognized the object. It was the rope-saw Xeke had used to decapitate one of the Ushers back in the Mutilation Zone. And she remembered how efficiently it had sawn through the creature's muscular neck.

Be careful, be careful! she thought.

Xeke leapt. . . .

Go!

His quick leap landed him on Blackwell's broad back, then he clamped on tight by wrapping his legs around the monster's waist.

The sound of the Grand Duke's objection sounded like high-explosives going off. The long room shook as if struck repeatedly by a wrecking ball. Then the vicious frenzy began.

Blackwell fruitlessly tried to reach behind him, to swipe at Xeke with his long claws, but Xeke had already slung the rope-saw around the demon's neck. Veins fattened at once under the stricture.

Blackwell's face darkened.

"What's all the fuss?" Xeke joked. "I'm just measuring you for a tie!"

Blackwell stumbled clumsily around the room as the rope-saw ground deeper, Xeke yanking the saw's handles vigorously back and forth with all his might. The sound of the implement cutting deeper and deeper was a sickening see-saw-like rasp, like lumbermen tearing away at the thickest tree but where sawdust and wood-pulp would be flying away from the toil of lumbermen, it was black blood that flew out of the deepening groove.

Repeatedly, Blackwell tried but failed to fling Xeke off, and then he let out another deafening bellow. The room seemed to convulse from the bellow's inhuman concussion. But the objection didn't last much longer. Blackwell turned silent the instant—

thunk

—his head fell off.

The head rolled a few times and stopped on the carpet, the scarlet eyes staring up in outrage.

Xeke *yahoo'd* when he jumped off.

He did it! Cassie rejoiced.

But the mammoth body continued to stumble around.

Xeke grabbed a wide-bladed ax off the wall and—

thwack! thwack! thwack!

—took to laying the great blade deep into Blackwell's chest. The giant headless body fell over, and after a few more swipes, Xeke had ravaged the chest cavity. He bent over and reached in, tearing out the football-sized heart and throwing it against the wall with a bloody splat.

When the body attempted to get up again, Xeke scratched his head and commented, "Oops. Forgot about the head."

thwack! thwack! thwack!

He chopped the severed head into neat, fist-sized chunks. With his boot, he kicked the chunks across the carpeted floor much like a child would kick cans in the street.

"Who says it's hard to kill a Grand Duke?" he jovially remarked, wiping sweat off his brow. His smile of relief beamed; he looked to Cassie. "Are you all right?"

"Yes," she said, but it was just a wisp from her throat. She could still barely talk or move. The after-effects of the broken spell from the Power Relic left her dizzy and weak, like a nagging flu. It didn't seem to be wearing off very fast.

"It was no walk in the park, I'll tell ya," Xeke said. Then he winked at her. "You probably thought I was mincemeat by now."

Cassie nodded. "We saw the wanted posters, then saw on TV how you'd escaped from the Commission. But . . ." Suddenly, the question bloomed in her mind. "How did you know Blackwell had brought us here?"

Xeke ignored the question, rubbing his hands together. "And I'll bet you even might've thought that I went to the other side."

"Yeah," Cassie said. "Via did, at least, and Hush too, I think. But I never really thought that myself."

"Well you should have," Xeke said.

Cassie's eyes thinned. "What?"

"Because it would be true." Now Xeke stood cockily before her, hands on hips. "How else would the Constabulary be able to guess your every move? How else could a trap like this be set?" He smiled broadly now. "How else could they *know* you had the ability to activate a Power Relic? It was your sister, you dumbass."

"My . . . sister?"

"Your sister hates you. If it hadn't been for you, she wouldn't have been condemned to Hell, would she? *You're* the one who slutted after her boyfriend, tried to steal him from her—"

341

"That's not how it happened!" Cassie cried.

"—and when she caught the two of you together, Lissa was so shattered, so heart-broken and betrayed, that she killed herself in despair. The despair that *you* brought on her."

"No!"

"And all this time you've been trying to find her, like telling her you're *sorry* would mean anything. Well, fat chance on that, honey. You wanna know who told the Constabulary about you? It was Lissa."

"Lissa," Cassie's whispered.

"Still don't get it?"

Cassie felt lost in a fog, tears hot in her eyes.

"Well, check *this* out," and then Xeke brought a hand to his face.

His fingers closed.

Then, as if he were turning a tight stocking mask around, he turned his *face* around.

Cassie felt drowning in shock.

It was *Lissa's* face that looked back at her.

"Nifty, huh? It's the very latest in Transfiguration surgery. No more skin hanging around your neck; they put the new face on the other side of your head. Works like a charm."

Lissa. A Bi-Facer. She planned it all from the start. . . .

Now the figure shucked off the leather jacket, peeled off the punk t-shirt.

It was Lissa's body. Cassie could see the scars from where her breasts had been removed, could even see the barbed-wire tattoo around her navel.

342

But right above her navel was another tattoo now. Cassie squinted.

No, not a tattoo.

It was a small branding mark seared into the skin.

A pentagram.

"It wasn't hard duping Via and Hush—they're just a couple of stupid Plebes. Infiltrating them as 'Xeke' was a piece of cake. Christ, Via's so stupid, she was even falling in love with me! From there it was just gaining confidence. You moved into a *Deadpass,* for God's sake. What better way to get the twin sister into Hell? Do you have any idea how *valuable* you are? A true Etheress? A living flesh-and-blood woman in Hell? The Ethereal energy you have in that pea brain of yours can give the Mephistopolis a power that's never been seen before. It can put devils on the earth. It can destroy God's blessing to mankind. It'll be *glorious!* It'll change *everything!*"

But Cassie remained in shock, crushed now in this total defeat.

Lissa strutted around, glanced down at Blackwell's headless body amid all the gore. "And look at this big dumb dolt. He gets Grand Duke status, but all he cares about is his fuckin' *reward.* Whatever happened to real servitude? Whatever happened to *faith?*" Lissa grinned again. "Lucifer knows all. Lucifer knows who truly serves him. And Ezoriel—ha! We ground up a couple thousand of his people tonight; it was like dropping steak into a grinder. But do you think he'll ever learn? Fuck no."

Cassie shivered as she watched her sister turn toward Via.

"Asshole," Lissa said. "Snooty tramp." Another smile. "Hmm, a Paresis Spell, huh? That's great. It'll make her easier to skin. That'll be a *lot* of fun. Oh, and what have we here?" Now Lissa was looking down at Hush. "I think I'll have some fun with this little bitch right *now,*" and then she dragged Hush up and lay her down on the dolmen.

"Poor little Hush. Poor little innocent Hush. I think I'll cut your head off and pulp it right here on the floor. Yeah. Then your soul can spend eternity in the body of a little shit-worm."

"No please don't!" Cassie croaked out a sob, but Lissa had already wound the rope-saw around Hush's neck. The finely barbed chain cut quickly with its sickening sound.

"Stop it stop it!" Cassie wailed. "She never did anything to you!"

Lissa grinned as her hands yanked the saw handles briskly back and forth. "I know, and that's exactly why I'm doing it."

Tears flowed down Cassie's face.

Still paralyzed, Hush's body quivered on the slab. Lissa zipped right through the rest of her neck—
thunk
—and then Hush's head fell off.

"Why did you *do* that!" Cassie wailed.

Lissa shrugged. " 'Cos it was fun. But don't worry, that's nothing compared to what I'm gonna do to Via. I'm gonna *really* fuck *her* up."

All that horror at once, all that anger and outrage and despair, caused something in Cassie to snap like a twig. She squeezed her eyes closed, *forced* herself to break out of her own pain and paralysis. Her face turned pink in the effort as she strained, strained further. . . .

"Ah, but I gotta finish one job first, right? Before I start cutting on Via. . . ." Lissa chose a long iron sledgehammer from the wall of Blackwell's instruments of torture. She weighed it in her hands, nodding satisfaction. "Yeah, this'll do the trick. This'll turn Hush's noggin to mush in one swipe."

"GET AWAY!" Cassie screamed. Her Ethereal Powers had broken back to the surface of her consciousness, and with a throat-flaying scream, she hurled the most violent thought of her life at Lissa.

The projection tore the room up as it fired forward, carrying its hot freight of rage like a wild bull suddenly unleashed from the stable. Anything on the wall was suddenly knocked to the floor. The carpeting flew apart in fat strips, and the surface of the walls themselves began to crack.

Then all that Etheric energy collided into Lissa. . . .

Lissa just laughed, shaking her head.

Cassie stared in horror.

"That hocus-pocus doesn't work on me," Lissa remarked.

She raised the sledgehammer high into the air, arcing up over Hush's severed head.

Cassie collapsed back against the couch.

"Get ready to eat shit forever, you little Goth floozy!" Lissa celebrated.

The hammer hovered. The eyes in Hush's severed head widened in terror, her mouth opening in a voiceless scream. And just as the hammer's flat face would be slammed to the floor, crushing Hush's head and sending her soul into the physical body of some hellish vermin—

The room rocked.

It began to tremor worse than the force from Cassie's last projection.

But . . . *It's not me,* Cassie realized.

Some *other* force had entered the room, and after the following triage of sound—

Sssssssssssssssssss-ONK!

Sssssssssssssssssss-ONK!

Sssssssssssssssssss-ONK!

—Cassie knew what it was.

Three more Nectoports opened in their concussive wallops and wobbling flashes of swamp-green light. In less time than it took for Cassie to register her next thought, Blackwell's Victorian chamber was full of the armed black knights of the Contumacy. They surrounded Lissa in a deep circle, their broadswords at the ready, the points of their halberd shafts and spears forming a ring of metal teeth around Lissa and the stone dolmen on which lay Hush's decapitated body.

The room fell pin-drop silent.

Lissa cast the sledgehammer aside. She seemed unafraid, as well as unimpressed by the sudden invasion of insurgent soldiers.

Behind the mass of knights, Cassie was tended to by several more black guards; one picked her up and held her in his gauntleted arms, while others stood before her as living shields. Between the figures standing before her, she could barely see anything, but she could see enough.

Lissa stood with her hands on her hips, a sly smirk on her face.

"Well?" she said. "Come out, unless you're afraid."

Through the ranks, then, Ezoriel stepped forward in his bloodied battledress. His burned wings were drawn in behind his back, and his bronze helmet gleamed in spite of the dents from countless blows. In his large hand he grasped a sword.

"Might it have been a stray whisper from God that led me to this place?" Ezoriel's luminous voice issued.

"God's not here," Lissa said back to him. "He cast you out. Remember?"

"Then perhaps it's just that I'm smarter than you."

"You probably are smarter than me, but so stupid in your faith. Faith in *what?*"

"I'm not sure. But that hardly matters."

Lissa smiled. "We used to be friends. We can be again. Consider the power here, Ezoriel. We'll share in it—if you give your faith to me."

"On the coldest day of winter, I wouldn't give you the steam off my shit," Ezoriel replied.

"So what now? You'll stand aside and watch your peons chop me up. You know how pointless that would be."

"I suspect so."

"Just you and me then—unless, of course, you're still a coward."

Ezoriel dropped his sword and helmet to the floor.

Lissa looked back at him, displeased.

Then she said, "Fuck off," and simply disappeared.

Chapter Seventeen

(I)

The little that Cassie could see and hear of those final moments in Blackwell's chamber were utterly inexplicable. Too much had happened just too quickly for her to properly calculate any of it.

About the only thing she *could* comprehend, though, was Lissa's diabolical hatred of her twin sister, which left Cassie feeling even more morose and helpless. Who else could Lissa blame for her damnation but Cassie? Thinking back to that night in the bar—the night Lissa had shot Radu and then herself—it had been Cassie's own drunkenness and inner-angst that had spurred the weakness which had urged her into Radu's arms. His own sexual designs for her were really no excuse, nor was his deceit, his overt lying, and his willingness to cheat on Lissa.

In Cassie's heart and mind, none of these facts could ever pardon her from what had happened that night.

And she knew she would carry that blame around with her, like a satchel of heavy bricks, for the rest of her life.

It was a burden that would never fully be relieved.

(II)

After the showdown at Blackwell's, Cassie had been safely Nectoported back to Ezoriel's hidden fortress, to the Fallen Angel's chateau and the very headquarters of the Satan Park Contumacy. By now she was used to the queen-like treatment, considering her power as well as her status as an Etheress and the First Saint of Hell. She was washed, fed, and cared for by every conceivable personal attendant and metaphysical doctor, then left under guard to recover from the incapacitating aftereffects of her manipulation of the Power Relic. The much-needed rest rejuvenated her much more quickly than she would've thought.

As for Ezoriel and his militia, their defeat at the Flesh Warrens was a considerable one, but not a fatal one. Countless thousands of the Fallen Angel's soldiers had been destroyed, though their loss was not totally in vain. This largest invasion of the Warrens provided them with much in the way of logistical and intelligence information, and such surveys would serve them well in future assaults against the Demonocracy of Lucifer.

Of that, Cassie felt sure.

There would be more assaults indeed. Ezoriel and his army would never retreat from their goal of deposing God's former-favorite.

But the question of Lissa continued to nag at Cassie's sensibilities. There was so much to assess. Lissa's ploy, at least, was now much easier to see after Cassie had had time to think about it. Certainly her masquerading as "Xeke" via the latest and most sophisticated techniques of Transfiguration surgery would allow for a simple yet effective infiltration among the likes of non-Hierarchals such as Via and Hush. As a Bi-Facer, Lissa could easily pose as one of them, undermine their confidence, pretend to share in their ideals as renegades of the damned. The specifications of a true Etheress would be just as easily reckoned by Lissa, a sexual virgin in the Living World, and the twin sister of another virgin: Cassie.

The rest was elementary, simply by the designs of Hell itself, and the diabolical motivations that were the status quo there.

Eternal damnation breeds eternal hatred.

And eternal greed.

What cruxed Cassie the most, however, were some of the very last things she'd witnessed back at Blackwell's chamber before her rescue.

For one, how had Lissa so quickly disappeared from the spot, and why? Cassie could only assume that since her sister was clearly in league with the Agency of the Constabulary, she must've had access to other, newer provisions of the Constabulary's sorcery-based transportation technologies. No Nectoport had appeared at that last moment to secret Lissa away.

Instead, she'd simply vanished.

Odder still were Lissa's final words. She'd acted as though she *knew* Ezoriel. She'd implied that they'd once been friends.

Cassie couldn't figure how such a thing could be possible—

Until she asked Ezoriel himself.

(III)

She stood on a high rampart, on the highest turret of Ezoriel's fortress. This hidden track of the Nether-Spheres seemed to defy all understanding of geography, even in Hell. Was it a fortress in the clouds? Did it exist in some other domain of the Mephistopolis? The first time she'd come here, Via had even told her that the Nether-Spheres occupied a plane of physical existence in some proximity to Heaven.

But here, she knew, a simple inch could equal a million miles by her own understanding.

The sky wasn't scarlet here; instead it seemed indescribably colorless, yet wisps of blue-tinted clouds breezed by, and the air was so fresh it seemed to mildly intoxicate her. Paradise in the domain of the Damned. But in all its luxury and freshness, this stronghold of Ezoriel proved his dedication. He could elect to simply spend eternity here amid this beauty—quite a powerful temptation, in this place that had been *created* by temptation—but instead he choose to brave the horrific streets and alleys of the city in order to pursue his battle against the injustice of Lucifer and his government.

The breeze caressed her living skin. When she peered into the infinite distance, she thought she saw a sparrow fly by.

Footsteps approached.

When she turned against the stone rampart, she saw Ezoriel, in a shining silver breastplate, coming toward her along the narrow passage.

His voice continued to remind her of bright light.

"Have you any needs, Holy One?"

"No," Cassie said.

"Though our battle was lost, we've gained much—to fight again. And that is how it will always be. Your presence has blessed us, and for that you have our eternal thanks."

"I didn't really do anything," she said. "I tried to but it all got screwed up."

"You've done more than you can ever imagine. Not only have you served Lucifer the greatest insult of his reign, you've given myself and my legions a gift beyond measure."

A gift? she wondered. "What gift?"

"Hope," the Fallen Angel said. "In the realm of the hopeless."

Cassie shrugged, despondent.

"Even if you never return to Hell—a circumstance that I ardently advise—your time with us will never be forgotten, ever. Your spirit and your presence has granted us an unflagging strength."

"Well, that's nice of you to say," she limply replied. "I'd like to come back and help you sometime, but . . ." What could she say? That she was scared? Of course she was. "I have a father—and a life—somewhere else."

"Of course. You don't belong here."

If I came back, I could get killed, she realized. How many times had she nearly died already?

Her voice darkened. "What happens if an Etheress dies? I mean, if she dies in Hell?"

"I cannot say," Ezoriel's voice shined. "It's a secret."

Terrific, Cassie thought, leaning against the rampart with her chin in her hands. But Ezoriel was right, and even if it was fear that most motivated her to never come back here, she was right too. Her life—her living body and mind—was a precious thing; life itself was precious, and she knew that now. Being in Hell, being among all this misery and endless despair, had taught her that at least.

She cringed to think back on the times when she'd hated her life, and the times she'd wanted to end it. Now she knew better.

Now she knew she would never take the Living World for granted again.

Then the thought rekindled as she remained there on the rampart with the Angel.

Lissa.

"When we were at Blackwell's," she began, "Lissa said some things I couldn't understand. She indicated that she knew you, didn't she? She said that the two of you had been friends once."

"Yes."

"How is that possible?"

"I trust you noticed the brand on her abdomen," Ezoriel said. "The pentagram. It was a band of Transposition. In your world, ranchers brand their cattle to prove ownership. It works similarly here, too, but there's something more."

She figured at least this much: the brand meant that Lissa was *owned*. By someone here, someone in Hell. "Transposition," she spoke the word. "Wasn't it a Transposition Spell that allowed me to use the Power Relic, to put my spirit into the bones?"

"To *transpose* your spirit, yes. Your spirit left your physical body, to occupy something else." Ezoriel looked down at her. "So I hope that you will find at least some solace."

Cassie's own glance back showed him that she didn't understand.

The voice, like strange light, explained. "Just as your spirit was transposed, so was the spirit of your sister— hence, the brand."

"You mean—"

"It wasn't actually Lissa whom we confronted in Blackwell's chamber," the Fallen Angel said. "It was Lissa's body, transposed with the spirit of someone else."

Someone else. . . .

"Who?" she asked.

"Someone I used to be friends with," Ezoriel said.

(IV)

"You get drunk again last night?" Mrs. Conner whispered fiercely to her rather disheveled son. Had she been home, she wouldn't be whispering, she'd be yelling. But she didn't dare yell at him now, not here at Blackwell Hall. It simply wouldn't do for Mr. Heydon to overhear a family spat. *Cain't have that wonderful man thinkin' we're just a bunch of backwoods hillbillies,* she told herself.

Instead, she'd confronted Jervis outside, when he'd arrived an hour late to start mowing the lawn. He looked a sight, a big bump on his head, a cut on his face, and he appeared exhausted with dark circles under his eyes.

"I ain't lyin' to ya, Ma," he pleaded. "I didn't drink a thing last night, I'se swear to ya." He rubbed the back of his head. "Must've fallen out of bed and hit my head. And, lord, did I have some weird dreams."

Weird dreams, Mrs. Conner thought. She'd had a few herself, but they'd been less weird than wild. She blushed slightly thinking about it now. *Dreamed I was makin' some serious bacon with Mr. Heydon.*

To her, it was a terrific dream.

"Just get on about your work and straighten yourself up, boy," she ordered. "We got ourselves some fine jobs here at the house and I ain't gonna let you mess it all up for us by comin' to work late and lookin' like you slept in a cement mixer. So get to work! And try not to be seen by Mr. Heydon. Honestly, you look like a perfect rube, boy."

Jervis sluggishly yanked up on the cord, started the mower, and just as sluggishly began cutting the front lawn.

Mrs. Conner scurried back inside, her formidable bosom jogging up and down. She got back to cleaning the front bow windows as quick as she could, streaking her squeegee and squinting against the high morning sun. Hard as she tried to appear normal, she had to admit she was a little off kilter. *Those were some dreams,* she thought. Naughtily erotic, thrillingly dirty. Her crush on Mr. Heydon was clearly manifesting itself. Making love to him in the dream had seemed alarmingly real.

In fact, she wouldn't mind having *more* dreams like that.

But what bothered her was her memory. Dreams aside, there was something definitely peculiar about last night. She couldn't remember anything from eleven p.m. or so, to four in the morning when she woke up in the bed in her trailer, naked. Mrs. Conner never slept naked. And her clothes were strewn on the floor as if dropped there. This was not her style at all.

I ain't old enough to be gettin' senile, she thought.

She stepped up higher on the footstool, reaching up toward a higher pane.

"Good morning."

Mrs. Conner nearly fell off the footstool. Mr. Heydon stood behind her looking up. She didn't know why she thought it, but she had the oddest feeling that he might have been standing there for a while, looking at her. The thought flattered her, but she knew it was just a fantasy.

"Mornin', Mr. Heydon. Lovely day, isn't it?"

"It certainly is. A good-to-be-alive day."

She steadied herself and looked back down. Handsome man, if a bit fat, but Mrs. Conner liked a man with some meat on his bones. *Even if he wasn't rich,* she mused, *I'd jump his bones in a second,* and then she thought, *Lordy, what's gotten into me thinking such things!*

"How are you today, Mr. Heydon?"

Bill Heydon arched his back as though it were sore, then rubbed his eyes. He looked very tired. "Feeling pretty beat to tell you the truth. Didn't sleep that great." He seemed to frown at himself, as if remembering something nonsensical. "I had the weirdest dreams last night."

Mrs. Conner's brow tittered. *You and me both.* But she couldn't believe what she said next. "Sometimes if you talk out your dreams, it helps you understand yerself better. What did ya dream about?"

Did he chuckle under his breath? "Never, uh, never mind, Mrs. Conner."

She was blushing again in the recollection of her own dreams, then tried to change the subject. "How's Miss Cassie feelin'? She seemed a bit under the weather the past few days."

"She's still in bed, I just checked on her. I think she just got too much sun. She'll be fine in no time."

"I sure hope so, Mr. Heydon. She's a right nice gal, she is." She polished more glass, desperate for something more to say. She didn't want him to leave. "Oh, just so ya know, Jervis is out front mowin' the yard, and I should be done with these windows in an hour or so. Then I thought I'd start scrubbing the floors in some of the rooms upstairs, that is, if ya like."

Bill looked distractedly at his watch. "Don't bother. I don't care about those old rooms." He paused, looking at her. "Say, I was wondering . . ."

"Yes, Mr. Heydon?"

"I was thinking of driving up to Pulaski. Would you like to go with me? We could have lunch somewhere."

Again, Mrs. Conner nearly fell off the footstool. "Why—I—why sure, Mr. Heydon. That'd be lovely. . . ."

"Forget about the windows. Let's go now."

Mrs. Conner could barely speak. "I'm, uh, ready when you are, Mr. Heydon."

"I'll be right back. Let me get my keys. Oh, and call me Bill."

(V)

Did I just ask my housekeeper out on a lunch date? Bill shrugged. *To hell with it. I can do what I want.*

And, man, what a body. . . .

He went back to his bedroom, grabbed the keys to the Caddie. Something caused him to pause, though, and look around the room.

He'd wakened in the wee hours, naked in bed.

Bill Heydon never slept naked, or at least not for years.

And why were his t-shirt and shorts scattered about the room?

Weird, he thought. Another thing he'd noticed was a broken lamp on the floor, and it infuriated him that he couldn't explain it. It must've fallen off the nightstand or something.

His body was sore, and this morning when he looked in the bathroom mirror, he noticed some bruises on his chest and scratchmarks on his shoulders and back.

He could remember nothing of last night . . . except the dreams.

Man, he thought again. *What a body. . . .*

It was just one of those things, he supposed. Upon waking, some nameless fear had seized him. *Cassie,* he'd thought. But when he'd rushed upstairs to her room, he found her safely asleep in bed.

Bill just shook his head at the whole perplexity and left the bedroom. Better just to forget about it.

It was time for his lunch date. . . .

Epilogue

(I)

"Eight-ball in the corner," Roy said, awkwardly lining up the shot. *He's getting cocky, I guess,* Cassie thought. Only some expert English by a pro pool player could make such a shot, and the rest of the bar's patrons laughed when Roy called it.

Too bad I can't tell him why he's really winning.
click

Via, unseen to all but Cassie, flicked the ball into the pocket. The crowd around the table cheered.

"Rack 'em," Roy said to the next challenger.

Things were settling down now. It hadn't taken Cassie long to recuperate from her sojourn to Hell. She felt fine now, rested, healed, and surprisingly normal. Her father had some serious ga-ga eyes for Mrs. Conner, and the feeling was clearly mutual. Soon, they'd be officially dating, which was perfectly okay with Cassie. Jervis, for reasons only Cassie could understand, never came into the house anymore; he stuck to working strictly outside, so there'd be no more peeping.

And Roy still hadn't realized the coincidence that any time Cassie happened to be in the Crossroads Tavern, he won big at the billiards table. And when she *wasn't* there, he pretty much sucked. Of course, he'd never know why.

Indeed, life was returning to normal, or at least as normal as could be hoped for.

"Hey, look," Via said, "here comes that asshole again."

Cassie, from her bar stool, glanced at the door, and in walked Chester with a black eye and bandage on his nose.

"Want me to have some fun with him?" Via asked. "I'll kick him right in the stomach."

The tiny cut on Cassie's hand would make that possible to their sheer delight. "Let's wait and see if he acts up first," she told Via.

"What's that?" the towering barkeep asked. "You say somethin', Cassie?"

"Just talking to myself," she said.

Chester, obviously ashamed, walked right up to Roy at the table and handed him some cash. "Here's your money from the other night, Roy," he said, embarrassed. "I'm really sorry 'bout what happened. Some things never change, ya know? Beer plus Chester equals asshole."

"No problem, Chester," Roy said. The two men shook hands. "Wanna game?" Roy asked, gesturing the lit table.

"Hail no!" Chester said, and then everyone laughed.

Can you believe this? Cassie thought. *I'm a Goth girl hanging out in a redneck bar . . . and I'm fitting in.*

It was funny. Cassie was really beginning to like this place.

"There's my good luck charm," Roy said and came back to the bar. "Can you believe all this money I'm winnin'?"

"You're a hot shot, Roy."

He nodded over his beer. "Yeah, it looks like I am."

There'd be no romance between them, but Cassie really liked Roy. In fact, he was her best friend out here.

Her best friend that was *alive,* that is.

Via scuffed around invisibly. "He's got the hots for you, you know?"

"I know," Cassie said, but then instantly thought, *Damn! I keep doing it!*

Roy looked at her oddly. "You know what?"

"Nothing."

Roy sipped more beer, suddenly shaking his head.

"Something wrong?"

"Can't stop thinkin' about it," he said. "Been buggin' me for days, and I probably shouldn't even tell ya."

"What, Roy?"

"Aw, you'd think I was whacked in the head."

"Probably not. Try me."

Then he laughed under his breath. "I had the weirdest dream the other night, damn stupidest dream I ever had in my life."

"Yeah?"

"Yeah? I dreamed that . . . I was helpin' you dig up a grave. . . ."

Via laughed out loud.

"Kind of a strange thing to dream, don't you think?"

"And you want to know whose grave it was?"

"Hmm, let me guess. Uh . . . Fenton Blackwell's?"

Roy sat up straight. "Yeah!"

"You're right, Roy. You're whacked in the head."

Cassie remained in the bar a while longer, drinking Cokes and watching Roy—with Via's help—rule the billiards table. But eventually the country and western jukebox began to get on her nerves; she could only take so much of The Judds. Some Nine Inch Nails was what she needed, or maybe even some Aldinoch.

"Gotta go now, Roy. See ya later."

"Yeah, see ya!"

"The poor sap'll probably lose it all now," Via said when they left the tavern.

"He'll learn."

"You ever gonna tell him?"

"Naw."

The hot summer night teemed in moonlight and cricket sounds. They began to walk back up the path, toward Blackwell Hall. They dawdled back, Cassie's mind aswarm with doubts.

She knew she had some options to consider but she was pretty sure that her mind was made up now.

"I guess you've been thinking about—well, you know."

"Yeah," Cassie divulged.

"Have you decided?"

"Going back to the Mephistopolis? Risking death and eternal imprisonment? Returning to Hell as Lucifer's worst enemy to help a Fallen Angel who looks like Brad Pitt wage war against him, and being hunted by every Usher, Golem, Conscript, and any other grossout homicidal hellborn creature in the city? Yeah, I've decided." Cassie gulped. "I'm going to go back."

"Cool!" Via celebrated, hugging her.

What else could she do?

"Lissa's still there somewhere, and, damn it, I'm going to find her."

"Yeah, and we'll have a friggin' *blast!*"

Cassie wasn't sure about that part. But she was an Etheress. She was the First Saint of Hell.

Might as well go with the flow. It beats sitting around on my butt all day watching MTV and a bunch of White Zombie videos.

"Use the power," Via said. "It's yours. You can make history."

Cassie supposed she could.

Sudden footsteps crunching down the dark path startled them for a moment, but then Via said, "There she is!"

It was Hush who approached them, short and spooky with her wan white face and flowing black dress.

"Hi, Hush," Cassie said.

"Hey, guess what?" Via excitedly informed. "Cassie's decided that she's gonna go back to the city!"

Hush smiled back at them. Ezoriel's own team of Transfigurists had sewn her hand and head back on, and they'd even implanted a new voice-box in her throat.

She pointed to the next trail, the Rive out of the Deadpass.

"Then why fuck around?" Hush said. "The next train leaves in ten minutes. Let's go back to Hell right now and kick some demon ass!"

(II)

The sky churns dark-scarlet. The moon is black. It has been midnight here for millennia, and it always will be. The scape of the city stretches on in an endless sprawl. Just as endless are the screams, which fly away into the eternal night only to be immediately replaced by more of the same.

It is an incontestable cycle of human history, 5000 years old:

Cities rise, then they fall.

But not *this* city.

Not the Mephistopolis.

INFERNAL ANGEL
EDWARD LEE

Hell is an endless metropolis bristling with black skyscrapers, raging in eternal horror. Screams rip down streets and through alleys. The people trudge down sidewalks on their way to work or to stores, just like in other cities. There is only one difference. In this city the people are all dead.

But two living humans discover the greatest of all occult secrets. They have the ability to enter this city of the damned, with powers beyond those of even a fallen angel. One plans to foil an unspeakably diabolical plot. The other plans to set it in motion—and bring all the evils of Hell to the land of the living.

EDWARD LEE
FLESH GOTHIC

Hildreth House isn't like other mansions. One warm night in early spring, fourteen people entered Hildreth House's labyrinthine halls to partake in diabolical debauchery. When the orgy was over, the slaughter began. The next morning, thirteen of the revelers were found naked and butchered. Dismembered. Mutilated. But the fourteenth body was never found.

The screams have faded and the blood has dried, but the house remains…watching. Now five very special people have dared to enter the infamous house of horrors. Who—or what—awaits them? And who will live to tell Hildreth House's ghastly secrets?

OFFSPRING

JACK KETCHUM

The local sheriff of Dead River, Maine, thought he had killed them off ten years ago—a primitive, cave-dwelling tribe of cannibalistic savages. But somehow the clan survived. To breed. To hunt. To kill and eat. And now the peaceful residents of this isolated town are fighting for their lives....

ISBN 10: 0-8439-5864-2
ISBN 13: 978-0-8439-5864-5 $7.99 US/$9.99 CAN

RICHARD LAYMON

SAVAGE

Whitechapel, November 1888: Jack the Ripper is hard at work. He's safe behind locked doors in a one-room hovel with his unfortunate victim, Mary Kelly. With no need to hurry for once, he takes his time gleefully eviscerating the young woman. He doesn't know that a fifteen-year-old boy is cowering under Mary's bed....

Trevor Bentley's life would never be the same after that night. What he saw and heard would have driven many men mad. But for Trevor it was the beginning of a quest, an obsession to stop the most notorious murderer in history. The killer's trail of blood will lead Trevor from the fog-shrouded alleys of London to the streets of New York and beyond. But Trevor will not stop until he comes face to face with the ultimate horror.

ISBN 10: 0-8439-5751-4
ISBN 13: 978-0-8439-5751-8

To order a book or to request a catalog call:
1–800–481–9191
This book is also available at your local bookstore, or you can check out our Web site **www.dorchesterpub.com** where you can look up your favorite authors, read excerpts, or glance at our discussion forum to see what people have to say about your favorite books.

PEACEABLE
KINGDOM
JACK KETCHUM

When it comes to chilling the blood, fraying the nerves, or quickening the pulse, no writer comes close to Jack Ketchum. He's able to grab readers from the first sentence, pulling them inescapably into his story, compelling them to turn the pages as fast as they can, refusing to release them until they have reached the shattering conclusion.

This landmark collection gathers more than thirty of Jack Ketchum's most thrilling stories. "Gone" and "The Box" were honored with the prestigious Bram Stoker Award. Whether you are already familiar with Ketchum's unique brand of suspense or are experiencing it for the first time, here is a book no afficionado of fear can do without.

SIMON CLARK

THIS RAGE OF ECHOES

The future looked good for Mason until the night he was attacked…by someone who looked exactly like him. Soon he will understand that something monstrous is happening—something that transforms ordinary people into replicas of him, duplicates driven by irresistible bloodlust.

As the body count rises, Mason fights to keep one step ahead of the Echomen, the duplicates who hunt not only him but also his family and friends, and who perform gruesome experiments on their own kind. But the attacks are not as mindless as they seem. The killers have an unimaginable agenda, one straight from a fevered nightmare.

ISBN 10: 0-8439-5494-9
ISBN 13: 978-0-8439-5494-4

TO WAKE THE DEAD

RICHARD LAYMON

Amara was once the beautiful Princess of Egypt. Now, 4000 years later, she and her coffin are merely prized exhibits of the Charles Ward Museum. If you were to look at her today, you would see only a brittle bundle of bones and dried skin. But looks can be very deceiving, as Barney, the museum's night watchman, finds out. . . .

Barney is the first to make the shocking discovery that the mummy's coffin has been broken open. But he doesn't have a chance to do anything about it. Amara is once again freed from the cramped confines of her coffin, free to walk the earth. Free to kill. Nothing can satisfy her bloodlust. And no one can stop her. You cannot kill what is already dead.
